KU-779-018

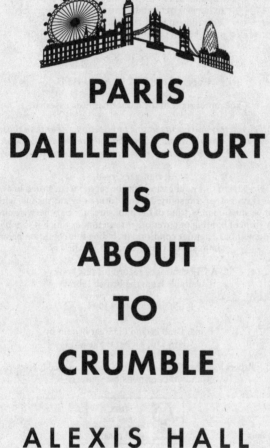

PARIS
DAILLENCOURT
IS
ABOUT
TO
CRUMBLE

ALEXIS HALL

PIATKUS

PIATKUS

First published in the US in 2022 by Forever,
an imprint of Grand Central Publishing,
a division of Hachette Book Group, Inc
First published in Great Britain in 2022 by Piatkus

1 3 5 7 9 10 8 6 4 2

Copyright © 2022 by Alexis Hall

The moral right of the author has been asserted.

*All characters and events in this publication, other than those
clearly in the public domain, are fictitious and any resemblance
to real persons, living or dead, is purely coincidental.*

All rights reserved.
No part of this publication may be reproduced, stored in a
retrieval system, or transmitted in any form or by any means, without
the prior permission in writing of the publisher, nor be otherwise circulated
in any form of binding or cover other than that in which it is published
and without a similar condition including this condition being
imposed on the subsequent purchaser.

A CIP catalogue record for this book
is available from the British Library.

ISBN 9-780-349-42994-6

Printed and bound in Great Britain by
Clays Ltd, Elcograf S.p.A.

Papers used by Piatkus are from well-managed forests
and other responsible sources.

Piatkus
An imprint of
Little, Brown Book Group
Carmelite House
50 Victoria Embankment
London EC4Y 0DZ

An Hachette UK Company
www.hachette.co.uk

www.littlebrown.co.uk

Content Guidance

Main character with an undiagnosed anxiety disorder (that does get diagnosed), on-page panic attack, hospital stay due to panic attack, treatment plan for anxiety disorder discussed, emotionally unavailable parents, very graphic swearing, cyberbullying, religious and racial microaggressions, Islamophobia (challenged).

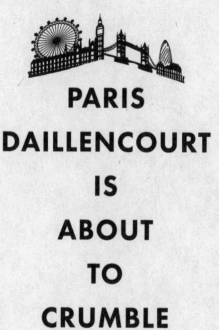

PARIS DAILLENCOURT IS ABOUT TO CRUMBLE

Summer

Friday

PARIS DAILLENCOURT WAS removing his biscuits from the oven while a naked man he'd never seen before raided the fridge for beer.

"Those look nice," said the stranger, who, as well as being entirely undressed, was distractingly built and had the telltale marks of Paris's housemate's teeth, fingernails, and riding crop over much of his back and arse.

"Thanks." Paris got that warm, cosy feeling he always got when someone complimented his baking that was strangely distinct from the hot, uncomfortable feeling he got when they complimented anything else about him. "They're biscuits roses de Reims."

Cracking open his beer, the man retreated to the lounge area of the apartment's open-plan living space. There he lowered himself into an armchair, swiftly learned the error of his ways, and stood up again with a strangled yelp. "What's a biskwee?"

"Biscuits for pricks." Morag—the housemate, riding crop

artiste and self-styled fat Glaswegian sex goddess—emerged from her room. Unlike her guest, she was fully clothed, with only her tangled hair betraying the fact that she'd been fucking extensively and loudly approximately eight minutes earlier.

"They're not for pricks," Paris protested. "It's French."

Morag adjusted the neckline of her strawberry-print sundress in order to better frame her magnificent bosom. "So pricks then?"

"You can't call the whole nation of France pricks."

"I fucking can. In fact, we're both fucking culturally required to. The only people who are bigger pricks than the French are the English."

If Paris didn't carve his biscuits into even rectangles soon, they'd harden and therefore be difficult to carve into even rectangles. So he grabbed a knife and began rectangling evenly. "I'm English. *And* I grew up in France."

"Sometimes, Paris," said Morag, "you make it too easy."

The naked man, who would probably have found the prick debate hard enough to navigate even if his own hadn't been hanging there like a chorizo in a delicatessen window, had come to peer over Paris's shoulder. "So these are, like, French Hobnobs?"

Morag shook her head. "No, these are for posh bastards. They were invented specifically to be eaten out of Marie Antoinette's vagina."

The naked man looked interested. "Really?"

"No," cried Paris. "They were designed to be dipped in champagne and not to go anywhere near anyone's genitals." He looked down at the chorizo. "No offence."

"None taken. Can I try one?"

"If you like." Paris added a sprinkle of powdered sugar and nudged over one of his better-evened biscuits. "But they really are better with champagne."

"Or," suggested Morag, "in a vagina. Most things are." She paused. "Except Mars bars because the batter comes off."

The naked man crunched appreciatively. "I'm game if you are."

"Is it okay"—Paris didn't quite wring his hands, but he moved his hands in a wringular direction—"if we don't make my biscuits roses de Reims into a sex thing? I have childhood memories of these."

Morag fixed him with an affectionate glare. "Oh, I bet you did. You probably had them in your packed lunch, next to your caviar sandwiches and your squeezy box full of Dom Pérignon."

Paris tried to glare back, but he didn't have a face for glaring. He suspected he probably looked like a mildly upset sheep. "I did not have a squeezy box full of Dom Pérignon."

"But you did have caviar sandwiches?"

The problem with being baited was that the bait would just sit there wriggling until you bit on it. And Paris couldn't stand to have something sitting there wriggling. "You don't put caviar in sandwiches."

"Well," Morag finished triumphantly. "I wouldn't know. Because I'm not a posh bastard."

"To be fair," said the naked man apologetically, "you must be a bit of a posh bastard because you live in a fancy flat in central London with a man who makes biskwee roses de Reims."

Morag put her actual hands on her actual hips. "How fucking dare you? I'm as common as fucking muck and fucking proud of it. The closest I got to fine wine when I was growing up was a Capri Sun that had been left by the radiator. The flat's his." She jerked a thumb at Paris. "I just rent a room off him with money that I don't have and he doesn't need."

The rent had, in fact, been a bit of a sore point when they'd first started sharing, because it'd felt weird to Paris that Morag was technically paying more to live there than he was. "I said you didn't have to."

"And I said I've never been a freeloader in my life and I'm not going to start now."

Morag had guests over fairly often—something that Paris at least semi-appreciated since otherwise it would just have been her, him, and a skittish Russian Blue that a long-since-forgotten whim had led him to name Neferneferuaten—and so he was fairly used to seeing the look of confusion he was currently seeing.

"And how," the naked man asked, "did you two meet exactly?"

"It's a long story," said Morag at the same time Paris said, "At university."

Morag considered this for a moment. "Okay, so it's not that long a story. Basically, I spent the whole of first year listening to people going *what's up with that weird Paris guy. He never talks to anyone and lives alone in a big mansion like he's Norma fucking Desmond.*"

"I talk to people," protested Paris.

"*Hello* and *yes, you can borrow my pen* are not talking to people. Anyway, the point is that I wasn't going to let some lanky Sassenach scare me off with his *oh I'm so aloof* routine, so I pinned him down after lectures one day and asked if he wanted to fuck me hard in the toilets. And he said *actually I'm gay*, and I said *okay, do you want to get coffee then*. And we've been friends ever since. Then in second year I asked if he wanted to live together so he'd look like less of a lonely wee loser, and here we are."

From the way the naked guy was peering around, there was still something about the arrangement that wasn't quite making sense to him. Probably it was the fact that while "we met at university and she felt sorry for me" was a reasonable explanation for why Morag and Paris were living together, it didn't explain why there were biscuits roses de Reims spread over every available surface. "So now," he tried, with an un-reassured edge to his voice, "you share a luxury flat in central London and spend most of your time"—he picked up a biscuit—"making one very specific type of expensive biscuit?"

As was her habit, Morag did the explaining for both of them. "He's on *Bake Expectations*."

"What?" The naked man looked mildly interested. "The thing with people baking cakes in a ballroom?"

Morag nodded. "When we first started hanging out together, we had two things in common, which were Catullus and that fucking baking show. And he said he'd always wanted to go on it—"

"Once," interrupted Paris. He didn't usually like interrupting people, but with Morag you interrupted or held your peace like an extra at a movie wedding. "I said that once. Because I'd had wine and I was feeling hubristic."

"Aye, and I listened. Because I'm great with people, me. Also *I might like to go on that TV show one day* isn't hubristic. It's at best mildly ambitious. Anyway it soon became extremely clear that he wasn't going to enter himself, so I entered him—I mean I entered him into the competition, not with one of my many strap-ons—and out of thousands of contestants he's been selected as one of Britain's ten best amateur bakers."

Slinking over to the sitting area, Paris shrank down into an armchair and tried to hide behind Neferneferuaten, who had finally emerged from naked-stranger-induced hiding. "Don't. I'm really not. It's just it's series seven, and they're obviously scraping the bottom of the barrel a bit."

"Shut up, Paris."

"You know what I think?" offered the naked man. "I think you've got a shot. These are good biscuits. They've got a decent crunch to them, and the rose is coming through."

Morag stared at him in utter bewilderment. "Who do you think you are? Marianne fucking Wolvercote?"

"Marianne who?" asked the naked man, whose name Paris was pretty sure he'd now left it too late to ask.

"You know, the mean judge on the show we're all talking about?"

The naked man gave a shrug, which wound up being a very different gesture when attached to a buff man with his wang hanging out. "Never really watched it. And anyway I was just trying to be nice."

"He doesn't need you to be nice. He needs to get his head out of his arse." Morag waved a frustrated hand in Paris's direction. "It's not just the baking, he's like this with everything. He says he's having an essay crisis and it comes back with a first. He'll buy some new kecks and be all, do these make my bum too apricoty."

"I did not say that," insisted Paris, blushing. "I was just worried they'd make me come across like I was trying too hard."

"Like that time you sat me down and asked me very sincerely if I thought your cheekbones were too high?"

In his mind, at the time, it had been a very sensible thing to ask, so Paris tried not to sound too flustered when he replied, "A guy said I looked like an elf."

"He was a LARPer. He was trying to pull you."

Paris peeped between Neferneferuaten's ears. "No he wasn't."

"Yes, he was." Morag joined him in the sitting area, drawing her still-not-ready-for-furniture guest with her. "That's why he asked for your phone number."

"He said he was going to invite me into his D&D game."

"That's nerdspeak for 'I want to fuck you.' I know, because I've fucked a lot of nerds and never played a single game of Dungeons and Dragons."

"That's you." To Paris's dismay, Neferneferuaten had got bored of being emotionally supportive and gone to investigate the naked man. "Everyone's attracted to you."

"Well, I'd say that's because I'm a fat Glaswegian sex goddess, but mostly it's because I fucking ask them if they want to have sex with me."

The naked man raised one hand while using the other to shield his genitals from Neferneferuaten's scrutiny. "Worked for me."

Paris glanced at him. "Where did you two even meet?"

"Sainsbury's."

Paris gave a little moan. "I could never do that. I'd go up to someone and say, *hello, do you want to come home with me*, and they'd say, *no, you're clearly unwell, I'm calling the police*."

"You don't have to be on my level yet," said Morag, "but there are places you can go and apps you can download full of horny boys who'd be happy to stick one up your bumhole."

"Um…" Paris could feel himself getting blushy again. "That's not actually what I'm looking for."

"You should try it. It's great fun."

"She's right," agreed the naked man. "Anal's not just for gays anymore."

Paris's blushing gave way to squirming. "I'm not saying I've never. I'm just saying I'm looking for more than a bumhole."

"That's your problem," Morag told him, for about the hundred and fortieth time. "You can't just look for things. You have to go out and get them."

"Yes, but what if—"

She folded her arms. "What if what?"

And, for about the hundred and fortieth time, Paris couldn't answer.

Saturday

EARLY NEXT MORNING, Morag dropped Paris off at Patchley House, the sprawling stately home where *Bake Expectations* was filmed. It felt unnervingly like his first day of school, partly because he'd just been taken to a strange place full of strangers by somebody who had their shit far more together than he did and partly because, in many ways, his old school had looked quite a lot like Patchley House.

Hawton Abbey was one of those private schools so old that it was called a public school because it had been founded back when the idea of sending your kids away to be taught instead of paying for teachers to come to your kids had seemed terribly, terribly common. Paris's years there had been by far the worst of his life, and while he was sure the crew and contestants of *Bake Expectations* would be at least twenty percent less sociopathic than English public school boys, he was getting that same I-hope-they'll-like-me-they-won't-like-me-will-they feeling that had crept up on him every time he'd been introduced to a new social situation. At least, every time since he'd first looked on the gabled cloisters of Hawton. He sometimes remembered being different before.

Trying not to over-gloom, Paris trudged his way up the long path to the house and, to his surprise, found his mood lifting. He'd been a fan of the show since—well—since school. And as awful as the other boys had been, as little common ground as they had shared in every other aspect of their lives, *everybody* loved *Bake Expectations*. They'd gather in the common room on a Tuesday evening and watch the new episode, and for a while Paris would feel like he belonged. At least until they went back to their rooms and the other boys started yammering on enthusiastically about which of the contestants they'd most like to have sex with despite, Paris belatedly realised, being children and knowing about as little about sex as they did about baking.

So Patchley House felt—not like home exactly—but ephemerally familiar, like a place he'd seen in a dream, or a person that you've heard so many other people talk about that you forget you've never met them.

He'd never seen it like this, of course, with the camera operators moving around in some dance whose steps he didn't know (in Paris's experience, that was all dances). With crew swarming everywhere pointing at things and shouting instructions that Paris couldn't help but think were meant for him, even when they couldn't be.

"Paris Daillencourt?" asked a small, friendly-looking man with a clipboard.

"Yes." That was, Paris suspected, the only question he'd be confident answering that day.

"Colin. Colin Thrimp. And it's lovely to see you so early." He smiled at Paris with what seemed genuine relief. "The other contestants are just coming up from breakfast, and Jennifer will be starting the briefing as soon as everybody's together. Can you find the ballroom yourself?"

Paris said that he could out of a kind of reflex but realised after he'd said it that he actually could. A pair of vast glass-panelled doors led direct from the ballroom to the gardens at the rear of the house, and for the past six years Paris had watched contestants walk apprehensively through them at the start of the series and triumphantly out of them at the end.

And although he was still in the *apprehensive* phase and triumph was a fairly alien emotion to him, he felt confident that he could at least find his way through a big hole in a wall into one of the most famous rooms on British television.

So he skirted the house, found the doors, and—having reassured at least three members of the production crew that yes he was a contestant and no he wasn't a tourist—made his way into the ballroom.

It had always been a bit incongruous now he thought about it, people doing something so homey in a setting so unsuited for it, but that had been part of the magic of the show. Besides, it was an orderly incongruity. Everybody had their own special work-station, arranged in its own special place, and there was something comforting about that. It was, Paris thought, part of what he found comforting about cooking in general.

The contestants gathered together on stools and—shit, they'd all got there the night before, hadn't they? Which meant they'd already know each other, and if they already knew each other, then Paris would be stuck on the outside looking in again, for the whole eight weeks. Or until he went out. So for the whole one week.

From a certain perspective, ten people wasn't a *lot* of people. It wasn't even a complete football team. But trying to keep track of everyone quickly got overwhelming. *There* was a nice-looking man in a nice-looking cardigan talking to a willowy woman in earth tones. *There* was a man in thick-rimmed glasses being largely ignored by an older lady Paris tried really hard not to think of as hatchet-faced while a tall, thickset man—actually he was probably a *bloke*, there were certain men who looked like *blokes*—pulled up stools for people who hadn't already found their own.

Once they were all settled, a woman walked in who Paris knew at once was Jennifer Hallet, the show's producer and general mastermind. She looked younger than Paris had expected, but then again he'd never been good at judging people's ages. Or, really, anything else about them.

"Right," she began, "we've got a lot to do so I'll keep this short. These things"—she pointed at the cameras—"are cameras. Ignore them or you will fuck up all our shots and make yourself look like a fucking weirdo who keeps staring at people. *These* things"—she indicated several of the people standing near the cameras—"are my production staff. They will ask you questions, and you will answer those questions as if you *aren't* answering a question, clear?"

Paris would have been too afraid to admit if it wasn't, but one or two of his fellow contestants looked like they were about to say something before Jennifer cut them off.

"Good. First aid is *there*"—she pointed to one side of the room. "Don't bother them unless you've lost enough blood to fill a mixing bowl. Technical is *there*"—she pointed to a different side of the room. "Don't bother them unless you're *really* certain that whatever problem you're having isn't your fault, and, spoiler warning, my little bags of joy and jism, it almost certainly *is* your fault. Finally my trailer is out *there*"—she pointed out of the doors and into the gardens. "Don't bother me *at all*, *ever* for *any* reason. Colin." She turned to the pleasant man who had greeted Paris when he'd arrived. "Tell Grace we're ready for her. It's time to start turning this pack of arseholes"—she waved a hand to indicate the contestants—"into the ten most beloved people in this shitty fucking nation."

Colin nodded once, sharply, and scampered away. While he was scampering, the contestants were shepherded to their stations, and when he scampered back, it was with Grace Forsythe, the show's terrifyingly Oxbridge, dangerously ebullient host in tow. She took her place at the front of the room and addressed the contestants, the cameras, and—through the strange time travel of pre-recorded television—the Great British Public with the confidence of a woman who had been showing off in front of an audience since the Thatcher years.

"Welcome," she began, gesticulating like a tweed windmill, "to the seventh season of *Bake Expectations*."

And out of nowhere, it hit him. He was really here. He was really doing this. And it was all a terrible mistake.

"Over the next eight weeks, you'll be pushed to the limit of your pastriological prowess, you'll be brought to the brink of your bakerly abilities, and also you'll probably make some cakes."

He couldn't do this. Not on television.

"As always, you'll be flashing your baps and whipping out your baguettes for the pleasure of our two esteemed judges, the fragrant and delicious Marianne Wolvercote, and the crusty but surprisingly light Wilfred Honey."

The judges stepped forward, Wilfred Honey smiling like the sort of storybook grandfather who would always remember your birthday. "My advice to you is to stay calm, try to enjoy it, and remember at the end of the day it's only baking."

"And my advice," drawled Marianne Wolvercote, looking less grandparental and more like she wanted to make a coat out of your children, "is to plan carefully, pay attention to detail, and remember that it *is* a competition."

Feeling panic rise slowly but inevitably past his intestines and into his chest, Paris glanced wildly around the ballroom. He wanted to see if anyone else had noticed that the judges had just completely contradicted each other—that they'd implicitly suggested that whatever you did, no matter how hard you tried, one of them would be disappointed. But the other contestants were all just smiling and nodding as if everything made sense and nothing was a disaster waiting to happen.

"So the first blind bake of the series," Grace Forsythe was saying, "is taking us right back to basics. Wilfred and Marianne want you to make two dozen perfect chocolate chip cookies." She raised a finger. "You have one hour and thirty minutes, starting on the count of three. *Three*, darlings."

Okay, that could have been a lot worse. It was chocolate chip cookies. Paris knew how to make chocolate chip cookies. Except, no. Wait. He'd seen this before. It was a trap. They'd give you something really simple and the bakers would all be saying *well, this should be all right, I whipped up a batch of these just the other day*, and then the camera would cut to Marianne Wolvercote saying, "The thing about chocolate chip cookies is that they're such a *simple* bake that there's nothing to hide behind." Which meant whoever wound up in the bottom would be there because their chips were at slightly the wrong angle or their cookies weren't completely circular. But nobody watching the show would remember the context, so if Paris didn't totally nail this, he'd be going home, and for the rest of his life he'd be the guy who went out in round one because he couldn't make a biscuit.

"Are you all right, my love?" asked Grace Forsythe, popping up in front of him, a camera operator at her shoulder. "Or is this a new strategy that involves absorbing the recipe by osmosis?"

Paris blinked—realising that everyone around him already had their bowls out. "Sorry. No. I'm just—I'm going to mess this up, aren't I?"

"Tell you what, if you do, I'll distract the judges, you run out of the ballroom, and we'll have a helicopter waiting for you in the garden. It'll take you to a secret location and we'll sort you out with a new identity."

"Oh, okay." Amused in spite of his mounting terror, Paris nodded. "That sounds good and in proportion."

She turned to the camera. "Right, I'm going to go and radio for the chopper. You'd be surprised how often this happens at the BBC."

The timely intervention of a beloved '90s comedian had made Paris feel a little less like he was going to cryvomit in front of a watching, judgemental nation. But running away and never being seen or heard of again still seemed like a really tempting strategy. Unfortunately, it was too late. He was here now, and he couldn't waste any more time thinking about how embarrassing it was going to be when it all went wrong.

Very conscious he was already falling behind, he began assembling the ingredients of a basic cookie mixture while skimming the recipe. And, to his relief, found the instructions matched pretty closely to what he'd been going to do anyway. It was, however, only a small relief, because *pretty close* wasn't what he was going to need. Taking a deep breath and doing his best to centre himself, Paris tried to think very serious thoughts about cookies.

Honestly, they weren't his favourite bake. What he liked about cooking was the mastery of it, the precision of it, the knowing it was something he could always do *right* and be sure he'd done right. Being able to share it with people he cared about was just a bonus—and given the state of his social life quite a theoretical one.

The thought crossed his mind that perhaps Marianne Wolvercote thought the same way. That the reason she set this kind of deceptive simplicity challenge was because she, like Paris, delighted in the details.

So the trick would be to work out which details would delight her.

Making the dough, Paris suspected, would be the easy bit. The problem was that a proper soft-yet-chewy cookie needed to be chilled for as long as possible, then left to soften at room temperature before it could be rolled out and put in the oven. And that was going to be the catch, wasn't it? This week's blind bake would be all about having the nerve to leave the actual baking to the last possible minute.

It was the Cuban Missile Crisis in biscuit form. And for just a moment, Paris entertained the real possibility that he could be Kennedy.

"I don't normally work with this kind of dough," one of the other bakers—the willowy woman in the floral dress—explained. "At home, I normally use chickpea flour, and I'm pretty sure this chocolate isn't organic. But I hope if I channel enough positive energy into the mixture, the universe will forgive me."

A tiny voice at the back of Paris's mind pointed out that *he* wasn't channelling. Just whisking and worrying. Was that a problem? It had never been a problem before.

He had to concentrate. Except it was hard to concentrate, because he was in a hot room full of strangers and their voices kept creeping into his head.

"Yeah, I make these for my kids all the time." That was the man in the cardigan. "Well, not all the time. Sometimes, if they've been good. So be good, girls."

"Personally, I don't hold with this sort of thing," the series' obligatory older woman was saying. "We had shortbread in my day, and we were grateful for it."

A woman about Paris's age, who was somehow managing to make dungarees work, even with the apron, was dividing her dough with an actual ruler. "I think cooking is kind of like art. It's meant to be subjective, but everyone knows when it's bad."

It hadn't occurred to Paris to bring a ruler—just as it hadn't occurred to him to channel energy or have an adorable family to dedicate things to—but he was becoming increasingly convinced his dough wasn't quite right. Perhaps he needed to be firmer with it. *Remember, girls, be good.* Or would that just make it overworked? *I'm channelling energy into the mixture.* Or if he didn't, would it be underworked? And which would be worse? *Everyone knows when it's bad.* Either way, he had to get it in the fridge soon, which meant he couldn't just start fisting it in the middle of the room. Shit, why was he thinking about fisting? *Personally, I don't hold with this sort of thing.*

Staring despairingly into his bowl and doing his best to banish fisting from his thoughts in case it came out at an inappropriate moment, Paris tried to cling to what he knew. The dough was ready. There was nothing more he could do if he hadn't done it right. And it needed to chill, probably for a long time. So he needed to get it chilling now. Committing himself to the fridge-now-ask-questions-later strategy, Paris dashed to his allocated refrigerator and yanked open the door.

There was a thud. Followed by "Ow. Seriously, ow."

Oh God. That was someone's face. He'd hit someone in the face. With a fridge. On the first episode.

"Oh my God," Paris said. "That's your face."

The door swung gently closed to reveal a young man with a very natty shirt and a very bloody nose, partially covered by one hand. His fingernails were painted in jewel-bright rainbows. And his dough was on the floor.

"Oh my God," said Paris again. "That's your dough."

Cameras were already swarming around them like overexcited wasps.

"It's okay, it's okay," said the doughless stranger, pinching his nose. "It's covered and I don't think—"

A middle-aged woman in an orange blouse beneath her standard-issue apron approached briskly from the back of the room. "Let's not worry about the dough for now—"

"I've got the dough." Grace Forsythe darted forward, sweeping up the fallen bowl, which seemed to have survived the drop intact. "I feel like mountain rescue except for baking and also we're not in the mountains. Er, what shall I do with it?"

"Oh God," cried Paris. "I've hit you in the face with a fridge."

His victim put his other hand to his nose. "It's fine. It happens all the time."

"People hit you in the face with fridges," Grace Forsythe asked, "all the time?"

"Well. No. I just mean—accidents happen. In general. To people."

Distraught, Paris clutched at his hair. "I've assaulted you. I've assaulted and battered you. I've done ABH on national television."

The woman who'd come over—Paris thought her name might be Tanya—put her hands on her hips. "Will you all stop messing around? You"—here she pointed at Paris—"put your dough in the fridge. You"—that was to Grace Forsythe—"put *his* dough in the fridge. And you"—she took the casualty by the arm—"sit here, be quiet, tip your head forward, and pinch the bridge of your nose for at least ten minutes."

"My word." Grace Forsythe gazed at her with unabashed adoration. "You must have the best-run classroom in the country."

Tanya laughed. "Compared to my year nines these guys are nothing. Now get to it or you're all coming back to see me at lunchtime."

"Um." This new interruption came from Colin Thrimp, who seemed a lot less pleasant now Paris had hit someone in the face with a fridge. "While this is all very lovely and I'm sure we can work with it, the rules do say that you're not supposed to talk to each other during the blind bake."

"ButIhithiminthefacewithafridge," Paris protested while, at the same time, Grace Forsythe offered the more succinct, "Oh, do shut up, Colin."

"This man is bleeding," said Tanya firmly. "He needs a first aider and everyone else was too busy filming him."

"Filming is their fucking job." Jennifer Hallet came striding in from whatever monitoring station she'd been using to watch

Paris mess everything up. "Colin, tell me we got as much of that as possible. As for you"—she pointed at Tanya—"the take-charge thing was cute and it'll play well in the home counties, but this is a competition so fuck off back to your biscuits." She descended upon the injured contestant, who was still following Tanya's nosebleed instructions. "Everything okay here?"

"I'll be fine"—the fridgee's voice was getting increasingly burbly—"I just need one of those blue plasters on my whole face. Is my dough all right?"

"Chilling like a villain who is certain her crimes have gone undetected," confirmed Grace Forsythe happily.

Jennifer Hallet glared. "Just to remind you, Tariq, *Bake Expectations* is in no way liable for any incidents that take place on set. Colin, get him to a first aider."

Colin Thrimp wrung his hands and then began guiding Tariq out of the ballroom.

"Bub by dough!"

"The dough doesn't matter." Colin Thrimp's eyes were wide. "We can't have you bleeding everywhere. We'll be sued."

"Nobody is fucking suing anybody," insisted Jennifer Hallet.

Tariq gave an outraged bubble, but since blood was beginning to seep between his fingers, he didn't really have much room to protest.

"Your dough's in the fridge," said Grace Forsythe, "where it must remain for a length of time we're not allowed to tell you, but is certainly long enough for you to go and get your nose reattached."

"What should I do?" asked Paris plaintively.

"Darling." Grace Forsythe put a hand on his shoulder. "I know you might find this difficult, but the best thing you can do for everybody is to not hit anyone else in the face with a fridge."

"Oh my God," Paris told a production assistant tearfully, "that must be the worst first day anyone has ever had. I mean, I hit a guy with a fridge and I'm sure my cookies were underbaked. Let's face it, I'm probably going home."

Released from his interview duties, Paris wiped his eyes, kicked himself for crying—partly on principle, partly because it seemed particularly inappropriate when he wasn't the injured party—and drifted after the rest of the contestants towards the hotel, where a wraps-and-sandwiches-style lunch was laid out on a series of silvery cardboard trays. Honestly, with the spectre of his terrible cookies and inevitable public disgrace hanging over him, Paris wasn't sure he could eat.

Because this, this right here, was exactly why he'd hesitated to come on the show in the first place. Okay, not *exactly* this, even in his worst nightmares—and he'd had several, not all of them involving public nudity—he hadn't actually maimed anybody. But there had, on bad days at least, been this general sense that he was definitely going to fuck it up and that people were going to laugh at him.

Staring forlornly at a curly sandwich, Paris tried to recapture that sense of not-everything-being-awful-forever that he dimly recalled feeling when he'd first arrived only a couple of hours earlier. Except he couldn't. He knew that there had been a time—even a fairly recent time—when he didn't feel miserable and hate himself, and he knew that there would be a time—perhaps even quite soon—when he'd be unmiserable and self-nonhating again. But he knew it in the same detached, abstract way that he knew that his whole body was made entirely of empty space held together with electric fields. It might have been true, but it didn't really *mean* anything.

For a moment, he sort of hovered, wondering if he should hide in his room for the next half hour instead of showing his face-fridge-hitting face amongst the other contestants. After all, they probably had better things to do than talk to the guy who hit the other guy with a fridge and was probably getting eliminated for hitting a guy with a fridge and making crap cookies so there was no point getting to know him anyway. Of course, then he'd be the creepy hovering guy.

The creepy hovering guy who hit a guy with a fridge.

Desperately needing something to do with his hands, he pulled out his phone and texted his mum.

You know how I told you I was going on that baking show? Well I'm on that baking show.

He waited a minute or two. It was fine to wait for a minute or two. Staring-at-a-phone guy was way better than hovering guy. Besides, he didn't even know what time zone his parents were in at the moment. Or even if they were in the same one.

I don't think I'm doing very well.

He waited another minute. Maybe she was in…Australia? It would be really late in Australia. Especially if she was in Adelaide or Kingston or somewhere.

"Hello." Someone actually pounced on him from behind. Like a full-on Tigger pounce, rainbow fingernails hooking gently over his shoulders. "You hit me in the face with a fridge."

Paris froze, not quite daring to turn around. "I know. I'm really sorry. Are you okay? Is anything broken?"

"Yes, I'm scarred for life. I'm going to have to wear a *Phantom of the Opera* mask forever." Tariq emerged from behind Paris, his arm cast melodramatically across his brow. "I'll have to live in the cellar beneath a bakery and there'll be a young ingénue who can smell my baking and one day the senior baker will throw a strop and refuse to bake anymore so the ingénue will bake something amazing, and I'll be sitting there in the shadows, going bravi, bravi, bravissimi."

"You realise," Paris said, "this scenario doesn't end well for you."

"I don't know. I get a cool lasso."

"Which is ironic. Because you really should have kept your hand at the level of your eyes today." Paris raised a hand to indicate the lasso-and-fridge-door-blocking gesture he was suggesting.

"Did you just make a joke," Tariq asked, "about my very serious facial injury that you caused?"

Yes. Yes he had. He was awful. He was an awful person who

made jokes about other people's suffering. "Shit shit sorry no, I didn't, I mean—"

Tariq was getting that look that Paris saw a lot. The look that said *there's something wrong with you, and I'm not certain I like it.* Then he laughed. "Honey, it's fine. I'm fine."

"It's not fine." Paris wilted all over the lawn. "I hit you and then I thought I'd try to be funny about it. Who does that? I'm the school bully on a baking show."

"Come on." Slipping his arm through Paris's, Tariq tugged him gently towards the buffet. "Let's do lunch."

"Oh, I'm not, I don't think I can—"

"How can you resist when we have these"—Tariq scrutinised the range of offerings—"beautiful coronation chicken wraps, some of which actually contain chicken, these lovely sandwiches, at least three of which haven't disintegrated yet, and this…thing, which I think is supposed to be a rocket salad but is actually just some rocket."

Still not really wanting to eat anything, but definitely not wanting to seem ungrateful, Paris helped himself to a bowl of leaves that did, indeed, turn out to be nothing but rocket. And then he followed Tariq through the already-crowded tables to a grassy verge where they both sat down. It had taken them a while to get there because Tariq had stopped and said hi to pretty much everybody.

"We've been here two minutes," said Paris. "How can you know so many people's names already?"

Tariq smiled. "Oh, I've got a trick for it. What you do is, when someone introduces themselves, you visualise a famous person or something you'd definitely remember with the same name, and then you remember that."

"Wait, there are tricks?" Paris had always suspected there were. That everybody else got some kind of be-good-in-social-situations manual that they were perversely refusing to share with him. "Nobody told me there were tricks. I just thought I sucked."

"My mum's a university lecturer. She says if you suck at something, it just means you haven't learned to do it yet.

Look"—Tariq pulled a knee up, resting an elegant hand on top of it—"I'll give you a demo. So the guy in the dad cardy over there is called Rodney—and okay, he's a bad example, because he's called Rodney and the only Rodneys I can think of are someone who might be called Rodney Dangerfield and the younger brother on a sitcom my dad watches about—actually I don't know what it's about. But anyway, I remember Rodney because if you look at him and think *if that guy had a name, what would it be*, you immediately go *Rodney*."

The man called Rodney was showing pictures of his kids to the thoroughly uninterested woman next to him. "He does look kind of Rodneyey," admitted Paris.

"Rodneyey?" repeated Tariq, his eyes twinkling. "Are you sure that's the right word?"

Paris thought about it. Probably too seriously. "Rodnesque? Rodnoid?"

"Rhodnodendron?"

"That sounds like a flower," Paris pointed out.

"Well"—Tariq gave a little huff—"Rodnoid sounds like a thing you'd get called in the playground. And then you'd go crying to your mum and be all *Billy Dawson called me a rodnoid again*."

"Who's Billy Dawson?"

The smile was never far from Tariq's mouth, and now it inched closer. "Don't worry, honey. He's a fictional bully."

"But fictional bullies are the worst," said Paris, realising too late that he'd sounded way more sincere than he'd intended to. He'd been aiming for light banter but had accidentally vomited up an off-putting hairball of personality quirks. "I mean, don't you ever—like when somebody is mean in, I don't know, a book or a film or on TV, and you can't do anything about it because it's not real, doesn't that make you feel really..." There was no good way to end that sentence. Or at least, no way that was both good and honest. Hitting a man in the face with a fridge was bad enough; hitting him in the face with a fridge and then telling him you were frequently made to feel helpless and nauseated by stock bully characters in children's shows was probably a really bad call.

To his relief, Tariq agreed, or at least agreed with the less-messed-up version of the sentence he'd obligingly filled in on Paris's behalf. "Yeah, I get what you mean. Like you'll really wish you could step up and do something, but you can't because the thing you're trying to step up and do something about only exists on a screen and the person you're angry with is just an actor." He smiled again. "But don't worry, Billy Dawson gets his comeuppance in the end."

"Oh." Paris tried to recover his composure, although the spectre of the wholly invented Billy Dawson was still floating dimly at the back of his mind, calling him a rodnoid. "So…who else did you do your trick on then?"

Tariq tilted his head as he considered the rest of the contestants. "Well, next to Rodney is Catherine Parr, who you can remember because she's called Catherine Parr. And she definitely looks like she'd outlive Henry the Eighth."

"She looks like she'd behead him to be honest. Oh my God." Paris covered his mouth with his hands. "I can't believe I said that."

Tariq gave a theatrical gasp. "Wow. You've said a slightly catty thing about an unpleasant woman. You're a monster."

"Don't." Paris tried to fold himself inside himself like human origami. "I feel really bad."

"I'm not going to tell her. That'd involve speaking to her."

Still suffering the sting of his Henry VIII comment, Paris tried to summon some doubts to give her the benefit of. "She's probably secretly nice. She's probably just got resting crone face."

"Nope. We had a five-minute conversation in which she told me it was inappropriate for a man to be wearing nail varnish on a family TV show and expressed surprise that my sister has a job."

"You mean because…" Paris realised there was no way to finish that sentence either.

Tariq laughed. "Yeah, I think so. Or she just thinks women shouldn't have jobs in general, and I'm not sure which is worse."

There was a crash from the buffet area as a thin, bespectacled man dropped his plate of sandwiches, backed up sharply, and knocked an entire tray of cutlery onto the floor.

"Now that," Tariq went on, "is Bernard, who is nice but a bit hopeless. And you can remember his name because if you put a *Saint* on the front, you get a species of dog that is nice, but a bit hopeless."

"Don't they kind of rescue people when they're stuck up mountains and things?"

"Yes, but look at their silly faces." Tariq did an honestly not very effective impression of a St. Bernard. He was not, Paris felt, very well constructed for it, being slight and slim, with a narrow chin and strong cheekbones, and a noticeable lack of jowls or, for that matter, fur. He also had far better fashion sense, since he was wearing well-tailored trousers and a dark shirt with a delicately patterned, almost cowboy-style collar which made him look like the world's most exquisite gunslinger.

Paris always envied men who knew how to dress. Since both his parents were in fashion, he was acutely and perpetually aware of how much better it was possible for him to look, which made actually trying to buy clothes a nightmare of second-guessing and self-recrimination. And so his wardrobe had, over the years, devolved into jeans, T-shirts, and oversized jumpers—one of which, despite the heat, he was currently wearing.

And he suddenly realised he was staring at Tariq in that awful noticing-someone-was-very-attractive-and-wishing-you-were-more-attractive way.

"What about, um, me?" he asked in an effort to distract them both. Which only made it worse because now Tariq was staring right back.

"Well, my options are plaster, Hilton, judgement, or France. And I think I'm leaning towards judgement."

"Do I look particularly like I go around giving out apples?"

"It *is* a baking show. We'll get to fruit eventually. But I more sort of meant you have a"—Tariq framed him in a finger square—"classical vibe."

"Doesn't that just mean 'tiny penis'?"

Tariq's eyes widened. "Um…I…How did you get there? Because I really didn't mean to suggest anything about your penis at all. I'm sure your penis is, um, fine. Lovely even. But none of my business."

"No, no…" Paris waved his hands frantically. "I don't want you to think about my penis. I didn't mean to insert my penis into the conversation at all."

"Look. I hope this won't make me sound like a prude, but can we maybe have about ten percent less penis in this conversation?"

"I'm sorry." Putting his rocket leaves aside, Paris curled up in a ball on the ground and covered his head with his hands. "It's just I'm a classicist and, actually, in that era large penises were considered vulgar because they were associated with excess and the Greeks valued moderation. Plus there's the idealisation of the youthful form to consider and some complex beliefs about fertility involving sperm losing heat if it has to travel too far along the…um…shaft."

"You do know you're making this worse?"

"I'm not making it worse. The ancient Greeks are making it worse." Paris strongly suspected he should stop talking or change the subject, but his mouth and his inner ancient history nerd had other plans. "If you look at any art or sculpture from the era, the young men are always very athletic and always have very, very small…phalli."

"I just meant you looked handsome," yelled Tariq over Paris's penile babbling. "And sort of clean-cut. I didn't think this was going to go the way it has apparently gone."

"Neither did I. I'm sorry. I shouldn't be allowed."

They were still frozen in a tableau of phallically induced embarrassment when a soft voice said "Tamir?" and Paris uncoiled to see universe-love-putting woman—who he thought might be called Gretchen—standing over them.

"It's Tariq," replied Tariq.

She nodded and smiled. "Mhm. I noticed you had a bit of an accident earlier, and I'm actually a qualified Reiki practitioner.

So I wondered if you wanted me to do anything for you." Her hands waved intrusively close to his face. "I can see your energy is somewhat disrupted."

Tariq leaned backwards like he was entering a seated limbo competition. "That's really kind of you, but I think my energy'll be okay."

"Oh, it's no trouble." Her hands pursued him as he pulled away, creating a kind of feedback loop that Paris suspected was going to lead to someone falling over very soon. "And you won't feel anything. It's not invasive like western"—she withdrew her hands briefly to make air quotes—"'medicine.'"

Tariq looked the opposite of reassured. "I'm fine with aspirin, thanks."

"You know that was invented by the Nazis."

"Um," said Paris. "I don't think that's true."

"Yeah." Tariq tried to nod without getting his face too close to Gretchen's healing energy. "I think you're getting it mixed up with Fanta."

"You shouldn't drink that," she told them earnestly. "It's full of chemicals."

Tariq, who was practically supine now, opened his mouth, then closed it again. And then mercifully they were called back to the ballroom, so Paris could learn how terrible his cookies had been.

Judging was awful. They were lined up on their stools like they'd all been picked last for sports at school while Marianne Wolvercote and Wilfred Honey prowled—at least Marianne prowled, Wilfred more sort of ambled—up and down the table of cookies, pausing occasionally to scrutinise some unfathomable element of somebody's bake.

"These," declared Wilfred Honey as they approached Tariq's tray of rather pale cookies, "are underbaked."

Marianne Wolvercote nodded. "Yes, they don't need long in the oven, but these are about two minutes short of long enough."

They'd been firmly instructed not to react to the judges' critiques for the blind bake, and Tariq did a far better job of that than Paris, because Paris knew the underbaking was kind of his fault. Even with the dough taking a while to cool, the first aiders hadn't let Tariq back into the ballroom until it was slightly too late to finish his cookies properly. Tanya, at least, had not suffered too horribly from her part in the Great Refrigerator Catastrophe of season seven, with Wilfred Honey noting her cookies were "exactly the right level of chewy and a lovely golden colour."

The rest began to blur, some too dry, some too moist, this a little too brown, that inexplicably two cookies short. And then it was Paris's turn.

Until right then, he hadn't quite been prepared for the enormity of having his baking judged by two professional baking people on an internationally syndicated television show.

It was, it turned out, a truly enormous level of enormity.

For a moment, he wondered why he'd signed himself up for such an obviously and objectively terrible experience. Then he remembered that he hadn't. That Morag had signed him up for it and then inertia and Paris's fear of saying no had done the rest. He'd have been angry with her, but the dread and anticipation curdling in his stomach like a truly ruined custard were pushing all other possible feelings out of the way.

"Now, these look promising," said Marianne Wolvercote grudgingly, and Paris silently braced himself for the hammer-blow of criticism that was going to follow. "The colour's good, the chocolate chips are evenly distributed and have neither over- nor undermelted."

"But of course," Wilfred Honey added, "what really matters is how they taste."

This was it. They were going to taste awful. They were going to taste titanically, cataclysmically, biblically awful. Paris was going to have used salt instead of sugar, or rabbit droppings instead of chocolate chips, and Marianne was going to try one and then say *don't eat that, Wilfred*, which was the worst thing that she could possibly say.

"Now, that"—Wilfred Honey chewed meditatively—"is a proper biccy."

Marianne offered the camera one of her rare smiles. "Yes, whoever baked this has done very well. The secret is to remember they carry on cooking for a while after you remove them from the oven, so when you first take them out, they need be a little paler than you might expect. These have a perfect texture and the flavour is spot-on."

Oh God, he should never have let Morag sig—wait. What?

"I...I...won?" said Paris to Colin Thrimp's camera operator a few minutes later. "I was so sure I'd messed that up. When they said it was me, I thought they'd made a mistake. But, um, obviously I'm really...happy and grateful and...a bit scared. Because there's still the baketacular and now they'll be expecting me to do well and I probably won't."

Meanwhile, Bernard was standing under a tree explaining the mystery of the missing cookies. "So what happened was, I was worried that something might go wrong, so I thought, *I know, I'll make fourteen and that way I can pick the twelve best*. So I did that, and I took the two worst ones, and I put them aside. Then I checked to see where they were, but they weren't where I thought I'd put them, so I thought I'd just not done it, and I'd forgotten, so I put them aside again. And then there were only ten and by the time I noticed it was too late. But"—he smiled—"I found the first two in the end. They were in my apron pocket. Look." And with an air of profound triumph, he produced two now slightly crumbly cookies.

"That's great," said the production assistant who was conducting the interview. "But can we just get it again, because I think a bird crapped on your shoulder."

"You know, I reckon I did all right"—that was Tariq, sparkling into the camera like he'd been doing it his whole life instead of since that morning—"given I got hit in the face with a fridge."

I came first on day one, Paris texted. **It probably doesn't mean anything but it's nice.**

He paused. **Hope things are going well where you are. Love to Dad if you see him.**

"Boo." Tariq Tiggered him from behind again. "A bunch of us are going to the bar. Are you coming?"

Paris turned, still not feeling entirely unshitty for the whole face-fridge incident. "I'm really sorry about your cookies."

"It's fine. I've got tomorrow. And a bunch of people did worse than me despite not being hit in the face with a fridge, so I'm taking that as a good sign."

"But...but..."

"No." Tariq wagged a glittery finger in his face. "I'm the one who got hit in the face, so I get to decide when you stop apologising. And that *when* is, like, three hours ago. So let's go to the bar, okay?"

"I..." Picking at the sleeves of his jumper, Paris squirmed helplessly. "...I think I'm just going to head back to my room."

Tariq sighed. "Are you always like this?"

"Probably." A pause. "Um, like what?"

"Like"—his hands described circles in the air that were perhaps less expressive than he hoped they would be—"you know *Romeo and Juliet*? Well, if that was you, you'd be 'if I profane with my unworthiest hand, oh no I've profaned, sorry for profaning, I profaned you didn't I?' and later you'd pop up under the balcony and be all 'I'm sorry for profaning you earlier,' and she'd be all 'a rose by any other name would smell as sweet,' and you'd be all 'yes but can we get back to the profaning?'"

Paris thought about it. "I...I'm not...Oh God, I am, I'm totally like that, aren't I?"

"Yes. But you're also really pretty."

That was fair. He had been kind of awf—then Paris's brain caught up with his ears and he almost winced. "Wait? What?"

"Come. To. The. Bar."

And because Paris didn't know how to address the pretty question without sounding incredibly needy, they went to the bar.

There was a small crowd already sitting round a table with a variety of drinks and snacks between them.

"Do you want anything?" called out Bernard. "It's my round."

Tariq slipped into the space available. "Sorry to be difficult, and I know it's a social thing, but I don't do rounds. I don't drink, so I just wind up subsidising other people's beer with my student loan."

"Don't be silly," Bernard called back. "I can shout you a lemonade. What about you, Paris?"

"Oh. Um. Sparkling water?"

Bernard grinned at them. "Look at you two, Generation Sensible. That's what happens when you grow up in a housing crisis."

A couple of minutes later, holding three glasses in a sort of triangle between his fingers, with a packet of cracked black pepper Kettle Chips hanging from his teeth, Bernard made his way carefully back to the table. "Beer for me, lemonade for Tariq, sparkling water for Paris, and crisps for the table."

He opened the crisps and laid them ceremoniously between the glasses and the bowls of olives. Then, in an effort to make them more accessible, he began tearing one side open with, as it turned out, far too much force. The packet jerked upwards sharply, sending cracked black pepper Kettle Chips fountaining in the air, before they rained gently down on the gathering.

"Thanks, Bernard." Tanya fished one out of her wineglass, nibbled it, and then tucked it quietly under a paper napkin.

"Do you all know Paris?" asked Tariq, mostly, Paris suspected, as a polite way to fill the space in which everyone was picking crisps out of their hair, food, and, in one case, cleavage. "Paris, you've met Bernard and Tanya, of course, from the time you assaulted me. This is Joan." He gestured to a no-nonsense kind of woman with a buzz cut and a denim shirt. "She's in carpentry, which honestly I didn't even realise was a thing anymore."

Joan gave him a flat stare. "Where do you think banisters come from?"

"Factories?"

"And how do you think they get into your house?"

"The magic staircase elves?"

"Or"—Joan's voice had a permanent edge of sarcasm, but she didn't seem actually offended—"as we prefer to be called: carpenters."

"You know," said Bernard, "I've never really understood how carpenters are different from joiners."

Joan stroked her chin. "Well, joiners tend to work off-site, with things that need large machinery. Whereas carpenters tend to start major world religions."

There was a moment of silence. And then Bernard gave a little bounce. "Oh, like Jesus. I was thinking of the band."

Not even Tariq seemed to know how to respond to that.

Eventually Tanya rallied, turning to Paris with the sort of smile you gave a student who'd handed in their maths homework early. "Good job on the cookies."

"Oh, don't." He cringed. "I got lucky. And I know I'm going to mess up tomorrow because it's going to be really complicated."

"It's just biscuits on some biscuits," Joan pointed out.

Paris was still mid-cringe. "It's not, though, is it? It's your best biscuit served on an edible display stand that's also made out of biscuit. And it has to be two different *types* of biscuit, which means you've got two chances of it going wrong, and I know one of mine is going to snap and drop the other one on the floor."

"And if they do"—Tanya discovered a spare Kettle Chip still clinging to her hair—"you pick them up and you serve what's left."

This was probably supposed to be reassuring. But having had his cookies scrutinised more than anyone should ever have their cookies scrutinised, Paris could imagine, all too vividly, the way Marianne Wolvercote and Wilfred Honey would look at him as he presented them with the crumbling remains of his sugar cookie stand and two surviving biscuits roses de Reims. Wilfred Honey would be deeply sorrowful and say something like *now, you've had an accident, haven't you, lad*, as if Paris was a toddler who'd wet himself in front of the class. And Marianne Wolvercote would raise an eyebrow and say something arch and cutting like *fuck you, you're shit*. Okay, maybe not that. Maybe something a bit more BBC.

Like *fuck you, you're shit, and your biscuits are shit and—*

"What about you, Paris?" Bernard was asking.

Uh-oh. "What about me what?"

"What are you making tomorrow?" He smiled encouragingly. "Joan here's making a bookcase. Tariq is doing bee biscuit on a honeycomb stand. Tanya's doing ginger chemical reaction biscuits which, if I'm honest, I don't really know what they are. And I'm doing lemon shortbread on a vanilla shortbread table."

Paris stared at them in horror. Because, with the possible exception of shortbread on shortbread—which he thought might be the biscuit equivalent of denim on denim—they all sounded so much better than his idea. "I was going to make biscuits roses de Reims. But now I'm worried it'll look really pretentious."

"Don't be silly," said Joan. "What could possibly be pretentious about making a biscuit with a French name that nobody's ever heard of."

"Oh no." Paris hid his face in his hands. "I'm going to be the guy who cheated on the blind bake by smacking someone with a fridge, then made biscuits nobody had ever heard of, then went out."

Draining the last of his lemonade-and-Kettle-Chip cocktail, Tariq blinked in outrage. "Excuse me. I've heard of them. They're the thing you dip in champagne. They're very chic. Although I think Leopold the Second of Belgium liked them and he was famously a mass murderer."

"Well"—Tanya shrugged—"it'll stop people complaining about liberal bias on the BBC."

"Don't be silly," said Tariq. "*Nothing* could stop people complaining about liberal bias on the BBC."

That wasn't, to Paris, entirely comforting. And while he tried to relax into the evening and enjoy the flow of conversation, his mind kept circling back to *what if I've made biscuits with unintentionally colonialist implications?* and from there to *everybody is going to hate me* and from there to *I should never leave my house and never do anything.*

Sunday

"OH NO," **SAID PARIS.** Normally baking was calming, but this was anything but calm. This was doing for his love of baking what A-level English literature had done for his love of poetry. "Oh no, oh no, oh no."

Grace Forsythe materialised at his side. "Is there a problem, my little cupcake?"

There was no problem. Not really. He'd made biscuits roses de Reims a hundred times before, and they were going about the same way they always had. But this was TV and somebody had asked him a question, so he tried to answer it honestly. "I'm worried that my meringues are going to settle while I'm beating these egg yolks and then the whole thing will be dense and won't work."

"Tell you what." Grace Forsythe adopted an attitude of military alertness. "I'll guard the meringues, and if I see the little buggers settling, I'll sound the alarm."

"Would you?" He gave her a look of unalloyed gratitude.

"Absolutely. There's just one slight hitch. I'm not totally sure what a settling meringue looks like. I'm assuming it's a meringue that's hit forty, realised it's still single, and married the first other meringue who'd have it."

Paris's look of gratitude alloyed slightly, and he eyed his bowl nervously. "I just sort of mean...I don't want them to collapse or deflate or absorb too much moisture."

It was at this moment that the judges began their approach. And this wasn't good. It wasn't good at all. He'd come on national television because he thought—well, Morag thought, but also *he* thought—that he was shit-hot at baking, and he'd tried to do something really complex and impressive and it was going to turn out that he was actually much less hot and much more shit than anybody had expected.

"Oh no," said Paris, looking around for somewhere to hide and seriously considering the oven. "Oh no, oh no, oh no."

"Don't worry." Grace Forsythe patted him on the shoulder. "They don't bite. Well, Wilfred doesn't."

"So what are you making here, lad?" Wilfred Honey took up his customary position at the end of the bench.

Paris knew what he was making. He was making biscuits roses de Reims. But saying it aloud suddenly felt impossible. Like he was confessing to a crime.

"Now this"—Marianne Wolvercote pounced on his bottle of champagne—"is promising us something special. I hope you can deliver. From the ingredients and"—she glanced back at the bottle—"accompaniment, it looks like you're making biscuits roses de Reims."

"Yeah," Paris admitted. "But I'm going to mess it up."

Wilfred Honey had that concerned sagely look Paris had seen on TV. Usually when contestants had grossly overreached. "They *are* very technical. And this is only the first week, so I hope you know what you're doing."

"I don't." Paris blinked against a sudden prickle of tears. "I thought I did. But I don't. I'm really sorry. I'm going to serve you awful, terrible biscuits."

Marianne Wolvercote's gaze became fleetingly less steely. "I'm sure you won't, Paris. Just keep a lightness of touch, and when you're adding the dry ingredients, remember to check the bottom of the bowl for lurking flour."

"Oh, thank you." He gave her a weak smile. And, feeling less reassured than he thought he was supposed to, wiped his eyes with a fresh tissue and got on with beating his yolks.

Everyone else's biscuits were much better than Paris's biscuits. And even his interview had been a failure because he'd been sniffling too much to give them any usable footage. Still, at least he wouldn't have to do this again next week. And while going home first would be embarrassing and humiliating and dreadful and devastating, at least he'd be able to tell Morag he told her so.

Not that he would.

Rodney in the Cardigan and the tall man Paris hadn't been able to use Tariq's name trick on had already been judged, and they'd received okay comments. Not the excoriation of disappointment Paris both was expecting and probably deserved. Next up was Gretchen, the woman who'd tried to nonconsensually Reiki Tariq over lunch yesterday. Her biscuits didn't, if Paris forced himself to look past his haze of despair, seem like they'd come out the way she'd been hoping. Of course, from what little he knew of her, Gretchen was slightly, well, slightly eccentric. Which meant it wasn't impossible that "pile of broken biscuit parts in irregular, shapes, sizes, and colours" had been her plan all along. Perhaps it was a statement on the unseen harmonies of the universe.

Or perhaps her biscuits had just collapsed.

"So these," Gretchen explained in much the same voice she'd explained that she was going to heal Tariq's nose by magic, "are spelt and hemp biscuits served on a pair of giving hands, one modelled in vanilla shortbread, the other in chocolate shortbread."

Marianne Wolvercote stared at the crumbled mounds in front of her. "I'm not really getting hands. So much as ... nothing."

"But you know, Marianne," said Wilfred Honey quickly, "what really matters is the taste."

"Part of the challenge was making a biscuit that could support another biscuit. These"—Marianne picked up a piece of far-too-soft shortbread—"couldn't support their own weight."

Wilfred Honey selected one of the bullet-like hemp biscuits that languished amidst the rubble of the giving hands. "Never mind, though. Let's give them a try." He was still trying about thirty seconds later. At which point he turned decorously away from the camera and spat something into a handkerchief. "I think," he said, "they're a little dry. And while the flavours are interesting, they're not quite to my taste."

"That's all right." Gretchen smiled sweetly. "I appreciate that you tried."

Paris was sweating through his jumper as the next few contestants took their turn before the judges. Joan had made an intricate bookcase—far better than anything Paris could have constructed—and received a lot of praise for her presentation, even if her flavours didn't quite live up to it. Tariq had run slightly out of time, which meant his beehive was mostly just a slab of honeycomb biscuit with some very prettily iced bees sitting on top of it. And Bernard's shortbread-on-shortbread was so remarkably unremarkable they had to do two takes because neither Marianne Wolvercote nor Wilfred Honey could think of anything to say.

Then it was Paris. And he picked up his wobbly stand of catastrophically overbaked biscuits with a sense of dread so profound it tasted like blood and felt like nausea. He was trembling so hard it was a wonder he didn't lose the whole stack as he staggered the twenty-seven thousand miles from his workstation to the judges' table.

"I'm sorry," he cried, as soon as he was in range, "I'm so sorry. These went really wrong. And the whole thing's just a complete state. And…I'm sorry. I'm just so, so sorry."

There was a low buzzing in his ears like Tariq's bees had decided to move into his head. A buzzing that, in Paris's experience, usually presaged the sort of faint that got you kicked out of PE for a week and mocked in the dorms for a month.

⬤

"I thought I was going to faint," Paris told Colin Thrimp in the post-show interview. "I was sure I'd ruined everything. I can't believe I won." He blinked his damp eyelashes and risked a shy smile for the camera. Then something occurred to him. "Oh no. That means they'll expect me to do well next week too. Oh, this is so much stress. Oh no."

They let him go not long after this, and he wove his way carefully through the rest of the contestants who were still finishing their interviews.

So, he texted his mum. **That baking show I'm on? Where I did quite well yesterday? I won the first week. Go me.**

"Well," Gretchen was saying, looking far more contented than Paris would have if he'd been eliminated. "I put my intent out into the universe and, on this occasion, the universe has told me to move on. But I'll never forget all the wonderful people I met in my time on *Bake Expectations*."

Paris was heading for the car park, where Morag was already waiting for him, when Tariq Tiggered him from behind for the third time that weekend.

"Congratulations," he said. "And after all that fuss you made yesterday. And—" He paused "—today."

Paris drooped. "Oh, don't. I feel really silly. I think I must have got in my head or something. And, anyway, it was just a fluke."

"You're right." Tariq was smiling at but, Paris hoped, laughing with him. "Definitely a fluke. People are always making technically flawless meringue-based biscuits by accident."

"They've gone wrong every other time I've made them." Not catastrophically badly, of course, but flawed, definitely flawed. Touched with an edge of not-quite-good-enough like everything else.

"Have they, though? Or are you just saying that to make me feel better about my beehive getting colony collapse?"

"I'm not," Paris explained earnestly. "They've genuinely gone really badly." True, Morag and her naked friend had seemed to enjoy them, but they'd probably just been humouring him.

"And there I was thinking you were being nice to me. But you're insisting that no, you just suck."

Paris gave a little flail. "Um. No. I mean, yes. I mean your bees were great. And you probably only lost track of time because I hit you in the face with a fridge."

"Yes." Tariq nodded. "You hit me in the face yesterday so hard that you knocked my sense of temporoception clean out of my head."

"I'm sorry. I'm really—"

"I'm *joking*."

"I know, but you shouldn't have to. Because I shouldn't have hit you in the face with a fridge."

Given how bad Paris was at reading people, he took the fact that he *thought* Tariq was looking at him affectionately as a sign of deeply misunderstood scorn. "Didn't we agree yesterday that you have to stop apologising for that?"

"Actually"—Paris risked a smile—"you said I had to. But I didn't agree to anything and I can apologise a lot. It's sorry all the way down."

"Is it?" Tariq stopped, his eyes travelling very slowly from the top of Paris's head all the way to the tips of his battered Converses.

"Um. What's happening? What are you doing right now?"

Tariq quickly looked up again. "Sorry. I assumed this…all this…was a kind of weird flirtation technique."

"What? No?" Fuck, now the guy he'd hit with a fridge thought Paris was sexually harassing him. He took a respectful-but-too-sharp step backwards. "How would that work?"

"I have no idea. I thought it was like the opposite of a neg. You know, instead of insulting me so I'll feel bad about myself and be off my guard when you ask me out, you're insulting yourself so I'll…Actually that's about as far as I've got."

"Oh my God, no." Paris had that too-hot, too-cold, too-everything feeling again. "I wasn't going to ask you out. I'd never ask you out."

There was a pause like someone had dropped a knife on their foot.

"Wow. Well. Okay. That clears that up." Tariq pulled his

shoulders back with more dignity than Paris had ever been able to muster in his life. "So I'm going to my car. See you next week."

"Shit. No. I didn't mean because you're not. I mean because I'm—"

Tariq had gone. And an irate Glaswegian was already beeping her horn from across the car park.

Saturday

THE DRIVE TO Patchley House, once they got out of London, took them through some very pretty scenery, and Paris was trying hard to enjoy it. After breaking down on camera last week he'd come home and told Morag all about it, and she'd reprimanded him in her usual way, pointing out that he'd won, that he had nothing to complain about, and that he should stop whinging like the pampered English bastard he was and get on with his life.

And he had, pretty much. He'd disappeared into his history books and his practice bakes, and for a while he'd been able to go back to his little world where everything was safe.

The quiet confines of his flat with his neat, familiar kitchen and Neferneferuaten staring quizzically up at him, where nobody was going to slice his pies open like an autopsy and assess the thickness of his pastry or the evenness of his filling. Now, though, he'd left all that behind and was returning, inevitably, to the ballroom where he'd have to bake, once more, for people who knew nothing about him. Who he couldn't trust to be kind.

"I don't think I can do this," he told Morag out of what must have seemed to her like nowhere.

She kept her eyes on the road, which was good because it meant Paris couldn't see the look in them. "You fucking can. You fucking have. You fucking will."

"I got lucky last week, but what if it goes wrong this time?"

The way Morag shrugged suggested that you could fit all of the shits she gave about the possibility of it all going wrong into a carton of eggs that already contained a dozen eggs. "Then it goes wrong. Things do, you know, people still get by."

Paris didn't really have an answer for that, although he privately suspected that *what if x? / then x* was rather a cheap rhetorical trick and not one Aristotle would have approved of.

The journey continued quietly for a while, and then another thought bubbled up through Paris's subconscious and out of his mouth without him getting much say in the matter. "But I hit a guy with a—"

"Fridge. I know." Morag still didn't look at him, but from the tone in her voice Paris was firmly convinced that she was sick of the fridge story. "And you said he told you to drop it. Also, he clearly fancied you."

"He did—"

"Pariiis."

"You weren't even—"

"Pariiis."

"No I mean really this ti—"

Morag made a sound that weirdly put Paris in mind of Neferneferuaten when she was in a bad, hungry, or just especially feline mood. "Paris. We go through this every time. You are an annoyingly good-looking man in a posh, obvious sort of way. Boys like you. *This* boy likes you so much that you hit him in the face with a fridge and the first thing he did afterwards was jump on your back and start flirting with you."

That didn't sound right. "But I also told him I'd never ask him out."

"You what?" It was a detail of the story that Paris had, for the past week, managed to elide.

"*He* said *he* thought *I* was trying to flirt with *him*," explained Paris, not quite sure how Tariq's lack of interest in him wasn't obvious from the context. "And because I didn't want him to think I was harassing him or being a fetishist, I reassured him that I wasn't going to ask him out, and he seemed to find that really insulting."

"Oh, I *wonder why*." The car juddered over a cattle grid as they turned onto the narrow country road that would lead them, far sooner than later, to Patchley House.

"I didn't mean it like that."

"How did you mean it?"

"Reassuringly?" Paris tried, although it sounded weak even to him.

"Paris." Morag gave a deep, rightly exasperated sigh. "You're hopeless. Did you *want* to ask him out?"

"No. I mean not *no* no. Just it didn't come up."

"It doesn't, you know, unless you make it. And I'd assume that you'd only want to"—here Morag's voice became sarcastic in a way only a Glaswegian can be sarcastic—"*reassure* him that you weren't going to ask him out if at least a bit of you was thinking of it."

"I wasn't, I sw—"

One of many things Paris envied-slash-admired about Morag was her ability to interrupt people just by looking at them in the right way. She was looking at him in the right way now.

"Okay, maybe a tiny, tiny part of me was thinking about it. He was nice, and cute, and seemed to be able to put up with me even though I hit him with a fridge. But I wasn't going to actually do it."

"Now, *that* I believe. You want my advice, go back, cook whatever you're meant to cook this week, then tell this guy you're sorry that you were such a soggy wankbiscuit and that you'd actually like to go out with him thanks."

"But—"

"No buts. Talk to him."

"But the show…my bakes…" Paris wasn't quite sure if he was putting together a reasonable objection or just naming things he happened to be able to think of.

"The show and the bakes will look after themselves. You did fine last week. You are going to do fine this week. You just need to get out of your own way and stop being such a titanic fucking prick to yourself."

Paris could, at least, accept that he was being a titanic fucking prick, so now they were quibbling over the victims of his titanic prickishness.

"Really, though," Morag continued as they reached the main gates and the long driveway, "you'll do well. At the baking, I mean. Dating, you're a fucking high-speed-train derailment."

That, Paris understood, was probably intended as reassurance, much as his assertion that he'd never date Tariq had been. Unfortunately it was about as ineffective. "I hope so. But what if the blind bake is something I've never heard of before?"

Morag shrugged. "Then it'll be something you've never heard of before. And you'll deal."

It was something he'd never heard of before.

He was not dealing.

"Are you all right there, my darling?" Grace Forsythe put a gentle hand on Paris's arm.

"I'm fine," he said, staring at his bench of flour and potatoes. "It's just I don't know what a knish is. I've never heard of a knish. And I'm worried that makes me come across as culturally ignorant. But then I'm worried that I'm just making my cultural ignorance about me and not the people whose culture I'm ignorant about and—"

Grace made a *you're being peculiar* noise. "If it's any consolation, Paris, right after I do the introduction there'll be a cutaway where I go and speak to someone who makes traditional knishes and explains all about the history. So if you want to learn about them you can watch the show when it airs. Or just Google it when you get your phone back."

On some level, this made sense to Paris. On another level, he was convinced that the fact he didn't already know it made him a terrible person.

It was at this moment that Colin Thrimp scurried over. "Grace, we've talked about you being meta before. It never gives us usable footage."

"The footage, Colin," retorted Grace, glaring, "would be perfectly usable if only Jennifer trusted my sense of humour and the great British public."

Colin put a hand to his earpiece. "Jennifer wants you to tell her when trusting the great British public last ended well for anyone."

For a moment, Grace looked stymied, which wasn't a look Paris had ever seen her have before, at least on TV. "You're both being colossal pains in my perineum. Now kindly fuck off and leave Paris to his gentile guilt and baking."

Unsurprisingly, Colin Thrimp fucked off as directed.

"I'm sorry," said Paris again, very aware he was making everything worse for everyone as usual. "I get really freaked out when I don't know what I'm doing. And the instructions just say 'make the dough' and they don't say preheat the oven yet, and it's a long challenge. Which makes me think something weird is going on."

Grace Forsythe shrugged consolingly. "Well. That's the way it goes sometimes. And if knishes were horses…"

"…horses would mostly be found in areas with a large Jewish community?" suggested Paris.

"Something like that." And, with a last cheeky glance to camera, Grace Forsythe wandered off to support someone else.

This left Paris alone with some unhelpful instructions, a half-filled food processor, and the crushing awareness he was already behind everyone else. He'd thought having to make perfect cookies was bad enough, but at least he'd known what a perfect chocolate chip cookie was meant to look like. They'd been told that a knish was some kind of filled pastry, so he was intending to treat it like a pasty and hope. But that seemed both culturally insensitive and not a very good strategy.

Which meant after lunch he was going to be standing there with something in front of him that looked nothing like anything anyone else had made. And Wilfred Honey would be all *well, somebody's clearly never had a knish before* and Marianne Wolvercote would be all *yes, these are just pasties, and not very good pasties at that* and then the entire nation would be all *wow, that guy's racist and shit at baking. It's a good job he's going out.* And later, Morag would say *well, I wouldn't have put you forward if I knew how badly you were going to fuck this up.* And his mum and dad would say—

Actually he didn't know what they'd say.

But they'd probably be pretty upset. Also they probably knew what a knish was.

"I don't hold," Catherine Parr was saying loudly to a flinching camera operator, "with them asking us to make ethnic food. *Bake Expectations* is a celebration of British baking. And this is not British."

Okay. Maybe he was overreacting. Clearly, Paris wasn't the only one who was having trouble here. Although he really didn't want to think of himself as being in the same boat as Catherine Parr, because that was a boat for terrible people who believed terrible things.

And that was about all the reassurance he could muster. And as it turned out, all the reassurance he was going to get.

"Yeah," Tariq was saying, "I've actually made these a couple of times. I got the recipe from a guy in my interfaith group at uni."

Oh God. Tariq was going to win and Paris was going to be eliminated. They'd probably only kept him in so that the audience would find it really satisfying when the guy who smacked the other guy in the face got knocked out of the competition by that guy a week later. And to Tariq he'd forever be that weirdo who said he'd never ask him out. Then left the competition.

For making a shit knish.

The whole shit-knish-wouldn't-ask-you-out-actually-really-want-to-ask-you-out fiasco was still buzzing around Paris's head all through judging. In an effort to make it debuzz, he resolved to talk to Tariq at lunch and apologise, and maybe explain why he'd been so awful. Then, after he failed to do any of that at lunch, he resolved to do it at dinner.

Week two of the competition, he texted his mum. **Not going so well.**

Although, actually, he'd done okay. His knish wasn't the worst knish. Annoyingly Catherine Parr's knish wasn't the worst knish either. That distinction had gone to the very tall guy Paris thought might be called Chris. He'd have been more certain he was called Chris if he'd managed to execute Tariq's name trick properly, but he'd heard "Chris" and gone immediately to Hemsworth and now, for the rest of his life, was doomed to be uncertain whether that particular man—who he also thought may have been a policeman—was named Chris, Liam, or Luke.

Once they'd announced the worst knish, they then had to announce the best knish. And the judges tried to act like it was close but this was one of those weeks where only one of them had known what they were doing. And that was obviously Tariq.

"It's amazing," he said in his interview afterwards, "what you can achieve when you don't get smacked in the face with a fridge."

Okay, it was now or never. Well, it was now or bottle out and try again in about eight to twelve minutes. Repeat until bedtime.

"Tariq?" Paris burst out of the rhododendron bush where he'd been definitely not hiding.

Tariq turned, his expression more apprehensive than Paris

would have liked. He'd also slung a tailored jacket over the peacock-print shirt he'd had under his apron, which made him look devastatingly cool and not the kind of guy Paris would have dared approach in a million years under any other circumstance. "Hi?"

"Hi. I, um. So." Paris paused for breath. This wasn't a disastrous start. But you'd have needed to be exceptionally generous to call it a good start. "The thing is. I mean. So. Um."

"Are you all right?" asked Tariq, hovering somewhere between concern and perplexity.

"Oh yes. Um. I just. Um."

Tariq's phone bleeped, and he slid it out of the pocket of his very well-tailored jeans to check it. "Hold that thought. Whatever that thought was. I'm going to go and pray."

"There's an app? That tells you when to do that?"

"Honey, you can get apps that tell you when to drink water, which is something your body does automatically. Keeping track of a schedule that changes day-to-day and month-to-month depending on where the sun is and where you are is complex and matters to millions of people all over the world. *Of course* there's an app for it."

Oh God, it was the knish all over again. Not only had he demonstrated complete ignorance of Jewish cuisine, he'd also accidentally implied that he didn't think Muslims knew how to use technology. "Sorry that was—"

"Look"—Tariq's fingers, the nails painted metallic turquoise this week, fluttered impatiently—"we've been here before. I know how long your apologies take. I've got a religious obligation. I'll come find you later."

"Sorry. I mean—"

Tariq was gone. And for a moment Paris just stood there, not knowing what to do with himself. Because if he went away and did something else, that would make him look like he didn't give a shit. And if he hung around waiting, that would make him look like a stalker. In desperation he fumbled for his phone and googled "how long do prayers take if you're a Muslim," which did not help with his growing suspicion that he might secretly be a giant racist.

According to the internet, it took five to ten minutes to do the actual praying bit, but Tariq would also have to walk to the Lodge, find where Mecca was—however you did that, there was probably another app, wasn't there—and get himself set up. Then he'd have to put everything away and decide whether he was coming back at all. Or if he'd rather be doing literally anything else than talking to Paris.

And by the time Paris had decided that standing around having a crisis wasn't helping, and that he should at least sit around having a crisis...and then found somewhere to sit...and then realised that it was just a log and maybe you weren't supposed to sit on a log because it wasn't a chair and there might be spiders in it or woodlice...and then decided that no, this was a planned garden and they wouldn't leave a log lying around at sitting-on height if they didn't want people to sit on it...and—

By the time all that had happened, Tariq was back.

"Um," said Paris again. "Hi."

Tariq put his hands on his hips. "Hi. And just so you know, I've got another set of prayers coming up in about four hours, so you might want to speed this up."

"ImreallysorryIsaidIdneveraskyouout."

"Okay, maybe not that much."

"I'm really sorry I said I'd never ask you out." Paris took a deep breath. "I just meant that I wasn't making any assumptions or trying to harass you or anything. I mean, it's the twenty-first century, I shouldn't even really be assuming that the fact you wear nail varnish means you're into guys. Or even that you are a guy. Shit, have I been misgendering you? Like, I don't remember talking about you specifically, but I think I might have done? Because obviously when I'm talking to you, I use *you*, which is non-gendered but, for all I know—"

Tariq was giving him a look that might have been amused. But was also a little bewildered. "Slow your roll, honey. Yes, I like guys. Yes, my pronouns are *he* and *him*, although I will answer to *girl* and, on special occasions, *queen*."

"I don't think I've ever called anyone girl or queen," Paris told him. "I don't think I even call *girls* girl because that would be sexist. And I'd probably call the Queen...Your Majesty? I think that's what you call her? Or is it ma'am? Or Your Highness?"

Something about Tariq's sparkly, TV-confident presence was oddly soothing, and Paris found his brain slowly de-spiralling. "But I suppose I'll never meet the Queen," he recovered. "Unless I win and I have to make her a birthday cake, like the guy who won season two. Wouldn't that be embarrassing, though, making a cake for the Queen and calling her the wrong thing?" Paris smiled to show it was a joke and thought he half succeeded.

"Okay, all of *this*?" Tariq was making an encompassing gesture. "It's adorable, but it's a hot mess. I'm not secretly straight, or secretly nonbinary, and you're not going to randomly have to meet the Queen, and by the way how freaking *blessed* is your life if your biggest fear is having to meet a royal because you won ten grand and the nation's favourite baking show?"

Paris squirmed. "That's not my biggest fear."

"Oh?" Perhaps Paris was wrong—he was probably wrong—but Tariq seemed slightly less impatient than he had every right to be. "What is?"

"Spiders." Strictly speaking, it wasn't his biggest fear, but it was the biggest fear Paris was comfortable naming aloud to a man who had correctly identified him as a hot mess less than twenty seconds ago. "I have to get Morag or Neferneferuaten to kill them for me, and then I feel bad because they're not doing any harm and I'm probably messing up the food chain."

"You have a friend called Neferneferuaten? How from Chelsea can you be?"

"Technically, I think she's from Russia? Although I got her from a rescue home so..."

To Paris's surprise, Tariq came and sat next to him. Not super close next to him. But next to him enough. "Now it sounds like you have a mail-order bride."

"She's a cat."

"Your mail-order bride's a cat? I think that's illegal on two levels."

This was the good kind of teasing, Paris decided. The kind of teasing you got from people who didn't hate you. Not the kind of teasing he was used to. "I'm not married to my cat. She's just a cat."

"And you named her after an ambiguously gendered Egyptian pharaoh, why?"

Paris blinked. "I thought it might be a good way to start conversations? I thought people might be *hey, that's a beautiful cat*, and I could be like *yes, her name's Neferneferuaten*. And then they could be *that's an interesting name, where does it come from?* And I could say *oh, it's the name of an ambiguously gendered Egyptian pharaoh*. Except you already knew that. So it hasn't worked."

"Sorry, honey," said Tariq, laughing. "Let me try that again. That's an interesting name for a cat. Where does it come from?"

"Oh. It's the name of an ambiguously gendered Egyptian pharaoh."

Tariq arched a beautifully shaped brow. "Fancy that."

"Although actually"—the part of Paris that unironically loved his subject temporarily overrode the part of his brain that knew when it was time to shut up—"I think she's not ambiguously gendered anymore. I think they've done trace DNA analysis or something. They're still not sure if she's the same Neferneferuaten that was Tutankhamun's dad's wife. Or if she's a different, independent Neferneferuaten."

"Wow, you really do know a lot about Neferneferuaten."

"Well, since it was my cunning plan to make people talk to me, I thought I'd better."

There was a thoughtful silence. "While I appreciate you going to this much effort for an icebreaker," Tariq said finally, "are there not several major problems with this strategy?"

"To be fair, I think most people don't already know who Neferneferuaten was."

"What can I say? She was the original fierce queen."

"Um"—Paris twitched, still caught between his instinctive desire to ancient-history-nerd and his more instinctive desire not to sound like a complete arsehole—"that might have been Merneith."

Tariq paused just long enough for Paris to convince himself he'd fallen squarely into the arsehole box. "Good to know. But actually I was thinking more that cats aren't...you know, they're not like dogs. You don't go to the park and walk your cat. So if someone finds out you've got a cat, you've either told them, in which case they're already talking to you, or they've seen you with her, in which case they're probably already in your house."

"You'd be surprised"—there was a moment of uncomfortable squirm—"how often I need a conversation starter even if both those things are true."

"You know"—Tariq gave him a smile that Paris couldn't help but be surprised by—"I really wouldn't."

There was no way to reply to that. At least, there was no way Paris could think of to reply to that. Not that he could think of good ways to reply to most things. So he let the silence blossom for a moment, like some kind of fungus, then said, "See."

"Yeah. Maybe you need to get another cat."

"I don't think Neferneferuaten would like that. She's really skittish around other animals."

The silence-fungus started creeping back. Then Tariq said, "So...about how you're not *not* going to ask me out?"

Shit. They were back on this topic. And Paris was suddenly very hot and a bit nauseous. "Yeah. Like I say, I'm really sorry and I didn't mean to insult you or anything."

"That wasn't quite what I—"

Seized by a sudden urge to talk about literally anything else or to be literally anywhere else, Paris glanced at his phone as if it had just buzzed, which it definitely hadn't. If only there was an app that would detect when you'd fucked up a social situation so badly you needed to bail. And then bail you. "I think they're going to be serving dinner soon. I'll—I'll talk to you after maybe?"

Tariq looked if not shocked, then at least a little zapped. "Okay? Good chat. Learned a lot about early Egyptian monarchs."

"Actually," Paris's mouth said before his brain could stop it, "Neferneferuaten is from the Eighteenth Dynasty, which was really the beginning of the New Kingdom."

And before he could see how Tariq responded to that, he dropped a quick "fuck sorry" and ran.

Sunday

PARIS HAD NOT, in fact, spoken to Tariq after dinner. He'd wanted to, but there'd always been a really good reason why he couldn't. Like Tariq was talking to someone else. Or Paris was talking to someone else. Or Tariq was going for dessert and probably didn't want to be bothered while he was going for dessert. Or Paris was holding a used paper plate and wasn't sure where to put it, and thought going up to a guy you liked with a used paper plate covered in smeary bits of ketchup and sausage grease was probably kind of insulting. And wasn't it a bit early? Or a bit late? And what if he brought up the not-asking-him-out thing again? Or the cat thing. Or the fridge-in-the-face thing. So in the end Paris had gone and hid in his room.

And now he was having to make a winter pie and a summer tart—wait, it *was* a winter pie and a summer tart, wasn't it? Not a winter tart and a summer pie? No, that was stupid because he'd been planning these all week and he'd have noticed if he'd had it the wrong way round. Fuck. He would have noticed, wouldn't he? He'd checked. He'd definitely checked. He thought he remembered checking on Tuesday, but maybe he'd been checking something else.

"So what have you got for us this week?" asked a voice at his elbow.

And Paris got halfway through a description of his summer vegetable pesto rose tart before he realised it wasn't actually one of the presenters, it was Tariq.

Who was grinning at him.

"Are you"—Paris glanced around wildly in case they were dragged off by the baking police or, worse, Jennifer Hallet—"are we…allowed to do this?"

"It's fine. My filo's cooling. And we're not in prison. We're on television."

"But don't Marianne and Wilfred usually do this bit?"

Tariq rolled his eyes. "Yeah, they've not hired me instead. In case you haven't noticed, we're not actually being filmed. It's just you look so serious, I thought you could use a laugh. Although what I seem to be getting is a blank stare."

"I wasn't doing a blank stare."

"You were doing a blank stare."

Oh no. He was doing a blank stare. And now he was thinking about how he was doing a blank stare. And he needed to say something. He needed to say anything. "I like your shirt."

"Thanks. It's the same one I was wearing yesterday because of continuity."

"I liked it yesterday as well. I just didn't get around to saying."

"No"—Tariq gave him a half-playful, half-challenging look—"you were too busy running away."

"I didn't."

"Yes. Yes you did. Blank stares and running away are your whole thing."

"That's not true," protested Paris. "I sometimes assault you with kitchenware and talk about classical penises."

This was enough to summon Grace Forsythe like a smutty Beetlejuice. "Is this a penis conversation anyone can join?"

Paris winced. "It wasn't really a penis conversation. It was just a conversation in which I happened to reference a penis. Not even a penis. More sort of a past allusion to a penis. Not even a real penis. An artistic representation of a penis from a culture that felt quite differently about penises."

"Ahhh." Grace Forsythe was nodding sagely. "For now we see through a penis darkly; but then face-to-face."

This, of course, was too much for Colin Thrimp. Which was good, because it was also too much for Paris. "You start earlier every season, Grace."

"I know. It's like phallic Christmas shopping."

"You only do it to get me into trouble." Colin Thrimp did not have a face for outrage, but he was compensating well.

"Colin, darling, if you believe that, then you have a *terribly* overstated sense of your own importance."

In fairness, Paris thought that was unlikely. And while some of the other contestants found Colin Thrimp difficult, Paris couldn't help sympathising with him. Because he understood that instinct to see everything in terms of how it could go wrong, or reflect badly on you, or blow up in your face.

"I think"—Tariq cast a cagey eye towards the row of fridges that covered half the length of the ballroom—"I might need to go check on my filo."

Paris had ruined it again. He'd brought penises into a perfectly good conversation that wasn't about penises and then Grace Forsythe had jumped onto the penises and Colin Thrimp had heard about the penises and now the whole set would think he was the one who couldn't stop talking about penises. Which meant he was probably also playing into homophobic stereotypes, or at least heterosexist stereotypes. Or normative stereotypes and…Shit. He was alone, and he had pesto to make, and the clock was ticking. He took a deep breath and, when that didn't work, took several more. Eventually, he got it together enough to reach for his basil.

By the time judging descended upon them, Paris was sure he was going home. The petals on his pesto rose tart weren't even, and he'd concluded about half an hour ago that pear and Gruyère pie—while it had sounded cool when he'd thought of it—was going to come across as gimmicky. And Wilfred Honey was going to say *well, I'm a simple man, and I like a pear pie or a cheese pie, and not both*. And Marianne Wolvercote would say *fuck you, Paris, you talentless shit*.

Bernard was first, with his mince (of the Christmas, rather than meat variety) pie and a giant jam tart, both of which the judges thought were a bit too simple, being, as they were, a mince pie and a jam tart but big. He was followed by Tanya, who'd done not exactly a matched pair but a sort of complementary duet: a fresh, zesty summer fruit tart coupled with a rich, deep-filled spiced fruit pie for the winter.

"Now, I love the way you've addressed the brief here," Marianne was saying. "Just looking at them, they immediately capture the season. The pattern of the fruit and the design you've baked into the crust here are equally artful. And if it tastes good, we should have something special."

Wilfred Honey forked a piece of tart into his mouth. "It tastes good," he confirmed. "It's clean and zingy and exactly what you'd imagine taking on a picnic if you were going somewhere really nice."

The spiced fruit pie received equal praise, and Paris was reduced to staring at a bit of exposed pear, wondering what the fuck he'd been thinking. He, too, could have done something that captured the essence of wintertime. But instead, he'd had to put fucking cheese in it. Because he was a fucking ponce.

Being raised, more or less, by two people so sophisticated they didn't have jobs so much as a series of things they were "in," he'd always felt he should have elevated tastes. And he did in a way—he'd had his first sip of vintage champagne at the age of eight (he'd said it was like lemonade that had gone off)—but whenever he tried to share those tastes, he always wound up feeling like a total prick. Especially with people from uni. He'd once been volunteered to organise an end-of-term dinner for his coursemates and had been seriously looking into reservations at Le Gavroche before Morag had reminded him that the budget was supposed to be thirty quid a head and suggested PizzaExpress might be nearer the mark.

The blood roaring in his ears made it hard for Paris to follow the next round of judging. He thought Rodney in the Cardigan and Catherine Parr had done okay, while Joan (of Arc, Tariq's name trick reminded him) the carpenter and Lili (she toils not, neither does she spin, which was unfair because, being an art student, she probably did both), the one who'd impressed with her dungarees and presentation in the first week, had fallen down on flavours.

"Um." Colin Thrimp was nudging him in the ribs so gently that Paris could barely feel it. "It's you."

Paris jerked up from his stool. "Sorry. Sorry. I'm here." Stumbling forward with his offerings, he placed them somewhat haphazardly before Marianne Wolvercote and Wilfred Honey. "I'm so sorry. I messed this up. This one is supposed to be a rose. But you can see it's sort of burned on here—"

"Paris." Marianne Wolvercote cut him off. Which, while it wasn't the worst thing that could happen to you on *Bake Expectations*, was still pretty bad. "Stop sabotaging yourself."

"Sorry."

"Now, I'll be honest," said Wilfred Honey. "I'd normally say that I like a pear pie or a cheese pie but not both together. But actually this does work."

"It's a difficult balance to get right," added Marianne Wolvercote, "but I think you've judged it very well. The sharpness of the Gruyère offsets the sweetness of the pear nicely. Now, as for the rose—"

Unable to contain his conviction of abject failure, Paris put his hands to his mouth and was assailed by a sudden, intense memory of the chemical one of the nannies had painted on his nails to stop him biting them. "Oh God oh God oh God."

"—I think it's a little darker over here," continued Marianne Wolvercote, "but I don't think it's burned."

Wilfred Honey offered a reassuring, grandfatherly smile. "But we'll be able to tell for sure when we try a piece."

"Oh God oh God oh God," burbled Paris.

The judges popped fragments of rose into their mouths and did not immediately regurgitate them in disgust.

Marianne nodded thoughtfully. "Pleasant. It's not mindblowing but the flavours are subtle and work together."

"You've done well, lad," Wilfred Honey told him. "Just have a bit more confidence in yourself next time."

Paris barely made it back to his station. It was slowly dawning on him that maybe he wouldn't go home. Which was good. Except it was also bad, because it meant he would have to come back. Only coming back would be good, because it meant he'd done well. And because he'd get to see Tariq again. And maybe keep failing to ask him out until one day he failed at failing.

Chris-Liam-Luke the Probably-a-Policeman was up next. Paris already knew he'd baked a lemon tart, because he'd overheard Marianne Wolvercote doing a bit to camera about how, with lemon tarts, there was nowhere to hide so it was going to have to be perfect. Although, come to think of it, Paris couldn't quite imagine Marianne Wolvercote ever doing a bit to camera where she said *well, this is quite a complicated dish, so if you fuck some of it up, we probably won't notice.*

As it turned out, Marianne Wolvercote was never going to get the opportunity to assess the perfection level of Chris-Liam-Luke's lemon tart. Because he'd also made a pie. Quite a big and, by Paris's estimation, quite a burned pie that swayed with a disconcerting fullness that suggested not all of its contents had cooked. And while Chris-Liam-Luke was navigating the difficult business of setting this pastry behemoth before the judges, he managed to tilt the plate with his tart on it to a steep enough angle that it began to slide. Which, not that Paris had been great at physics in school, shifted its centre of mass just past the point of balance, so it pulled the whole thing off his arm, upside down and onto the floor with a thud, a squelch, and spangling of broken crockery.

Somebody screamed.

Cameras swarmed in.

Colin Thrimp dashed forward listening intently to his earpiece and instructing everybody to freeze exactly where they were. "Please stay out of the aisles," he was saying. "Jennifer will want this filmed from as *many* angles as possible. Chris, that face you're doing is perfect. Camera two on Chris, do we have camera two on Chris? Camera five, other contestants please. Lovely reactions, everybody. Do watch out for the little bits of china, we'll have cleanup in *just* one moment but before we do—camera nine, please stop filming the pie, we have all day to film the pie."

Eventually the chaos subsided, the cleaning crew came and went like the sort of people that Paris imagined the Mafia might use to get rid of bodies, and Chris (definitely Chris, then) stepped forward to face judgement of his pie and his plate that once had a lemon tart on it.

"For obvious reasons," said Marianne Wolvercote, "we won't be able to determine the quality of your summer tart. So we'll need to make our decision based entirely on your winter pie."

"And honestly, lad," added Wilfred Honey, "it's not looking too happy with itself, is it?"

Chris hung his head, visibly defeated, as they sliced into his overburdened meat pie, which wept fatty gravy onto the plate.

"I think," said Marianne Wolvercote in the unexpectedly gentle voice she reserved for people who not even Wilfred Honey could say anything nice to, "I can see what you were going for. But you may have got a little carried away with the filling."

Once Chris had shuffled back to his place, carrying the burned wreckage of his TV baking dreams, that just left Tariq. What with having made a perfect knish and his own filo, Paris thought—hoped maybe—that there was a good chance that Tariq would take this. Right now, Tanya and Catherine Parr seemed to be the front-runners, and he'd rather Tariq win than either of them. Because—well, partly it was probably still fridge guilt, and wouldn't-ask-you-out guilt, and the general nonspecific guilt Paris felt most of the time about most things—but Tariq *deserved* a win. He was, Paris thought slightly yearningly, the kind of person who deserved wins in general.

"—a spanakopita," Tariq was saying, "and a Croatian fig tart."

Fuck. Paris hadn't been paying attention.

"This is interesting," Marianne Wolvercote was saying. "And filo was a risk in the time."

"Well, you know what they say"—Paris couldn't see Tariq's face, but he could imagine his smile well enough, all bright eyes and playfulness—"go flaky or go home."

Wilfred Honey nodded. "I understand you're joking, lad. But filo and flaky are very different things, and we take pastry very seriously in the Honey household."

"It *is* flaky, though," Marianne Wolvercote was observing, cracking through the pristine golden top of Tariq's spanakopita with a cake slice. "And in exactly the right way." One of the cameras wheeled in to catch the profile. "The lamination here is excellent."

It was at this point that Wilfred Honey made his habitual observation that what really mattered was the taste, and then the judges tucked in. They were quiet for a while, which was usually a good sign, because it meant they were actually eating the food rather than tasting it, and then moved on to the tart.

"Now, those are both *lovely*," Wilfred Honey declared. It wasn't quite a *by 'eck it's gorgeous*, which was his not-literally-trademarked-but-you-wouldn't-want-to-call-a-cookbook-that-or-you'd-get-sued code for "this is really good and probably winning." Except he normally didn't break that out before week three, and a *lovely* was a decent second place.

"But," said Marianne Wolvercote. Paris had heard that *but* a hundred times on the show, and it always cut through the ballroom like a gunshot through Ford's Theatre. "I do have a criticism."

Even though Tariq was looking away, Paris could see tension creep into his shoulders under his peacock-print shirt.

"The spinach and feta is a beautiful, classic combination," Marianne Wolvercote continued, "and has a wonderful lightness to it that's almost refreshing. But the brief was a *winter* pie, and this feels far more like a *summer* pie to me. While the tart—figs in a custard base—that more brings to mind the *autumn*."

Wilfred Honey was nodding his sagest nod. "When I think of the winter, I think of something warming and filling. Not something Mediterranean."

"They do"—for a second it sounded like Tariq wasn't going to finish, but only for a second—"they do have winter in the Mediterranean *as well*."

"That they do, that they do." Wilfred Honey was nodding. "Just giving a bit of feedback as relates to the brief."

"Mmhm," said Tariq. "Thanks."

So Paris wasn't going home. Well, he was going home. But in the immediate, physical sense rather than the "kicked off the show in disgrace" sense. It took him a while to pack because he always brought too much with him in case there was something he needed (there never was) and then, on the way out, he'd spend forever going to and from his room, convinced he'd left something behind. Eventually, when he'd managed to convince himself that, even if he *had* left something behind, it wasn't the end of the world and it would still be there next week, or he could get another one of whatever it was, he set off through the gardens with his trundly suitcase ploughing deep furrows in the grass behind him.

He was just past the sitting log, where he and Tariq had sat, when he noticed that Tariq was once again sitting on it. And he looked so unTariqishly down, with his chin plonked on his hands, his shoulders slumped, and his toes turned in, that Paris temporarily forgot that he was too embarrassed to talk to him.

"Sorry you didn't win," he said, perching himself on the log— in open defiance of any spiders, woodlice, or snakes that might be lurking.

Tariq glanced his way, almost smiling. "I'm going to ban you from apologising for things. I'm going to make you put ten pence in a jar every time you say you're sorry."

"Oh God, I'm so—hang on. That doesn't count. I wasn't apologising, I was expressing consolation. That's a different linguistic function that happens to be represented by the same word."

"Is it weird," Tariq asked, "that quibbling over a minor point of grammar is the most assertive I've ever seen you?"

There was a lot of truth to that. But if assertiveness about petty points of linguistics got a positive reaction, it seemed like a good direction to go in. "Actually that's not grammar, it's usage."

There was a long silence. "If your plan is to distract me from my humiliating defeat by annoying me and looking pretty then…" Tariq paused again. "…honestly it's kind of working."

Having never learned to take a compliment, Paris strategically ignored "pretty." It wasn't the first time Tariq had mentioned that, maybe, Paris was kind of all right looking. But Paris knew from experience that people thinking he was all right looking wasn't enough to make them like him. "It wasn't a humiliating defeat. Tanya had done really well, too, and it was obviously close."

"Don't get me wrong," Tariq said quickly. "Tanya deserved it. I think I'm just…annoyed at myself for being annoyed."

That was something Paris completely understood. Although he suspected that when it came to beating yourself up for beating yourself up for beating yourself up about something, Tariq was an amateur by comparison.

And he'd nearly found the perfect words to express how wise and intuitive and getting-it he was when Tariq went on. "The thing is, I knew it was a risk going with Mediterranean flavours because, obviously, when they said winter, they meant suet, cinnamon, and dead animals. And actually, I'm fine with suet, cinnamon, and dead animals. I just thought everyone would do that. And I was right. It's just that Tanya did it best and she won."

"I'd have given it to you," offered Paris. "But I did use to spend a lot of Christmases in the south of France."

At that, Tariq started giggling. "Sorry, are you trying to cheer me up by bragging about how rich and cosmopolitan you are?"

The problem with having an unusual childhood was that you could never tell what things would clue people in to the fact you'd had an unusual childhood. "What? No? I'm sorry, my parents are weird."

"Okay. You owe me ten p."

"That's not fair," protested Paris. "You challenged an incorrect apology earlier, so *you* should owe *me* ten p."

"All right. Fine." Tariq lifted his hips in an unconsciously slinky way and hooked his wallet out of his jeans. After a small amount of rummaging, he fished out a ten-pence piece and handed it to Paris. "There you go."

Paris took it uncertainly, feeling like he'd accidentally performed a very small mugging.

"Now give it back."

He gave it back.

And somehow, Tariq did seem to be looking happier. And that made Paris happy for the five seconds before he started to panic. Because if you could make someone happy, you could also make them unhappy. And it was way easier to make people unhappy.

They sat on the log in silence for a second or so.

"You know," said Tariq, "I think I could take a bit more parental weirdness if my family spent more time in France instead of Bethnal Green."

"I don't go there anymore. My parents are quite busy and I've got my own thing..." He hadn't got his own thing, but admitting it seemed both self-pitying and faintly pathetic. "...so I usually just spend Christmas in the flat with Neferneferuaten."

"You parents make you spend Christmas alone with a cat?"

"They don't make me. I'm sure, if I asked, they'd..." Unfortunately, Paris wasn't at all sure what "they'd" if he asked. He assumed that they'd probably sort something out. But he didn't like to think about it too much in case they, well, didn't. "Anyway, it's fine."

"I'll be honest." Tariq was giving him the sort of look Paris didn't enjoy receiving, although to be fair there were few looks he did. "It doesn't seem especially fine to me, and my family doesn't even do Christmas. Well, my dad does, but I think he just likes the excuse to play Slade really loudly."

Paris squirmed on the log. "I've probably not explained it well. It's not that I don't see my parents or anything. It's just they're..." He was about to say *very busy* but he felt like he was saying that too much. "...very international. Which means it's not always easy to keep a conventional schedule. The important thing is being with people. Not being with them on a particular day."

"Okay, honey. It's your family."

That was nice. But also…Paris was feeling a bit uncomfortable. "Um. You've just said you don't do Christmas either. Why's it such a big deal to you if I do?"

"I'm not saying you have to have a turkey and a tree. But it's cold and dark and the whole country has stopped, and everybody is eating, partying, or doing conspicuous consumption. And you"—Tariq made an expressive palace with his fingers—"have a cat?"

"I like my cat," Paris wailed. "And Morag's around for a lot of it."

"Be honest. Is she another cat?"

"No. She's my flatmate. She's a fat Glaswegian sex goddess. I mean, that's what she calls herself. I'm not labelling her. And she normally brings hot guys home. So that's fun? And I could always go and stay with her family if I wanted to. It's just, I feel like intruding on someone else's Christmas would be weird."

"Why?" asked Tariq. "If it's just about being with people. But not about being with people on a particular day?"

Paris thought he might actually be pouting. "That's mean. You're not allowed to use my own words against me. I think you should give me ten p for the using-my-own-words-against-me jar."

Dutifully, Tariq handed the ten p back, half turning on the log so he was facing Paris directly. His eyes were deep and dark and full of laughter. "You really are pretty, you know."

"Oh don't. I'm…I…just…It's genetics. It doesn't mean anything."

"You're also hopeless."

"I know. I'm sorry." He handed the ten pence back.

And then Tariq put a gentle hand on his knee, the nails so bright against Paris's quite boring and ill-advisedly warm corduroy trousers. "I think maybe we should revisit the never-asking-me-out conversation. Also, I'm aware that's using your words against you, so…"

Paris took the ten p. "I…um…"

"Ask me out, Paris."

This was scary. It was very scary. Paris felt like the stars were falling out of the sky despite the fact that it was midafternoon at best and the middle of summer. "Do you…Um…I mean… shit, sorry." The ten p changed hands again. "Do you want to go out with me? Like for dinner or something. Or a drink—shit, wait, no you don't, do you—coffee? Is that too—I don't know—I just meant…"

Tariq laughed. "Coffee would be great. Dinner would be lovely."

Wednesday

"YOU KNOW"—MORAG PASSED a critical eye over the range of syrups, antipasti, and charcuterie that was currently overrunning their kitchen benches—"the amount you've spent on this, you could probably have just hired a rent boy. I mean, probably not for full sex but you could at least get a blow job."

Paris looked up from the pasta machine he was currently hand-cranking. "Do you often need to do sex-work-to-picnic-food conversions?"

"No, but then I don't usually spend fifty quid on cold meat just to get laid."

"Yes, but you're *you*. I'm not the sort of person who can just walk up to a guy and say *nice dick, would you like somewhere to stick it?*"

"Hey now, I only tried that line once."

"And it worked."

"It was a student goth night. Everything works at a student goth night."

The end of the pasta flolloped onto the work surface, and Paris paused to finish the conversation before moving on to the next step. "Well, this isn't a student goth night. It's a cute guy I met on a TV baking show who is clearly way too cool for me. And unless I can distract him from...from..."

"From what?" asked Morag.

"From me? From everything?"

There was a silence, during which Neferneferuaten started nosing curiously towards the embryonic picnic. "Let me get this straight." Morag scooped up the cat and moved her to a less unhygienic position. "You like this man, and he likes you enough to come over here and be alone in a flat with you even though for all he knows you're a serial killer—"

"Oh my God. Do you think he thinks I'm a serial killer?"

"Well no. Because, *like I said*, if he thought you were a serial killer, he wouldn't be coming."

"Sorry. Sorry. It's just he'll be here soon and I'm in my head and—"

"Paris, are you ever anywhere else?"

"No. No, I'm not." He started cutting out his ravioli discs. "But there's a lot of things that can go wrong here. And I thought I'd taken them all into account. Except I hadn't factored in the possibility he might think I'm going to sexmurder him."

Neferneferuaten gave a soft mew that Paris chose to interpret as meaning *I don't think you're a sexmurderer and I should know because I'm a cat* rather than *I want to eat your egg yolks*.

"Out of a morbid curiosity I should really be over by now," said Morag, "you've invited somebody to dinner, what do you think could possibly go wrong?"

"My egg ravioli might not work, so he'll think I'm a pretentious shit who can't really cook. Or I could give him food poisoning, and then he'll spend the evening vomiting in my toilet." Paris started counting things off on his fingers. "Or he could be allergic to one of the ingredients, and then he'll spend the evening being dead."

"That seems very un—" Morag began.

"Or maybe Neferneferuaten won't like him or he won't like her, and then I'll have to choose, and I'm not sure which I'd choose because, on the one hand, he's a human being and she's not. But on the other hand, I've had Neferneferuaten for a long time whereas Tariq and I have only just met."

"I'm beginning to regret ask—"

"Or," Paris went on, "he could get lost on the way here and think I've given him a false address, because I hate him. Or I could open the door with my fly undone…" He paused, instinctively checking his fly, and then realised too late that he'd just wiped flour on himself. "Or I could do that. So now I'm meeting him with white powder on my trousers, so he's going to think that I spend my evenings snorting cocaine off my own dick."

"To be fair, if he thought you could do that, you'd definitely be in. It'd be one hell of a party trick."

Paris gazed despairingly between the uncut pasta and his lightly dusted crotch. "Fuck, now I need to change. And it took me ages to pick these jea—"

The intercom buzzed.

"Fuck," Paris wailed. "Fuck fuck fuck. Do I go to get changed or do I go to the door or what if he leaves and—"

Morag was already picking up the internal phone. "Hello, is that Tariq? This is Paris's housemate. He can't come to the door right now because he's having a trouser-related emergency…"

"That makes it sound like I've pissed myself."

"He also wants you to know he definitely hasn't pissed himself."

"That makes it sound *more* like I've pissed myself."

"I'll buzz you up."

Frantically, Paris tried to brush the flour from his jeans, but since his hands were still floury, that just floured him further. With a little wail, he dashed into his bedroom and yanked open his wardrobe. If nothing else, his long-term strategy of overcoming his fashion-induced paralysis by exclusively buying clothes that were more or less identical to clothes he already owned made selecting a new pair of jeans relatively non-excruciating. Although having to change into them in a hurry somehow caused Paris's legs to become the most high-friction surfaces in the known universe. He was sitting on his bed with his thighs and knees still very much exposed when he heard the front door open.

"Hello," Morag was saying. "Don't worry. It takes him a while to get his kecks on."

"Hi," came Tariq's voice. "I'm Tariq. You must be Morag?"

"Oh aye." Somehow Paris could hear her raising an eyebrow. "What's he told you?"

"He told me you were a fat Glaswegian sex goddess. But also said that was your language not his."

"It should be everybody's fucking language. It's what I fucking am. You'd be amazed what I can do with a fritter roll."

"Well"—to Paris's relief Tariq did not sound too traumatised—"I'm *super* gay and I try to avoid fried food, so I'm probably never going to find out."

Standing up and yanking his trousers hastily over his hips, Paris dashed into the corridor. "Hello. I'm here." It was meant to sound relaxed and calm. But was definitely not. "Thank you for coming. Sorry about the—everything."

Tariq held his hand out.

"Can I owe you? I left my wallet in my other jeans."

"I thought you said this man wasn't a prostitute." Morag glanced between them. "I thought that was the whole point of rolling your own pasta."

"First of all," said Tariq, "he owes me ten pence and I'd like to think I wouldn't be quite that cheap. Secondly, have you really rolled your own pasta?"

Paris blushed. "Yes, but, um, temper your expectations. I got a machine for Christmas a couple of years ago, and I haven't used it very much."

"Don't listen to him. It's fucking perfect." Maybe it was Morag's accent that made insults and compliments sound interchangeable, or maybe it was just her personality. "Anyway, I'm going to leave you boys to it. I've very kindly decided to go and stay with a friend this evening. And by friend I mean man I met at a bus stop."

"Isn't that a bit dangerous?" Tariq asked.

"Oh no, I've given him a safeword. It was nice to meet you, Tariq." Grabbing a bulging bag, the contents of which Paris did not like to speculate about, Morag gave him a quick hug. "You have a lovely time. Don't do anything I wouldn't do. And more important, don't do anything you *would* do. I'll see you in the morning." She was halfway out the door when she turned back. "By the way, your fly's undone."

With a frantic yelp, Paris urgently zipped himself. "Shit. Shit. Sorry—that wasn't a…It wasn't a—it was an accident because of the…"

"It's fine," Tariq told him. "I hadn't even noticed."

Did that make it worse or better? It meant that there was an alternative sequence of events where nobody had spotted Paris's fly was undone until the evening was over or he was nipping to the loo or something and he'd have got away with it completely. But it also meant that there was an alternative sequence of events where they were just sitting down on a sofa to eat some egg yolk ravioli and his dick slipped out, like it was what he'd been planning all along. Like he was saying *enjoy this delicious pasta and also my penis*.

It was at about this point that Paris realised he had two choices: either he could stand there forever speculating about all the ways he could have ruined the evening, thus ruining the evening, or he could put it behind him, try to be a good host, and put off ruining the evening for a few minutes at least.

"Anyway." Paris made what he hoped was a *let's stop talking about my crotch* gesture. "Please come in. It's not a very big flat but there's chairs. You can sit in a chair, if you like chairs."

Tariq laughed. "I will admit, I'm a big fan of chairs. I'd love to see your chairs."

Oh God. He'd invited a man round and offered to show him his chairs. And the man in question was nice enough to pretend that this was a thing normal people did.

"So," Paris explained, as he led Tariq the short distance into the combined kitchen and living area, "these are the chairs. One of them has a cat in it."

As if she knew she was the subject of conversation, Neferneferuaten flicked back an ear and stretched in a way that very much communicated *this chair is mine now*.

Tariq was looking around him in…in…something. "If you got this through your uni, I am suing Birmingham."

The problem with having incredible, artsy, international parents—not that there really was a problem with having incredible, artsy, international parents—was that you just got used to everything being effortlessly beautiful all the time. They'd bought the flat as a sort of pied-à-terre sometime in the '90s, spent a couple of years making it perfect, and finally got bored with it. Then they'd let Paris live in it after they'd got bored with him.

"It's," he admitted, "it's my mum and dad's?"

Tariq practically had cartoon heart eyes. "It's *amazing*."

And he was right. It was. Only his parents could have a dark gold sofa opposite two hardwood armchairs upholstered in midnight-blue velvet and make it work. Maybe there'd come a day when Paris would stop being made to feel inadequate by furniture, but that day was not this day. "Thanks. I mean. On their behalf."

"Sorry." Tariq did his best to rein his eyes in. "I didn't mean to go all Elizabeth Bennet at you. Remember, I agreed to this date before I saw your magnificent grounds at Pemberley."

"Probably for the best because I think I'd make a pretty terrible Mr. Darcy."

"I don't know." Tariq gave him a playful look from beneath his eyelashes. "You're rich, white, and awkward."

There was only one element of that characterisation to which Paris felt he could object. "I'm not rich."

"He says from the vintage Bohemian wonderland he was given by his parents."

"They're not rich." Paris squirmed. "They're just fashion people, so they have a lot of things."

"A lot of things that cost a lot of money that most people don't have because they can't afford them?"

The squirming continued. Because Tariq was right, wasn't he? "Okay, maybe they're a *bit* rich? But not *rich* rich. I don't think they're millionaires?"

Tariq looked around again. "This is a fairly big flat in central London. If they weren't millionaires when they bought it, they definitely are now."

On some level, Paris thought this was probably going okay. It definitely felt like *banter* and not like *contempt*, which was the response Paris usually felt he deserved, kind of in general. On another level, though, he really badly wanted to change the subject to something that wasn't the opulent wealth of his family.

"Food." Shit. That was meant to be a sentence.

"Glorious food?" offered Tariq in response, moving his hands very slowly into the beginning of a dance routine.

"I made some. I mean, it probably won't be glorious—I mean—sorry—"

"Twenty p and counting."

"There's charcuterie," Paris pressed on valiantly. "And a range of syrups for lemonade because you said you didn't drink. And all the meat's from a halal deli I found because I thought you probably were—probably did keep halal, I mean, but if that's wrong and I've just made a huge assumption, I can run out and go get some bacon and—"

"No, it's fine. I do and it's sweet you made the effort." Tariq glanced over at the—now the whole opulence issue had been pointed out—noticeably granite kitchen surfaces. "What's the deal with the pasta?"

"I'm also making egg yolk ravioli."

"Wow. You must really like me." To Paris's surprise, Tariq didn't sound remotely sarcastic. Playful, yes, but secretly loathing him, no.

Heat rushed to Paris's cheeks. "I do. I mean. Not in a creepy way. I don't know you very well. I just mean I wanted to do something a bit special."

For a moment, it looked like Tariq was going to say something teasing. But instead he put a hand—the nails shining a deep silver-blue—on Paris's arm, went up on his toes, and brushed a kiss against his cheek. "Thank you. This is lovely."

Paris froze, trying to be suave. But Tariq's hand was warm against him. And his lips were…also warm. And very…*there*. And he smelled of violets and cedarwood, like he had a signature cologne. Which was the sort of thing that Paris had always wanted but had always talked himself out of.

"Illgogetthecharcuterie," he squeaked.

While Paris flailed in the kitchen area, trying to look in control of the situation, Tariq selected one of the unencattenated chairs and settled himself into it. Leaning against the midnight-blue velvet, with one leg draped elegantly over the other, he seemed like the kind of person who actually belonged in a vintage Bohemian wonderland. Unlike Paris, who just lived in one.

"Drink?" Paris gestured towards the row of bottles that, now it came to it, he couldn't quite bring himself to call the soda bar. "I've got basil and apricot—not together—although I don't know why I made basil, because I don't think that would be good in lemonade anyway. And mint and rose and raspberry and orange and peppercorn—those are together—and—"

"I think I'll try the raspberry."

Paris rallied enough to manage a mischievous look. "Not the basil?"

"You made it, you drink it."

"I bet you say that to all the boys."

There was a long silence. "I really don't."

"I'm sorry." Paris was un-rallying rapidly. "That sounded flirty in my head. But it came out really…semeny."

There was another long silence. Then, "I bet *you* say that to all the boys."

"Actually, I find unique ways to embarrass myself with each boy individually."

Tariq was laughing again. Thank fuck. "That makes me feel very special."

Balancing plates and glasses, Paris made his way to what he suddenly realised was an intimidatingly exquisite glass coffee table. There was a dining area in one corner of the room, but it was permanently occupied by his laptop and a stack of whatever books he needed for his course—currently various translations of Xenophon.

"I don't know why I'm shocked," Tariq said, observing the spread in front of him, "because I met you on a TV cooking show. But even so, this seems like a lot of work."

Paris perched on the edge of the sofa like he was suddenly afraid of his own house. "Not really. I made the chestnut pâté from scratch, obviously I baked the bread, but the olives are just olives and I didn't cure my own meat or anything."

"Oh well." Tariq waved his fingers dismissively. "This date is over and I feel totally taken for granted."

"That's a joke, right? You are joking?"

"No, this is my deadly serious face. Can't you tell?"

To be honest, Paris had been avoiding looking at Tariq's face too much. Because it was bright and lively and fascinating and made him feel boring and lumpen by comparison. "I just wanted to check. Because I didn't want to be all *ha-ha* while you were walking out the door and calling a taxi."

"Actually I drove, so I can walk out with dignity whenever I want."

"I'm not reassured that you planned that in advance."

"Honey, it's not personal." Tariq helped himself to a slice of cured beef and a piece of bread. "I had this guy over a few months ago, and things went really south and I had to ask him to leave, but it was dark and cold and he didn't have a car. And there was no way I was driving him anywhere, so we had this dismal half hour of him sitting in my kitchen, sulking and glaring at my housemates, while we waited for an Uber to show up. And then he tried to get me to reimburse him for the cost."

"Well, you'll be okay with me because I'd be far too embarrassed to do any of those things. I'd just stand outside in the snow, hoping my ride showed up before my nose froze off."

Tariq flashed him a smile. "Good to know. I'd say I feel more comfortable inviting you over now, but I'm living with four other students in a house in Birmingham with one bathroom and rising damp."

"Oh, don't. I know I've got it really good here what with my probably-actually-millionaire-actually parents letting me stay in their—"

"Vintage Bohemian wonderland?"

Paris gave an uncomfortable nod. "Yeah. In their—their that—rent free instead of living in halls like other people my age, but I'm still just—me? And I sometimes think it'd be nice to live somewhere that was mine instead of somebody else's."

"Hold on a moment." Tariq wiped the last of the charcuterie from his fingers on a tastefully embroidered serviette before wagging it in Paris's general direction. "You don't get to turn this into a whole big Princess Jasmine—on second thoughts forget I said anything, I want to see you dress up as a peasant and go running around the city stealing bread for orphans before falling in with a lovable street rat."

"Are you the lovable street rat in this scenario?"

Tariq seemed to be giving the which-*Aladdin*-character-are-you question far more thought than Paris might have expected. "I don't know, I always found him a bit of a jerk. He pretends to be all man-of-the-people, but the moment he gets any money he's like *hey check out my fifty elephants*." He went back to contemplating this very serious conundrum. "I think I'd probably be Jafar."

"The bad guy?"

"The obviously queer-coded guy who's trying to achieve something instead of sitting around waiting for a magic lamp to fall into his lap."

Wanting to play along but not quite able to top Tariq's analysis, Paris went with the first thing that came into his head. "I think I'd be the monkey. No real reason to be in it, spending most of my time sitting on the protagonist's shoulder. Regularly losing arguments with a rug."

"Honey, you're Jasmine. You're clearly Jasmine."

"But if you're Jafar, doesn't that mean you're going to trap me in an hourglass or demand I be sent to your bedchamber?"

"As we've established, I'm a student. All I've *got* is a bedchamber."

To be honest, Paris could imagine worse places to be sent. And worse people to be sent there by. But he thought saying that aloud would probably end up implying he had a kinky hourglass fetish. "Shall I put the ravioli on?" he suggested, instead.

"That'd be fabulous. But fair warning, I'll be watching you make them because it's either going to be really impressive or a hilarious disaster."

Paris twitched anxiously. "Please don't watch. It'll probably be a boring disaster and I'll overcook them and you'll have a hard-boiled egg in rubbery pasta, or I'll undercook them and you'll get salmonella."

"Okay, now I'm definitely watching."

Being watched was not one of Paris's favourite things—he was very much a sex-with-the-lights-off kind of guy—but Tariq was his guest and saying *no you have to sit twelve feet away from me and take it on trust I'm not going to poison you* would probably go down like an undercooked egg yolk. He drifted back to the kitchen area, set a pan of water to simmer, and finished cutting out his ravioli.

"So, pet," said Tariq, in a better Yorkshire accent than Paris could have managed. "What have you got for us this week?"

"Oh, don't. It's bad enough on the show."

"Why are you even *on* the show? You seem to hate everything about it."

Taking his piping bag from the fridge, Paris began piping rings of fonduta onto his pasta discs. "Morag put me in for it. I think she just wanted me out of the flat."

"*Or* she could have thought you were really good, which you clearly are. And been a bit aggressive about communicating it, which she clearly is."

"I had a lucky first week. I'm actually pretty average."

"He says while making egg yolk ravioli like it's something he does all the time."

Paris whimpered under this barrage of unfair compliments. "It's easier than it looks."

"It looks really difficult."

"It's not." He cracked two eggs into a dish. "All you have to do is scoop them up like this…" He scooped. "…and then lay it in the middle of the ring." He laid.

"If you say so." Stepping forward, Tariq picked up his own yolk, which slithered in his fingers and then burst into a drizzle of sunshine-yellow liquid.

"You did that on purpose to make me feel better."

Tariq went to the sink to wash his hands. "You think I got myself covered in egg yolk on purpose?"

"Yes. I think you're very nice and it's exactly the kind of thing you'd do."

Breaking open a fresh egg, Paris juggled it between his palms to separate it. There was something instantly calming about the action. The routine of it, the repetition. The knowledge that he was doing something he was good at, sharing something he cared about with somebody he…liked? It seemed too early to say more than that, but could he compromise on *was interested in*? When all the traces of the white were gone, Paris slid the yolk carefully into the second raviolo. From there it was just a matter of seasoning, topping, crimping, trimming, and the barest dip in the pan to cook.

Tariq stayed leaning against the sink, watching with quiet curiosity while Paris plated up. And Paris tried to focus on his grating Parmigiano Reggiano rather than ogling his date, which Tariq wasn't making easy. He'd chosen quite an understated ensemble for the evening—slim-fit jeans and a well-tailored blazer over a black-and-gold-print shirt—but it had that immaculate, effortless coherence that suggested he knew himself and knew fashion and was comfortable with both.

"Is that white truffle?" Tariq asked, visibly wincing. "Don't use that. I'll feel incredibly guilty. That probably cost more than my car."

"It's fine. I checked it was halal-certified. And anyway, it's just a seasoning."

"Anything that needs a dedicated shaving tool isn't just a seasoning."

Paris glanced from the truffle to the dedicating shaving tool and back again. "But I've bought it now."

"Honey, why? What is it about me that says, this is a man who expects white truffle?"

There were lots of things he could say to that—things like *you're amazing and exquisite and I'm just me and I wanted to give you something as wonderful as you are*—but they sounded way too intense now he was articulating them. "I guess I...I thought it would be nice?"

"I'm not saying it isn't *nice*. It's all *nice*. Except the basil syrup, which I think was probably a misfire. But this"—Tariq had crossed the room now and taken the truffle and the truffle shaver gently out of Paris's hands, making Paris shake slightly from embarrassment and from the nearness of him—"this doesn't feel like it's about me. This feels like it's about...I don't know."

Shit. Shit, he was looking like a show-off. Like he was saying *hey, come check out the expensive London flat I live in and let me show you how easily I can drop a couple of hundred quid on a picnic ingredient*. It was a fuckup. It was a fucking fuckup and he'd fucking fucked it up again like he always did. "I...I'm sorry."

"Thirty p."

"That's not fair. I've actually got something to be sorry for this time."

"Forty p. And no, this isn't a *sorry* thing. It's an *I'm really not sure what you're trying to do* thing." Tariq ran a hand through his perfectly coiffed hair. "You're a student, I'm a student, I know we met on a cooking show, but I'd have been perfectly happy to get a Chinese, or for you to whack a frozen pizza in the oven. And if this is you trying to impress me, I'm not sure what it says about the sorts of things you think I'm impressed by."

Paris flapped in despair. "Well, I mean, I did...I do...want to make an effort. And I wasn't really thinking about the money, which I know is probably a big, um, Princess Jasmine thing. But the recipe said serve with shaved white truffle, and I thought *oh, I haven't got any white truffle, I should get some white truffle.* Not *oh, I think Tariq will really like me if I have white truffle.* I didn't mean to suggest you were some kind of…tuber prostitute."

"Okay." Tariq gave a controlled sigh. "I'm glad we've reached the *I don't think you're a prostitute* stage of the relationship. But for future reference, a date to me is a restaurant where your main course costs about twenty quid, or you maybe spring for popcorn at the cinema. It doesn't need to involve this much effort, and it certainly doesn't need to involve this much money."

"Yes, but then there'll just be me."

Tariq looked at Paris earnestly. "I think I'm beginning to see what this is about, so let's get some things clear. First off, I don't mind that you're rich."

"I'm n—"

"Expensive flat, truffles, constantly denying how rich you are? You're *textbook* rich. That's okay. It's even kind of cute. Believe me, this"—he indicated his ensemble—"is not how you dress when you're trying to start a proletarian revolution. It doesn't bother me at all that you're one of the tiny number of extremely lucky people who could get away with literally never working a day in their lives. I'm pretty lucky myself, it's just that my parents are *have good jobs and can pay my way through uni* levels of well off, not *here, take our spare flat* levels."

"Then—" Paris began, but Tariq checked him with a finger-wave.

"Nope, still talking. The point is that I don't care you've got money, I care that you just seem to be throwing it at me like it's the only thing I could want from you. It's making me think that you're not Princess Jasmine after all."

Paris wasn't sure he wanted to know what the alternative was, but he asked anyway. "So who am I?"

Spreading his arms wide, Tariq affected a deeper, growlier voice. "*You like it? Then it's yours.*"

"That's not fair," Paris protested. "The Beast had anger issues.

I do *not* have anger issues. Also the library scene was *sweet and thoughtful*. It was the moment where the Beast finally showed he understood Belle as a person by—"

"Demonstrating that he'd spotted her most obvious character trait?" asked Tariq with a grin.

Although he'd never had the trick of standing up for himself, Paris felt a strong need to defend the honour of a wealthy cartoon monster. "It *is* a children's movie."

"True, but either way *this*"—with a circular, encompassing gesture, Tariq indicated the traitorous egg yolk ravioli—"isn't a library. It's the bit at the beginning of the movie where the Beast is convinced nobody can ever love him for himself, so he's just hiding away and leaving everything to his servants. These truffle shavings are…They're the culinary equivalent of an over-sexed candelabra with a French accent."

Paris took a deep breath. "Okay," he tried. "You make some good points. But you've got to admit that if I got a jar of caviar out the fridge right now and said *try the grey stuff, it's delicious*, that would be pretty cool."

"Yeah. That would have been cool. But don't think I can't see you deflecting."

Paris hadn't thought he was deflecting. Then again he suspected he might deflect a lot. "Sor—I mean, right. Good catch. I probably was a bit. I just…Look, I'm bad at this."

"Bad at what?" Tariq tilted his head slightly.

Everything seemed too self-pitying an answer. "Dating?" Paris suggested nervously. "Or maybe just people in general. And I really wanted this to go well. And it's probably unattractively revealing that the only thing I could think of that might make it go well was white truffle egg yolk ravioli."

"It's *revealing*. I think you might have to work a little bit harder at unattractive."

And there it was again: that unencompassable observation that people thought Paris looked a certain way and it was a certain way that some of them thought was good. Except it always just floated there, not really connected to anything, and then melted like a snowflake when it finally landed on him. "How about"—Paris scooped up the egg yolk ravioli and strode purposefully towards the bin—"we get rid of this and we can order a pizza or something."

"Oh no you don't." Tariq put himself very firmly in Paris's way. "I'll admit I was a bit surprised that you went so totally extra, but now that you've *gone* so totally extra it'd be a crime not to at least sample the fruits of your extraness. You made me egg yolk ravioli, I am *going* to eat the egg yolk ravioli."

"Are…are you sure?"

Folding his arms, Tariq adopted a posture of whole-body sarcasm. "No, I'm deeply uncertain about whether I want to eat this beautifully made, if rapidly cooling, hand-rolled pasta dish brimming with fancy ingredients. Now gimme."

Paris…gavehimed? And they returned to the sofa, where they resettled themselves and started eating. Honestly, Paris's appetite had mostly deserted him. While he'd told Tariq that his greatest fear was spiders, his *real* greatest fear was trying to do a good thing and it turning into a bad thing—like if you bought a lovely toy for an adorable kitten but it wasn't a pet-safe toy, and so the kitten choked to death and what had been intended as a wonderful happy moment of perfect innocence turned into pain and death and a baby cat fighting to breathe.

Steadying himself, Paris took a forkful of the dead kitten ravioli.

It had turned out perfectly. Absolutely *fucking* perfectly. The butter was rich, the cheese was exquisitely sharp, the pasta neither flabby nor rubbery, and the egg yolk flowed over the plate like the roads of El Dorado. And to all that the truffle brought a deep, earthy quality that, in context, turned to ashes in Paris's regretful mouth. Probably this was the best thing he'd ever made, or ever would make, and it rebuked him with its unnecessary extravagance.

Maybe he looked as traumatised as he felt, because Tariq gave a soft hum of gastronomic pleasure. "Okay, this is actually really good. Just don't buy any more truffles on my account."

Paris was never buying truffles again. They'd give him flash-backs forever.

And now they were sitting in silence, and Paris was getting more and more certain that he needed to find a new topic to talk about or else he'd just be this awful guy who threw money at things and couldn't keep a conversation going for more than eighteen seconds without it all getting awkward and terrible. Except he didn't really know much about Tariq except that he was attractive, gay, at least slightly religious, and on the same baking show that Paris was on. But maybe that was enough.

"So," Paris tried as casually as he could manage. "Why did you sign up?"

"For the show, you mean?" asked Tariq. And for once, somebody else was doing the squirming. Tariq might even have blushed a little. "I'm aware how this sounds, but I think I just really wanted to be on TV?"

"Um…" Paris stared at him. Then he realised that wasn't a particularly useful response. So he said, "Um…"

Tariq kept squirming. It was charming on him, though. "Don't get me wrong, I really love cooking and I'm a huge fan of *Bake Expectations*, and I know *I kind of want to be famous* isn't a very admirable ambition. But I think I'd make quite a good D-list celebrity. I tick multiple diversity boxes, I dress really well, I like talking to people, and I wouldn't be too proud to open a supermarket in Croydon or turn on the Christmas lights in Burnley."

"Um…" This was so outside anything Paris could imagine wanting that it was borderline impossible for him to engage with. "And that…and you…and um."

"Thanks for your support."

"I'm sorry. I'm being crap." He took a breath and a moment to think. "Maybe it's because there's sort of a taboo about admitting that you're on a reality TV show because you want to be on television. Nobody goes on *Dragons' Den* and says, I don't want your money or expert mentorship, I just want two minutes of free advertising on the BBC. Even the people on *Love Island* pretend that they're there for romance, despite the fact they're all professional influencers."

Tariq nodded. "Yeah, I get that. And believe me, I did not tell the producers, yes, I quite like baking but my masterplan is to get to the semifinal, be good and look cute enough to get a BBC Three cooking series called *Fabulous Halal*, and then a couple of years down the line be invited onto *Strictly* and dance with Janette Manrara."

"You know she's retired now?"

"Yes, but in my perfect fantasy she comes out of retirement just to dance with me." Tariq paused for long enough that Paris almost thought he'd finished, but then he went on. "We make it to the week after Blackpool, but then I have to do a rumba and it's fine, but it's not what they're expecting at that stage in the competition, and so I wind up in the dance-off against some bloke off *EastEnders* and I lose."

"You've...really thought this through."

"Well, I had to. My original plan was to study environmental science and save the planet, but then I realised it involved quite a lot of hard maths and I wasn't very good at it. So I tried student theatre, because I thought *hey, you're gay and you like people looking at you, why not be an actor*. Except"—Tariq made a what-you-gonna-do kind of gesture—"it turns out I'm quite bad at pretending to be other people. That left *Love Island*, and I'm not straight enough or buff enough, or *The Apprentice* but I hate business and I'm not a horrible person. Besides, I don't actually *like* either of those shows."

All this "having a plan" was slightly overwhelming to Paris, who sometimes got anxious trying to decide what he was going to cook for dinner. "And...," he asked. "And I don't mean this in a bad way, but is this something you actually expect to happen? Or is it sort of a, well, joke?"

To Paris's relief, Tariq did not immediately throw the remains of the egg yolk ravioli in his face. "I admit, Janette might be a pipe dream. But *Bake Expectations* is an opportunity. And it's silly to go into something without knowing what you want to get out of it."

"That makes sense," said Paris, who had no idea what he wanted to get out of anything. "But what if it…goes wrong? Or doesn't happen?"

"Then it'll go wrong or not happen. I'll do something else. I'll become a social media consultant or work in a shoe shop."

"What if the shoe shop closes down because of Amazon?"

"Then I'll take out a loan and start some kind of online bespoke shoe company. Or maybe a shoe subscription box because everything's a subscription box these days. And then I *will* go on *Dragons' Den*."

"And none of this scares you or makes you worried what people will think?"

At this, Tariq laughed. "In case you haven't noticed, I'm a short, gay British Bangladeshi Muslim. What people think about me is just the background noise of my life."

"Oh God"—Paris cringed—"sorry."

"Did you just try to apologise on behalf of institutionalised-racism-slash-homophobia across multiple cultures and subcultures?"

"No, I mean. Sort of? I mean, more for not being more… aware, I guess?"

"You haven't noticed I'm short, gay, and Asian?"

Just when Paris thought he didn't have any cringe left in him, he cringed a little harder. "Well I asked you on a date, so I obviously noticed the gay bit. And I'm not one of those people who say they don't see colour, when they totally do. But shouldn't I have been more, you know, knowledgeable about the reality of your, I don't know, experience?"

"Three things." Tariq put his empty plate aside. "One, I am currently choosing to see this as adorable. If it continues much longer, I may not. Which leads us to two: this is going to get very tiring for me if I can't mention my ethnicity or religion without you panicking. And three, no, you obviously shouldn't know what my life is like, because you're not me and we've met exactly three times. I was just doing banter. I wasn't trying to trigger your white guilt."

"Oh you must have noticed," Paris told him, trying not to think about how near to each other they were now, "that my guilt comes pre-triggered."

Tariq's hand was on his arm again, the silver in his nails making the grey of Paris's jumper seem especially drab. "I'll admit it took me a minute"—Paris suspected it had taken him a lot less than a minute—"but I'm beginning to work it out."

"And you showed up anyway?"

"Well, the way I see it you're sort of an angel cake."

"Garishly pink?" suggested Paris. "Slightly cloying? Already done in season two?"

"You come in layers. On the top you've got"—his free hand waved around Paris's face—"all of this. And that's very intimidating."

This was sounding increasingly not good. "My face is…my face is intimidating?"

"Yes. You look like someone stuck a baggy jumper on Michelangelo's *David*."

Paris picked helplessly at his sleeve. "It's my mum. She's a model. I've got her cheekbones."

"Hang on. Your mum's a model and you think it's weird I want to be on TV."

"She didn't want to be a model. She was walking down the street one day, and my dad saw her and said *you have to be the face of my new range of lingerie*, and that was that."

"I can't tell if that's incredibly romantic or incredibly creepy and inappropriate. But anyway: layer one." Tariq did the wave again. "*That*. There's no way *that* could be interested in anybody like me. Layer two: oh wait, it's fine, he's actually a total mess."

"That's fair," Paris admitted. "But I'm not sure it reflects well on you."

"Hang on. I'm not that desperate. We haven't got to layer three yet."

"Is that the pink one? Or the neon-yellow one?"

Tariq's eyes flicked up to Paris's, holding his gaze in a way that made Paris want to run either towards or away from him very fast indeed. "It's the one where I think you're probably a sweet, funny, clever guy under all the icing and sponge, which, in this terrible metaphor, represents a lot of nonsense."

"But…but what if you're wrong? What if I only have two layers? The Mr. Kipling ones only have two layers."

"I don't believe you've ever had a Mr. Kipling cake in your life."

"I have. Morag buys them. And I could still be a mess right down to the bottom."

"You know what?" Tariq smiled at him, bright and inviting and filled with a certainty Paris couldn't help envying. "I'm willing to take that risk."

He was wrong, of course. If Paris was any kind of cake, he was one of those dense fruit ones you got at weddings: way too intense, and every mouthful finds a new and interesting way to disappoint you. But it was good for a moment to imagine that things could be different. People had been telling him he looked some variant of hot his whole life, but this was the first time he could remember somebody telling him that there might be a universe in which he was more than just a pretty ball of irresolvable neuroses.

So for the first time in as long as he could remember, Paris took a chance and kissed somebody.

And despite everything, Tariq did not recoil in horror. Instead his hands came up to cup Paris's face, and the whole thing turned into, like, a proper kiss. And not just Paris mashing his lips awkwardly against some guy who was too polite to say *fuck off, you're a wanker and I hate you.*

Anyway, it was fine. Actually, it was lovely. Far slower and softer than Paris was used to, since most of the guys he'd been with had treated kissing like the prelude to the good bit. Of course, the problem with someone spending a lot of time on the kissing was that it offered Paris a lot of scope to worry about all the ways his mouth could ruin this for him. It could be too wet or too dry, or still have bits of truffle in it, or his tongue could be weird and invasive, or weird and not invasive enough, or just weird. Maybe he had a weird tongue?

Or maybe he just wasn't very good at kissing.

"Are you okay?" Tariq drew back a couple of inches. "I assumed the fact you kissed me meant you, um, wanted to? But now you've gone all…peculiar?"

Oh my God, he *did* have a weird tongue. "Sorry…it was really nice. I just suddenly started thinking of all the ways it might not be. Or ways I could mess everything up. Which, ironically, has messed everything up."

"Yes," said Tariq thoughtfully, "that is ironic. Is there anything I can do to stop it happening?"

That wasn't a question anyone had asked him before. And, actually, it hadn't really occurred to Paris that sex for other people wasn't fifty percent—okay, maybe seventy percent—stressing out over whether you were doing it wrong. "I don't think it's anything you're doing or not doing? I think it's just, you know, me?"

"How about I tell you I really liked it? And I thought it was going well. And I'd like to keep going. But I'm also happy to take a beat and talk about…whatever."

This was also new territory. In all Paris's previous relationships, he'd had the strong sense that backing off was a sign of failure. It meant you either weren't into it, which raised the worrying spectre of being not gay enough, or hadn't done a good job of getting the other person into it, which raised the even more worrying spectre of being shit in bed. "Let's try again. I can do better."

"I'm not sure I want you to treat me like your homework."

"But I always did my homework really well."

"And that would be good to know if I was a maths problem."

"Actually," Paris admitted, "I did maths quite badly. But you'd be in for a great time if you were an essay on how Shakespeare uses metaphors related to darkness in *Macbeth*."

Tariq flashed him a far too indulgent grin. "Call me a hopeless romantic, but I haven't entirely given up on having a great time being me."

The idea of having a great time being yourself was something else Paris wasn't really used to. But he smiled back anyway. "Okay?"

"How about we take this slow?"

And with that Tariq slid delicately into Paris's lap and kissed him again. And for a few blissful minutes, the sheer shock and intensity of having Tariq *right there*—mouth on his mouth, hips beneath his hands—blanked out Paris's brain completely. Which turned out to be really helpful. Since it left him with nothing but how soft Tariq's lips were, how sweet he tasted, how warm and sleek he was pressed up against Paris. And perhaps because Paris had been lobotomised with pleasure, the kiss went on, and on, and on until he wanted to curl up inside it and live there. In this strange, wonderful place where everything was simple and nothing mattered except the two of them.

Except unfortunately Paris's brain had other plans. It crept back slowly, starting with little suggestions like *maybe your hand's in the wrong place* or *did your teeth clack right there*. And then worked its way up to *he must be so bored right now, it's been ages*. And finally reclaimed its throne with *he's been so nice to you but nobody is this patient. What can he possibly be getting out of it?*

And, oh God, his brain—that is, he?—was right. When you invited a guy round for dinner, he expected more than a single raviolo and a bit of PG wriggling on your parents' very expensive sofa. Probably this was going to go down in history as Tariq's most awful date ever. No, worse than that, it was going to go down in history as Tariq's most nothingy date ever. *I don't know what to say*, he'd tell his friends. *I mean, I literally don't know what to say. I went round to his place, we had some food and kissed a bit, and then I went home. What a wanker.*

It was the least helpful thing to do when you were kissing someone, but Paris opened his eyes a crack. Of course, Tariq looked ridiculously perfect up close, with his lashes fanned against his cheeks, and an expression of gentle absorption on his face. Some tiny, neglected bit of Paris's subconscious suggested that maybe, just maybe, this meant everything was going the way it should. That Tariq was not, in fact, hating and resenting every second of it. And—for whatever reason—wouldn't actually mind if he spent the rest of his evening kissing Paris into blissful brain silence.

But the rest of his subconscious, and for that matter most of his conscious, said *no mate, you're having a laugh*.

So he attempted to communicate that he was ready for things to go further through the universal language of the dick grab.

"Um." Tariq's eyes jolted open. "Can you move your hand please?"

Tariq definitely wasn't bored. Paris adjusted his grip slightly. "How do you want me to move it?" he asked, in his best sultry voice.

"Off? Away?"

"Sorry. Oh my God sorry. I thought you meant—sorry." Paris pulled both of his hands back as quickly as he could and, for good measure, shifted his whole body to one side in a way that was meant to be nonthreatening but ended up dumping Tariq squarely into the remains of the egg yolk ravioli and charcuterie plate.

It was the closest Tariq had looked to annoyed, even counting the time Paris had smacked him in the face with a fridge. He peeled a slice of cecina de León from his arse. "Okay, I meant stop groping me. Not use me in a reverse food fight."

"Sorry. I panicked. I didn't mean to assault you. In, like, a food way or any other way." Paris gazed at Tariq in growing mortification. His fears that the evening would be unmemorable had proven unfounded, but that was turning out not to be a good thing. "Did I do something wrong?"

"Yes. Yes. You threw me on a table full of cold meat and eggs."

"No. Before that. When I—did you not—I thought you were into it."

Tariq was slowly wiping bits of everything off his everything. "Can you find me something to change into before we have this conversation?"

The fact it was going to be a conversation did not bode well. Although it boded better than Tariq just storming out the door, beef and olives still clinging to his blazer. And having chucked the guy into a picnic, sorting him out a change of clothes was very much the least Paris could do.

Ten minutes later, Tariq's beautifully put together ensemble had been carefully folded into a Waitrose bag and replaced by a pair of extremely ill-fitting lounge trousers and a jumper whose sleeves extended well past his hands. Paris didn't say anything—because Tariq was still scowling—but he did look kind of adorable.

"Why on earth," asked Tariq, rolling up the legs of his trousers, "do you dress like this?"

"Well, they fit me. Which makes a difference."

"They don't fit you. They cover you. It's not the same thing."

Paris pulled at his own sleeves. "I don't know. I just feel safe in them."

"The really annoying thing"—Tariq stroked the cashmere—"is that this would be a really nice jumper on someone ten stone heavier and eight years older than you."

"My parents are the ones who work in fashion. I…I buy clothes."

"Yeah, but this is Ralph Lauren. You could buy ten shitty jumpers that make you look terrible for what this cost."

It was one thing to suspect he looked awful. Quite another to have it confirmed. "I knew you were lying when you said I looked…" Paris couldn't quite bring himself to say "like Michelangelo's *David*." "…nice?"

"You do look nice. But you dress appallingly. And also expensively, which is…" Tariq made a gesture of frustration. "…gah. And why are we talking about your clothes?"

"Because you had to put some of them on. Because I threw you into dinner. Because I, um, went for your penis? Because I am the worst date ever."

Sighing, Tariq lowered himself back into the blue armchair. "I'm sorry. I'm just a bit ratty because my favourite jeans are covered in eggs and I'm dressed like a ten-year-old who raided the wardrobe of his older brother with no taste."

"You picked the trousers," Paris pointed out.

"They were the least bad trousers. Anyway, the thing is—and while I hadn't expected you to either grab my crotch or launch me into food—I should probably have made it a bit clearer that when I said *shall we take it slowly* I meant for me as much as for you."

Okay. Maybe this wasn't unsalvageable. "We can definitely take it slowly. We don't have to have sex tonight. Or, you know, even on our next date if that happens."

"Yeah." Tariq raised a finger. "Put a pin in that."

"Oh my God. You're just not into me, are you? Is it the jumpers? I can buy better jumpers."

"No, I promise I'm very into you. I'm just not going to have sex with you."

Shit. He was that bad at kissing. "Am I that bad at kissing?"

"No. It's not you. It's…I…" Tariq shrank back, which, in the enormous jumper, made him look very small indeed. "I don't believe in sex before marriage."

This was not something Paris's previous relationships had prepared him for. "That might be a bit of a problem, because I think it's very soon to be talking about marriage."

Tariq laughed. "Honey, hold your horses. I'm not saying I want to marry you. I'm just saying that I want the guy I marry to be the only guy I have sex with. And that guy might not be you. And, spoilers, given how tonight's gone, probably will not be you."

"But why?" Paris asked, aghast. "I mean, not why don't you want to marry me. I mean why don't you want to have sex with me. Or anyone. But right now, mostly me?"

Tariq sighed. It wasn't one of his patient sighs. "You know that bit in the Ten Commandments about not committing adultery? I think that still applies. And before you say anything, there's stuff about it in the Quran as well, but I figured you'd have heard of the Ten Commandments."

"Well, yes, in a can-name-six sort of way. Only I don't quite see what that's got to do with anything? Plenty of Christians have sex outside marriage."

This was not going well. Tariq had uncurled and flopped back in the universal gesture of *what is this, I don't even*. "And a lot don't. And a lot of Muslims do. And a lot don't. It's almost like these things are complicated and people disagree about them."

"Okay, but…" This was entirely outside of Paris's sphere of experience. He was used to guys showing up, getting annoyed with him being weird and in his head all the time, and then making it pretty clear that they expected to get laid. That was *how it worked* and nothing in Paris's admittedly unhelpful brain could explain how it could work differently. "But then why are you even here?"

Social cues were not Paris's strong point, but even he could tell that had been the wrong thing to say. It had been *I'd never ask you out* all over again but with a deeper undertone of being a sexual predator. And Tariq was staring at him with an expression that was almost betrayal.

"I…That's not what I meant." It was a poor attempt at a recovery and Paris knew it. "I just…It's just…I'm not really used to…I just really don't. It's just you say different people believe different things, and I just want to know why you're agreeing with the ones who say you…y'know…shouldn't?"

Tariq looked like he was trying not to—actually Paris wasn't sure, not to cry? Not to lose his temper? Whatever it was, he was trying not to do it. "I agree with them," he said very carefully, "because I think love matters and I think sex matters and I think family matters and I want my faith to be part of all those things. And I *really* want to believe that you're asking me this because you want to understand me better—"

"I *am*," Paris insisted perhaps slightly too forcefully.

"That's what people always say." Tariq looked down. "The thing is I've had this conversation a lot and I've always come away feeling it had an undertone of *explain your weird foreign religion to me*."

"If it helps," Paris offered, "I'd say the same if you were a Christian."

From the look on his face, Tariq did not seem very reassured. "I don't think it does. I think it just makes you equal opportunities condescending."

"I'm not being condescending. I'm trying to understand."

"Two things." Tariq squared his shoulders. "One, tough, it's not my job to play Google for you. Two, even if you don't understand, you should trust that I've thought this through."

That was...Paris supposed it was fair. But that didn't make it less confusing. And he didn't think he was being judgemental, or not-trust-showing. He was just being curious. Although if he was being honest with himself, there *was* something about "I won't have sex before marriage" that bothered him in a way that "I won't eat pork" didn't.

"What if it was still 2013?" Paris asked. "And you couldn't get married at all?"

Tariq took a deep breath. "Okay. The thing is, Paris, you seem like a nice guy and I don't think you're trying to be a jerk about this, but it still feels to me kind of like you're asking me to justify my choices."

"No. I'm trying to...to..." Actually, what was he trying to? He was just sort of saying whatever came into his head. Well, about a tenth of what came into his head. Because, when you got right down to it, there were only so many times you could make egg yolk ravioli for someone. And if Tariq wasn't interested in sex—or a steady supply of white truffle—what else did Paris have to offer? "I just don't get how...and this isn't about any one religion...I just don't see how it fits?"

"Fits?" repeated Tariq flatly.

"Well, it's not like, and I'm sure Christianity is the same, it's not like those sorts of religions are, you know, super down with homosexuality?"

Tariq stood up. He seemed—not angry, exactly, more sort

of hurt. "Okay. I think I'm going home now. It's nothing—it's not—I just really thought you'd be...Oh never mind. What you've got to understand is, people in both my communities have been asking me that question my whole life. And I just...I was here to have a nice time. Not to explain who I am again." Blinking, he looked away and was quiet a moment. "I'm going to get these"—he indicated his borrowed nonsemble—"washed and back to you as soon as I can. Thank you for dinner."

Oh God. "You don't have to go."

"You're right, honey, I don't. But I'm choosing to."

Oh God. "Look, I'm sorry, I didn't mean—"

"I know you didn't. That's part of the problem." Tariq picked up the Waitrose bag containing his original outfit and made his way to the door, with Paris trailing forlornly behind him. He paused on the threshold. "I'm just so bored of it being this hard. Have a lovely evening. See you Saturday."

He closed the door with a polite little click, leaving Paris to reflect on how the hell he'd managed to fuck things up even worse than he'd thought he might.

Thursday

PARIS WAS PICKING at a bowl of dry granola when Morag bounced in the next morning.

"How'd it go?" she said, flinging herself down opposite him.

"I sexually assaulted him, then insulted his religion."

There was the slightest of pauses. "Did you actually or are you just being a prick like usual?"

"We were kissing and I was worried he might be getting bored—"

"You were worried he was getting bored? What were you kissing him with? A Monopoly set?"

Paris picked even more pickily at his granola. "No, but, like, when you're kissing someone, you expect it to go somewhere?"

"That depends quite a lot on who it is."

"Well, everyone I've been with has expected it to go somewhere. So where I went was…I put my hand on his dick. And he didn't like it."

Rising, Morag crossed to the cupboard where Paris kept his mason jar of homemade granola. She brought it back to the table, along with a mug, a carton of Greek yoghurt, and a pot of honey. "Put something on your breakfast, man. You're not a fucking monk."

"I wish I was," said Paris mournfully. "Then I wouldn't have invited a guy over to my flat and grabbed his dick."

"You've really not seen any news about the Catholic Church in the last couple of years, have you?"

"Not where I was going with that."

Morag shrugged. "Oh come on. We've all done a misjudged dick grab. You go for the cock, you get a *sorry love, not up for that yet*, and you say *ach, no worries, do you want to lick my tits?*"

"I don't have tits. And even if I did have tits, he wouldn't want to lick them, because he doesn't want to have sex with me."

The look on Morag's face was justifiably suspicious. "How do you know he doesn't want to have sex with you? Not liking one bit of a thing doesn't mean you don't like the whole thing. I hate glacé cherries, I still eat Chelsea buns."

"Yeah." Paris drooped a pathetic teaspoon of yoghurt onto his shame granola. "He explicitly told me he didn't want to have sex with me because he doesn't believe in sex before marriage."

"I take it that this is the part where you insulted his religion."

"I didn't *mean* to. I just don't understand why anyone would...believe something like that?"

"Pretty sure it's none of your fucking business, Paris."

"It's my business if it stops me having a boyfriend," he wailed.

"Do you not think"—Morag's voice had the tone of wary patience that she used at some point in at least forty percent of her conversations with Paris—"that maybe it was the insulting his religion that's stopping him being your boyfriend?"

Of all people, Paris would have expected Morag to understand why a no-shagging policy was a dealbreaker. "But it's not just that, is it? Isn't sex kind of a huge part of the package in a grown-up relationship?"

She actually rolled her actual eyes. "Maybe if you're fucking fifteen and you've got no other way to prove what a big fucking adult you are. But if you're old enough to vote, then you're old enough to realise that the Netflix-to-chill ratio is very much up for negotiation."

"You say that, but it's not like you'd—"

"Don't you tell me *what I'd*, you wee shit."

Normally, Paris didn't like to push back against Morag. Of course, he didn't like to push back against anybody. But he particularly didn't like to push back against Morag since that was a recipe for getting his teeth metaphorically knocked in. On this occasion, though, he thought he was one hundred percent in the right. "No but seriously. You would never be in a relationship where you weren't getting any."

"Have you not noticed that I don't have boyfriends?" Morag had that *you have fucked with me and you will regret it* glint in her eye. "Why would I think the point of dating somebody was to get something I could get anywhere?"

Paris's metaphorical teeth were rattling. "But surely you should get at least as much as you could get somewhere else."

"You've seen how much I get. That would be fucking impossible. The man would be dead."

"Okay okay," he conceded quickly. "If you were in a monogamous relationship, you'd have to settle for less. But there's a difference between less and none."

"Aye, but then we're just haggling over the price. If you want sex, go out and get sex. If you want somebody who'll eat your fucking ravioli and put up with your endless river of bullshit, then do that instead. But they're not the same thing."

"And you don't think"—Paris was starting to feel he'd lost this argument, despite being right in every particular—"that after this hypothetical guy eats my fucking ravioli and puts up with my endless river of bullshit, he should at least get an orgasm out of it."

Morag plonked her elbows firmly on the table. "If you need sex to be happy in a relationship, that's your choice. But it sounds like you're saying other people need sex to put up with you. And I'll be honest, some days I can see why you think that. Frankly, after I've finished this conversation, I'm going to go and have a therapeutic wank myself."

"Sorry. After all that, are you agreeing with me?"

"No, I'm insulting you. It's a different thing."

"And you wonder why I have self-esteem issues."

"Oh no." She shook her head. "You were like this long before I got to you. Anyway, point is you found a man who came all the way out here just to spend time with you and didn't even want you to suck him off at the end of it."

"Yes, and people dump me even when I *am* sucking them off. So how am I going to get someone to stick around when I don't have that option?"

Having finished her granola, Morag stood and went to rinse the bowl. "I don't know, Paris. Maybe you just have to trust he likes your personality. Now I'm going to bed. I didn't get any sleep last night. You know, because of all the sex I was having without being in a long-term relationship."

Paris hadn't slept much last night, either, on account of the guilt, shame, and nausea which he hoped was stress rather than salmonella. He was about to go back to picking at his granola in solitary gloom when Neferneferuaten leapt onto the table and almost stuck her tail up his nose. It was an ambiguous gesture, even for a cat, but he chose to interpret it as broadly supportive.

Abandoning breakfast as a bad job, he stroked her head instead and thought about everything that had happened and everything Morag had said. It felt like an impossible emotional Sudoku. Because how could you tell whether you wanted something or just thought someone else would want you to want it?

All things being equal, he probably *did* want to have sex with Tariq. But he wasn't sure he wanted it so much that not being able to was worth giving up any hope of being with him at all.

And anyway, he'd been single for months now. So it wasn't like he'd actually be giving anything up. And he'd be getting a hot, funny, clever guy who was way too good for him and had given every impression of quite liking Paris until he'd turned into a raging sex maniac.

Which would have been bad enough if he *was* a raging sex maniac. But he wasn't. It was just Morag was—annoyingly— right. And he'd fallen into a pattern of assuming that sex and relationships were the same thing. When they didn't have to be and clearly weren't.

Oh God, he was an idiot. Though, in his own defence, he was pretty sure most people, at least most people he'd been with, made the same assumption.

Neferneferuaten was beginning to get far too interested in his granola. He lifted her gently into his lap, where she circled like she was making a permanent nest. Finally, she settled down and casually picked at his pyjamas with her claws.

"Stop that," Paris told her, without much hope that she'd actually stop that.

Since Tariq had left, Paris had been low-key speculating about ways the evening could have gone better. Mostly things like *I wish I hadn't dropped him onto a table* and *I wish he'd been less prickly about the sex thing*. But now he was veering in the direction of *I wish I'd been more aware of how awful I was being*.

Because—whatever his messed-up brain was telling him about what he had to offer—he'd as good as told Tariq that if they weren't going to fuck, he didn't see the point in spending time with him. And that was a horrible thing to say to someone, even if it didn't come double-dipped with *also I think your religious beliefs are stupid*.

"Oh, Neferneferuaten," he said. "I'm a total arsehole."

Saturday

"WELCOME," ANNOUNCED Grace Forsythe, "my oblectatious octet of oxygeusians to—"

Colin Thrimp stepped forward, one hand on his earpiece. "Jennifer says, and I quote, 'Stop fucking about and use normal words, you miserable sack of overeducated, overpaid, overrated shit.'"

"I've always taken a certain pride in being overrated," Grace Forsythe mused in a way that made it very clear she wasn't actually *replying* to him so much as riffing on what he'd just said. "I take it as a tribute to my skills as a performer."

"She says, 'Fuck off and stick to the fucking script.'"

"Darling, I've not read a script in twenty years."

"Jennifer says, 'That's because you're too busy staying up late, reading through a thesaurus looking for obscure words that alliterate so everybody will forget you actually got a lower second.'" He paused. "She also says, and again I should stress I'm quoting here: 'Now do your fucking job, you talentless hack.'"

Grace Forsythe sighed as Hercules might have sighed upon being told, having slain the Nemean Lion and the Lernaean Hydra, and then captured the Ceryneian Hind and the Erymanthian Boar, he would subsequently be required to spend the day shovelling shit.

"Welcome, bakers," Grace said, still very much at an eleven, "to week three of *Bake Expectations*. Over the last seven years we've asked our contestants to make French brioche and Swedish prinsesstårta, Spanish almendrados and Polish szarlotka. But today the producers have obviously run out of ideas, because we've resorted to the fucking Americans."

"Grace," roared Jennifer Hallet, striding into the ballroom

like Darth Vader. "Stop pissing about or I'll tell the press you had a tragic workplace accident and are going to have to spend the next eight weeks in hospital having a three-tiered cake stand removed from your pyloric sphincter."

"I"—Grace Forsythe pulled herself up to her full height, which couldn't have been more than five foot four—"am the glue that holds this show together."

"The thing about glue, sunshine, is that you can get it from any old broken-down horse in the knacker's yard. And I can always replace you with an out-of-work actor doing a bad impression of David Attenborough."

The two women glared at each other while the bakers stood around with the paralysed expressions of people who knew they were still being filmed.

Grace Forsythe did her aggrieved-Hercules sigh again. "Fine. But I want it on record that I think we're really scraping the bottom of the barrel with this one."

"Excuse me, I've got more barrels than you can fit up your arse. But there's three hundred million people in America, and if we want them to keep paying attention, either we mention them occasionally or you start co-hosting with Pat Sajak."

"Fine." With a world-weary gesture, Grace Forsythe waved to the cameras. "Once more from the top, darlings. Yippee ki-yay, mothercluckers. On today's show we're paying tribute to the greatest nation on God's green earth, except Britain. That's right, it's American week. I fucking hate you, Jennifer."

The bake, as it turned out, was donuts—the pink kind, with the sprinkles, like Homer Simpson would eat. Except they all had to be very careful not to mention Homer Simpson for trademark reasons.

The recipe started with "bloom the yeast," which Paris thought meant sprinkling it in warm water until it foamed. He'd actually made donuts before—Morag had dragged him to a couple of parties with their coursemates over the last year, and he'd found showing up with baked goods made him feel less like an unwelcome intruder—so was less thrown than some of the other contestants.

"This is arrant nonsense," Catherine Parr was telling Colin Thrimp. "Last week it was the Jews, this week it's the Yanks. I thought this was a British show, not some kind of non-denominational, multicultural, let's ban Enid Blyton and Winston Churchill BBC community project."

Colin Thrimp wriggled helplessly. "I don't suppose you could rephrase some of that ever so slightly, could you? Perhaps you could say something like *well I've not done much American cooking*? Or *I don't have a deep fat fryer at home*."

"I *don't* have a deep fat fryer at home. Because I went to a proper school and didn't get pregnant at nineteen."

"Well." Colin gave her the blandest of his very bland smiles. "Thank you very much."

Paris was already adding the wet ingredients to the dry ingredients in the stand mixer, which had come pre-fitted with a dough hook. He felt oddly calm. At least, calm about baking. He was a lot less calm about having been a complete dick to Tariq and about having totally failed to find him and apologise on either the Friday evening or the Saturday morning.

But maybe having one specific and important source of stress meant that all his usual sources of stress—messing things up, letting people down, making nebulously defined mistakes—seemed kind of trivial? After all, it was hard to worry about something that might go wrong somehow in the future when you'd definitely ruined something that was right in front of you and hurt somebody you could have been starting to care about.

"What are you doing?" asked a passing member of the production crew, camera operator in tow.

What Paris's mind was doing was endlessly rehearsing and re-rehearsing ways to tell Tariq that he knew he'd fucked up and would try not to fuck up again. His hands, however, were laying his freshly cut donuts on a baking tray where they would wait until his fryer came up to temperature.

He glanced up distractedly. "I've just got my first batch ready. And when the oil hits about…" The recipe hadn't actually specified a temperature, but it was always between a hundred and seventy and a hundred and ninety degrees. "...a hundred and eighty degrees, I'll pop them in and hope for the best."

The producer moved on. And Paris couldn't help looking towards Tariq's workstation. In the heat of the ballroom, a single lock of hair had escaped his usually perfectly maintained... whatever that kind of I-know-what-I'm-doing-up-here hairstyle was called. But no matter what Tariq was currently feeling, it was almost certainly donut related, and not the lingering aftereffects of a single shitty date.

Paris wasn't expecting a second chance. Honestly, he wasn't sure he deserved one. Or that he'd deserved a first chance, really. But he'd thought about it a lot—like, *a lot* a lot—and there was no getting away from the fact that, regardless of the outcome, he owed Tariq an apology. A proper apology with details and personal growth and shit. Not just his usual aura of being sorry for existing.

In an ideal world, of course, he wouldn't have done anything he needed to apologise for in the first place. But since he had, there was something almost comforting about having a clear idea of what he needed to do and why he needed to do it. Why, for that matter, he wanted to, when some days he couldn't even say why he wanted to get out of bed.

Paris delicately lifted his first donut from the tray and dropped it, with a soft plop, into the oil.

The donuts he'd made in a distracted trance had come out pretty well. They got an honourable mention from Marianne Wolvercote, although Rodney (in yet another cardigan) had taken the top spot because, obviously, he made donuts for his girls all the time. And by all the time, he meant a parentally responsible amount of the time. The rest of them had fallen somewhere from mediocre to bad. Joan's dough had been too dense, Catherine Parr seemed to have taken a certain pride in refusing to even try, and Tanya—as she explained to the camera afterwards—had made the mistake of assuming a deep fat fryer worked like a piece of lab equipment rather than a piece of kitchenware.

"I don't cook a lot of fried food," she said, "because I've taught enough year sevens about the importance of a balanced diet that I'd feel really hypocritical. Anyway, I tried to adjust for the fact that most oils have a much lower thermal conductivity than water, which, looking back, was probably overthinking it."

Meanwhile Paris was making slightly halfhearted *well, I think I did pretty well* noises at Colin Thrimp while doing his best not to keep glancing around for Tariq when he was supposed to be giving an interview.

Liberated at last, he made for the bar in the main building since while Tariq—unlike Paris—didn't drink, he did—unlike Paris—find it easy to approach large groups of people. And if you were going to interrupt someone else's perfectly pleasant evening to say sorry for being a dick, ambushing them in a crowd was probably marginally less obnoxious than knocking on their door while they were praying.

Once he was in the bar, however, he realised that his plan had a fatal flaw. Which was that a bunch of his fellow contestants were already there, already talking to each other, and now Paris was going to have to walk up to them and say *hi, stop the thing you're enjoying doing and focus on me for twenty seconds while I make it very clear I'm looking for someone who isn't any of you.*

He sidled over to the table and stood there, waiting for a gap in the conversation that steadfastly refused to arrive.

"So run this by me again," Joan was saying. "You do art but only on computers?"

She was addressing Lili, the vibrantly dressed art student who Paris had said precisely six words to throughout the entire competition. "With computational technology."

"So it's not just…Photoshop?" Tanya asked.

Lili flapped a hand, half-amused, half-exasperated. "I'm not doing a BA in Photoshop studies. I'm exploring the ways in which twenty-first-century technology can enhance or integrate with artistic expression."

"Like what?" Joan seemed sceptical at best.

"Okay, so let's take sculpture…"

"Sculpture's just carpentry with airs."

"That's a different argument, for a different day," said Lili, with another hand flap. "The point is, there's a lot you can do with laser cutting or injection moulding or 3-D printing that you couldn't do even ten years ago. So if you want to really, really simplify it, it's a perfectly normal art course except instead of working with a chisel or a paintbrush I'm working with a hot-wire cutter and a machine learning algorithm."

"You what now?" This was Bernard, ambling back to the table with a bag of crisps and three drinks. "Hello, Paris. How long have you been standing there?"

Paris gave a little jump. "Oh, not long. Just didn't want to interrupt."

"You should have interrupted," Lili told him. "Explaining what I actually do usually takes a very long time."

"I still don't get it." Joan folded her arms. "It sounds like bollocks."

Taking her wine from Bernard, Tanya put her teacher face on. "Why don't we try not calling each other's careers bollocks."

"It's fine." Lili took her own drink and leaned back with a confidence that Paris instantly envied. "I'm not the one with an obsolete skill set."

This garnered the sort of eye roll from Joan that would have made Paris shrink under the table in abject mortification. "Tell you what, I'll live in a house with no art. And you live in a house with no furniture. And we'll see who has the better time."

"I'll live in a world with no wood," Lili threw back, "and you live in a world with no plastic. And we'll see who has the better time."

"To be fair"—Tanya seemed to have given neutrality up as a bad job—"right now we definitely have too little wood and too much plastic."

"But we do," Bernard announced, with the air of a man desperate to change the subject, "have crisps for the table."

"Why don't you let—" started Tanya.

Before Bernard, once again, tore the pack open with enough force to scatter sea salt and balsamic vinegar Kettle Chips across the gathering like slightly greasy confetti. "Dearie me." Unperturbed, he laid what remained of his offering ceremoniously in front of the group.

"Um." Realising he might never get a better opportunity than the window in which people were picking crisps out of their hair, Paris hurled himself off the cliff edge of the conversation. "Has anybody seen Tariq?"

Bernard's eyes lit up. "Ooh, are you going to ask him out? You should definitely ask him out. I think he likes you."

"Actually"—that was Lili—"he might need a bit of space."

"No, no." Bernard shook his head with fatal certainty. "Just last week he was telling me what a nice lad he thought young Paris was. Well, actually I was saying what a nice lad I thought you were. But he was agreeing very strongly."

Lili was giving Paris a look. A look that said *it would be a bad idea to take relationship advice from a fifty-year-old man who can't open a packet of crisps*.

"So," Paris asked, "how much space on average would you say he needed?"

She gave the kind of pause that Paris felt certain was not going to lead to a sincere answer. "Three-point-seven cubic give-me-a-breaks."

"Thanks. I'll...um. Thanks."

"Hang on." Joan looked up from her newly de-crisped beer. "It's been two weeks. Have you blown it already?"

"Oh, you'd be amazed," Paris told her, "how quickly I can blow—wait, that's coming out really wrong."

In consolation, Bernard proffered the remains of the Kettle Chips. "Crisp?"

"I might go back to my room."

"Or stay," suggested Joan. "Get drunk and forget all about it."

Drinking to forget never really worked for Paris. Everyone knew alcohol was supposed to lower your inhibitions, but the particular inhibitions he'd found it removed were the ones stopping his brain spiralling down the plughole of improbable catastrophe. "No, I think an early night is what I really need. Thanks, though."

Joan shrugged. "Wuss."

"Oh, be nice." Bernard looked faintly pained.

"Oh, piss off."

"Shan't."

A lifetime of avoiding anything remotely resembling conflict had given Paris pretty sharp instincts for the difference between an actual argument and free-spirited bants, and he was pretty sure this was the latter. In any case, he took advantage of the distraction to slink quietly away. And it was only when he'd slunk far enough that he couldn't really unslink that he realised he was now not only failing to apologise to Tariq but also failing baseline human interaction.

Because, actually, it might have been quite nice to hang out with Lili, Bernard, and Joan for a bit. He'd been telling himself he had nothing in common with them—and they probably wouldn't like him anyway—but they didn't really have anything in common with each other, either, and they were still clearly getting on fine. Besides, they had a mutual love of baking and fear of Marianne Wolvercote to fall back on. And then he could have gone home to Morag and said *I did a sociable, be proud of me* instead of *I sat alone in my room feeling too self-conscious to leave.*

Spotting the sitting-down log and having no pressing reason to be anywhere, Paris stopped for a moment and sat down. Then realised he didn't have a pressing reason to do that, either, and now he was sitting alone on a log and people might see him sitting alone on a log and think *why is that guy sitting alone on a log, what a wanker.* Though, of course, if he got up, people might see him, sitting down and standing up, sitting down and standing up, and think *why is that guy doing an incredibly low-impact exercise routine in the grounds of a stately home, what a wanker.*

He pulled out his phone and texted his mum. **Hi. Hope whatever you're doing is going well. I'm still on the baking show. It's week three and I've done okay so far.** He wasn't exactly waiting for a reply—he still didn't know what time zone she was in—but there was something about just sending the message. Something that felt like connection. For a while, anyway. Until it faded.

Glancing up from the screen, he spotted Tariq emerging from the Lodge. Which would have been a brilliant opportunity to catch him and apologise. Apart from the bit where he was supposed to be giving him space. Except if he didn't apologise at all, he'd just be a dick who never apologised. And he wasn't sure whether Tariq would prefer *doesn't respect my personal boundaries* guy or *refuses to admit he's done anything wrong* guy.

In the end, he decided to err on the side of not respecting boundaries. Because, actually, all he really knew about how Tariq was feeling was something he'd said to someone else at some indeterminate point in the past. Pleased with this unusual decisiveness, Paris leapt to his feet and strode purposefully across the lawn.

Unfortunately, he'd badly misjudged the distance, which meant by the time he'd purposefully stridden halfway, Tariq was already wandering towards the woods that edged the grounds. Committed now, Paris broke into the sort of abashed jog you did when you were trying really hard to look like you weren't running for a bus when you definitely were.

"Uh," he gasped. He'd intended it to be an *um*, but he was more out of breath than he thought he should be. "T-Tariq?"

Tariq turned, making Paris acutely aware that only one of them had recently undertaken an impromptu hundred-meter dash. "Are you chasing me?"

"No. I just saw you. And wanted to…" Probably Paris should have gone to a gym, like, ever. Because, right now, he was sweaty and lacked the oxygen for long sentences. "Wanted to say sorr— to say I've been thinking and you were right."

"Right about what exactly?"

The air situation was still making this harder than it needed to be. "Everything. The truffle. And how I was being. And all the assumptions. And the whole how things need to…with…your penis."

There was a silence. In Paris's head, it had been a much more coherent apology.

"Well," said Tariq finally. "I'm glad to know you think I'm right about my own penis."

"No, I mean yes, I mean obviously. It's your…Okay, I'm going to try to stop saying *penis* now. Because it's not really about the penis. It's about everything that's attached to the penis."

"For someone who's trying to stop saying *penis*, you're still saying *penis* a lot."

"I know. I think it's called ironic processing. I looked it up once."

Tariq folded his arms. He wasn't wearing nail varnish this evening, and Paris tried not to read too much into that. "All right. Thanks. I guess? I was actually just going for a walk, so I think I'll get back to it, if that's okay with you?"

While Paris hadn't quite expected Tariq to fall immediately back into his arms, he'd hoped for slightly more than *kthanx-bai*. And although he wouldn't have said he *deserved* more than *kthanxbai*—because wasn't part of the point here to be owning his entitlement and accepting Tariq's right to his boundaries?— he thought it was probably okay to give it one more go. If only so he could try to do this without saying the word *penis*. "I messed up and I'm sorry. And I messed up saying sorry as well. In my defence, I'd just run quite a long way. But I do…I mean I have… I'd be different if you…but you don't have to."

There was another silence. It was longer than the last one, and Tariq was frowning slightly in a way that seemed thought-ful rather than repulsed or infuriated. Which Paris was taking as a semi-win. "Tell you what. I'm going for a stroll by the river. Why don't you come with me and see if you can form a complete sentence?"

"Mhm," said Paris eagerly. "That sounds…yeah."

They wandered quietly for a while, Paris trying to relax enough to actually get words out. Had his multitudinous fuckups not been hovering around him like wasps at a picnic, it would have been his perfect evening. Of course, he could never have admitted it, because being into long walks with nice men through sun-dappled woodlands was a god-awful cliché. But then maybe that was the same self-defeating mindset that led you to grab someone's dick in a fit of anxiety when you were having a really nice first date.

"So," he tried, "I think what I meant to say..." Then he paused, struggling to get his thoughts in the right order. Which made the pause last long enough that he realised he'd probably have to start over. Which made the pause start over as well. "What I meant to say," he tried again, "is that I was talking to my housemate and I realised—sorry this is going to sound really rehearsed now..."

Tariq almost smiled. "Honey, if this is you sounding rehearsed, do not go into improv."

"I can honestly say that's one of the few mistakes I'm not at risk of making. But, anyway. I was talking to my housemate and I realised that I'd, um, been a total dick. And I'd been so wrapped up in what everything I was doing said about me, and so worried that I didn't have anything to offer you, or anyone really, that wasn't truffles or sex or...or...actually, that's kind of it?"

Perhaps it was Paris's imagination, but Tariq winced.

"Anyway, I was so wrapped up in those things that I wasn't thinking about your actual, like, needs or feelings. Which was a pretty basic dating fail? And also a pretty basic human being fail. And so I'd, you know, completely get it if you wanted me to fuck off and never talk to you again. But if you don't, then I really will try to be less...um...shit?"

"Wow." Tariq definitely was smiling now. "I'm not sure *I promise I'll try to be less, um, shit* is going to go down as one of the all-time great romantic declarations."

"I'd say we'd always have Paris. But that's my name, so it has some really unfortunate implications."

"I know this is a massive cultural taboo, but given the choice between you promising to be less shit and you telling me to go with another guy because I'm"—Tariq did spectacularly extravagant air quotes—"'part of his work,' I'll take less shit every time."

Paris gazed at him. "Sorry but…are you telling me you don't like *Casablanca*?"

"Yep," Tariq told him gleefully. "I don't drink, I don't believe in sex before marriage, and, for me, a truly romantic story doesn't involve the heroine getting regifted like a box of unwanted bath bombs against a background of explicit propaganda."

Paris continued gazing at him—lost in his eyes and his smile and the moment. "I really like you."

"Because of my hot takes on eighty-year-old movies?"

"Sort of? I mean, not literally. Just I'd never be able to say I didn't like *Casablanca*. Even if I didn't like *Casablanca*. And also you're, like, really hot. And good at kissing. And dress well, and things. And probably, if this situation was reversed, which it wouldn't be because you wouldn't fuck up as badly in the first place, you'd say all this stuff way better."

"Well"—Tariq cast him a look that was bordering on affectionate—"the jury's still out on the complete-sentence thing. But points for sincerity."

They paused in an odd little glade in front of an even odder stone archway. It was hard to tell how this was going. But Paris was hoping not terribly?

He glanced back at Tariq, somewhat imploringly. "And I honestly *honestly* will try to be less shit. Not a Mr. Kipling. I just get in my head. In a really big way. And I know when that happens, I…I'm not always thinking about other people."

"I have noticed that. Both bits of that." Tariq's hand came to rest lightly on Paris's forearm. "But you don't really think you've got nothing to offer except sex and truffles, do you?"

"Um, not exactly. It's hard to come up with a list."

"I don't think most of us have lists?"

"Yes, but then…how do you know what's good about you?"

Tariq shrugged. "You don't. You mostly assume you're okay."

This was beginning to sound very improbable. Perhaps impossible. "I'm not sure that would work for me," said Paris, in a small voice.

"All right, angel cake." Tariq got that faintly thoughtful, faintly challenging expression. "What's on your list?"

"I just told you. Without sex and truffles I've got nothing."

"Don't be silly." Stepping closer, Tariq put his other hand on Paris's shoulder. His face was faintly upturned, almost like he was waiting for a kiss. "You're ridiculously good looking. You're an amazing cook. When you remember to be, you're incredibly sweet. And when you don't, you work it out eventually. Plus, you make me laugh."

"With or at?" asked Paris.

"Little from column A, little from column B."

"I'll take it."

"You're also a pretty decent kisser. And"—Tariq went up on his tiptoes—"you are way too tall."

So Paris leaned down and pressed his lips to Tariq's. And, weirdly, without the pressure of truffle and egg ravioli and fretting about getting laid, it was different. And better. And—

What was that prickling on the back of his neck?

He raised his head. "Can we go somewhere? Because this… arch thing is really creeping me out."

"Yeah." Tariq peered around him. "I've no idea what it is or why it's here."

"Is it some kind of burial mound? Are we making out in front of someone's dead wife?"

Disentangling himself, Tariq crept towards the archway and stuck his head inside. "Actually, I don't want to go in there. It's just a dingy hole and I think a badger lives in it. It smells like a badger lives in it."

"Can you really identify badgers by smell?"

"Honey, I'm from Bethnal Green. The animals I can identify are cats, pigeons, and fish and chips. But something is definitely using this place as a toilet, and I prefer to believe it's a badger rather than a serial killer."

"Okay," said Paris. "Now I really want to go somewhere else."

"Back to my room?"

"Is that...Would you be comfortable?"

Tariq rolled his eyes. "Yes. I'm religious. I'm not an unmarried woman in a Jane Austen novel."

"Right. Sorry. Just wanted to, you know, check?"

"That's kind of you. But how about we trust that I can set my own boundaries?"

"Are you sure?" Paris asked. "Because you might be overwhelmed by my intense self-confidence and raw animal magnetism."

"Honey"—Tariq was clearly laughing in that little from column A, little from column B way that Paris was beginning to let himself—"you're cute as heck, but whatever animal magnetism you have is definitely well done."

"It's probably overdone to be honest."

Tariq gave him a look of mock exasperation. "Are you seriously asking me to reassure you about how your animal magnetism is cooked?"

"No, I'm being charming. This is me being charming."

"Fine, I'm charmed." Tariq took Paris's hand, their fingers twining together in a way that—for all his tendency to see the worst in things—Paris couldn't help thinking was a good sign. "Come on, let's get out of here and you can charm me some more."

They walked away from the oddly smelling den that might still have contained a serial killer and back towards the Lodge. Where, if Paris is lucky, there'd be a lot more kissing and a lot less potential murder. And while, in Paris's experience, even the remote threat of a serial killer or, for that matter, a badger would gnaw at the back of his mind like, well, like a badger for hours even after the initial threat had passed, tonight it didn't.

Heading back through the woods, talking to Tariq, knowing—or at least hoping—that he would soon be able to kiss him again, all the thoughts of knives and claws slipped away. It felt a little strange, but it also felt safe. Or perhaps more to the point it felt strange *to* feel safe. From a lifetime of living with his brain, Paris knew that if he examined the sensation too closely, it would vanish, and, for once, he didn't examine it anyway. He just let himself enjoy the walk, and the night, and being with Tariq. And dared to wonder a little bit if, perhaps, he wasn't the total wreck he feared he might be.

Sunday

"SO"—TARIQ POPPED UP at Paris's workstation and twinkled at him—"what are you making for us?"

Grace Forsythe also popped. "You realise I have one job and you are stealing it?"

"I prefer to think of it as an homage," Tariq told her.

"Maybe," Paris suggested, "you could go and look after his bake?"

Placing a theatrical hand over her heart, Grace Forsythe gave an equally theatrical shudder. "Darling, ever since the Victoria sponge incident in season two I'm contractually obliged never to be alone with a cake again."

Tariq smiled his smiliest smile. "Honestly, I'm just playing around while I'm waiting for my base to set."

"Well, I admire your generation's commitment to flirting."

Paris's heart squeezed nervously. "Oh my God, does this look like flirting? Are we going to be flirting on TV?"

"Angel cake." It was Tariq's soothing voice. Paris had made him do soothing voice already. "I just came over to see you. They're not going to show this. It'd make awful television."

"Actually"—Colin Thrimp called from across the ballroom, hand to his earpiece—"Jennifer thinks it's a late enough season we can start doing self-referential material. Also she likes that it's making Grace insecure."

"It's not making me insecure," Grace snapped insecurely.

Colin Thrimp listened for a moment. "She says it should. The kid has promise. And he'd probably be way cheaper than you."

"Should I be offended by that?" asked Tariq.

"No, darling." Grace patted him on the shoulder. "She means

because you're young and easily exploited. Not because you're a raging manslapper."

This was all getting a bit much for Paris, especially since he had a tart to make. But now the spectre of flirting was hovering over his bench, he felt he couldn't really say *can you go away please, I need to get my pastry in the fridge.* And he was, on principle, eager to avoid any situation that involved a fridge-Tariq interface.

"Um," he squeaked. "So what I'm doing right now is I'm just making the dough into a ball, and then I'm going to wrap it in cling film, and then it needs to go into the refrigerator for about half an hour."

Grace Forsythe was giving him something that felt a lot like side-eye. "Who are you narrating that to? The cameras are over there."

"Don't worry." Colin Thrimp made an incomprehensible hand gesture, and a camera operator swung back towards Paris's workstation. "Let's have it one more time."

"But I," protested Paris, "...but..."

"Tell you what." Grace Forsythe looked worryingly like she had an idea. "If it helps, I'll be Marianne, Tariq can be Wilfred, and you can explain it to the two of us."

With the alacrity of an inveterate joiner-in, Tariq offered a cheery, "Eh up, lad, what've you got for us?"

"Well...Wilfred," said Paris uncertainly, "I've just balled up my pastry, and now I need to wrap it in cling film and put it in the fridge."

Grace-as-Marianne looked down her nose in a way that was almost as terrifying as the real thing. "Interesting. Of course that's actually quite a technical process, so you *are* taking a risk here."

"Oh now, Marianne, don't be so hard on the lad—and *wow*"—Tariq broke character—"sorry, that might be the worst Yorkshire accent anybody has ever done. I sound like an Australian Ned Stark."

"Well, Paris." Grace Forsythe, somehow, stayed full Marianne. "Wilfred and I will have to bid you…g'day, mate."

"I think," Tariq said, "I'm going to slink back to Winterfell and check on my base."

Grace Forsythe lit up like Christmas. Or, perhaps, like an '80s comedian, spotting an opportunity for a truly atrocious gag. "You do that, darling. After all, as a great woman once said, it's all about that base."

They both departed, leaving Paris to his actual baking. Having bunged his pastry safely in the fridge and, amazingly, done so without bloodshed, he began tossing his remaining ingredients into the food processor. This probably wasn't going to be the best bake—the theme was supposed to be a dessert showcasing peanut butter, which could have meant basically anything, and Paris, frankly, had been distracted even before Tariq and Grace had showed up.

And, unusually, not in a bad way.

Because last night had been…lovely? Really lovely. Of course, it had started with a difficult conversation, but it had ended with them going back to Tariq's room. And they'd kissed, and not kissed, and talked, and not talked, and Paris had only apologised three times for things that weren't his fault.

All in all, the least stressful date Paris could remember having basically ever. And while it probably *hadn't* been the least stressful date Tariq had ever been on, he'd still seemed broadly content to be with Paris. Maybe even more than broadly content? Maybe happy? As if making someone happy was a thing that Paris was somehow able to do.

Without truffles or blow jobs or anything.

Just him. Oh God, that was weird.

No. No, he'd decided he wasn't going to do that. And he wasn't.

He was going to let himself float happily, like a kitten on a surfboard, and enjoy whatever the hell was going on for however long it lasted. And if that meant he didn't care about getting his peanut butter and jelly Bakewell tart exactly perfect, then so be it.

Humming softly, he set the food processor to blitz.

Despite Tariq's playful—shit, Paris hoped they were playful—protestations that they were wasting perfectly good sunlight, they'd gone to sit under a tree.

"I just get really hot," he explainogised, "and then I'll get sweaty and uncomfortable."

Tariq perched in his lap and ran a finger lightly underneath Paris's collar. "Did you ever think that maybe an enormous fuzzy jumper wasn't the best choice of outfit for July?"

"I know. I know. Every year I tell myself I'm going to pay attention to the weather and start dressing cooler when it gets sunny, except then I wake up and I think *but it's cold now, what if it stays cold, what if it gets colder.*"

"But once you're out," Tariq suggested, "you could take it off and tie it round your shoulders like you're in a movie about gay cricketers in the 'twenties."

"I don't want to look like a gay cricketer in the 'twenties."

"Because you're incredibly modern, don't like cricket, or have a tonne of internalised homophobia?"

Paris blinked at him. "Um, um. Those all sound really bad?"

"Let's be clear. One is worse than the other two."

"Oh I know. My school was very big on cricket."

"Of course," said Tariq laughing, "you went to a school that was big on cricket. I bet you had one of those uniforms with a pointy collar as well."

"Yes, but it wasn't Eton."

There was a pause while Tariq thought about this. Then his eyes glinted. "Do you still have the uniform?"

"Probably. Somewhere."

Leaning in, Tariq nipped at his chin. "You should get it out for me sometime."

"Is that…Are you…" Now Paris was feeling hot and flustered in a way that had nothing to do with his jumper. "Are you secretly kinky?"

Tariq held his fingers a fraction of an inch apart. "Maybe a tiny bit?"

"How tiny a bit are we talking?" asked Paris, trying to suppress the part of his mind that went once again to the awful penis conversation.

"This tiny." Tariq put his fingers back in the indicating-small-amounts-of-abstract-concepts position. "Or maybe this tiny." He made the distance between them infinitesimally larger.

"So," Paris asked hesitantly, "what would happen—in theory—if I did know where my uniform was?"

"I suppose we'd go make out behind a bike shed? Or, for the real posh school experience, a bike valet service?"

"We had bicycle sheds. Where do you think we kept the school bicycles?"

"And did you ever make out behind them?"

"Well no. But I sometimes…borrowed a bike? To go for a ride in the woods?"

"Did you make out there?"

"No. Mostly I just, um, looked at trees? And then went back to school."

"Wow." Tariq gazed at him. "You rebel you."

"Actually"—Paris gazed as good as he got—"it *was* pretty rebellious because everyone else in my year was getting drunk on imported vodka and trying to sneak into the girls' dormitories."

"All the more reason then to dress up in your school uniform while I take discreet but candid photographs on my phone."

"You're not going to really take photos of me, are you?"

"No. Although"—Tariq was still smiling mischievously—"you would look really hot."

Secretly, Paris doubted this. Then again, it was hard to have a uniform fetish when you lived in one every day for your entire adolescence. Well, hard or probably—for some people—far too easy. But he decided that telling this to Tariq would just spoil his fun, so he kissed him shyly instead.

"Oi," shouted Joan. "Get a room. This is a baking show. Not

Love Island. Or *The Bachelor*. Or *Too Hot to Handle*. Or *The Bachelorette*. Or *Love Is Blind*."

In a moment of panic, Paris squirmed out from under Tariq, causing him to keel off sideways into a patch of moss.

"You have to stop doing that," Tariq said, pushing himself onto his elbows. "Also, Joan, how many dating shows do you watch?"

"Me: none? My husband: all of them, all the time." She paused. "I sometimes wonder if he's trying to tell me something."

"What would he be trying to tell you?" asked Tariq.

She shrugged. "I don't know. That we need a better streaming service?"

"Or," Paris suggested, "that he wants more romance in his life?"

"Don't think so. I made him a chair the other day. Can't get more romantic than that. Anyway, Colin says they're starting judging in five minutes."

Once Tariq had picked himself up, and Paris had apologised, they trooped back up the hill with Joan.

"I've got a bad feeling about this week," she said.

Paris usually had a bad feeling as well. But he'd apparently been too distracted to develop one. "I'm sure you'll be fine."

"We were supposed to do a dessert showcasing peanut butter. And I've made them some biscuits."

"Well," offered Tariq with a wince, "I made a giant Reese's Peanut Butter Cup and—I won't lie—it looks amazing. But I've suddenly realised that I've come on a baking show and made something that involves no baking."

Joan clapped him on the shoulder. "Oh. Maybe I'll be all right then."

"Thanks for that." Tariq shot her a look of mock outrage. "I was trying to reassure you."

"Yeah, and it worked. Tell you what, if you go out, I'll do you up a stool."

"No chair for me then?" asked Tariq.

"Don't think so. I'm not trying to have sex with you."

Which left Paris wondering if he'd ever think of chairs the same way again.

———

Paris was so the opposite of with it that when he took his peanut butter and jelly Bakewell tart up to the judges, he even forgot to apologise.

"Another beautifully presented bake, Paris," said Marianne Wolvercote, approvingly.

"And I've got to say," added Wilfred Honey, wielding an eager cake slice, "I do enjoy a Bakewell. Though I'm a bit nervous because I'm not sure what peanut butter is bringing to the table."

That, Paris felt, was a little bit unfair since peanut butter was kind of the whole point.

Marianne Wolvercote brushed a fork gently across the surface of Paris's bake. "But peanut butter and—as the Americans have it—*jelly* is a classic combination for a reason. And I think it's rather clever that you've paired it with something as quintessentially English as a Bakewell tart."

Having finished judging his ideas, they moved on to judging Paris's flavours.

"By 'eck," exclaimed Wilfred Honey, "it's gorgeous."

Paris blinked. "Thanks."

Marianne Wolvercote gave a stately nod. "I agree. It's an unexpected combination, but it's technically perfect and very on brief."

"Thanks," said Paris again, before stumbling back to his place.

The rest of the contestants' bakes went by in a bit of a daze. Joan had been right that her peanut butter biscuits (*cookies* for the American theme) came across as a bit lacking compared to some of the other offerings, like Catherine Parr's peanut butter and chocolate banana bread. And Tariq had also been right that going for a non-baked good on a baking show was a strategic error. Which Paris thought was a shame because his Giant-Other-Cup-Shaped-Peanut-Butter-Confections-Are-Available was visually impressive, tasted great, and was probably the most archetypally American of all the other American-week offerings.

As the peanut-buttery surprises kept coming and nobody did obviously better than Paris, at least in terms of judges' feedback, he found himself wondering why he wasn't feeling happier. He'd got the first *by 'eck it's gorgeous* of the series, and he was more concerned with the fact that Tariq's technically-not-a-bake wasn't getting as much attention as he thought it deserved.

And maybe that was it. Not the bake, obviously. Although he still thought a giant peanut butter cup was a good idea—and a very *Tariq* idea if Paris had any insight—but maybe he was just capped out on happiness. Two days ago he'd been unable to worry about the risk of messing up his donuts when he thought he'd messed up his relationship, and now it was hard to be happy about doing well with his Bakewell when he was already happy about doing so well with his…boyfriend? Maybe boyfriend? Pre-boyfriend? Boyfriend-in-waiting?

In any case, whatever his official relationship status was, the fact remained that Paris's dating-related feelings were definitely pushing out his baking-related feelings. And the part of his brain that firmly believed he shouldn't have nice things was not-so-politely asking him whether that wasn't a bit weird? Like he was basically one of the fairies from *Peter Pan*, so small that he only had room for one emotion at a time. Although if Tinker Bell rules were what he was stuck with, right now he was okay with that. It was a whole lot better than having endless space for a thousand different ways to beat himself up.

"Thank you, everyone"—Grace Forsythe stepped forward—"for your platters of peanutty pulchritude. Marianne and Wilfred will—"

"Er?" Bernard waved his hand in the air. "You haven't done me yet."

Grace Forsythe struck a pose of comical dismay. "Oh my God, Bernard my darling. I am so sorry. I assure you the blame lies squarely between all the pastries I've eaten recently and the cocaine I did in the 'eighties."

"Okay," said Colin Thrimp. "From Marianne's last mark please. And if you could all do your best to look as much like this never happened as you possibly can."

"How do we look like that?" asked Bernard.

Marianne Wolvercote made a beckoning gesture that cried out for a cigarette holder. "Just come here, Bernard."

Bernard obediently went there. "So this," he said, doing a surprisingly good impression of someone who hadn't been completely forgotten or didn't mind that he had been, "is a bread and peanut butter pudding."

"This is very…" Marianne Wolvercote seemed at a rare loss for words.

"Well," Wilfred Honey chimed in, "it's very homey." *Homey* was Wilfred Honey's code for "a mess." "But sometimes homey is exactly what you want. And I, for one, love a bit of bread-and-butter pudding."

Marianne Wolvercote swept up a bready, peanut-buttery forkful. It took her longer to eat it than was traditionally a good sign on *Bake Expectations*, but she laid down her fork with an expression of grudging approval. "This is not normally the kind of dessert I like, and as you progress in the competition you'll need to seriously work on your presentation, but I think this is made exceptionally well."

"Hits the spot, that does," agreed Wilfred Honey, taking another helping. "Almost as good as my mam's."

Beaming, Bernard collected his pudding and trotted away.

Strangely enough, at this point, he was probably Paris's strongest competition. Although, as it turned out, there was no way Marianne Wolvercote was letting something quite that "homey" win in a week where there was any other option.

So…Paris won.

Which was nice.

And Joan went home.

Which wasn't.

Thursday

PARIS COULD DO this. It was just a train. And Tariq had come all the way from Birmingham to London last week, so he could return the favour and go from London to Birmingham now.

And it was fine. It'd be fine. It was just Birmingham.

A large, well-populated city that millions of people lived in perfectly happily their whole lives and that probably contained no more murderers per capita than anywhere else in England. Which didn't stop Paris using the fourteen-minute wait for his train to google *Birmingham crime rates* only to realise that it wasn't much help to be told that Birmingham was slightly more dangerous than Wolverhampton and slightly safer than Stoke-on-Trent when he had been to neither of those places.

He was also really beginning to wish he'd booked himself a first-class ticket. He'd been meaning to, but then he'd remembered the whole truffle incident and decided against it. Tariq was going to meet him at the station, and if he saw Paris getting out of first class, it'd be really embarrassing. Like Paris was saying *hi, yeah, I had to slum it in a first-class train carriage because my chauffeur was taking my private jet to be detailed*.

But that meant he was going to have to crowd onto a tiny chair that wouldn't have enough legroom and would probably have at least two suspicious stains and would smell of something nonspecifically organic. When he could have been reclining in the relative luxury of a seat with slightly more legroom and at most one suspicious stain, and have had its nonspecifically organic smell covered up with something else that was nonspecifically chemical.

Mostly it was the legroom that bothered him. He'd inherited height from both sides of his family, and public transport almost always required him to bend his legs in ways that were a recipe for cramps and—eventually, probably—deep vein thrombosis.

But it was too late now. Or maybe it wasn't? Maybe he could just make his way up to first class anyway, and then ask for an upgrade when the conductor came round? But if that didn't work, he could be fined, and while he could probably *afford* a fine, he might also have to go to court and then he'd have a criminal record.

He made his way up the aisle, trying not to go too fast or too slow, or to hit anyone with his overnight bag, looking for the least objectionable space, and panicking in case the real least objectionable space turned out to be the one he'd just walked past and now couldn't go back to.

Eventually he forced himself to settle *somewhere*, deciding at the last minute to pick the seat with the cigarette burn over the one with discarded remains of a KFC Boneless Banquet for One, while strangers flowed past, bizarrely untraumatised by being packed into a smelly metal tube. Thankfully, there was just enough space in the smelly metal tube that nobody had to sit next to anybody they didn't come aboard with. Then, with an animalistic screech and a confidence-sapping jolt, they were under way.

Paris had done it. He had potential-boyfriended successfully and was bound for Birmingham.

His journey began, as did every long trip by public transport, with Paris checking to see if his motion sickness had miraculously cured itself since last time. It hadn't. So he shoved his needlessly hardback copy of *The White Ship* back into his bag and fished out his phone instead.

Hi Dad. Hope you and mum are okay. I'm still doing well on the show. Won last week. Might have a boyfriend. He's on the show too.

He waited a bit.

Off to Birmingham to see him now.

He waited a bit longer.

And then had to put his phone away, too, because staring at the screen was making his stomach churn.

Only an hour and forty-something minutes to go.

Shutting his eyes, he leaned back, tried not to think about headrests and germs and the possibility of someone's discarded chewing gum getting in his hair, and did his best to relax.

An hour and forty-something minutes later he was still very much unrelaxed. It was too hot, and no air was circulating, and someone two seats down had produced a paper bag from nowhere that was giving off that unmistakeable McDonald's smell that somehow managed to evoke a brand instead of a food.

Also, Paris had needed the toilet for the past eighteen minutes, but the thought of using the tiny, chlorine-drenched receptacle at the end of the carriage was just too horrifying to deal with. Even leaving aside all the terrible things a previous user could have done, there was a risk of the door swinging open while Paris had his trousers down, or of not swinging open when he was trying to get out, or of the train making a sudden lurch at a critical moment, which would mean Paris arrived at his date covered in—if he was lucky—his own urine.

And on top of all this, was a rising dread that, despite his best intentions, he was going to be a total wreck in front of the guy he'd sincerely promised to be non-wrecky with. And Tariq would look at him tenderly and go *oh honey, what happened?* And Paris would have to say *nothing, I'm just an overprivileged piece of*

shit who can't even get on a train without having a breakdown.
And then Tariq would realise Paris wasn't worth it and dump
him, and he'd have to go all the way back to London on, ironically, a train.

"Oh honey," asked Tariq, "what happened?"

Paris tried frantically to look slightly more together than
he felt, which was to say even remotely together. "First Great
Western?"

"Say no more." Tariq put a hand, the fingers rainbow-polished,
lightly against Paris's chest—making him flinch slightly from
both the public statementiness of it, and the knowledge his heart
was still pounding from the journey. "I hear they're being investi-
gated by Amnesty International."

That was funny. Tariq was being funny. And Paris needed to
laugh, the way a normal, healthy, not-at-all-fucked-in-the-head
person would laugh. "Ha-ha-ha," he said.

Tariq squinted up at him. "Are you all right?"

"Um. Yes. I mean, yes. Why wouldn't I be?"

"I don't know. It's like you're a rabbit who's just discovered
that big loud heavy things sometimes go up the weird black river
very fast indeed."

This was not good boyfriending. This was not even good
potential-boyfriending. "Sorry, I just, um, need the loo? Quite
badly."

"Okay. Let's put a pin in the romantic meeting while you go
and...do that? I think there's a toilet over where that sign clearly
says there's a toilet."

"Back soon. Sorry."

Paris dashed. In his surprisingly detailed internal hierarchy
of awful places to urinate, station toilets were well above train
toilets but significantly below anywhere he was comfortable. He
did not, however, have a choice—at least not one that wouldn't
end in a public indecency charge. Which was several points lower

on the comfort-o-meter and would definitely have tanked his chances with Tariq.

In any case, getting to spend a few moments alone in a box—years at boarding school had taught him that urinals were just an invitation for people to laugh at your penis—helped him...if not gather his thoughts, then sweep them into a rough pile.

This was fine. Everything was fine. It was going to be fine. He'd made it to Birmingham and he hadn't sat in anything or been stabbed by anyone. All he had to do was pretend to be a nice, normal person for whom this was a nice, normal date. And not a private hell of uncontrolled spaces and unexpected experiences.

"Better?" asked Tariq when Paris emerged, very casually, trying to look like he hadn't been balancing on one leg and operating the door handle with his foot.

"Absolutely. Completely. Yep."

"So, as I was trying to say"—catching him by the sleeves of his jumper, Tariq drew Paris gently towards him—"it's lovely to see you, angel cake. Thank you for coming."

And then, while Paris was frozen and reflustering, Tariq kissed him right on the lips.

In the middle of a railway station.

Where anybody could see. Even a homophobe with a knife.

Tariq's head tilted in quizzical bemusement. "Are you sure you're okay? Because you usually enjoy this a lot more."

"No, no, I'm fine. It's great. It's just...I'm not used to... Birmingham?"

"Not used to," Tariq repeated, "...Birmingham?"

"I've never been here before. And people might be... different?"

"What? Brummie?"

"No." This was not going well. "Just like, London's very... And other places might not be so...About..."

"You know this is Birmingham, England, not Birmingham, Alabama? I've been very gay here for nearly two years, and nobody's even tried to give me a pamphlet about Jesus."

"That could be because you…"

"Honey, don't finish that sentence. You won't like how it ends."

Paris hid his face in his hands, then wished he hadn't because they still smelled faintly of that weird pink soap you always got in public toilets. "I'm sorry. I'm fucking this up already."

"It's fine." Tariq gave an indulgent sigh. "I'm from London, too. I know we're contractually obliged to think everywhere else in the entire country is some kind of medieval backwater with ankle-deep manure and live pigs in the street. But guess what? It's quite nice up here. They've got a Lush and everything."

Paris had been into a branch of Lush exactly once. And the staff had been so horrifyingly attentive that he'd fled, never to return. "Oh thank God. I came all this way, and then I realised I'd forgotten to bring a facial scrub with a self-consciously quirky name."

"Don't worry," Tariq told him, laughing. "When it comes to facial scrubs with self-consciously quirky names, I've got you covered. Now come on, you can throw your bag in my car and then I'm taking you on a picnic."

Paris nearly asked *what if your car gets broken into, because I was checking the internet and Birmingham does actually have an usually high level of vehicle crime despite otherwise only having the seventy-second-highest crime rate in the country?* But then thought better of it. He did, however, make sure his bag was well out of sight of the window.

And then he let Tariq lead him into the streets of a strange city. Which wasn't terrifying at all and which he would be totally comfortable relying on his phone to navigate if they got separated. For a few minutes, they walked in silence through some kind of…shoppingy area type place full of the sorts of people who didn't freak out if they had to go into a brick-and-mortar store to buy a thing from a human instead of doing it all online where it was nice and safe and detached. And from there, wider streets, and that strange tangle of architectural styles that said *not all of these buildings survived the Luftwaffe.*

"So…" Tariq had an uncertain look in his eyes, which was a look Paris was most used to seeing about an hour and a half before somebody decided to break up with him. "I was going to hold your hand, but you're sort of acting like you're not into PDA. And if you aren't, that's cool because boundaries"—he made a little square with his fingers—"are…something important that rhymes with boundaries?"

"Foundaries?"

"I think it's pronounced foundries? Also I'm pretty sure that's totally meaningless."

"Sound—aries?"

"Okay, I think the rhyme thing might not be helping us. I just mean that I've got my things and it's okay for you to have yours, and if you're private about relationships in general, that's great."

And that would have been great. But Paris had an inkling the conversation wasn't going to end there.

"The thing is, though," Tariq went on. "I sort of got the impression that maybe you were not so much uncomfortable with public displays of affection as…how can I put this…public displays of gayness."

"Can't they be the same thing?" asked Paris, slightly more desperately than he'd intended.

Tariq thought about it for a second or two. "Maybe? It's just one of them feels like a choice a person might make for a variety of reasons, and the other feels the tiniest bit…the opposite of everything I believe in and how I live my life."

"Oh," said Paris. Obviously, he needed to say it was the first one. And he really wanted to be able to say it was the first one. But…He glanced at Tariq, who was looking all amazing, in slinky jeans and a vertically striped blazer over a horizontally striped T-shirt, in a combination that said *I am not afraid of making a statement or kissing boys in public*. And who wouldn't want to hold his hand and have people look at them and go *wow, how did that lanky prick get with the cool guy with the effortless sense of style*. Except what if then people were saying *oh wow, look at the lanky prick and the cool guy with the effortless sense of style, it's such a shame they got brutally murdered in Birmingham by a gang of teenage bigots.*

"I'm an out gay Muslim," Tariq went on, "and I don't want to hide any aspects of who I am. Not for anybody. Even someone as sweet and pretty as you."

Paris choke-blushed. Because that was a lot of conflicting… feelstuff. To go with all the conflicted feelstuff he'd been stacking up since he left London. Or possibly, since he was born. "I…I…"

"It's okay." Tariq's hand brushed lightly over Paris's sleeve in a gesture that could have been any sort of person-to-person type reassurance. "You don't have to do anything now. I know I put you on the spot a bit."

"A bit," Paris admitted. And somewhere in the back of his brain a timer—one of those old, twisty kitchen timers—started ticking down the seconds until he had to confront his own emotional bullshit.

Because, realistically, he knew they wouldn't get murdered. Well, probably wouldn't get murdered. It was very unlikely they would get murdered. But knowing that just didn't help. It had never helped. With anything.

Tariq was giving him a slightly wide-eyed, undeniably vulnerable look. "Will you think about it? For me?"

And Paris just nodded.

It was probably a lovely picnic. No, it was definitely a lovely picnic. The problem, as ever, was Paris. Tariq had taken him to a sort of grassy square surrounding a pretty stone church that glowed white-gold in the sunlight. It was clearly a popular spot because there were families and couples all around them. More families and couples than Paris would ideally have preferred.

Out of deference to Paris's jumper, they'd found a place in the shade, and Tariq had laid out sandwiches and fruit and absolutely no truffle of any kind. There'd also been Mr. Kipling Angel Slices, which, being slightly overwrought and trying to pretend he wasn't, Paris had initially worried was a gastronomic dig. But after a heart-stopping half second he let himself accept that they'd been intended to be cute. And while Tariq had talked and laughed, and waved his glittering hands, he hadn't touched Paris once. Which was clearly good and respectful. And also awful and not what he wanted.

And, of course, Paris could have solved the problem at any time by leaning over to kiss Tariq or taking his hand or just scooching a little farther along the very traditional picnic blanket. But every time he thought about it, he also thought about the upward trend in hate crimes and how if he was found beaten to death next to a canal, there'd be no-one to tell his parents. At least Morag could feed Neferneferuaten.

Except Morag probably wouldn't want to commit to staying home every evening to look after her, so she'd end up in a cat shelter, and those places had really low adoption rates, so she'd get put down. Which meant not only would Paris be dead but his cat would be dead and it would all be his fault.

So probably best just to sit there and nibble another angel slice. Even though they tasted of nothing and fear.

"See," said Tariq. "Isn't this nice? We're two guys, having a picnic, and nobody's staring, or yelling names, or trying to start anything. Because actually, ninety-nine times out of a hundred *people are fine.*"

"Y—"

"And before you say *yes, but what about the one time in a hundred when they aren't fine,*" Tariq went on, "you just can't let it get to you. Because yeah, obviously sometimes I get shit. I mean look at me."

He gave Paris a moment to look at him, and Paris looked, and carried on looking for a while because he was so worth looking at. Rationally, he understood what Tariq meant—if there was ever a combination that was going to be the proverbial red rag to the proverbial bull of the hypothetical roving bigot, it was a South Asian guy in nail varnish. But lying there, peeling the film off an individually wrapped Mr. Kipling slice, Tariq seemed so invincible that Paris couldn't quite imagine anything bad happening anywhere near him. And there was a comfort in that, a kind of reflected invulnerability that he felt like he could get used to. "You look amazing. Like you always do." Paris let out a slightly wistful sigh. "I just wish I could be half as…everything as you are."

"Honey, I wish *I* was half as everything as you think I am."

"What do you mean?" Paris blinked at him.

"Oh, you know…" Tariq fluttered his fingers, half dismissive, half self-conscious. "We both have our defence mechanisms. The only difference between us is that mine are fabulous and yours are"—his gesture morphed into a stirring-the-bowl-of-you pattern—"um."

"Unfabulous?" Paris offered. "Schlumpy? Totally rubbish?"

"Gorgeous and aloof?"

For a moment Paris wasn't sure who Tariq was talking about. Like he was pretty sure he was the only one there, but he couldn't connect the words he was hearing to any part of his self-image. "Who, me? I'm not aloof."

"So you admit you're gorgeous?" Tariq flashed him a checkmatey grin.

"What? No. You cheated."

Apparently not at all concerned at having tricked Paris into accepting a compliment, Tariq continued grinning. "Hey, it worked. And you're right, you're not really aloof, and I'm not really a one-man Pride parade, but we both sometimes act like we are because the alternative is letting people see how scared we get."

It was hard, with Tariq sparkling in the sunlight, for Paris to imagine him being scared of anything ever. Except now he was relaxing more he was able to see that for the massive empathy fail it was. After all, everybody got nervous occasionally. It was just that most people didn't let it chew on them like a rat on Winston Smith's face. Biting his lip and holding his breath, Paris stretched a hand across the picnic blanket and let Tariq take hold of it. And screw what Birmingham, or the people of Birmingham, or hypothetical wandering homophobes might think.

It only lasted a moment. They had nics to pic, and once he'd retrieved his hand to eat a sandwich, Paris didn't quite have the courage to reach out again. But while it had lasted it had been good. Normal even. Like maybe Paris was a gorgeous, aloof guy who touched his fabulous maybe-boyfriend in public.

Once they were done with the food, and early afternoon had started fading into late afternoon, they cleared up the picnic things and made their way back to Tariq's car, which hadn't been broken into, and from there to his house. Or rather the house he shared. Shared with four other people, none of whom Paris knew, and who would probably think Paris was a total wanker. And there was second-guessing Paris again. He never went far. He was reliable that way.

"Hi, Dave," said Tariq to Guy Paris Didn't Know Who Would Probably Think He Was a Total Wanker Number One. "Dave, this is Paris. Paris, this is Gay Dave."

Gay Dave, who was the kind of man who put Paris off going to the gym, gave a cheerful wave. "Hi, Paris."

The question at the forefront of Paris's mind was whether it was vitally important to ask why Tariq had introduced his house-mate in a way that specifically referenced his sexuality or vitally important not to. "Hello."

"Can you just take care of Paris for a moment?" As far as things Tariq could have said to make Paris feel reassured, this was hovering right next to *we need to talk* and *what's that crawling up your leg?* "I'm nipping upstairs to pray."

And with that, Tariq nipped. Leaving Paris alone in a strange house in a strange city with a strange man in a very tight vest.

"Do you want anything?" asked Gay Dave.

"I think I'm good?" Paris wriggled uncertainly in the doorway for a bit and then realised he should probably sit down. Which left the question of whether he should sit next to Gay Dave on the sofa and risk looking like he was hitting on him, or else sit on a chair on the opposite side of the room and risk looking like he was trying too hard to avoid looking like he was hitting on him.

He went sofa.

There was a long silence. Gay Dave was very absorbed in his phone, but Paris was pretty sure bringing out his own would be rude.

"What do you think of this?" Gay Dave slid across the sofa and waved a picture under Paris's nose.

Paris stared at it for a long moment. "Is that a penis?"

"I'm a bit concerned you had to ask."

"No, I mean. I'm aware it's a penis. I just wasn't sure if you intended to show me a penis."

"Bloke just sent it," explained Gay Dave. "Wanted a second opinion."

What was going to happen when Tariq came downstairs and found Paris looking at digitised wangs with another man? "I don't really…What kind of opinion?"

"You know, size, shape, general aesthetic."

"Don't they all, um, look a bit the same?"

Gay Dave seemed genuinely horrified. "No. You've got your long thin ones, your short thick ones, your long thick ones, your short thin ones, circumcised, uncircumcised, big head, small head, your Prince Alberts, your ladders, the ones with a weird bend, the ones that don't bend at all, which I'm not personally a fan of."

"It looks," said Paris faintly, "very nice."

"Do you think? I'm worried it'll have a weird mouthfeel."

Up until this exact point in his life Paris had managed to avoid worrying about the mouthfeel of his penis. "Is that a thing?"

"Oh my God, it's totally a thing."

"But how can you tell from a picture?"

"It's just a vibe you get. I'm getting a spongy vibe." Gay Dave swiped decisively left. "He messaged like a guy with a spongy cock."

Any possibility that Paris might ever have signed up for any kind of dating app evaporated. He would definitely message like a guy with a spongy cock.

"Okay"—Gay Dave leaned in closer—"how about this one?"

The door swung open, and a tall man with a shock of orangey-red hair stepped into the room. "Dave. Stop showing the guest dick pics."

"It's fine," protested Gay Dave. "He's gay. He understands."

The newcomer folded his arms. "Steve was gay. He didn't understand. Karim was gay. He didn't understand. Helen was gay. She *certainly* didn't understand."

"Whatever, *Mum*." Gay Dave put his phone away. "Paris, this is Ginger Dave. Ginger Dave, this is Paris."

That at least solved the Gay Dave mystery.

"So," asked Paris. "Do I call you…Dave? Or Ginger Dave?"

"Dave if there's only me." Ginger Dave was giving him a *this is obvious, what is wrong with you* look. "Ginger Dave if I'm in sufficient proximity to another Dave that confusion might arise."

"Sorry," said Paris. "Sorry."

There was another brief silence, while Paris tried desperately to think of something charming to say to two men named Dave.

"Anyway." Ginger Dave plonked himself on the arm of the sofa, which now sort of left Paris as the filling of a Dave sandwich. "What's your…thing? Apart from getting low-key sexually harassed by my housemate."

Gay Dave rolled his eyes. "It's not harassment. It's a celebration of my sexuality."

"Ignore him. He's only been out for ten minutes and it's gone to his head."

"Excuse me," huffed Gay Dave, "I've been out since first year."

"Since the end of first year. You were insisting you were straight all the way up to exams."

"Look, I played a lot of sport, I didn't have time to date, I made a lot of assumptions." Pausing, Gay Dave scratched his head. "I think maybe I'm just not very introspective."

"I've dissected flatworms with more self-awareness." Ginger Dave's phone buzzed, and he glanced down. "That's Welsh Dave, he says he's going to be late for dinner."

They were joking. They had to be joking. "You've got another housemate called Dave?"

Gay Dave nodded. "Yeah, Jewish Dave."

"Welsh Dave is Jewish?" This was getting complex.

"No, Jewish Dave is Jewish. Welsh Dave is Welsh." Ginger Dave slid his phone back into his pocket. "It's a pretty simple system, once you've got the basics down."

It was at this moment that Tariq hurried into the room.

Gay Dave and Ginger Dave both threw their arms into the air. "Bangladeshi Dave!"

"Sorry," said Tariq. "I should have warned you. All my housemates are called Dave. It's a whole thing. And they don't actually call me Bangladeshi Dave except sometimes as a joke. And, anyway, hi again."

What Paris really wanted right now was to go and have an enormous hug that didn't stop for, like, five or six hours. He'd got a train, he'd done a picnic, he'd spoken to two people he hadn't met before, both of whom had the same name, and one of whom had shown him the penis of a third person he technically also hadn't met before. And so he was exhausted—stretched like Bilbo Baggins over too much bread—and he just wanted to be with Tariq. Very quietly.

Unfortunately, everyone was looking at him like there was a social cue he'd missed. And, after a couple of seconds, he found what he hoped was it. "How did you...I mean...with the whole Dave situation?"

"Okay, so," started Ginger Dave.

Yes. Good. That was the cue.

But then Gay Dave cut him off. "The thing is, I was dating Tariq in first year."

"You were not dating Tariq," said Tariq. "We had one dinner, at the end of which I said to you *by the way, Dave, have you considered the possibility you might be gay*."

"Yeah." Gay Dave was nodding. "It was two gay men having dinner together. That's a date."

Crossing to the sofa, where Paris was still wedged between

Daves, Tariq hovered like he was considering sitting on Paris's lap—which, frankly, Paris would have welcomed—but since they'd still not established where they were on the PDA thing, he sat on the floor instead, vaguely in the vicinity of Paris's knees.

"Honey, it was one gay man and his deeply confused friend in a PizzaExpress. But anyway, I knew Gay Dave from not dating him and I knew Jewish Dave from my interfaith group. And we decided we'd get a house together for second year and—"

"And Gay Dave knew me." Paris forced his attention back to Ginger Dave—it wasn't that Ginger Dave was hard to pay attention to, but the number of people speaking at once was beginning to throb in Paris's head like he was at a rave. "Because, when I came to uni, I decided I was going to change my life and be who I always wanted to be, so I took up rowing for two weeks, then quit because it sucked and I realised I prefer being unfit. But I stayed in touch with Dave because he'd borrowed my Nutribullet and I wanted it back, and by the way he still hasn't given it back—"

"It's in the kitchen," protested Gay Dave. "It's not my fault you don't use it."

"Then," Ginger Dave went on, "we realised that we had a house of four people, three of them called Dave, and we needed a fourth to complete the set. So we put up posters around campus with Gay Dave's phone number on them saying *Are you called Dave? Do you like bants? Do you want to live with three other guys called Dave and one guy who isn't?*"

Gay Dave took over the story with practised ease. "And a couple of days later, I got a text that just said **yes** and we knew that was our Dave."

"And you didn't know him at all?" asked Paris, caught between awestruck and aghast. "What if he'd been a serial killer?"

"Then we'd have called him Serial Killer Dave," said Ginger Dave.

"But he was Welsh," added Gay Dave, "so we called him Welsh Dave." And then, with barely a gap, "What's for dinner, Tariq?"

Ginger Dave winced. "I should clarify that we take turns cooking and it's Tariq's turn. We don't just make the Asian guy do the food."

"We should, though." That was Gay Dave, with a thoughtful look on his face.

"You do mean"—Ginger Dave cast a concerned look at his friend—"because he's the best cook? And not because we need to change your name to Racist Dave?"

"To be fair," said Tariq, "you two are really bad." He glanced up at Paris. "The other week, Gay Dave made, I kid you not, bacon and banana bolognaise."

Gay Dave gave an unconcerned shrug. "It's what was in the fridge."

"Yeah"—Tariq was leaning slightly against Paris's leg now, a shadow of warmth that wasn't quite enough to soothe him—"there's a reason most recipes don't go *open the fridge, put everything in a bowl, eat*. Anyway." He bounced to his feet, leaving Paris suddenly warmthless. "I should actually go get cooking. You can come help but you're a guest, so if you want to just hang—"

"I'll help," said Paris, slightly too quickly.

And then raced after Tariq.

If anything, the kitchen was even more crowded because, while it contained fewer people, it was much, much smaller. It was one of those galley kitchens that had clearly been bunged onto the back of the house so they could convert the previous kitchen into another bedroom and then charge students higher rents. But for all the chaos that came from five guys and a semi-communal Nutribullet jostling for space it was, by the admittedly low standards of kitchens in shared accommodation, scrupulously clean.

"Are you all right, honey?" Tariq asked.

The only answer was yes. "Yes."

"No, really?" Tariq rested his hands on Paris's hips and gazed searchingly into his eyes. "Are you all right?"

Paris swallowed. "It's…it's really…I appreciate…I'm not…"

"The Daves are a lot. But, and I admit this is only slightly comforting, Gay Dave and Ginger Dave are the most a lot."

"Okay," said Paris gratefully, trying very hard to be re-assured. Because Tariq had invited him to Birmingham, taken him on a picnic, and was now making him dinner—well, making him and four guys named Dave dinner—and Paris wanted to be the sort of person that you could just do that for. And not leave them overwhelmed and scared and weirdly lonely.

"What can I do to help?"

And Tariq was suddenly all business. "Can you chop the onions while I do the shatkora?"

"The...the what?"

"Onions? They're round. Make you cry if you cut them wrong."

"Ha-ha. Yes, I'm ignorant. I'm just usually really good with ingredients."

Tariq shot him a sparkly look from where he was washing his hands. "It's kind of a citrus fruit."

While Paris was also washing his hands—something he was diligent about even when he wasn't about to cook for strangers—Tariq cleared space on the bench, moving a Breville sandwich toaster and one of the kitchen's two kettles. "Can you grab the chopping boards with the green electrical tape on them?"

"Did your chopping board suddenly...lose power?"

Tariq laughed. "They're the halal ones. And sort of also the no-pork ones because Jewish Dave isn't super orthodox kosher but does mostly keep kosher."

Obediently Paris retrieved the appropriately marked chopping boards. "What are we making?"

"Literally just called beef shatkora. It's a curry with beef and shatkora in it."

For a few minutes they chopped and diced in companionable silence, Paris making short work of his onions with the help of what Tariq called "the good knives" that came out of a special box labelled *Tariq's Knives. No Daves Allowed.*

"Wow." Tariq, who was segmenting a knobbly fruit, gave him

an admiring glance. "That's some YouTube-video-level chopping. The wow-look-at-this-person-be-cool kind of YouTube video. Not the wow-look-at-this-person-messed-up kind of YouTube video."

Paris cringed. "Please don't make me think about it. If I think about it, I can't do it, because I'll be worried about cutting my fingers off."

"Can you sauté those with some minced garlic and ginger?"

That Paris could definitely do. He got sautéing. And, for the first time all day, felt something close to calm.

"You're totally spoiling me," Tariq said, with a smile. "What am I going to do when I don't have you to be my sous chef?"

This made Paris feel so warm and fuzzy, he was actually embarrassed. "Get one of the Daves to do it?"

"You've met fifty percent of the Daves. Ginger Dave won't take instructions, Gay Dave is constantly on Grindr, Jewish Dave does everything so carefully that it's quicker to do it myself, and Welsh Dave does everything so carelessly I have to do it myself again."

"Well..." Paris risked a shy smile back. "I honestly kind of like sous-ing for you?"

Once Paris had finished his sautéing, Tariq took over, adding beef, spices, and chillies to the pan with the casual ease of a man who somehow avoided freaking out over the last microgram.

"This is the wait-for-it stage," he explained as he filled a kettle and got some rice going. "We can go back to the front room if you want. But we don't have to."

"Maybe I'll do some washing up?" Paris suggested, because it sounded way better than *please don't make me talk to your friends again*.

"*Definitely* an improvement on the Daves."

For a moment, Paris just washed and rinsed and washed, enjoying the quiet routine of it. It probably said depressingly dull things about him, but there was something about washing up he found grounding. You knew what was expected of you, you knew what success looked like, and you knew when you'd finished. When most things in life offered one of those three at best. Of course he couldn't just stand there in bubbly silence because then Tariq would probably think he was a weird Fairy Liquid zombie.

"Um," he asked. "Do you cook this a lot?"

"Ish. I try to do a variety."

"Oh?"

It was one of Paris's *please keep talking* noises and, to his delight, Tariq kept talking. "Don't get me wrong, I grew up eating this kind of food, and I love it but I don't want to be the guy who makes curries. That's why I've not done the"—Paris wasn't looking but, from the tone, he caught the air quotes—"'Asian flavours' thing on the show." He laughed. "Not that the 'diverse and eclectic' strategy is working out for me so far."

Paris glanced over his shoulder. "You've had some good comments."

"And you've won two weeks out of three."

Hearing it like that it seemed alien, like it had happened to somebody else. "I just got lucky."

"Paris"—Tariq's tone sharpened slightly—"you know that's really annoying, right?"

"Is it?"

"You're not just putting yourself down, you're kind of putting everyone down. If you coming top doesn't mean that you did best that week, then we're all wasting our time. Do you think Tanya just got lucky in week two as well?"

Paris spun away from the washing up so abruptly he nearly knocked a plate off the drying rack. "What? No. She did really well."

"Then that must mean"—Tariq tapped him emphatically on the chest with a single finger—"that the system works and you've won twice because you're good. And when I beat you in the final, it'll be because I'm good."

"I'll never get to the fi—"

"You are so lucky you're pretty."

And with that Tariq kissed him soundly, and it only felt a little bit like he was doing it to make Paris be quiet.

Dinner was served on the coffee table, from pans that Tariq balanced on two hardback books next to a stack of mismatched bowls.

The books, though. They made Paris wince.

"Shouldn't you," he said. "I mean won't they...Aren't we going to damage them?"

Tariq twisted one slightly towards him, revealing the grinning image of a smug man in sunglasses and the title *Sweet Revenge: The Intimate Life of Simon Cowell*. "A couple of months ago we sent Ginger Dave out to buy coasters. And he—"

"And I," Ginger Dave cut in, "decided very sensibly to go and buy a job lot of hardback books from the fifty p bucket in a charity shop and use those instead."

"Because apparently"—this from a newcomer who from his punctuality Paris deduced was not Welsh Dave and was therefore Jewish Dave—"aesthetics can go fuck themselves."

Ginger Dave folded his arms. "Look, I don't want to trade in stereotypes, but this is a student house shared by a bunch of blokes in their early twenties. I thought cheap and disposable was the way to go."

Out of morbid curiosity, Paris peeped at the other book-coaster. It was a 2018 *Star Wars* annual. In his moment of distraction, Gay Dave reached past him and grabbed one of the serving spoons.

"Were you born in a barn, Dave?" demanded Jewish Dave. "Tariq's got a guest. Can you not make us all look like dicks?"

Gay Dave froze, bowl in one hand, spoon in the other. "I'm encouraging him to help himself to the food by demonstrating that this is a self-service situation."

"No, you're not. You're trying to nick all the beef out the curry."

"I need the protein," protested Gay Dave. "The meat doesn't maintain itself."

"Mate"—that was Ginger Dave—"don't talk about your meat at the dinner table."

There was a long, expectant pause, everyone looking hungrily at Paris like the hyenas in *The Lion King*. Which did not make helping himself to curry—was this enough, was it too much, what if he splashed the carpet or knocked the whole thing over?—any less stressful. Eventually he retreated to the sofa with what he was pretty sure was a neither insultingly small nor gluttonously large helping of beef shatkora in a panda bowl he hoped was no-one's favourite.

"Remember," said Tariq, as the rest of them dug in, "leave some for Welsh Dave. You know what he's like when he's hangry."

This felt like a social cue for Paris again. "What's he like when he's hangry?"

Ginger Dave glanced up from the pot. "Just, like, really sullen? Like he sucks energy out of the room."

"Yeah." Jewish Dave nodded. "Like a black hole."

"Actually," Ginger Dave said completely unironically, "black holes don't suck things in. Their gravitational field isn't any stronger than any other object with an equivalent mass. Which is obvious when you think about it."

Jewish Dave blinked. "Thanks. That really got to the heart of my point."

There was a brief, fooding silence.

"Is it obvious, though?" asked Gay Dave. "Because if it's a hole, how does it have mass?"

Ginger Dave dropped his head briefly into his hands. "Oh God, what have I done? Because, Dave, it's not actually a hole."

"Why's it called a hole then?"

"For the same reason tinfoil's not made of tin."

Gay Dave's eyes were getting wider by the moment. "Tinfoil's not made of tin?"

"No, it's made of aluminium, you pillock."

"Then why," demanded Gay Dave, "is it not called aluminium foil?"

"It sometimes is. In America they call it *aloominum* foil."

"For what it's worth"—Tariq returned his fork to his slightly chipped bowl—"as the one who pays attention to these things, the stuff in our kitchen is technically called extra-strong roasting foil."

Gay Dave gave a chuckle. "Heh. Nice."

"Are you"—Jewish Dave was now also giving Gay Dave a look—"heh-nice-ing *extra strong* or *roasting*? Because neither of those are remotely sexual."

"You can get extra-strong condoms," pointed out Gay Dave. "And extra-strong lube."

Jewish Dave thumped his head back against his chair. "You can also get extra-strong mints."

Gay Dave considered this. "Heh. Nice."

"I'm getting flashbacks," said Tariq, "to how you wanted us to move into that absolute dump with dry rot and no washing machine just because of the house number. Which I wouldn't have minded but it was seventy-one."

"But that meant," Gay Dave began, "that next door—"

"We know," shouted everybody in the entire room except Paris.

And Paris tried very hard not to shrink into a sofa cushion. Because while he understood bants in theory, and this was clearly bants, it was also four people yelling at once in quite a small room.

"Hi." A heavyset man without a trace of a Welsh accent appeared in the door.

Tariq waved at him. "Paris, Welsh Dave. Welsh Dave, Paris."

"Hi," said Paris.

Welsh Dave moved his head almost imperceptibly. Then beelined for the curry.

"Ginger Dave"—almost immediately Gay Dave started talking again—"is trying to convince me that a black hole isn't a hole and tinfoil isn't tin."

"He's right," Welsh Dave told him.

"What is it, then? If it's not a hole?"

Ginger Dave put his head back in his hands. "It's a gravitational singularity."

"Then why," persisted Gay Dave, pouting, "isn't it called a gravitational singularity?"

"It *is* called a gravitational singularity." Ginger Dave was gesticulating in a way that put him at serious risk of spilling his curry. "Just like tinfoil is called aluminium foil or extra-whatever-it-was roasting foil. Things can have more than one name. Your middle name is Quentin."

"But that's still my name. It's the name a person can have—"

"Barely," put in Welsh Dave.

"Shut up. I was named after Quentin Tarantino. My dad was really into *Reservoir Dogs*."

"Well you got lucky then," said Tariq. "He could have called you Mr. Pink."

"Then I'd have two middle names. And one of them would be Mr. and then, in formal situations, I'd be Mr. David Mr. Pink Babington. But my point is, that my middle name is still a person's name. It's not, like, potato. Which would suggest I was a potato."

"I wish"—Ginger Dave gave a rueful sigh—"I'd never started this conversation."

Jewish Dave smirked at him. "Serves you right for being pedantic. You, my friend, have been hoist by your own petard."

A pause.

"What's a petard?" asked Gay Dave.

It was the longest evening. The sort of evening, full of food and friends and easy conversation, that any normal, non-rubbish person would have really enjoyed. Unfortunately, after an hour of polite questions, too many voices, and the occasional in-joke Paris had felt his level of rubbishness climbing rapidly. The Daves were all very nice, but if they weren't thinking *what is Tariq doing with this boring prick*, it was only because they'd forgotten Paris was there at all.

"So, Paris?" said Jewish Dave, making him jump. "You're at UCL, right?"

He nodded. "Yes."

"I applied to UCL but that would have meant living at home. And don't get me wrong, my parents are great, but they'd have to be much greater for me to want to spend the next three years with them."

Ginger Dave raised his eyebrows. "What? So you decided to spend them with us instead?"

"And it's a choice I regret every day."

"Never been to London," offered Welsh Dave. "Heard it's shit."

"Your rent"—Gay Dave looked up from his phone—"must be through the roof."

Tariq smiled. "He's fine. His millionaire parents bought him a palace."

"It's not a palace," protested Paris, blushing and squirming. "It's a flat. And they didn't buy it for me, they bought it for themselves in the 'nineties and they don't use it anymore."

"Oh right." Ginger Dave grinned. "Like normal people do."

"You should see it," said Tariq. "It's amazing. I got the fright of my life. I thought I'd met this nice guy who liked baking, and then I walked into his house and I was like, oh no, is he secretly a drug baron? Is he secretly a drug baron with exquisite taste?"

"I like that you're implying"—that was Jewish Dave—"that being a drug baron wasn't enough of a dealbreaker that his taste level was still relevant."

"I'm not." Paris thought it was probably important to make this clear. "I mean I'm not a drug baron and my parents decorated the flat, so I don't have exquisite taste either."

Tariq whirled on him dramatically. "Excuse me, I think you'll find you do."

"I meant my taste in decorating, not in guys. And actually, no offence, previously my taste in guys was quite variable."

Gay Dave looked up from his phone again, like he was seeing the annunciation. "If you've got a fancy London flat...you must get so much cock."

"Dave." Tariq threw a cushion at him. "That's my date. We're in a relationship. Can we not talk about him having sex with legions of other men, please?"

"I haven—" squeaked Paris.

"I meant before he met you," clarified Gay Dave unhelpfully, "or after he's dumped you."

"Can we just remember please"—it was Tariq's sharpest voice—"that I've been single for a while and I'd rather you didn't tell everyone I have a thing with to ditch me so they can bang other people."

Gay Dave looked faintly hurt. "I'm just saying, he's got the option because of the flat."

Frankly, Paris didn't want Tariq's mind going to a dumping space either—especially since he was, by any objective standard, giving terrible boyfriend right now. "It's not an option I really want to exercise. I'm happy with Tariq and my cat. I mean, in different ways. I'm not dating my cat. I live with my cat."

"You know"—Tariq's hand drifted down to rest on Paris's knee—"every time you feel the need to reassure someone you're not dating your cat, I get a little more worried."

"Well, they are living together," pointed out Jewish Dave. "That's pretty serious."

"I...," began Paris.

And then Tariq whispered in his ear. "He's joking. Nobody thinks you're in a sexual relationship with Neferneferuaten."

"Also"—Paris thought of something—"I'm gay and she's a girl."

"Angel cake, now you're suggesting that if she wasn't, it would make a difference."

"Sorry. Sorry."

"Putting aside," said Ginger Dave in a tone that made Paris uncertain whether this was a rescue or a trap, "the whole cat thing, can we go back to the palace thing?"

Paris was getting a hot, sweaty, *you are not like other people and they're starting to figure that out* feeling. "I told you, it's not a palace, it's a flat."

"A flat in central London," declared Ginger Dave, "is a palace in any other part of the country. What do your parents even do?"

"Um." Glancing at Tariq for help, Paris suddenly realised they hadn't actually had this conversation. "They're in fashion."

"That was vague." Ginger Dave turned to Tariq. "Maybe he really is a drug baron."

"I'm not a drug baron," cried Paris yet again. "My dad's Hugo Daillencourt, you know, the designer."

While this clearly meant nothing to his friends, Tariq was staring at him. "Your dad is Hugo Daillencourt?"

"Yes? Kind of. I mean, yes completely."

"Are we missing something?" asked Gay Dave.

"Well, *you* are," Tariq told him, "because you've got no sense of style."

Gay Dave flexed. "You don't need one if you've got these bad boys."

"Does no-one in this room"—Tariq sighed heavily—"own a single thing with a label on it?"

Welsh Dave pulled the collar of his T-shirt around. "Forty degrees. Wash whites separately."

"Okay, let's put this in words you lot might understand. He's very famous. He makes clothes. And he's married to Isabella Holloway."

That got a reaction.

"Isabella Holloway?" repeated Jewish Dave. "The one from the advert?"

Paris knew the advert he was talking about. Everyone knew the advert he was talking about. "She's been in a lot of adverts."

"Oh fuck." Ginger Dave had his hands over his mouth. "Tariq. I'm really sorry. I think I might have wanked to your boy-friend's mum."

"I'd apologise," said Tariq, while he was inflating the household air mattress with a foot pump. "But I'm honestly not sure that covers it. And I don't think they make cards that say *sorry my house-mate literally said he masturbated over pictures of your mother*."

Paris was lying on Tariq's bed in a position that while it wasn't foetal was also not *not* foetal. "It's okay."

"It really isn't. If there was ever a thought to keep to yourself."

"Honestly, I'm used to it. I got used to it at boarding school."

Delicately, Tariq balanced himself next to Paris. "I think that might make it worse."

"Everyone got picked on for something." Although some, admittedly, had been more picked on than others. "And I wasn't going to let a bunch of teenage boys stop me being proud of my mum."

"I still can't quite believe that when you're talking about your mother, you mean Isabella Holloway. She's an *icon*."

Paris nodded. "I know."

"I like you better, though."

"Really? I've never even been on the cover of *Vogue*."

"In those jumpers?" Tariq ran his fingers soothingly through Paris's hair. "I'm not surprised."

"You are obsessed with my jumpers."

"I just think you'd look better in literally anything else."

"Well...well, you're wrong," Paris told him. "I have skinny arms."

"If I picked my boyfriends on the basis of arm bigness, I'd be dating Gay Dave."

Paris gave him a little smile. "No you wouldn't."

"You're right. He's awful."

"Hey, at least he never wanked over my mum."

"Oh, he might have. He was really confused for a really long time." There was a pause. Then Tariq leaned down and kissed Paris on the forehead. "Are you sure you're okay? I know the Daves can be a bit much even when they're not being, well, even more inappropriate than normal."

Paris knew he'd been quiet, and probably really boring, so in a way all the mum talk had been quite a good excuse. It meant Tariq would continue thinking the problem was other people instead of Paris's fundamental crapitude. "I'm fine. Really, I'm fine."

Tariq's eyes narrowed thoughtfully, but—to Paris's relief—he let it go. "Do you think we should call it a night?"

It wasn't quite midnight. In fact it wasn't even quite not quite midnight. But it was still past the time of day when Paris got unaccountably tired and now well into the hours where he was awake, alert, and therefore fully able to remind himself every eight minutes that he should be going to sleep. "Sure," he said.

Rising from the bed, Tariq headed over to a wobbly MDF chest of drawers. "I should warn you, my alarm is set for half four. But just ignore it. I'll need to wash before praying, so you can get up whenever you're ready."

"I, um, I probably won't want to get up anywhere close to half four."

"Angel cake"—Tariq flashed him a reassuring smile—"that is completely fine. We've got the whole day to spend together. Well, I've got Friday prayers at one and at some point we need to go do that being-on-TV thing we've signed up for. But *otherwise* I'm all yours."

"Okay," said Paris.

Because it would be okay. It would be completely okay. He'd probably only get two hours of sleep, but he'd probably only have got two hours of sleep anyway.

Tariq had dug a pair of surprisingly—oh wait, not surprisingly at all—stylish silk pyjamas out of his bureau. "So…" His gaze lingered on Paris, a touch of heat in his eyes. "I'd better, um…I'm going to go and put these on. If you want to get changed too, that would be great. I'll knock so I don't walk in on anything and then…yeah."

"And," Paris asked belatedly, "it's okay me being here? Like this?"

"Scholars' opinions vary. I will confess that…" Once again, Tariq trailed off. Which Paris found weirdly flattering. "Like, the whole *you in my bed* situation is a bit more…than I realised it was going to be. But I wouldn't have suggested you stay over if it was a problem for me or, you know, God. And I assume you'd have said no if it was a problem for you."

It honestly hadn't occurred to Paris that he'd had the option. But then, if he'd said no, he'd have not only had to get on a train to Birmingham, he'd have had to get on a train back. And, on top of that, he might have given Tariq the impression that he didn't like him. "I can take the air mattress," he offered.

"Don't be silly. You're a guest."

And, before Paris could say anything more, Tariq disappeared, pyjamas in hand. Which, since he didn't want to give the impression that he was deliberately lingering in a state of undress, left Paris scrambling for his own sleepwear. This was a much less stylish pair of lounge trousers and an oversized T-shirt, which exposed his very skinny arms. Or would have, had he not buried himself under the covers and concealed them.

A few minutes later, Tariq knocked and then, when Paris made vaguely assenting noises, came in. Of course, he still looked ridiculously, amazingly perfect—like he was Mr. July in a calendar called Cosy Fully Clothed Men. "The bathroom is down the hall if you want to wash or clean your teeth or anything."

Ideally, Paris would have liked to stay completely hidden under Tariq's duvet. But that would mean letting Tariq think he had no sense of personal or dental hygiene. So he shuffled out of the room, skinny arms and all, clutching his leather bag of toiletries. The bathroom, despite his incipient sense of dread, exceeded his expectations. It contained enough disparate products belonging to enough disparate people that it was quite hard for Paris to put anything down, but it was clean. And he returned to Tariq only mildly traumatised from his adventures in unfamiliar bathrooms.

"Thank you for coming down," said Tariq as Paris balled himself back up in the duvet. "I had a lovely day."

"Me too," Paris…half lied. Because it could have been a lovely day. If it had involved less trains. And fewer strangers. And if Paris had been a completely different person.

There was a pause. "And you really shouldn't worry about your arms. They're fine. You're beautiful."

Paris opened his mouth, then closed it again. He'd never been able to take compliments. They never felt true. "Thank you?" he tried.

And he wished that he could tell Tariq that he was beautiful too—really beautiful, not just *my mother was a model* beautiful—except it would have felt like a cheap echo.

Then the moment was gone.

From beside the bed came blankety, air-mattressy noises as Tariq tucked himself up. " 'Night, Paris," he said with the effortless drowsiness of someone with healthy sleep patterns.

" 'Night, Tariq."

Silence settled over him and the kind of darkness that you only got in rooms that weren't your own—full of knobbly shadows you couldn't quite identify and sounds that said someone somewhere was moving. The LED on his phone, which he'd left on Tariq's desk, was an eerie blip that sometimes ebbed and flowed inexplicably like Gatsby's green light.

He stared at the grey-black haze of the ceiling, half-imagined details gradually coming into focus. Bits of old moulding from when this had been a different room in a different house for a different purpose. Patterns that might have been cracks in the plasterwork. Or the blood vessels in Paris's retinas.

His heart was striking him in the chest like it was trying to steal his lunch money. And the more he tried to calm it down, the more he remembered why that never worked.

He wondered how much time had passed. If it was hours or minutes. If it was going to be one of those nights that raced past and left him exhausted, or dragged past and left him exhausted. Some bits of him were getting too hot, and others too cold, but he knew he wouldn't sleep at all if he wasn't entirely wrapped in the duvet. Just in case something crawled on him or grabbed him in the night.

Gingerly, desperate not to disturb Tariq, he rolled onto his side and felt the breeze across his face.

The window was open.

It was fine. They were on the second floor. And, even though he couldn't see through the curtains, it was probably too small for anyone to fit through.

But the room was facing the street. And if he held his breath and listened carefully, he could hear footsteps going past outside. Receding into the distance. Stopping. A car door opening and closing.

Still gingerly, still desperate not to disturb Tariq, he rolled onto his other side. He couldn't feel the breeze anymore but now he knew the window was behind him. And whatever was going on out there could sneak up on him.

What if he just got up and closed the window, very carefully? Tariq probably wouldn't even notice. But he might knock something over or stand on something. And then he would have woken Tariq up and made a mess of his bedroom and revealed himself as a total freak who couldn't sleep in a room with an open window.

The same sort of total freak who couldn't get on a train to Birmingham. Hold a man's hand in public. Have dinner with strangers.

"Are you all right?" came Tariq's voice.

Paris gave the sort of yes that was so obviously a no it was embarrassing.

There was a stirring of bedclothes and Tariq sat up, his hair splayed in all directions by a suddenly raised sleep mask. "What's wrong?"

"Nothing. I just. It's just. I'm sorry I woke you up."

"Honey, it's fine. But you seem really upset."

This was worse than trying to sleep with the window open. Because now Tariq would know he'd been losing his shit over trying to sleep with the window open. "I just—I'm sorry I'm being stupid."

Another shifting noise came from Tariq's direction. "You're not being stupid, but you sound all shaken up."

"I—I'm not—I mean. Can we close the window?"

The air mattress squeaked, and Tariq walked across the room and pulled the window down. There was a slight scraping noise as he pushed on the bar that held it closed, and the part of Paris's brain that still wouldn't shut the fuck up made him wonder how secure it was. "I'm sorry. If I'd realised you were cold, I'd have shut it earlier. It's just with five guys in the house I like the ventilation."

Since he was pretty sure he was visibly sweating, Paris didn't think *I was cold* was going to fly as an excuse. And besides, he owed it to Tariq to explain why he'd dragged him out of bed at whatever time this was at night just to get him to make the room marginally less comfortable for both of them. "I wasn't cold. I was"—ironically he *was* feeling cold now, if only on the inside— "I didn't feel safe."

There was a *glinck* of springs as Tariq sat a very respectful distance away at the end of the bed. "You didn't feel safe?"

"I don't if—if the window's open. Especially not if it's a street window. And I know we're a long way up and I know it's probably irrational of me, but...there was this article on the BBC a couple of years ago." If Paris shut his eyes, he could practically see it in front of him. "At least I think it was the BBC. It had been about these two guys—they weren't even gay guys, I don't think, they'd just been sharing a room because rent was so high, and they'd left their window open because it was so hot and these other guys had come through the window and tied them up and robbed them and then they, like, properly cut them to pieces with knives."

"That sounds bad, angel cake," said Tariq very gently, "but are you sure it wasn't an urban legend?"

Some nights Paris did wonder if he'd imagined it, but it was so clear and so specific. He could remember looking at photographs of, well, he couldn't remember if it was the killers or the victims, but he remembered faces. Blank, staring faces. "No. No, it really happened. And I know it isn't the kind of thing that happens a lot and I know that people sleep with their windows open all the time, and that I'm more likely to die crossing the road, but when it's late and it's dark and I'm just lying there looking at the window, it keeps buzzing around my head. Because they'd probably be alive if they'd left the window closed, and I know it's silly and I know it's not really real except it was real and I just don't want to die because it was warm and I thought *oh this will be nice, this will be a nice thing that I will do for me and my boy-friend that will make us happier* and then..."

At some point Paris had started forgetting to breathe, and it was catching up with him. So now he was making choking, sob-bing noises. And then Tariq slid across the bed and enfolded him in a crisp pyjama-ed hug.

"I'm really sorry." Paris sniffed into Tariq's shoulder. "I know I said I'd do better and I'm not doing better."

"It's not the same. I was angry at you last time because you were an inconsiderate dick. Not because you had feelings."

"But my feelings are all messed up," Paris burbled, "and sometimes they make me act like an inconsiderate dick. Like I've woken you up and your alarm's set for half four and you'll have to sleep in a hot room and—"

Tariq shushed him and held him tighter. "You can't control how you feel. But in future can you just be a bit more open with me about it?"

"If I'm open about it, you'll realise how useless I am and dump me."

"Okay...so I guess we're having a talk then?" Drawing gently away, Tariq flicked on the bedside lamp and sat opposite Paris with his legs crossed and his sleep mask still scootching up his hair.

Paris pulled the duvet up to his nose. "Oh God? Are we hav-ing a We Need to Talk talk already?"

"No, we're just talking. But you seem to have this idea in your head of the kind of guy I want you to be. First it was truffles and blow jobs, and then it was big arms, and now it seems to be some macho stereotype with no fears or feelings or problems."

There was a pause while Paris tried to make enough space in the middle of his neuroses to think about this. "Then what do you want?"

"Well, that's the thing, I don't know. This is still quite new for both of us, and maybe it'll turn out that I'm not right for you or you're not right for me. But we're not going to find out if you decide on day one I'm going to hate the real you."

There were exactly two people in Paris's world who didn't hate the real him, and one of those was a cat. He made a half-hopeful, half-sceptical noise.

"I mean"—Tariq tapped his knee—"for all you know, my ideal type could be a hot mess in a baggy jumper."

"That's no-one's type."

"Okay, so maybe my type is men who are exceptionally good at baking. Or men who'll come up to Birmingham to spend a day with me. Or maybe I'm shallow and my type is men who are really, really pretty."

"But," said Paris, hardly knowing what was happening between his brain and mouth, "Birmingham was awful."

Tariq blinked. "Er. Okay."

"No, no, I mean…Birmingham is fine. I mean, not fine. More than fine. Lovely—it was lovely. And we went on a picnic and I met your friends and I was just so scared and crap the whole time. And now I'm taking your bed and keeping you awake because I can't sleep with the window open because I'm afraid of being murdered by two men from a newspaper article I read three years ago and might have made up."

There was a really long silence.

"Sorry," mumbled Paris. "Sorry." Partly because he was sorry and also to stuff the silence with something that wasn't his emotional dysfunction.

Eventually, while Paris picked at his already-well-picked nails, Tariq asked, "Do you really feel that way?"

"Um. Yes. Sort of. I'm sorry."

Tariq sat back on his heels. "Stop being sorry. I'm more thinking—stop me if this is out of line, but have you considered the possibility you might have, y'know, an actual mental health thing?"

The thought had crossed Paris's mind, and crossed it enough that he'd made occasional attempts down the years to look himself up on the internet. The last time he'd tried, Dr. Google had informed him that he had bipolar depression, narcissistic personality disorder, ADHD, psychopathic tendencies, clinical anxiety, and bowel cancer. "I don't think so," he said aloud. "I think I'm just a bit of a mess."

From the look on his face, Tariq wasn't quite buying that. "Honey, I know lots of people who are a bit of a mess. Most of them can leave a window open without worrying about getting murdered."

"I'm sor—"

"No." Tariq held up a finger. "This isn't a *sorry* thing. This is exactly the kind of thing you *don't* have to be sorry for. This is textbook *not your fault*. In fact it makes sense of some stuff."

That sounded bad. Paris didn't much like the thought of there being stuff that previously hadn't made sense but now did make sense when viewed through the label of a not-his-fault mental health issue. It felt a bit pathetic. "What stuff?"

"The no-PDA thing. You didn't have it on set so my guess is it was a—I'm guessing strange places are kind of a trigger for you?"

None of that was the language Paris would have used, but he was willing to go with it if it helped. "I suppose? When I'm somewhere I don't know, somewhere with lots of people, especially if it's a strange city, I just—"

"You assume that everybody's a violent homophobe who will beat you to death for doing a gay thing?"

Paris nodded sheepishly. "And I know they *aren't*. But it's just—what if they are?"

"It's the *what if they are* that makes me think you've probably got—I don't know—anxiety maybe?"

A hot ball of something was gently accumulating in Paris's chest. Because he could just about imagine a world in which Tariq was right and whatever had turned Paris into the useless sack of shit he was today was a medical thing he couldn't control. But it also felt like a massive cop-out: like he was appropriating a serious condition that other people had to justify his crappy behaviour. "I'm not sure I—" he began.

"It's okay." Tariq gave a reassuring half shrug. "If you've not thought about this stuff before, it can be quite scary, and you definitely don't have to put a label on it if you don't want to. But it doesn't have to be a big deal."

To Paris, *you're either mentally ill or a total fraud* sounded like a pretty big deal.

But before he could begin to articulate even a tiny fraction of that idea, Tariq had bounced on cheerfully. "I follow a bunch of people who are super open about this stuff. So you don't have to feel alone or judged or anything like that."

That was great in theory. But feeling alone and judged was Paris's whole thing. Or had become his whole thing. "And you don't mind that I'm...like this?"

For a while, Tariq just looked at him. Looked at him with a shocking lack of revulsion and a surprising lack of confusion. "It's who you are," he said at last. "And if it turns out you've got stuff to work through, then that's okay, because we can work through it together." He took Paris's hand and held it gently. "Besides, if you've been feeling this way and you did everything you did today—coming to Birmingham, dealing with the Daves, getting on trains..." The tiniest of pauses. "If you did all that for me. Then that was actually really sweet. And kind of brave."

"I don't think I'd call it bra—" began Paris, before Tariq enclosed him in a full-body hug.

They fell back against the pillows, Paris clutching slightly needily and Tariq a soft, sleep-scented ball against him. It didn't take long before Paris's needy clutching escalated into needy kissing, which—all too soon—Tariq gently eased out of.

Sitting back on his heels, he resettled his sleep mask. "We should probably take a minute. I'm very into this but"—he waved a slightly uncertain hand—"I'd like to keep it away from the general bed area."

"Fuck. Sorry."

"Not a problem. Just maintaining my boundaries and mostly avoiding temptations."

Paris gave him a slightly wide-eyed look. "I'm a temptation?"

"Honey, now you're just fishing."

"I'm not fishing. As we've established, I've got genuinely terrible self-esteem."

"That's still fishing. You just don't expect to catch anything." Moving to the end of the bed, Tariq scuffled the duvet out of the way and crossed his legs again. His expression grew serious and Paris's heart sank. "Look, I love that you came here for me, even though you apparently literally thought you were going to die half the time."

"Not half the time," Paris protested. Which wasn't a lie, because it was probably quite a bit more than half.

"But if this is going to work, we're going to need to trust each other and be honest with each other. I need to know I can say if things are going somewhere I'm not comfortable going, and you need to know you can say if you're getting"—he waved a hand around Paris's head—"Parisian."

That sounded workable. In theory, at least. And *let's be honest with each other* was way better than *I can't handle this, it's over*. For three seconds, Paris let himself appreciate the warm feeling of relief that Tariq was taking everything so well, then watched it drain away into the cold certainty that he was just letting a nice man make excuses for his own inadequacies. "Isn't me getting Parisian all the time going to be weird and frustrating?"

Tariq shrugged. "Maybe, maybe not. But I do need to know if I'm asking you to do something that's going to be really hard for you."

"That's the thing, though." Paris gazed at him solemnly. Agreeing to be honest was a lot easier than, well, being honest. "If you never ask me to do anything I'll find difficult, then we'll never do anything."

To his credit, Tariq was doing an excellent job of not looking horrified. "Is it really that bad?"

"I've no idea. I never used to be like this."

"What happened?"

That was the worst of it. "Nothing. I just…I used to not worry about anything. And now I worry about everything. When

I was a kid, my parents took me everywhere and I was…I didn't even think about it. They once left me with this family in Italy I'd never met and I had the best time."

Tariq was suddenly doing a less excellent job of not looking horrified. "They what?"

"I don't know. I think they had a vineyard. They were super nice to me. And it was really pretty. We used to drink wine and watch the sunsets."

"How old were you?"

"Twelve maybe?"

"Okay," said Tariq very gently. "I mean, I'm not a parent so I can't judge. But it feels to me like one of the important rules is never leave your child at a random vineyard."

"It was fine. It was just how things were. Like, I once got lost at the opera, and one of the sopranos took me to this café on Montmartre and—"

"Did she give you wine?"

"No, we had coffee and madeleines, and there was this artist who made pictures in sand."

"I honestly don't know what to say. I got lost in a supermarket once, and my mum called the police."

"Oh my God, were you okay?"

Tariq adopted an expression of sincerity that was so sincere even Paris could tell it wasn't. "No, Paris. I died. Of course I was okay. I was in the frozen foods aisle looking for ice-cream. And no-one even took me to a lifestyle eatery or fed me an age-inappropriate beverage."

Paris was getting the squirmy *oh fuck there's something wrong with me* feeling he had more often than not. "It wasn't age-inappropriate. You can have wine from the age of five at home."

"But not," Tariq pointed out, "in a vineyard."

"The vineyard *was* their home. And anyway, Italian laws are different. And I was different. And now I'm this…wreck who can't cope with anything."

Tariq reached over, took Paris's hand, and brushed his lips over the inside of his wrist. "You're not a wreck. You've got a…a brain thing that makes you overreact sometimes. And even if you overreact sometimes, you still do things. You're on TV. You came to Birmingham. You put up with the Daves, which is more than a lot of people manage."

"I sat in the corner, worrying you all thought I was boring."

"Okay." Tariq began counting on Paris's fingers. "One, the Daves never notice anything outside the Daveverse. Two, I thought you were stunned into silence by how amazing my curry was. Three, it's all right to be quiet."

"I didn't use to be quiet either." Having started on this wretched path of honesty, Paris couldn't seem to get off it. "I'd talk to anybody, in multiple languages. And now most of my conversations are me saying sorry, and other people saying *stop saying sorry, Paris, it's annoying*."

Tariq grinned. "It is pretty annoying."

"See."

"You know I'm joking. Mostly joking. And, anyway, change is part of growing up. You don't want to stay a kid forever. That's Peter Pan, and he is not the hero of that story."

This distracted Paris momentarily from his self-recrimination. "Wait. What? Of course he's the hero. The book's called *Peter Pan* and he does all the cool stuff, like hanging out with fairies and fighting pirates."

"The hero of *Peter Pan* is Wendy. Peter is trapped in a weird fantasy world constructed of his own fears. Wendy goes there, learns what she has to from it, then comes back and gets on with her life."

Paris thought about this. It made a terrible kind of sense. "Oh."

"Come on, you wouldn't want to live in Neverland."

"You say that. But when I left, I grew up into ... me."

"And I like you," Tariq insisted and, somehow, impossibly, Paris believed him. "I like the frequently insecure, often kind, secretly nerdy, weirdly funny, braver-than-he-thinks guy you grew up into. Plus, and I hope this goes without saying, I wouldn't want to date you if you were a twelve-year-old child."

"Um," said Paris. "Good to have that confirmed."

Tariq nodded. "Well, I did say we needed more honesty in this relationship."

"I wouldn't date you if you were a twelve-year-old child either. Or," Paris added, "a cat."

"Because you're still trying to convince me you don't date cats. Or because, if I was a cat, I wouldn't be your type."

Paris's eyes widened. "N-no, you'd definitely be my type if you were a cat."

"Angel cake," Tariq told him, giggling, "you make it too easy."

Friday

"—CANNOT BELIEVE," JENNIFER Hallet was saying, "after the shitstorm in a minefield we had last season that you two are fucking *fucking*. You've barely had time to separate an egg, and you're already smashing each other's trifles like you're in that porno we sued out of existence after season two."

Tariq and Paris, who'd barely arrived at Patchley House before Colin Thrimp had yoinked them into Jennifer's trailer, exchanged confused and clueless glances.

"What porno?" asked Paris.

Jennifer Hallet folded her arms. "It was called *Bake Sexpectations*, and it starred Wilfred Horny and Marianne Willbefucked and it was, in many ways, a masterpiece. But it never saw the light of day and it never will."

"And"—Tariq frowned—"what's that got to do with us?"

"What it's got to you with you, sunshine, is that the last time my contestants started rubbing their squashy bits together, it made my job more difficult. And there's nothing I enjoy less than people making my job more difficult."

"Sorry," mewed Paris instinctively.

"No, no, no," Tariq cut over him. "We are not sorry. We have a right to... Well, for a start, whether our relationship is sexual or not is nothing to do with you."

"Check your fucking contract. Everything's to do with me."

Now Tariq folded his arms. "Actually, I've read the contract and there's nothing that says we can't date."

"*Actually*, you've got morality clauses coming out your arse."

Paris glanced helplessly between Tariq and Jennifer Hallet, feeling absent but, unfortunately, only metaphorically. This was exactly the sort of thing he'd been worried about. Well, not specifically. But whenever anything bad happened, it always seemed to confirm his worst fears. Even if it wasn't something he'd had the foresight to be afraid of.

"And you don't think," said Tariq, an edge to his voice, "that counting a same-sex relationship as violating a morality clause might come across as, for example, incredibly homophobic?"

Jennifer Hallet seemed neither impressed nor cowed. "It won't come across as anything. This isn't going anywhere."

"Look." Tariq sprang out of his seat like Tigger if Tigger was really fucking angry. "Rosaline from last season is still dating the guy who went out in the semifinal. This is a blatant double standard."

"You won't understand this"—Jennifer Hallet and Tariq were now having a furious standoff—"but the fact you think that's the whole story really proves my point."

"I think," snapped Tariq, "it kind of proves mine. They obviously had a thing throughout the show, and everyone was really into it and it made really good TV. Someone even did a supercut of them looking at each other to 'Fire on Fire,' and it got a million views on YouTube."

"Your point being?"

"That you'd have no problem with this if we were a straight couple."

"Tariq," Paris protested weakly. "I'm sure Jennifer isn't actually saying…"

This did not seem to please Jennifer Hallet either. "No, no, carry on. The tall skinny one can tell me what I'm saying, and the little flouncy one can tell me what a massive bigot I am."

By some magic Paris could not comprehend, Tariq didn't run away screaming. "Don't get defensive. You're fine to have queer people on the show as long as we don't do anything that will upset the *Daily Mail*."

"If you think I'm scared of Rupert Pissing Murdoch, you know even less than I thought you did. And as for being scared of gay sex, sunshine, I've eaten more carpet than a swarm of moths.

I've stuck my fingers in more dykes than a little Dutch boy. So fuck off, you self-righteous prick."

Paris had sunk so far down in his chair that he was practically horizontal. This was everything that made his stomach turn to porridge: they were in trouble with an authority figure, and Tariq was accusing someone of homophobia who'd turned out to be LGBTQ+. Also there was a lot of bad language happening and people were raising their voices.

Tariq only rolled his eyes. "Oh, don't play the *queer people can't pander to a heteronormative audience* card."

"Relationships," growled Jennifer Hallet. "Cause. Problems. And don't get me wrong, if this ends well, you'll be doing the rounds giving lovely fucking interviews about your lovely fucking story, and about how fucking lovely and fucking inclusive the show is. But if it ends with someone getting punched in the face or sexually assaulted, then the two of you will disappear faster than spunk on a hot stove."

It was such a vile image that Paris actually whimpered.

"I can safely say"—Tariq cast a faintly frustrated look towards Paris—"that even my least successful relationships have avoided any kind of physical or sexual violence."

"Yeah, but you're fucking twenty. What do you know?"

"I know you can't actually force us to . . ." Tariq paused. "Wait a minute. What is it you want us to do?"

Jennifer Hallet cast herself into her Bond villain chair with a sigh of infinite weariness. "I want you to be quiet, I want you to be careful, and when this explodes like the lake of flammable pigshit it is—and it will because, I repeat, you're fucking twenty—I want you to keep the spackle of faeces and the smell of burning manure as far away from my show as is humanly possible. Good talk. Fuck off."

"You have no—" began Tariq.

"Was it the *off* or the *fuck* you didn't understand?"

Paris tugged at Tariq's sleeve. "Can we just go?"

"I'm not fini—"

"You fucking are," Jennifer Hallet told him.

And because she was in charge, they kind of had to be.

Outside, Paris was just beginning to congratulate himself for not fainting when Tariq whirled on him.

"Honey, what was that?"

Oh no. Somehow he'd annoyed both Jennifer Hallet *and* Tariq. "What...what was what?"

"You sat next to me and apologised for being who you are. And then, when I said that wasn't okay, you took her side."

Paris wrung his hands. "I didn't. I was trying to...trying to... defuse the situation."

"That implies the situation needed defusing. That wasn't a *defusing* situation. That was a *standing up for yourself* situation."

"Please don't shout at me."

"I'm not shouting," said Tariq. "I'm...having emotions, some of which are being conveyed in my voice."

"I'm sorry. It's just there's a lot of feelings coming at me and I'm finding that, um, quite difficult?"

Tariq glared at him. "And you didn't find the homophobia you were just subjected to quite difficult?"

"No, I mean. Yes, I mean. I don't think she was being homophobic."

"So you're taking her side *again*?"

"No," Paris said to Tariq's back. "I...It's...I..."

Tariq flung a hand in the air, his nails glinting a rebuking green in the evening light. "Whatever, Paris."

"Don't whatever me. I haven't earned a whatever."

"Oh"—Tariq spun back a moment—"so you'll find a backbone when you're defending your right to not support your boyfriend. But not when you're defending your right to have one in the first place."

For a moment, Paris felt like the breath had been knocked out of him, and by the time he recovered Tariq was halfway across the lawn back to the Lodge. Drawing in a trembling lungful of air, Paris sprinted after him. "Wa—wait."

With an exasperated slump, Tariq waited. "For what? For you to tell me I'm overreacting."

"No, I..." Paris stood panting for a moment. "I wouldn't—I don't—I'm sorry. I didn't mean to—I just wanted..."

"You've said all of this."

"I'm not sure I've said anything."

Despite everything, Tariq gave half a smile. "Exactly."

"I'm sorry I didn't back you up. I should have. I really should have. But—"

"I'm not going to like this *but*, am I?"

"Probably not? It's just I do think she's got a point."

"Angel cake"—and now Tariq just sounded sad—"I can cope with you being scared of trains and strangers and windows. But if you're not okay with being gay, or being with me in a way that people can see, that's a dealbreaker. And you know it's a dealbreaker."

Paris hung his head. He didn't think he had internalised homophobia—if only because he could spend hours listing things he didn't like about himself and never get to his sexuality. But he'd also never had to deal with someone who actually cared if he held his hand in public.

"I genuinely don't think," he said very slowly, "that Jennifer Hallet minds that we're gay. I think she's worried that"—he gestured between them—"whatever this is will go wrong in a way that's bad for the show. And knowing me, I can see why she's worried about that?"

"And you really think," asked Tariq with audible scepticism, "that Rosaline and whatshisface got the same speech?"

"Honestly? I think they probably did. And also they're...old? And were probably way more, you know, together and sensible about things?"

There was a long silence. Then the tension sagged out of the air like overstretched Blu Tack. Tariq sighed. "Maybe."

"And I'm not saying you're not right. And I should have... I could have...I hate I made you feel like I'm not on your side."

"Not gonna lie. I kind of hated it too."

"And I'm still learning how to show it, but I really do want to be with you and stuff."

"I guess," admitted Tariq finally, "we could both have handled that better. I think I'm just so conscious of how easy it would be to be invisible. And I never want to let that happen."

Paris took him by the hand and drew him closer. Then bent down and kissed the tips of his fingers. "Tariq, you could never be invisible."

"And you wonder why I like you, angel cake."

Tariq was smiling again. Which meant Paris could breathe again. And they were still a little way from sunset, so the sky had that hazy half-blue quality, softening the world and making everything seem, somehow, more possible than usual.

Including Paris himself.

So he kissed his boyfriend—his complicated, passionate, probably right boyfriend—and tried not to worry.

Saturday

AND MANAGED TO not worry all his way to a creditable St. Honoré cake that put him at the top of the blind bake.

Sunday

"PARIS," TARIQ WHISPERED, pulling at his jumper. "You have to check this out."

"Why are we whispering?" Paris whispered back.

"You have to see what Catherine Parr is making."

Paris assumed she was making cake pops like the rest of them. Thirty-six cake pops, a dozen in each of three different flavours. And probably, that was what Paris should have been focusing on. But Tariq was his boyfriend and his boyfriend seemed excited. So he let himself be led away from his workstation and, by a casually roundabout route, across the ballroom.

Tariq pushed him surreptitiously behind a camera operator and pointed at Catherine Parr's bench. "Look."

Looking, Paris beheld, each displayed upon their individual stick, a row of perfectly formed but eerily disembodied bums.

Needless to say, Grace Forsythe had caught the whiff of suggestive patisserie a mile away. "So," she said cheerfully, "these are very...round and juicy."

Catherine Parr gave her a stately look. "Those are peaches. Those are apples. And these are cherries."

"They are indeed," declared Grace Forsythe, "peachy."

"Well. Yes. They're peaches."

Paris could feel Tariq's shoulders beginning to shake.

"And was there anything on your mind while you were shaping them?" enquired Grace Forsythe. "Were you, perhaps, imagining a strapping young farmhand in a Mediterranean orchard?"

Catherine Parr frowned in mild confusion. "Actually, I was thinking about my husband."

"Then you're a fortunate woman, especially at your age."

"He likes fruit."

Lili had now joined Tariq and Paris. "Why is Catherine Parr," she murmured, "putting arses on sticks?"

"Well"—Tariq was actually stifling his giggles against Paris's arm—"if anyone knows about having a stick up your bum, it's her."

"Should someone tell her?" suggested Paris.

Tariq pushed him gently forward. "Off you go then. Go and tell an old lady that she's on national television with a dozen bums."

"Beautifully shaped bums," added Lili, making a hand signal that to Paris's limited understanding currently meant *perfection* but to the Elizabethans meant *vagina*. "Really emoji-worthy."

Any delusions they might have had as to their own subtlety evaporated when Catherine Parr turned and glared at them.

"And what are you three staring at?"

"Nothing," said Tariq and Lili together.

"Um." Paris shuffled forward.

Grace Forsythe, for the sake of either the cameras or the situation, had a butter-wouldn't-melt expression. "I'm sure they're just admiring your handiwork, Catherine."

"Well, they should go back to their own benches and stop gawping. This is, after all, a competition."

"You're right," said Grace Forsythe. "Nobody should be ogling your full, fleshy peaches."

At this, Lili started laughing and couldn't stop. And it *was* funny, but Paris, who listed "being laughed at" at about twenty-third on his list of his top one hundred fears, felt too guilty to enjoy it. It was just too easy to imagine a situation where he was Catherine Parr and everyone was laughing at him.

"Um," he tried again. "Catherine…"

Her glare lessened slightly for him, which, if anything, made him more uncomfortable. "Spit it out, Paris. I'd expect honesty from you if not from those two."

Lili was still too busy laughing to be bothered by this. But

Tariq asked, "Sorry, but what do you mean by 'those two'?" Probably more out of principle than because he expected a useful answer.

"Well?" Catherine Parr demanded.

Paris was starting to feel he'd made a not insignificant error. "It's just, your peach cake pops look...um..."

"Delicious?" offered Grace Forsythe. "Very realistic? Like something you'd really want to sink your teeth into?"

"Like bums," said Paris.

It was rare for the ballroom to be silent. It was, however, silent now as Catherine Parr looked from her creations to Paris to her creations. "Possibly," she said. "If one is a degenerate."

Grace Forsythe struck a pose with the air of a woman who not only gave no fucks, but was determined that fucks would be given by nobody. "Oh, Catherine, you flatter us." She stepped away from the bench and planted herself firmly in front of the cameras. "Thirty minutes, bakers. That's thirty minutes before the judges are popping your pops in their popholes. By which I mean mouths." She glanced towards Colin Thrimp. "Do I need to do that again?"

Lili, Tariq, and Paris took advantage of the obvious distraction— very obvious since the clock was clearly visible and there were actually thirty-six minutes left—to flee back to their own stations.

Tables at lunch, it was becoming increasingly apparent, were divided between those who felt able to tolerate Catherine Parr (in practice, Bernard and Rodney-in-the-cardigan) and everyone else.

"I can't believe," said Lili, "she managed to suck the fun out of bums."

Tanya gave a gloomy nod. "I know. Every year someone does a bum or a willy or some boobs, and it's always the best bit. Although it does mean the next day I have to start every class saying *yes, Tom, I saw that someone made a cake that looked like a penis. Now get on with your work or I'll make you draw a diagram on the board and label the vas deferens."*

"Should I know what a vas deferens is?" asked Paris. "Do I want to know?"

This clearly sent Tanya into full teacher mode. "Yes you should, because it's on the GCSE science syllabus. And yes you do, because knowledge is good."

Tariq wrinkled his nose thoughtfully. "Is it a tube? I've got a feeling it's a tube."

"They're ducts," Tanya told them, "that carry sperm from the epididymis to the ejaculatory ducts."

That sounded confusing, and thus faintly horrifying to Paris. "That's two ducts. Why do my genitalia contain multiple sets of ducts that lead into other ducts?"

"Oh, you cis men"—Lili gave an exaggerated sigh—"with your complicated reproductive systems. No wonder you're so irrational and moody all the time."

At that moment Bernard, who clearly couldn't stand the tension between the Parr and Non-Parr tables, drifted over. "Why are we talking about ejaculatory ducks?"

"Ducts, Bernard," explained Tanya. "Ducts."

He nodded. "Ooh. I had trouble with my ducts a couple of years ago."

Lili was eyeing her wilting wrap with the air of someone who expected it to soon become associated with an older gentleman's scrotum. "I'm not sure we want to hear about this."

"They were making terrible noises," Bernard went on, "and it was keeping my dad up all night. In the end, I had to get a man in to come and poke at them."

"And"—Tanya was clearly the only one brave enough to ask a follow-up question—"were they all right after that?"

"Right as rain. But you would not believe the muck that came out the end."

Lili thunked her head onto the table. "Bernard."

"Dust. Cobwebs. Paper clips. Mouse droppings, and I swear we've never had a mouse. Anyway"—he gave an oddly quiet clap as though his hands were made of marshmallow—"how does everybody think it's going?"

"Pretty well." Tariq nodded. "I'm doing sweet shop favourites with real crushed sweets on the outside, and they're looking really sparkly, and because I'm shallow that's literally all I care about."

It wasn't, Paris suspected, literally all Tariq cared about, but unlike Paris, Tariq could actually make a self-deprecating joke without it coming across as a deadly serious expression of self-loathing. Which, in Paris's case, it absolutely always was.

"I think mine'll be a crapshoot to be honest," said Tanya, looking more resigned than glum. "I meant to practise this week, but it's exam season and so I've been too busy running catch-up sessions, revision sessions, preparation sessions, and mock tests. It was very much work/baking/sleep, pick one and a half."

"Eh, that sounds rough," said Bernard with the unwavering sympathy of the largely clueless.

Tanya gave an acknowledging smile-shrug. "A bit, but it's the job. I was doing reproduction yesterday, which is probably why I've got vas deferens on the brain."

Slowly, and almost audibly, something clicked on in Bernard's head. "Oh, *those* ducts. My dad had a problem with them a couple of months back. Had to go see the doctor and get some special tablets."

Lili had just been raising her head from the table. "No," she insisted. "No, no, no."

And then—mercifully—they were called back for judging.

As she'd feared, Tanya's pops had come out badly. They were fine, if uninspired in concept, being three fairly generic cake types competently iced, but without a chance to practise her execution had been way off.

"Dry" was Marianne's one withering comment.

Which left Wilfred trying to smooth things over with "Sometimes simple is good. And if you'd just given these a touch less time in the oven, they could have been really nice. But as it is, I think you've had a bit of a bad week."

"Mmhm." Tanya nodded with the air of someone who had been weighed in the balance and found wanting. "Thanks."

Rodney, Lili, and Catherine Parr all did well, with their pops being neither dry nor raw and their themes generally coming together. Catherine Parr expressed mild disapproval at the whole notion of the cake pop, which she said she thought was *a little faddy*—a sentiment that Wilfred Honey wholeheartedly agreed with.

Then Tariq was up, his thirty-six boiled-sweet-themed cake pops glittering in what on television would look like sunlight but which was actually the powerful glare of two large lamps.

"Now these are very pretty," said Marianne Wolvercote, and Paris thought she meant it in the supportive way, not in the *I expect these to taste like shit* way she sometimes meant it. "What flavours do you have for us?"

Tariq pointed at each batch in turn. "This is sherbet lemon. This one's popping candy. And the last one is pear drops."

"And how have you flavoured the cakes?" asked Wilfred Honey. There was a *this is going somewhere* in his voice that Paris didn't like.

"Probably a bit obvious." Tariq was facing away from the workstations, but Paris liked to think he could see his smile anyway, bright and charming and impossible to say no to. "But the lemon sherbet is a lemon cake, the popping candy is a chocolate sponge, and the pear drops are—well, it's an apple cake recipe, but I swapped the apples for pears, so a pear cake."

With an inscrutable look in his eye, Wilfred Honey picked up a pear drop cake pop, which Paris thought should have got at least some points just for having a name that was fun to say. "That's what I was concerned about. Because maybe I'm misremembering but, to me, pear drops have never really tasted like pears so much as like"—he gave a pause that Paris was convinced he'd been practising—"nail polish remover."

"How do you know what nail polish remover tastes like, Wilfred?" asked Grace Forsythe.

"Let's just say we all got up to some very strange things in the 'seventies."

The judges each popped a pop and chewed for a moment in thoughtful silence.

"Wilfred's right," Marianne Wolvercote said at last. "The cake itself is well cooked and has a lovely subtle pear flavour, but the coating is—"

"Distinctly nail-polish-removery," finished Wilfred Honey.

"It's such a shame because there's no faulting the quality of your bake, they're just not tastes that go well together."

Paris didn't think anybody else noticed, but he saw just a little of the energy go out of Tariq's shoulders.

"Mhm," said Tariq. "Thanks."

Bernard was next, and he got the kind of feedback you'd expect for someone who'd done a chocolate cake pop with chocolate icing, a vanilla cake pop with vanilla icing, and a strawberry cake pop with strawberry icing. And then Paris.

Who did well. Who did really well?

With his Eton mess, crème brûlée, and lemon meringue cake pops being praised for their theme, their flavours, and their execution. All of which meant he won. Again. Somehow?

"I have no idea," he told Colin Thrimp afterwards. Before remembering what Tariq told him about how putting himself down undermined the success of other people. "I mean, I thought it was a strong concept. And I...put quite a lot of work in. But so did everybody else."

Tanya was sitting by the duck pond of destiny. "I just didn't have time to put the work in. Which is not a message I want to send my students. But since I didn't put the work in because of my students: you guys owe me one. I will see you in class, and I'll expect you all to have your homework with you."

"It's kind of a family weakness," Tariq was explaining to another camera operator. "We go all-in and then realise we've overlooked the single tiny insignificant flaw that ruins the whole thing. A couple of years ago, my dad found a really classic LP player on eBay, and he bought it and spent the whole weekend setting the front room up for perfect sound quality. Then remembered that he'd sold all of his vinyl in about 1995. And as for me,

I just got so hooked on my theme that I forgot pear drops are objectively the worst sweet."

Once his interview was over, Paris went to hug him. "They looked beautiful, though."

"So did yours. And they tasted good. Which is why you won. Again."

"Oh don't, I just got—" Paris cut himself off. "Yes. That definitely happened. I am filled with confidence in my own abilities."

Tariq leaned up to kiss him. "That was convincing. I'm very convinced. Although I'm starting to wonder if the rest of us should just go home."

"Please don't say that. I know you don't like me to say I'm getting lucky, but there is an element of luck to it. It's not Tanya's fault that exams were this week. Though"—Paris risked a smile—"it kind of was your fault you chose a really disgusting sweet."

"Shut up, angel cake." Tariq grinned back. "And congratulations."

While Paris was seldom actually on top of the world—and, if he was, he'd probably be too worried about falling off to enjoy it—he was feeling unexpectedly buoyant. "Um," he said. But buoyantly. "I don't suppose you want to come and—I promise I won't buy any more truffles. But I could make food for you in a better way? And not throw you on the table. Or insult you. So you wouldn't have to storm out."

Tariq was trying not to laugh. Though he wasn't trying very hard. "Not-storming-out is one of my favourite ways to spend an evening. So yes, that sounds lovely. What day do you want me?"

"Not Monday or Tuesday because I've got my dissertation to plan. And I guess Friday wouldn't be great for you unless you happen to know a mosque near where I live, which maybe you do?"

"I'm hearing midweek." Mercifully Tariq interrupted Paris's logistical rambling. "How about Wednesday?"

"That would be perfect."

"Great—oh wait. I can't."

The fact that this was still one of Paris's most successful

attempts to ask someone out did not say good things about his love life. "Oh."

"It's my dad's birthday. And it's his fiftieth and he's my dad. So I sort of have to go, and I would even if I didn't have to. Because, as I say, he's my dad."

"That's okay," said Paris quickly. "We can do something another time or the week after."

There was a pause, Tariq toeing the grass with one flawlessly polished loafer. "You could...be my date? If you want? It's in London so it won't be far. It *might* be really embarrassing, though."

It might be really embarrassing was a magical incantation designed specifically to make Paris not, under any circumstances, want to do something. "That sounds nice." His voice rose three octaves.

"Embarrassing for me, not for you."

Paris visibly relaxed. "How come?"

"Because the plan is for us to play laser tag and then go to an 'eighties-themed restaurant."

Since his own parents weren't generally around to model normalcy, Paris wasn't sure which part of this was the problem. "That doesn't seem embarrassing."

"We'll have to get dressed up in plastic armour. And you'll have to realise that my father is the kind of man who would spend his fiftieth birthday shooting pretend guns at his adult children."

"I don't mind," said Paris, realising, to his surprise, that he genuinely didn't. "It sounds nice."

"I know it's a bit early to be meeting the parents. But...well." Tariq shrugged. "Here we are. And, also, it *is* laser tag so there's a real ceiling on how serious this can get."

"As long as they won't...I don't know. Hate me."

"I think they'll just be glad I've got a boyfriend. It's been a while. Oh, and my mum will probably do the *you couldn't meet a nice Bangladeshi boy* joke. But she is eighty percent kidding."

"Um. Okay?"

There was a pause. And then Tariq put his hand on Paris's arm. "But. And, listen, because it's really important. If this is going to freak you out or make you feel scared or vulnerable, you don't have to do it, but you do have to tell me before it happens. Not after I've made you do it."

"I want to do it," said Paris.

And in that moment, he genuinely meant it.

Wednesday

THISWASFINETHISWASFINETHISWASFINE.

The problem was that when somebody had given you permission not to do a thing, and you'd insisted you could totally do it, that put you under a lot of pressure not to be a wreck. And for all that Tariq was patient and understanding and wonderful, Paris suspected there was only so much of a wreck he could be before he'd thoroughly exhaust his wreck privileges. So he'd got on the Tube, and then on another Tube, and then navigated his way through the streets of Bromley—an area for which he had diligently avoided looking up any crime statistics—using his phone. A phone that, despite the nagging voice in the back of his mind, nobody had mugged him for.

This, he told himself, was A+ boyfriending.

And he was only a little bit sweaty and terrified when he arrived at the venue. It was a...well...it was a blue cube in a car park with the words *Laser Vengeance* stencilled in white on the side. The lack of windows, coupled with the no-nonsense branding, made it look either like the kind of place suburban husbands went to buy porn in the '70s or else—actually, no, that was what it looked like.

This was beginning to feel like a joke. To pay him back for some terrible thing he'd probably done without realising it, Tariq had lured him out to a plywood cube in the middle of nowhere, and he'd get to the doors and there'd just be a Post-it note saying *ha-ha you suck*.

Paris tried to remember what they'd done for his father's fiftieth birthday. He thought they might have gone to the Guggenheim. At least his parents had—he'd read about it in *Hello!* a week later. Still, right now he'd have taken sitting alone while people swanned off to New York without him over standing alone in a car park outside a blue box that still might turn out to be full of murder.

Eventually, he did find a door, but he wasn't quite sure where it led. And he was now realising that *I'll meet you there*, while it had sounded breezy and casual at the time, was far too nonspecific. Was Tariq expecting to meet him inside? Or in the car park? Or under one of those big police tents after they discovered his body after he got *stabbed* in the car park? And of course he could text, but that might look needy or neurotic and what if Tariq was driving and he answered the text anyway and he went off the road and he died on the way to his dad's birthday?

A car door slammed close enough to make Paris jump but far enough away that he felt awkward looking at it. Except not looking at it began to feel increasingly worse on account of how pointed it seemed, and there was only so much interest you could feign in a blue wall with no signs on it. When he could feign no longer, he turned nonchalantly around and saw a woman approaching, talking on her phone. She was casually but elegantly dressed, in jeans, a flowing, long-sleeved top, and a light brown hijab. And, oh help, if Paris assumed she was part of Tariq's family, he would come across as super racist if she wasn't, and if she was, he'd come across as super racist for ignoring her.

"—middle of nowhere," she was saying, "outside some kind of blue warehouse and none of you are here, and there's a creepy guy in an expensive jumper staring at me." A pause as she listened to whatever was coming from the other end of the line. "Yeah, no. Really tall. And I wouldn't say ginger. But I cannot bring myself to use the word *auburn*." Another pause. "How long are you going to be?" Another pause. "You stopped for what? Can't you get that here? Why do you even need that?" She sighed. "All right. Fine. See you in a bit."

Tucking her phone into her handbag, she bore decisively down on Paris. "So I'm assuming you're either a weird stalker or my brother's boyfriend?"

"Yes." Paris nodded. "I mean, the second one. Definitely the second one. Not a weird stalker. Not that I wouldn't. I mean, you're very—I mean, I'm gay and stalking is wrong. Hi, I'm Paris?"

"You're where?"

"Paris. Like the city. It's my name. Sorry, my parents thought it would be romantic. Because I was, you know. Um. Sort of conceived there."

"Oh?" She arched a well-shaped brow. "I've got a friend whose parents did that. Good old Backseatofafordcortina. I really miss her."

Paris had managed to say "Why? What happened to her?" before he'd noticed it was a joke.

"Well, she's fictional, so nothing. I'm Salma, by the way. And my entire family are late because of course they are."

People criticising their own families was one of the many, many instances of social interaction that Paris could see no good way to handle. Either you agreed, and slagged off their family, or you disagreed and contradicted them. He made a kind of noncommittal noise and hoped that would suffice.

Thankfully, Salma seemed altogether better at humaning. "So Dad says that Tariq says that you met on the baking thing?"

"Yes."

"Not going to lie, but I was hoping for a longer answer."

"I, um, hit him in the face with a fridge?" Paris blurted out.

She thought about this for a moment. "Honestly, I don't blame you."

"What? No. It was an accident."

It was at this juncture that Tariq's car trundled into a nearby space and Tariq himself jumped out.

"They're running late," Salma told him, "because Dad wanted to stop at a petrol station for rhubarb and custards."

Tariq rolled his eyes. "I'm not even going to ask. But being late for his own party is peak Dad."

"On the subject of people being peak them"—Salma's eyes raked over Tariq—"what are you wearing?"

"My clothes?"

The clothes in question were white skinny jeans, a print shirt, and an electric-blue blazer. Which Paris thought looked amazing, but what did he know?

Salma gave a condescending elder-sibling frown. "Okay, but this is basically a warehouse. You are going to come out of here covered in dust, ketchup, and week-old chewing gum."

"But I'm going in"—Tariq gave a glittery wave—"looking fabulous. Anyway, I'm assuming you two have met but, Salma, this is Paris. Paris, this is my sister Salma. She's horrible."

"I'm not horrible," said Salma immediately. "You're annoying."

This seemed to be going really badly. But remembering the last time Tariq had felt un-stood-up-for, Paris tried to intervene. "He's not annoying. He's not annoying at all. Although, I'm sure you're also not horrible. But, I mean, I don't know you? So I probably shouldn't—"

Salma glanced at Tariq. "Is he all right?"

"He's an only child," explained Tariq, tucking himself in the nook of Paris's arm. "Paris, this is a sibling thing. We love each other very much. But we also really get on each other's nerves."

"Tariq was stealing my nail polish from the age of eleven. Which," Salma added, "I wouldn't have minded if he hadn't also been really catty about the colour choice."

"You had nothing exciting. It was all beige and nude and rose."

Salma flicked her fingers at him—the nails beautifully manicured in a subtle shade just shy of pink. "That's because I picked them to look good on me: a woman with taste. Not on you, her extremely extra kid brother."

"You should be grateful you had an extremely extra kid brother. Imagine if I'd been into, I don't know, cars or football or trying to sleep with your girlfriends."

"Honestly, I'd rather you tried to sleep with them. Instead of giving them fashion advice. That they then accepted."

It looked like they were settling in for a good long bicker, which, now he'd been reassured it was normal, Paris wouldn't have minded at all. He enjoyed social situations where his job was to be quiet and let other people get on with it. But then a generic family saloon lurched into a parking space, and the rest of the party began piling out.

"We're not late," insisted a man in a leather jacket and a T-shirt bearing a faded picture of Tears for Fears. He checked his watch. "We said we'd be here at half past. It's twenty to."

A woman in a loose-fitting blue dress and a black hijab climbed out of the passenger seat. "Ten minutes late is still late."

"Are you like this with your students?"

"Yes. Because otherwise they wouldn't show up on time for seminars."

"Dad. Mum," muttered the car's third occupant, a girl who looked precisely the wrong age to be standing behind her parents in a car park outside a blue cube. "Me and Tariq have both brought our boyfriends, and you're embarrassing us in front of them."

"This isn't embarrassing," said Tariq's dad. "This is my birthday. And it's cool."

His youngest daughter groaned and leaned her head on the

shoulder of the guy she was standing next to—a tall boy who radiated that effortless confidence that some teenagers were capable of.

He put an arm around his girlfriend. "It's fine, Mr. Hassan. Thanks for inviting me."

"Don't worry," said Mr. Hassan, with oblivious optimism. "You're going to really love this. I practically lived here when I was your age."

"You know what, Dad?" His daughter screwed up her nose. "I believe you."

They all trooped over to where Paris, Tariq, and Salma were waiting.

"Rhubarb and custard?" Tariq's dad held out a plastic bag full of red-and-yellow sweets.

"No," said Salma and Tariq together, at the same time Paris said, "Um, thank you," with the reflexive politeness of a six-year-old visiting relatives.

Tariq gestured vaguely amongst the assembly. "Everyone, this is Paris. Paris, this is my mum and my dad, and my other sister, Fariha, and her boyfriend Josh."

Fariha was too busy taking a selfie with her boyfriend to pay much attention to Paris.

"Pleased to meet you all," he offered, with an awkward head bob. "Thank you for inviting me, Mr. Hassan."

"Don't. Mr. Hassan's my father." Tariq's dad slipped the rhubarb and custards back into his pocket. "Call me Mo."

"I'm fine with Dr. Hassan," added his wife. "Because, unlike some people, I'm not trying to pretend I'm still twenty."

Mo pulled a deliberate pouty face. "Hey, it's my birthday, and I can do whatever I want."

"And what you've made a big deal about wanting"—Salma rolled her eyes—"is to play laser tag, and we're supposed to be doing that in three minutes. So we should—Fariha, are you actually wearing high heels?"

Fariha was still getting her hair selfie ready. "What?"

"You'll fall over in a dark warehouse full of dry ice. And

then I'll have to put up with you complaining for the rest of the evening."

"It'll be payback for me having to put up with you right now."

Looking like he was used to playing peacemaker, Tariq started out in the direction of the ominous door, dragging Paris with him. "Come on, if we stand around arguing for another hour, we really will be late."

Inside the blue box was a grey box, with a reception desk staffed by a bored-looking man in an equally grey T-shirt, and a café area full of plastic tables and plastic chairs, notably smaller than would be comfortable for the average adult.

Mo grabbed his wife's arm excitedly. "They've still got slush. They have the blue slush and the green slush and the red slush."

At which point he dashed off towards the refreshment kiosk.

Unperturbed, Dr. Hassan approached the bored receptionist and began to get the group checked in. Paris, feeling a lot less overwhelmed than he could have been but very much in the vicinity of whelming, slipped his hand into Tariq's.

"Thank you for coming," Tariq whispered to him. "This is genuinely a bit above and beyond."

"I don't mind."

"Dad's a lot. Actually, we're all a lot."

Paris sidled even closer. "It's fine. A lot's better than . . ."

He didn't know how to finish that sentence, but thankfully he didn't have to, because Mo jogged back, clutching a cup in which blueish, reddish, and greenish crushed ice were rapidly melting together into a chemical sludge. "I got them all," he cried triumphantly.

"And I'm very proud of you," Dr. Hassan told him.

Salma gave a long-suffering sigh. "You know you're not going to be able to take that in with you."

"Don't worry, I can drink it really fast." Mo took a long pull from the straw. Then winced and put a hand to his temples. "Argh. Brain freeze."

"Dad," groaned Fariha. "Why are you…" She made an expansive gesture that, for a moment, reminded Paris of Tariq. "Just *why*."

In the end, Mo had to leave his technicolour dream slush behind as they were shepherded through a set of grey doors, down a flight of neon-lit steps, and then into a tiny room lined with brightly coloured sets of laser-tagging apparatus.

Their guide was making an admirable attempt to disguise his boredom. "Okay, red team. In just a minute, you will be entering The Death Zone. But first you'll need to suit up. That means one vest and one blaster per person."

He proceeded to demonstrate, in some detail, how to put on and buckle the vest—Paris paying an almost painful amount of attention, for fear of doing it wrong, damaging expensive equipment, or looking like a fool. Well, more of a fool than a man wearing a tiny red plastic bib and holding a toy laser gun already looked.

"I can't believe we're on the red team." Tariq put a tragic hand to his forehead. "Had I known, I'd have worn a different jacket."

Salma gave him a consoling look. "But if we'd been on the blue team, it would have been too matchy-matchy."

"This isn't funny," said Fariha, sounding genuinely woeful. "It's stupid and I feel stupid."

Mo was already suited up and striking Rambo poses with his blaster. "This isn't stupid. It's an epic battle of wit and skill against an enemy that'll show you no mercy."

With his laser gun braced confidently against his shoulder, he slow-to-camera walked through to the briefing room, where the blue team were already assembled. In his defence, Paris reflected, they did seem pretty merciless.

On the other hand, they also seemed pretty small.

Fariha stopped dead in the doorway. "I don't believe it. It's eight-year-olds. Dad, you've dragged us out into the middle of nowhere to make us play a game for eight-year-olds *against* eight-year-olds. I hate you."

"Oi." One of the eight-year-olds sprang to her feet. "I'm nine. I'm nine today. And we are going to kick your arses."

Mo squared up. "Oh yeah?"

"Seriously." Salma tried to reel her father back in. "She's nine and—"

One of the other actual children got up and came to stand beside his friend. "So what? You wanna make something of it?"

"No," said Salma quickly. "Nobody's making anything out of anything. I just want us all to get out of here with our dignity."

Tariq was shaking his head. "Honey, that ship sailed when we walked in the door."

"Hey." Mr. Hassan turned a wounded gaze on Tariq. "This is laser tag. And in this building there are no 'adults' and no 'children.' There are only laser warriors."

"And losers," added the nine-year-old girl. "And you're going to be a loser."

"Not," shot back Tariq's dad, "if I make you a loser *first*."

She put her hands on her hips. "Not if I make you a loser first *first*."

"Not if I make you a loser first first fir—"

"Guys." That was the guide. "I need you to break this up because I've got to do the briefing. And also..." He snapped back into character. "Because here, at Laser Vengeance Bromley, we settle things...in the arena."

Mo and the nine-year-old gave each other one last cold glare and then went to sit down.

"I'm really not comfortable," Dr. Hassan whispered to her husband, "playing a competitive game against nine-year-olds. Also it's her birthday. I don't want to ruin a strange child's birthday."

Her husband leaned in. "Okay, one: not nine-year-olds, laser warriors. Two: it's my birthday as well. And three: this is war."

"Also"—Tariq leaned in too—"they're *definitely* going to beat us."

The guide took up his place at the front of the room. There

he spent five minutes hyping up the intensity of the experience to come, which, frankly, made Paris feel a little queasy. And then, very quickly, explained that competitors were also forbidden to run, make physical contact, lie down, climb on the scenery, or hold the gun with one hand, none of which Paris thought he would have tried but which he was now paranoid he was going to do by accident and get them all disqualified.

"When I open these doors," finished the guide, "you will enter The Death Zone."

The doors opened.

And the blue team, with a warlike whooping, immediately charged through.

"Um," said Paris. "I thought we weren't allowed to run?"

"To victory," yelled Mo, racing after the children.

His family followed him at a range of more sensible speeds, except for Fariha and Josh, who had taken the opportunity to hang back and kiss on a bench.

The guide cleared his throat. "You do actually need to enter The Death Zone."

Heaving a heavy sigh, and moving with surprising alacrity on her heels, Fariha dragged her boyfriend through the doors.

Inside The Death Zone, it was all of Paris's worst nightmares. It was dark, it was full of smoke, there were people literally chasing him with guns, and the floor was very slightly sticky.

"I told you," he heard Salma yelling, "not to wear white trousers."

And indeed, under the black lights Tariq was illuminated like a waist-down angel.

"Sorry, little brother," Salma continued, "but you chose to dress like that. I'm leaving you to die."

And with that, she vanished into the arena.

Tariq put a hand on Paris's arm.

And Paris leapt six feet in the air. "No physical contact. The rules say no physical contact."

"Angel cake, I'm on your team. In more ways than one. They just mean, like, don't shove each other. Or get into an actual fight."

"Oh."

"Anyway, you should probably get clear too. Because as much as I enjoy being the centre of attention, I'm looking a bit beacony."

"I'm not leaving you," protested Paris.

But before Tariq could reply, a klaxon sounded and a fake robot voice announced that "the laser war has begun." Two seconds after that, they were ambushed by two children who shot them to pieces and then darted out of sight.

"They're on us," shouted Tariq. "Take cover."

Remembering from the briefing that getting shot gave you a small window of invulnerability, Paris scampered off into the dark, heart pounding, hands already sweaty on the blaster, hoping that Tariq was behind him.

He wasn't.

And Paris was alone, his back against a plywood wall painted to look vaguely futuristic.

A child popped up from behind a three-foot barrel and shot him again.

The session was only meant to last twenty minutes but, to Paris, that was twenty excruciating eternities. He quickly adopted a strategy of hiding, getting attacked, running away, hiding, getting attacked, and running away in a sustainable cycle. Occasionally, he'd return fire. Mostly he'd miss, and the couple of times he didn't, he felt really bad because, for all Mr. Hassan had said about there only being laser warriors in the arena, the blue team still looked an awful lot like eight-year-olds to Paris.

Every so often he'd catch glimpses of his own team through the gloom. Mo was moving fast and staying low, picking off lone children like one of Captain Hook's pirates. His wife, by contrast, seemed about as reluctant to ruin a kid's birthday as Paris was, although her cries of "well done, you got me" every time she was shot drew a mixed reaction from the opposition. Salma, he suspected, was taking this more seriously than she admitted, because whenever he caught sight of her, she was edging cautiously along a wall, popping off precisely timed shots at, once again—it was hard to forget—actual children. Fariha and Josh, he didn't see at all and he suspected they'd gone off to a dark corner where they could break the letter if not the spirit of the no-physical-contact rule.

As for Tariq, he seemed to be doing wild circuits of The Death Zone, trailing a line of cheerfully sniping eight-year-olds like a mildly distressed Pied Piper.

"That's it, son," yelled Mo. "Draw them out in the open."

Tariq flailed his hands in the air. "They won't stop shooting me. I should not have worn this outfit."

"I told you so." That was Salma, leaning down from an overhead gantry to take out a bespectacled pre-tween. "You should always listen to your older sister."

Tariq's answer went something along the lines of "Ahhhhhh-hhhh!"

"Try to take cover," suggested Dr. Hassan.

"From my own trousers?"

Flattening himself to a pillar, Paris crept timorously closer to the action. In the crisscross of hazy red-green neon, Tariq was being herded slowly into a corner by a band of three armed moppets.

"Haven't you shot me enough already?" he asked plaintively.

The nine-year-old girl who had threatened, entirely accurately, to kick their arses, stalked forward. "That's the point of the game. Duh."

Tariq winced. "You are a mean little girl."

"I," she declared, "am a laser warrior."

Then she raised her blaster. And Paris, without really stopping to think, burst from behind his pillar, definitely violating both the letter and the spirit of the no-running rule, and threw himself in front of Tariq. He wasn't sure but he might have actually shouted "nooooooo."

His vest erupted into vibrations as he landed in a heap on the floor.

Tariq looked down at him. "Did you just take an imaginary bullet for me?"

"Um. Yes?"

"You are my hero." Tariq bent down and helped him to his feet. Then kissed him full on the mouth in the middle of The Death Zone.

"Are you boyfriends?" enquired the nine-year-old, blaster swinging casually by her side.

Paris looked at her. "Yes."

She thought about this for a moment. "That's nice."

Then she shot them both.

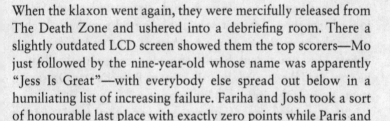

When the klaxon went again, they were mercifully released from The Death Zone and ushered into a debriefing room. There a slightly outdated LCD screen showed them the top scorers—Mo just followed by the nine-year-old whose name was apparently "Jess Is Great"—with everybody else spread out below in a humiliating list of increasing failure. Fariha and Josh took a sort of honourable last place with exactly zero points while Paris and Tariq hovered just above them, but still below everybody else, including literally all of the children.

On the next screen, a tally showed that the red team had lost by a margin that—having never played laser tag before and having no wish to play it again—Paris couldn't judge but suspected was crushing. Still, it didn't stop Mo from standing up and congratulating Jess Is Great on her win.

"Well fought, laser warrior," said Mr. Hassan.

Jess Is Great nodded solemnly. "You were a worthy adversary. Well, most of you sucked, but some of you were worthy adversaries."

After that, they piled into their various vehicles and drove the short distance to a slightly different bit of Bromley where Dr. Hassan had—in honour of her husband's less-vanished-than-one-might-expect youth—booked a table at a nostalgia-themed eatery called The Restaurant of Unusual Size. Reactions to this ran the gamut from "This is amazing, we should come here all the time" to "I hate you and wish you had died before I was born." But soon enough they were settled in a booth underneath a giant stuffed crocodile that Paris was convinced would fall and crush them. He perused the menu, which seemed to consist of generic diner food violently crowbarred into ill-fitting references to films Paris hadn't seen and songs Paris hadn't heard of.

Tariq put down his own copy of the menu. "None of this meat is going to be halal, is it?"

"I'm sorry," said Dr. Hassan. "It's one time. And you know your dad's—"

"Basically an infidel?" suggested Tariq.

Mo had just returned from the soda stream with a cup of what looked like three different soft drinks mixed together. "Yeah, I prefer the term *atheist*. Don't get me wrong, son. I respect your beliefs. I just don't want them to stop me getting a meal called"— he consulted the *Specials* board—"Ferris Burger's Day Off served to me by a waiter dressed as Indiana Jones."

"If I stabbed myself in the eye with this fork"—Fariha plucked a fork from the mug full of cutlery that sat at the end of the table—"would that stop you?"

"No," said her father cheerfully. "Because you're eighteen and about to go to university, which means you can stab whatever parts of your face you want and I'm not allowed to have an opinion about it."

Dr. Hassan glanced wryly at Mo. "We've not been allowed to have opinions about her for years."

"That," declared Fariha, "is because your opinions suck."

Salma leaned across the table. "Just so you know, Josh, Mum and Dad have been pretending they don't like you, just so Fariha will keep you around."

Josh thought about this a moment. Then fell back on "Thank you very much, Mr. Hassan."

While the other end of the table was debating the Hassans' secret plan to manipulate their daughter's love life, Paris squiffled a little closer to Tariq. "I think there's some vegetarian options here?"

Tariq did not seem very reassured. "What? A New Salad, The Salad Strikes Back, and Return of the Salad? That's going to be some lettuce, some lettuce with some rocket, and at the top level, if I'm very lucky, some lettuce, some rocket, and some slices of red onion."

"I think they do fish?" offered Paris. "Look, there's a big one called RoboCod. And a slighter smaller one called Children of a Lesser Cod."

A few minutes later, a Cockney teenager dressed as Flash Gordon came to take their orders (two RoboCods, the Ferris Burger, two salads, a Mystic Pizza, and, for Paris, Desperately Seeking Spaghetti). Then a rare silence descended over the table.

"So"—Dr. Hassan turned to Tariq with a grin—"you couldn't have found a nice Bangladeshi boy?"

Dinner had gone well, surprisingly well given how terrible Paris normally found interacting with new people. He had, however, been out of the house since quite early in the morning, and while he'd trained his bladder pretty effectively over the years to wait until he was somewhere not flesh-crawl-inducing, he eventually had to break and use the restaurant's toilets.

They were, to Paris's relief, of entirely *usual* size and, for an establishment that sold itself on the novelty rather than the quality of its dining experience, pretty reasonably maintained. Although the giant murals of the Teenage Mutant Ninja Turtles didn't exactly create a restful atmosphere.

He emerged, trying not to think too much about aerosolised faeces, and found Fariha slouching on the wall waiting for him. Perhaps it was the John-Hughes-themed décor, or the look of quintessentially adolescent defiance on her face, but somehow she managed to look like she was chewing gum even though she clearly wasn't.

"Want a word with you," she told Paris, who was immediately struck with the fear that his fly was undone, but since he was now standing directly in front of his boyfriend's teenage sister, he was in no way able to check.

"Oh?" he tried. It wasn't the worst possible response, but it was up there.

"What're you doing with my brother?" she asked with the unbreakable self-assurance that Paris normally associated only with fictional people.

Unfortunately he wasn't quite sure how to answer. "Well, we're—we're sort of dating."

She looked at him like he'd given the most pathetic answer it was possible for a truly pathetic person to give. "I know *that*, I just mean—you look after him, all right?"

"Look after him?" Paris echoed. He didn't feel qualified to look after himself most days; looking after somebody else as well seemed like a tall order.

"Or, you know, don't mess with him or whatever."

Paris didn't think he was going to. "I won't."

"See you don't. And don't go being all weird at him either."

This seemed to be getting personal. "All weird?"

She gave a *why is nobody as smart as me* sigh. "It's always the same way. He'll take up with some weird guy and be all *no, no, I can totally fix him*, and then he can't and it screws him up and it's annoying and it's stupid and he's stupid but that's what it is."

"Oh." Paris didn't *think* Tariq was trying to fix him. Then again he didn't think he could be fixed.

"Just"—Fariha waved her hands in a way that reminded Paris briefly of her brother—"I'm watching you, all right?"

"All right?" Paris could hear his voice climbing half an octave as he spoke, but he wasn't sure what else to say.

Straightening herself up, Fariha fixed her hair and made her way towards the ladies'. "Okay," she said. "Good talk."

Paris wasn't sure it had been, but he made a very firm decision not to think too much about it. He almost even succeeded.

"Your mum doesn't really wish I was a nice Bangladeshi boy, does she?" asked Paris. It was a safer question than *does your sister really think I'm a weirdo you're trying to fix?*

After dinner, Tariq had driven Paris back to his flat, and now they were curled up on the sofa together, Paris with his head in Tariq's lap, and Tariq's fingers playing lightly in Paris's hair.

"For the ninth time," Tariq told him, "no. It's a joke. She does it every time. It's her way of saying *I'm okay with you dating a boy.*"

"But sometimes jokes are, y'know, not jokes."

"This one definitely is. And, honestly, I think she's slightly over-compensating for the fact it took her a little while to come to terms with the gay thing. I mean"—Tariq made a sparkly gesture—"even though I've been the absolute gayest since I was eight."

Suddenly something occurred to Paris—something that made him feel a bit strange. "I...I don't think I've actually come out to my parents. I think they must know, and I do talk about boyfriends, but we've never had a conversation about it."

"Honestly..." Tariq glanced down at him. "I can't tell if that's really sad or really nice."

Paris couldn't tell either. "Yeah. Like, I'm sure they're cool with it. And I got to have the whole *it's okay, it doesn't change anything* moment with Sophie."

"Is Sophie another cat?"

"No. She's our housekeeper. And"—Paris hid his face against Tariq's leg—"now I've said that aloud it sounds really...um. Millionairey again?"

"Slightly," conceded Tariq. "But also slightly...your coming-out story is about your housekeeper."

"I spent a lot of time with her during the school holidays. She's the one who taught me to cook."

"Well"—Tariq was unexpectedly at a loss—"she seems like a really nice person?"

"She was. I mean, she is. I think she still works for my parents."

"You think?"

Paris squirmed. This was going to a place that was, at best, semi-comfortable. "I've not really spoken to her in a year or so. Or my parents really. It's just—I've just—everybody's been really busy."

While Paris was used to people looking confused, Tariq was currently looking full-on does-not-compute. "You've gone over a *year* without speaking to your parents? If I went a *week* without speaking to my parents, they'd assume I was dead."

"They've got a lot on. I'm sure they'll be back eventually." Paris's skin was beginning to burn, his mouth starting to feel dry.

"It sounds like Sophie might like to hear from you, though?" suggested Tariq.

"I don't think so. She's not—I don't mean this in a bad way, but it's not her job to care about me."

Tariq's body language took on a backing-away quality. Which was extra impressive considering how close they were. "Well no. But people can care about each other even when they *aren't* being paid to."

"I guess." This had definitely gone somewhere Paris would rather it hadn't gone. He was getting a feeling in his stomach like he'd tried to eat a whole sticky toffee pudding covered in custard made of regret. "But what about you?"

"Me?" asked Tariq. "I'm pretty okay with you being gay."

"No, I mean, before we went down this weird rabbit hole about me and my actual servant, you were talking about how it had been with your mum. And...well...if you don't want to talk about it, then that's...But if you do, it's also..."

For once it was Tariq's turn to look squirmy, although he did it with far more grace than Paris ever managed. "Not much to say really. It took her, like, a year and a lot of talking things through to get her head around it."

"What about your dad?"

That just made Tariq laugh. "You've met my dad. He was so determined to be cool with it that I found it slightly insulting. But at least we got through it quickly." There was a pause. "And even with Mum it wasn't so much that she had a problem with me being gay. It was just hard for her to accept that I could be gay and still a good Muslim."

Very gently, Paris levered himself out of Tariq's lap. "I... um. I really want to say something supportive here, but I don't want to make you feel judged again." His voice had gone slightly squeaky with not-wanting-to-fuck-up nerves. "But I also don't want you to feel you can't talk to me about this stuff because it's important to you. I guess I just... I don't know what I'd do if I... really believed in a religion that didn't believe in me?"

"I don't think it's the religion that doesn't believe in me," said Tariq softly. "It's all the"—another of his hand waves—"orthodoxy and patriarchy and tradition that's built up around it over the centuries. And to be honest, that's probably true of most religions."

"I've never really thought about it. I think I sort of assumed, y'know, faith wasn't for me. Or couldn't be."

Tariq grinned. "Faith is supposed to be for everyone. Or everyone who wants it anyway. That's kind of its whole deal. But I do know what you mean. And I think if religion hadn't always been part of my life, which it was because of my mum—which is why things with her got complicated for a while—I wouldn't necessarily have put the effort into..." The smile faded as Tariq cast about for words. "...*reconciling* all the different bits of who I am. But"—he shrugged—"it was, and it is, so I did. And for the record, I am aware that going on about how much my belief means to me is kind of unsexy."

"Well, how am I supposed to respond to that?" Paris didn't mean to sound quite as petulant as he feared he did. "I don't want to say it *is* sexy, because that seems disrespectful or like I have a really weird fetish."

"Yeah"—Tariq nodded—"maybe stick to cat dating?"

"I'm not dating my—oh stop it. I just mean, if it matters to you, then it matters to me."

"I know. I know. But I don't want you to think I'm uncool or brainwashed."

"Tariq," said Paris very seriously. "You're the coolest person I've ever been able to persuade to spend more than five minutes with me. Which, admittedly, is not the highest bar but it's still a bar. Why on earth would I think you were brainwashed?"

"Because, angel cake, quite a lot of people in the LGBTQ+ community think being queer and religious is letting the side down." With an oddly vulnerable look, Tariq drew Paris back down into his lap. "So it's like this...erasure sandwich because on the one side you've got *you can't be a proper Muslim if you're gay* and on the other side you've got *you can't be a proper gay if you're Muslim.* And I'm stuck in the middle saying *guys, I'm both and being both is really important to me.*"

It was not the right time for Paris to feel insecure. But he couldn't help noticing that Tariq had multiple things in his life that he felt passionately enough about to fight for. And Paris had a cat and a horny Glaswegian, both of whom could look after themselves. "I know this doesn't help, but I'm sorry people make you feel that way."

Tariq huffed out a resigned breath. "It's okay. And actually it kind of helped Mum get on board. She's really not down with people claiming you can't do this or can't be that because you're a Muslim. And she's a feminist, which means she's really used to getting the whole *but how can you follow a religion that oppresses you* thing." There was a mini-silence, Tariq's hands moving rhythmically but slightly absently through Paris's hair. "So in the end it came down to the same arguments she's been making for years about how a lot of preconceptions aren't actually based on Scripture, but come from later social traditions or questionably authentic hadith."

"Um"—Paris shivered slightly, Tariq's touches soothing him even if the conversation wasn't especially soothe-conductive— "should I ask you what that is now, or google it later?"

"Hadith? They're kind of reports of things that the Prophet

said or did that aren't in the Quran—and maybe weren't meant to be written down but sort of were." Tariq waved his hands in an *it's complicated and has context* kind of way. "And there's a lot of controversy about which ones actually happened and which ones didn't, and which ones genuinely reflect the actions and beliefs of the Prophet, and which ones are just other people projecting their own stuff onto him."

"And that…that helped with your mum?" ask-stated Paris, trying to show he was following without sounding like he was interrupting.

Tariq nodded. "It really did. Because it reminded us both that we come from a faith that's supposed to be about debating ideas and asking questions and being open to new interpretations of things we always took for granted. And actually, it's not like the Quran ever says it's wrong to be gay."

Caught by the conviction in Tariq's voice, and gentled beneath his hands, Paris blinked dazedly up at him. "That's lovely but aren't there, like, a lot of people who disagree with you?"

"There are and I wish there weren't. But I can't let other people take away what I think is important about my own faith. Which is"—Tariq's eyes were bright—"that God made all of us in all our diversity—all our different communities—so we can learn from each other. And I definitely don't think you get any closer to God by being straight or, for that matter, homophobic."

Paris thought about this. "Okay, but how do you know? What if you're just wrong? And God's not real and you're living your life like this and it's…I don't know. Pointless?"

"Then it was pointless," Tariq told him, apparently unperturbed by this possibility. "But I'll still have lived my life well, in a way that made me feel loved and free, and part of something beautiful."

For a second, Paris felt an unexpected sting of envy. From inside his world of what-ifs and second guesses, the whole concept of saying *this is who I am and I defy anybody to tell me not to celebrate it* was unthinkable. But he had no idea how to tell any of that to Tariq. So instead he sat up, took Tariq by the hand, and drew him into a long, lingering kiss.

And right then, for as long as it lasted, for as long as they were touching, Paris, too, felt loved and free, and part of something beautiful.

Friday

Hi Mum, Paris texted. **I know you're busy but I've got a lot of things happening in my life now and I really want to tell you about them. Please text me back. Love to Dad.**

    Hi Dad, Paris texted. **I know you're busy but I've got a load of things happening in my life now and I really want to tell you about them. Please text me back. Love to Mum.**

Saturday

WHEN MORAG—IN REMARKABLE good humour given the heat and the distance—dropped Paris off at Patchley House for the fifth weekend of filming, his parents still hadn't texted back.

And that wasn't exactly surprising, because they never did. But it stung more than normal because—actually why *did* it sting more than normal? Because he'd spoken to Tariq about them? Because for the first time since they'd left him at Hawton he actually had something worth telling them about? Something that mattered to him. Something that maybe, just maybe, he could expect them to be proud of. To care about.

Paris couldn't face breakfast, and he didn't really want to be sitting in a crowd trying to keep up his run of being-okay-at-people-stuff while his un-replied-to texts were burning holes in his phone case. So he stole away and sat on the sitting-down log. And there he sat, staring at his inbox, feeling a fool for waiting and caring. Like he had been his entire life.

Enough time passed that he'd soon be needed for filming, and the nothing he'd expected to happen had continued happening. And after a while the hollowness that Paris usually associated with texting his parents began to fill with something new. Something that almost felt like resentment. Because they were wherever they wanted to be, doing whatever they wanted to do, and he was here, doing—in theory at least—what *he* wanted to do, and he couldn't focus, because he was worrying about what they'd say. If they knew. If they could even be convinced to give a damn.

A shadow fell over the sitting log and Paris looked up, hoping to see Tariq standing beside him. But it wasn't. It was Bernard, looking droopier than ever in the heat but still smiling like somehow he'd got it all figured out. Even if his *it* wasn't quite the same as everybody else's *it*.

"Hello, lad," he said, taking a seat beside Paris. "You all right?"

Paris was about to say *yes*, but then he blinked and realised from the sting and the way his vision was blurring that he'd been crying. "Not really," he admitted, then wished he hadn't.

"Oh, I'm sorry." Bernard's frown was almost cartoonish. "What's the matter?"

"It's stupid."

That didn't go down so well with Bernard. "There's nothing stupid about being down in the dumps. It happens to everybody. When Norwich City got relegated, my dad was so shook up he wouldn't speak for two days."

Paris wasn't quite sure what point Bernard was making *specifically*, but he didn't doubt that it was well intended. "It's my parents."

"Ooh, that's tough." The look on Bernard's face was a picture of grave understanding. "Are they getting their bathroom redone?"

"Why would you think that?" asked Paris.

"Well, it can be very stressful. And there's a lot of memories in an old bathroom. When my dad got rid of the little china lady that used to sit over the toilet roll in our downstairs loo, I was quite taken aback."

Still cradling his phone like it was either an injured bird or an unexploded bomb, Paris looked up at Bernard as though he *hadn't* just shared a touching anecdote about a piece of kitschy toilet décor. "It's not that. It's just, I've been trying to text them to tell them how everything is going and they've—I haven't heard back from them."

"Well, not to worry." Paris suspected that Bernard had never sent a text in his life. "I'm sure they'll get back to you soon."

"I don't think they will. I don't know if they even know I'm on the show."

"I'm sure they do. Parents know things." It struck Paris that if there was one person who would be completely and entirely unable to empathise with his situation, it was Bernard, a man who—from what Paris understood of his domestic situation— had seen his own father every single day for the best part of fifty years.

"No," he said, more firmly. "I mean, I told them back in week one, but they never answered me. I really think they just aren't paying attention."

Saying it out loud, even to somebody who would never believe it, somehow made it feel realer than it had in a long while. Paris spent so much of his life in the hazy non-space that his mind built around him that he sometimes felt like he only existed in what people reflected back at him—their praise, more often their disappointment, their infrequent love. So his parents' absence had quickly settled for him into this quiet, anaesthetic fog. A childhood monster that couldn't hurt you as long as you didn't look at it.

Except now he *was* looking, and he couldn't say why. Things were so good in so many ways, he should have been able to let this one thing go, or at least to leave it be the way he had since he was thirteen. But he couldn't. He'd just be letting himself get comfortable—happy with his performance on the show, happy with Tariq, happy at home—and the thought would bob up unbidden that he'd been happy before. That he'd lived a charmed and perfect life before. And it had all gone away.

A signal came down from the house that they were needed on set. Bernard patted Paris cheerfully on the back. "Come on," he said. "I bet they'll have got back to you by lunch."

"Today's challenge," announced Grace Forsythe, "is an Italian pastry that legend has it was invented by a Neapolitan nun. Which is to say, a nun who resided in the vicinity of Naples, and not a nun who comprised equal segments chocolate, strawberry, and vanilla. It's a light, sweet pastry that rejoices in the difficult-to-spell name of *sfogliatella*. You have four and a half hours. Starting on three." Her trademark pause. "Three, darlings."

Turning over the recipe, Paris was greeted by the instructions: *Make dough with flour, salt, water, and honey*.

He frowned in nebulous confusion, trying to put the whole issue of the unanswered texts behind him. Hadn't he eaten sfogliatella before? The memory crept up on him like a homophobic mugger—subtly at first, trailing him through the dark alleys of his mind, before seizing his full attention with explosive violence.

He'd been with his mother in Naples, at one of those tiny, unbearably chic Italian patisseries that was all glass and marble and gold and history. He remembered the windows—so much of life was windows when you were a child, full of colours and wonders and mysteries—displaying an ever-dazzling array of breads and pastries and *Alice in Wonderland* jars. They'd gone every morning and sat at a little table outside. He would order something new every day, whatever seemed brightest or boldest, and she would order sfogliatella, and the blackest of black coffees. And when he'd finished his own cake, she'd always share what was left of hers.

The pastry warm and crisp, and flaking into perfect golden leaves. The richness of the filling, leaving a tang of citrus sparkling on his tongue. And his mother, dark glasses and red lips, the flame of her hair impossible against the blue sky of an Italian summer, laughing at something he'd said.

He was losing time. He stared again at the instructions. Crisp, flaky pastry—that probably meant lamination. Still slightly dazed, he mixed up a fairly stiff dough and left it to rest in the fridge.

They'd come to visit him once at boarding school. All the other parents had been tweedy or suity or twin-set-and-pearlsy. But Hugo Daillencourt and Isabella Holloway had been radiant—the only living things among all that ancient stone. They'd sat on an oak bench under a portrait of a dead headmaster, and Paris hadn't made them laugh once.

The dough had to be run through a pasta machine. Which—thanks to his recent adventures with try-hard ravioli—Paris managed without much difficulty. The next bit, however, did not go so well. He was supposed to be buttering the sheets and transforming them into a single large cylinder, but the butter was too firm and the pastry was too thin and so it was getting messy, and then messier, and there didn't seem to be any way to pull it back. He was just compounding mess with more mess, and that was making his heart race and his hands sweat, and dread pool in his stomach because it was going wrong. He was doing it wrong. And it was all his fault.

Because he sucked. And everything he did was rubbish.

And he'd never be that boy from the café in Naples again.

He'd watched his parents as they'd walked away. His mother's heels had clicked emptily against the cobbles. His father had his arm around her waist like he always did.

"I do hope," he'd murmured, or Paris had thought he'd murmured, or maybe he hadn't, "that an English education hasn't ruined our son."

Paris was crying into the duck pond, which seemed to be going down equally badly with the ducks and with Tariq.

"You did fine," he said. "It was a complicated pastry—"

"That I've eaten."

"Yeah, but not made. And you did kind of average, like the rest of us." He thwacked Paris playfully on the leg. "Welcome to real life."

Paris gave him a woeful glance. "That's the problem. I suck at real life."

"If by 'real life' you mean 'making fancy Italian pastries,' then…okay a bit. But not as much as Bernard. His was just a pile of gunge. And he was laughing about it."

"Well, Bernard's a *laughing about it* person. I'm a *feeling terrible about it* person."

"Okay but"—Tariq shuffled back a little and got all serious-faced—"you know you don't have to be, right?"

"I think I kinda do."

"I think you kinda don't," Tariq began, then checked himself. "Sorry, I just mean—you're probably like this because you've got a"—he waved a hand in a circle around Paris's head—"brain thing going on. And I know you're not comfortable putting a label on the brain thing you've got going on, but you can still try to do something about it. Saying *it's just the way I am* is the emotional equivalent of not studying for an exam so that when you fail, you can say *well yeah but I didn't do any revision*."

A small, teenage voice echoed in the back of Paris's brain, and he looked at Tariq suspiciously. "You're not... This isn't you trying to fix me, is it?"

"Fix you?" Tariq looked momentarily confused, then seemed to work something out. "Oh no, did Fariha get to you?"

"Sort of?" Admitting it seemed for the best, even if it was quite embarrassing in retrospect.

"Angel cake, she's eighteen. She thinks she knows everything, and she really, really doesn't. She's got this idea in her head that I'm fatally drawn to fixer-uppers, and it's sweet that she's protective but—"

"I am a *bit* of a fixer-upper, though?" Paris pointed out. "It's just—I just get all these feelings and they're big and intense and they make me feel like I'm not normal."

"Well you're not, in a way."

That wasn't the answer Paris had been expecting, except in the way he was always expecting to hear terrible things. "Wow, thanks."

"I didn't mean it like that. Nobody's normal. I'm not. You're not. Bernard's ability to be cheerful about everything, no matter how disastrous, is clearly very, very unusual. But it seems like his way of coping makes him happy and your way of coping makes you miserable. So..." Tariq's voice trailed away. "Think about that, maybe?"

"How am I supposed to think about how I think about

things?" asked Paris, in dismay. "That's like that Escher picture where there's a hand and it's drawing a hand and the hand it's drawing is drawing the hand that's drawing it."

Tariq blinked. "I might have lost you."

"There's these two hands and they're quite realistically drawn, but the cuffs are…pencil lines and both the hands are holding a pencil and they're, like, finishing off the cuffs of the—"

"Honey, I didn't ask for an art history lecture. I'm just saying, I know you take stuff hard, but you've still won most of this competition. So cut yourself some slack and maybe do some very gentle googling to see if there's anything you can do to make yourself feel better."

"Sorry." Paris drooped. "Sorry. I just feel like everything's unravelling and all I'm doing is making a fool of myself on national television. And everybody who's ever met me is going to see me fucking everything up and be like *oh yeah, that guy, no wonder I hated him*."

There was a long silence. Then Tariq let out an equally long breath. "Nobody is going to think that. Nobody hates you."

"No," Paris protested. "They actually do. Everybody hated me at school. They thought I was weird and pretentious, and they didn't even know I was gay."

"School doesn't count." Settling himself into Paris's lap, Tariq kissed him between the eyebrows. "Kids are—through no fault of their own—basically evil. And if people picked on you, that's about them, not about you."

"It felt about me."

"I'm sure it did. But you can't blame yourself for other people choosing to treat you badly."

Paris gave an *I hope you'll think I'm joking* smile. "Watch me."

"I'd rather not, actually. Because the thing is, and if this is just you fishing for compliments I'll be cross, you're a great person and you're doing great in the competition. And you can't let a few bad experiences shape your whole life."

This was why Paris liked Tariq. Well, one of the reasons he liked Tariq. He lived in a world where it really was that simple.

Where you could decide to do something and do it. Or decide to feel something and feel it. Or decide to be something and be it. It was like a window into a place Paris used to know. But that was the problem. It was a window, not a door.

"I suppose," he said. Which wasn't really an answer but looked like one if you squinted.

Sunday

IT WAS THE hottest day of the year so far. And the contestants were making delices—which meant they had to temper chocolate under studio lights while hoping against hope that their delicately flavoured custards would set in fridges that, like Paris's nerves, seemed wholly inadequate for the task before them. His parents still hadn't got back to him, and he was largely resigned to the fact that they wouldn't ever get back to him. They'd left him at Hawton and walked away, and now his place in the competition was slipping away as well, and while things with Tariq seemed to be going fine, it was only a matter of time before they went away too.

On any other day, the atmosphere in the ballroom would have been tense, but between the weather and the complexity of the challenge the tension was wilting away into a kind of flushed, sweaty focus. Even Tariq, who normally found time to bounce over and play with Paris at least once during the baketacular—especially one that involved downtime—was firmly ensconced at his bench, carving strawberries into little heart shapes.

Paris couldn't help missing him but also couldn't quite bring himself to go over and make contact. Because what if it *wasn't* the stress of the challenge that was keeping him away? They hadn't exactly had an argument the day before, but they also hadn't exactly *not* had an argument, and so perhaps furiously carving fruit was just Tariq's way of saying he needed a bit of space. And Paris was all about giving people space. And certainly wasn't about going over to Tariq's bench and saying *hi, why haven't you talked to me during this very high-pressure competitive thing we're doing* like some kind of weird needy creep. That would only push him away faster. Unless Fariha was right, of course, and he had a thing for weird needy creeps. But that was its own can of serpents.

Looking around, Paris saw Grace Forsythe meandering from bench to bench trying and—unusually—failing to coax competitors into making amusing comments about the work they were doing.

Fatally, he made eye contact, and she crossed the ballroom towards him before he could pretend to be busy.

"This is looking very colourful," she said, indicating the array of fruits and small pile of gold leaf that were still laid out on Paris's workbench.

"Yes." He should probably have given her more than that, but it was hot, and he was beginning to realise that everybody else's decorations were *far* more elaborate than his were. "They're to go on my delice au passion."

"Well…" Grace Forsythe looked distracted a moment, then shocked. "Fuck me, I don't think I've got anything. This fucking weather. I mean here I am in the business nearly forty years, and I can't think of something to do with delice au passion."

Paris wasn't sure if that was her fault or his fault. "Well, I suppose it *is* just a fruit custard."

"With the words 'au passion' in the name. *Surely* there's a joke in there somewhere. Something like…and *oh* you're looking very *passion*ate—no fuck, that's shit. That's a shit joke. Where *is* my head today?"

"Er…" Colin Thrimp scuttled forward. In the heat he was looking like a piece of spinach languishing in the bottom of a salad bag that should have been thrown away a week ago. "Jennifer says: 'It's up your arse, which is where it's been since John Major was prime minister.'"

"Tell Jennifer to go fuck herself." At which point Grace Forsythe strode to the back of the room, calling as she went: "Are any of these fridges free? I need to climb inside one of them."

Looking down at his bench, Paris started to get the nagging feeling that he was kind of…done? His decorations were mostly fruit, and unlike Tariq, he was leaving them more or less intact instead of cutting them into intricate shapes for presentation. And there was still more than half an hour left on the challenge and, yes, some of that would be used to decorate his delice, but most of it was just dead time.

While everybody else was frantically making caramel or twisting chocolate into weird shapes, he was going to be sitting around doing nothing. And then at the end of the day the judges would say *you seemed to finish very early, why didn't you use the time to do some sugar work?* and he'd say *I don't know, I guess it's because I suck, I'm sorry, I just fucking suck okay?* Except he wouldn't, because you couldn't say *fuck* in front of Marianne Wolvercote and Wilfred Honey. He'd just say *I don't know, I'm sorry, I didn't mean to and I should have and I'm sorry.*

Paris began to suspect that he was crying. In a spirit of scientific enquiry he touched his eyes and detected wetness: yes, definitely crying. He was going to be the one who did too little work to justify his spot in the competition and cried about it.

In an effort to distract himself, he tried staring at the clock. But that just left him with the same kind of weird time dilation effect that he always got in exams. Watching the hands somehow made each second stretch out forever, but then he'd blink and realise that so many forevers had passed that he'd wasted twenty minutes without noticing.

He'd wasted twenty minutes without noticing. And other contestants—contestants, admittedly, whose delices would probably involve a more complicated decorating process—were moving to take their bakes out of the refrigerators. So Paris hauled himself off his stool and went to check the damage.

Since they all had designated fridges, there was, at least, little chance of his accidentally assaulting somebody with the door, but he still couldn't quite bring himself to open it. Because what if it wasn't set? What if he just had to serve the judges vaguely fruity sludge dripping off a plate? And even if it *was* set, the best-case scenario was that he was going to serve up a perfectly adequate piece of patisserie opposite people who were serving pieces of patisserie that were much *better* than adequate, and then what would happen? He'd go out was what would happen. He'd be the guy that won three times and then fucked up so badly that he went out immediately and everybody would be *see, I knew that guy was shit*.

Taking a deep breath, he opened the door.

And it was, in fact, fine. The delice had set, it was a pleasant, cheery yellow colour with the seeds picking out black spots across the surface. It would look *good* when it was decorated. But *good* probably wouldn't be good enough.

From somewhere across the ballroom, Paris heard an "ooh, I think I'll give that another few minutes" from somebody who might have been Bernard, but right at that moment he didn't have the time to pay attention. He went back to his bench, slipped the steel ring from the edge of his delice, and, absurdly, started crying again when it didn't immediately collapse.

"What are you doing?" asked Colin Thrimp, diffusing towards his bench.

"I'm…" Paris blinked damply into the camera. "I'm just… I'm just really overwhelmed. And I sort of need to decorate but I'm just getting really in my head about it. Like what if… what if fruit isn't enough?"

As it turned out, the decorating in question was a quick job. Too quick. Paris had gone for a less-is-more approach with a spray of redcurrants for colour and a halved passion fruit because, well, it was a passion fruit delice, but when that was done, he was left with the unbearable conviction that less, in this particular case, was just less.

Through his tears, he tried to see the good in his creation, and to comfort himself with the thought that he had done what he set out to do. Except all that achieved was reminding him yet again of those high windows and bright colours in Naples when he could have been anything and gone anywhere. And instead he was here, sweating in a cheap hotel, staring at an underdecorated delice.

"Oh dear me. Now, that is *not* happy." It was *definitely* Bernard's voice and, wiping his eyes on the sleeve of his T-shirt,

Paris could see the rest of the contestants, even Catherine Parr, gathering around Bernard's creation.

"I'm sure it's fine," Grace Forsythe was saying reassuringly. "It's meant to be a *bit* wobbly."

Lili gave her a sceptical look. "That isn't wobbly, that's runny."

Close enough to see for himself now, Paris had to agree. Bernard's delice au chocolat hadn't even remotely set.

"Should I take the ring off?" Bernard asked the crowd.

"I really wouldn't." That was Tariq—still not looking at Paris, although to be fair at that moment there was something much more interesting going on. "It'll splurge."

Catherine Parr was looking down her nose at the mess. "Well, I don't know what you did wrong, Bernard. But it must have been something."

"I think it's just hot." This was Lili. "Things take longer to set when it's hot and it's not always predicta—"

"Well everybody *else's* has set," Catherine Parr insisted. "There's no sense making excuses for the man."

Lili sighed. "Catherine, can you stop being awful for, like, *five seconds?*"

"I don't recall asking for your opinion."

"Well"—Bernard carried the precarious ring of slop back to his bench with a look of oblivious optimism—"standing around gawping won't get the baby washed. Let's see how it stands up to decoration."

Paris watched in grim fascination as Bernard took a shard of tempered chocolate and tried to stand it up in the middle of his delice. For a moment, it almost seemed like it was going to hold. Then, with the slow inevitability of a declining civilisation, it fell gently onto one side before sinking completely out of sight.

"Maybe something lighter?" suggested Grace Forsythe gently.

Initially Bernard looked blank, which in many ways wasn't much of a deviation from his usual expression. But he soon brightened, grinning like a cartoon sun in a children's television show. "I've got just the thing." He turned to Colin Thrimp. "If you'll just let me pop out and get my coat, I've got a half pack of Maltesers in the pocket."

Colin Thrimp consented to this minor break from protocol, but Paris suspected that the last-minute Malteser play wasn't going to be enough to save Bernard from elimination. Which made him feel safe and happy for all of a third of a second, and then made him feel like a complete arsehole.

Lili was up first for judging and, afterwards, it was pretty clear that nobody else had a hope of winning that week. Like Bernard she'd gone with a classic delice au chocolat, but unlike Bernard hers had set. She'd also taken the slightly more daring serving option and, instead of producing a single large cake, made a batch of a dozen small rectangular ones, each individually dec-orated with carefully placed blackberries, caramel-dipped hazel-nuts, and delicate chocolate sculptures which she'd tempered on moulds that—she explained later—she had 3-D printed specially. They were abstract, geometric structures, all sharp angles and clean lines, that rose almost balletically above the delice-square below. They were the kind of food Paris felt bad eating because it meant destroying something wonderful.

"This," Marianne Wolvercote had said, "is genuinely artful."

Marianne Wolvercote didn't have an equivalent of Wilfred Honey's *by 'eck it's gorgeous*, but *this is genuinely artful* came close.

"I'm not ordinarily fond," she'd continued, "of people who rely too heavily on tools they've made themselves—that suggests it's the object doing the work rather than you—but I think these additions do bring something, and it's not quite anything I've seen before."

"And," added Wilfred Honey, who was already halfway through his slice of delice, "it tastes gradely. Would I be right if I said there was a hint of coffee in there with the chocolate?"

There was. Which, when combined with her presentation, made

Lili very much the one to beat with nobody in a strong position to
beat her. Tariq had made delice de framboises cut into the shape
of hearts, but while the judges had enjoyed both his flavours and
his presentation, it hadn't been quite as remarkable as Lili's. Neither had Catherine Parr's classic-to-the-point-of-austerity delice au
chocolat decorated with dark chocolate curls.

Rodney might have come close, his three-layered delice de
Kinder Egg apparently a tribute to his children's favourite chocolate, but he was marked down both for using plastic toys as
part of his decoration and for picking a theme that was almost
impossible to describe without mentioning a brand name.

With Bernard's offering, the judges were kind, and Wilfred
Honey observed that the flavours were good, and that he deserved
to be praised for making the best of a bad job.

"A lot of people," he explained, "would have just up and
chucked the whole thing in the bin. But you pushed through,
served us something, and even found a way to give us some
decoration."

"Although it is"—Marianne Wolvercote poked a Malteser
and watched it bob helplessly—"a little ... improvised."

That just left Paris. He came forward with his perfectly fine
delice au passion and set it down in front of the judges, who gave
him perfectly fine feedback.

"We did notice," Marianne Wolvercote was saying, and Paris
mentally filled in *that you're shit and you don't belong here*, "that
you seemed to finish a little earlier than the other contestants."

"Yes." Paris looked down. He was feeling very hot. Of course
it *was* very hot; that had been part of the problem. It was a hot
day under hot lights in a hot room. But this was the under-the-
skin hot that came from being told he'd done something wrong
and that there was nothing he could do now to fix it so all that
was left was shame and regret and ... "Yes," he repeated. "I think
I wanted it to be minimalist."

Marianne Wolvercote nodded. "I can understand that. And
I do see that there's a kind of a Continental style that you were
aiming for here and I think you mostly achieved."

"But," interjected Wilfred Honey, "this is *Bake Expectations*, lad. We expect you to go *bigger*. Because at the end of the day, it's a competition, and we want to see great things from you."

Slumped and dejected, Paris walked the thousand miles back to his workstation and waited for the inevitable judgement. And when it came, he congratulated Lili with as much sincerity as he could, and hugged Bernard goodbye with everybody else. Then he went outside for an exit interview. And, for no reason he could put into words, he cried. Again.

On the way to the car park, Tariq had asked if he wanted to meet up sometime in the week, and Paris had been so caught up with the failure of his delice that he'd reflexively told him that no, he needed to spend more time on his bakes.

He'd regretted it the moment he'd got in the car, and spent the whole trip home sobbing and feeling like a complete piece of shit.

Thursday

THE SCENT OF Paris's latest practice bake began to spread through the flat and, when it reached Morag's door, summoned her forth from the depths.

"Oh, not again," she said when she'd made the short trip to the kitchen, where Paris was carefully cleaning as he went. "I know you've got to get ready for the weekend, but I'm getting fucking sick of your braided loaves. I've eaten more braided loaves than the five fucking thousand, and at least they got fish to go with them."

Paris stared down at his creation. It was the wrong shade of brown, and the crust was already beginning to crack. "Sorry, I just have to—"

"They're fine. They've all been fine. You can do this, you great sack of angsty shite."

"They're not fine. And even if they were fine, *fine* isn't enough." To his mounting distress, Paris realised he was about to cry. He fought the tears back for a moment but knew it was a losing battle. "They have to be *perfect*."

Leaning back against the granite countertop, Morag scowled at him. "You realise," she said, "that you are actually *ruining the smell of fresh-baked bread* for me? I didn't think that was even possible. That's like ruining fucking sunsets or orgasms or kittens chasing laser pointers. There are some things you aren't supposed to get sick of, and you've actually managed to make me sick of it."

She was right. Paris knew she was right because he'd ruined it for himself as well. There'd been a time when baking a loaf of bread had been his way of relaxing, letting the here and now of kneading and shaping and proving take his head out of the dislocated neverwhen it usually lived in. "Sorry. I just—I did really badly last Sunday and the judges were really disappointed in me and then I had this big fight with Tariq, so I have to do well this time or else."

"Or else what?"

"Or else I'll go home." The thought of it made him sick. Although lately so had the thought of going back into the ballroom.

Morag shrugged. "Then you go home. You've done a decent job so far and you should be fucking proud of yourself."

"Well, I'm not." With a bigger-than-expected splash, Paris dropped his scourer into the washing-up bowl. "I'm—I'm just not."

"I swear I don't know what to do with you sometimes. I only put you in for the fucking show so you could see you're actually good at this crap."

"Well, it didn't work." Paris's breath was catching now, and he could taste something in his mouth that was almost like blood. "Because they hate me and think I'm terrible because I *am* terrible."

"Didn't you win three times in a row?"

"Twice in a row, three times in total," Paris corrected her, and was surprised to see that this didn't make it immediately clear to her how useless he was. "And that was just because I got lucky and bought a lot of expensive ingredients those weeks."

Morag made a noise between a growl and a sigh. "You really think that Marianne Wolvercote, a woman so posh that her shits probably come out in gift boxes, and Wilfred Honey, a man so wholesome he probably pisses butterscotch, are impressed because you used some slightly fancy toppings?"

"I mean, no. But—"

"If this was what your big fight was about, Tariq was in the fucking right."

He probably was. At least Paris assumed he was, but then he tended to assume that other people were right and he was wrong unless there was a really compelling reason to believe otherwise, like if they were saying something nice about him.

"It sort of was," he admitted. "And sort of wasn't. After the show we were both pretty upset we didn't do better, and really sad Bernard was going because we all liked Bernard. And Tariq asked if I wanted to come up and visit him again this week, and I said I couldn't because I had to practise. And then he said okay should he visit me then, and I said I still had to practise, and that maybe I'd see how things went but we probably shouldn't. And I think I said it wrong, because he seemed really hurt and I tried to say sorry but it got all tangled up. And we've been texting and it's probably fine? I think"—Paris fished out his phone and brandished an exchange that read: **How's it going? / Okay, you? / Okay**—"but I've been thinking about it, and I think thinking about it is getting in the way of practising anyway, so maybe I should've just said yes, only if I'd gone to Birmingham, it would have been a whole day of travel and then a whole day back and there's only really five days to work on our bakes and—"

Raising a hand, Morag put up the *I've heard enough* gesture, which she'd developed at a very early stage of her relationship with Paris and got a lot of use out of. "Sorry, was this *big fight* that conversation you had just as I was picking you up? The one where he said *do you want to get together this week* and you said *I can't, I want to focus on baking* and he said *fine*?"

Paris nodded.

"You complete fucking knobhead." *Complete fucking knob-head* was Morag's friendly name for Paris when she thought he was being a bit silly and overreacting. "That wasn't a fight, that was a mild scheduling issue. At *worst* you might have made him feel like he wasn't your priority, but you've only been dating a few weeks and you've both got ten grand and your fucking legacies on the line here."

The money didn't really mean anything to Paris (because he was an overprivileged piece of shit who thought ten thousand pounds was nothing because he'd never had to work a day in his life). His legacy didn't mean much either (for similar, piece-of-shit-related reasons). Even so Paris was dimly aware that Morag was trying to be reassuring. But reassurance didn't help when he could see his relationship evaporating in front of his eyes.

"I didn't mean to," he protested. "I mean I did mean to. I mean I didn't mean to make him not feel like a priority and did mean to not make him feel not like a priority. I was just really worried about my performance."

"Now if there's one thing I've learned," said Morag, "it's that worrying about your performance never improves your performance. Talk it through, be honest, and remember that this is actually the longest relationship you've ever had so you can't expect to be doing everything right straightaway."

This wasn't exactly slander, but it wasn't quite true either. "It's not my longest relationship, I was with Jon for three months."

"You got together at the end of first year, then he went away to Japan and didn't get around to breaking it off with you until Christmas."

"Long distance is a thing."

"When you're having phone sex every night, that's a long-distance relationship. When he fucks off to the other side of the world and doesn't even text, that's forgetting to dump you."

Paris tried to look indignant but failed. The tears weren't helping. "Okay, so this is my longest relationship. Doesn't that just mean it's past its—I don't know—sell-by date or something?"

The look in Morag's eyes turned several shades darker. "So help me, Paris, if you make this into a big complex reason why it's okay for you to start sabotaging yourself all of a sudden, I will braid your cock and balls together, stuff them with rosemary, and serve them up as a savoury yeasted loaf."

While he didn't want to think too much about how yeast got into the equation, Paris did at least take it as a cue to reverse out of that particular rabbit hole. "I really like him," he said instead. The words tasted gritty in his mouth, as if he didn't have a right to be saying them.

"Well, that's good. I'd not want you to have spent the last month going out with a guy you thought was a prick."

"But what if it goes wrong?"

"Then we'll pretend you *did* think he was a prick. That's the breakup rules."

"He's not a prick."

Morag rolled her eyes. "And *that* is why you should stop fucking about with focaccia or whatever it is."

"It's just a braided loaf, it doesn't have a specific name."

"Either way, stop fucking about with it and call him."

That would involve using his phone as an actual phone, which Paris honestly thought everyone had stopped doing sometime in 2015 even if they *didn't* have a crippling fear of speaking to people they couldn't see. Or, for that matter, people they could. "What if he's busy?"

"Then he'll say *sorry, Paris, I'm busy, can I call you back*. He's your fucking boyfriend, not a judge you've been had up in front of 'cause you got caught wanking in public. He'll like hearing from you. You prat." As if to add punctuation, she ripped a chunk off one of the three other practice loaves that were still lining the kitchen benches and then set off back to her room. "Call. Him."

She was right, of course. And the loaf would be a while longer in the oven. Paris had time to ring Tariq and say *Hi, Tariq, sorry I didn't make time for you, I should have made it clear that you're my priority and that I care more about you than I do about the competition, but I didn't because I got scared and confused, and*

I know I'm trying to do less of that but I hope you can still forgive me.

He navigated to the phone bit of the phone, and then down to Tariq's number. Then he stood there with his thumb hovering over the little green button that would make the calling-people app do the calling-people thing.

Then he clicked back, and into Messages, and onto the most recent text chain, and sent: **I'm still okay. Are you still okay?**

He felt like a coward.

Friday

THEY WERE RUNNING late. Well, technically Paris was running late. Well, even more technically Morag was running late because of Paris. He'd told himself that he wasn't going to do a final practice bake on the Friday afternoon because he'd once heard that you could over-study for exams and that had informed the way he had prepared for every high-pressure event in his life since.

The plan was always to establish a cutoff point after which he would relax and focus his mind and not think about whatever thing he had coming up, thus breezing through it with confidence and panache. In reality, he'd get to the cutoff point, spend about two hours feeling that he should be doing more prep and then feeling bad for feeling he should be doing more prep, before finally snapping and trying to cram in one last revision / rehearsal / baking session. Which would inevitably be a disaster because he was now rushed and stressed and leave him convinced that he'd ruined everything forever.

Thus, at about half past three that afternoon, Paris had launched into a three-hour bake despite needing to be out of the flat by six. And now they were speeding towards Patchley House, with an angry Morag in full club wear hunched over the steering wheel as if she could make the car go faster by sheer force of will.

"You realise," she said, "I'm missing happy hour to do this."

"I know, I know. You're great and I suck and I don't deserve you."

The car bombed past a flock of blurry sheep. "Oh stop it. I don't need you to be contrite. I need you to be considerate. Just occasionally."

"I could have got the train."

"No, you fucking couldn't. It took you three and a half hours to plan the route to Birmingham, and that's a direct line with no changes."

She was right, of course. From a totally selfish perspective the stress of having needlessly upset basically his only friend was way more dealable with than the stress of navigating public transport. "I just…" Paris shouldn't try to explain, he knew he shouldn't try to explain. He tried to explain. "I just started thinking what if there was something I was missing or doing wrong and if only I'd done one last batch, I'd have worked it out and got everything perfect, and I know that wasn't realistic but I just had to and…"

"Despite everything"—Morag's car screeched into the driveway of Patchley House and skidded to a halt in the begravelled carpark—"I do *actually* like you, Paris. But by fuck if you don't make it hard sometimes. I'll see you Sunday."

Before Paris could say anything else she leaned over and popped the door open for him. Murmuring a hundred indistinct apologies, he shuffled out. Morag was gone before he could even wave.

He was just about to trudge down the hill to the Lodge when he heard another screechy-gravelly-driving-too-fasty sound and turned just in time to see his housemate narrowly avoid ploughing her car into his boyfriend. It was dark enough that Paris could probably have fled, and more or less got away with it, but if he'd been caught in the gleam of Tariq's headlights, that would mean capping off a week of mild evasion with an obvious blanking.

This turned out to be the right call because Tariq pulled up alongside him and rolled down the window. "Hey," he said, as if everything was perfectly fine, "would you mind spotting me so I don't back into a flowerpot or a car I definitely can't afford to hit?"

Paris opened his mouth and closed it again. Because he was terrible at, well, anything that involved exercising personal judgement. But especially at things that involved exercising personal judgement in spheres of which he had no direct experience. Although probably you didn't need to be a driver to be able to tell if a car was about to hit something, it still felt as though he lacked the obscure vehicular gnosis necessary to understand how a tonne of metal death moved in a confined space.

But he didn't want to be a bad boyfriend. "Sure."

What followed was a prolonged dance of Tariq inching forward and back in the vague vicinity of a slightly-too-snug parking space between a wall and a van that probably belonged to one of the crew, while Paris made what he hoped were helpful hand gestures. Eventually, still very unparked, Tariq turned off the engine.

"Angel cake," he asked, "I'd really like to get out my car before we start filming tomorrow."

"Sorry. Sorry. I just—I'm really worried you'll hit something."

"Yes, and you're literally here to stop that happening."

"But what if I don't? What if I say, back a bit, it's fine, you've got plenty of room, and you don't, and it's not, and you go back a bit too much?"

Tariq made an exasperated noise and surged the car backwards, lightly clipping the wing mirror against the van. "There." Dragging his bag behind him, he slithered out of the driver's-side door. "It wasn't that difficult."

"Then what did you need me for?"

"Normally"—Tariq gave him a slightly ambiguous smile— "having someone helping you makes it easier."

"I'm sorry. I...I don't. Um, make things easier."

"Am I going to have to start fining you again?"

Oh God, Paris had promised he was going to do better. And he wasn't doing better. He was doing just like he always did. Trapped like Odysseus between the Scylla of how much he sucked and Charybdis of...how much he sucked. "No," he said carefully.

"Okay." Tariq was eyeing him, equally carefully. "Good?"

There was a long silence.

"So"—Paris made a desperate *this is normal, this is very normal* gesture—"how've you been?"

"Fine. Apart from my boyfriend being weird at me all week."

And here it was: Paris had been wondering how he'd be getting dumped this time. "Well, we had a fight and I—"

"Whoa, honey." There was an *I haven't got a clue what the fuck you're talking about* look on Tariq's face. "What fight? When did we have a fight?"

"Last Sunday?"

"You mean, when I asked if you wanted to hang out this week and you said no and I was a bit disappointed?"

Paris digested this like a biscuit. "Well. Yeah. But being disappointed in someone is really bad. I let you down and I made you feel that my braided yeasted loaves were more important to me than you, a human being who I'm going out with."

"Okay. Yes. You're a monster."

"I know," wailed Paris.

"Angel cake"—it was Tariq's gentle voice, or something close to it—"you're not a monster. You were slightly selfish and you slightly hurt my feelings. But then you hurt my feelings even more by being super arm's-lengthy for a week."

This was more than Paris's brain was willing to take on. It definitely got *monster* and *selfish* and *hurt my feelings*. And if there was context to those words, it just didn't care. "I didn't know what to do. I'd said I was going to be...not rubbish and then I was rubbish."

There was a pause. "You do realise"—this was not Tariq's gentle voice—"that there's a difference between *I don't want to make plans this week* and *come to my home so I can fail to respect your boundaries and then make you justify your religious beliefs.*"

Paris cringed. Of course he knew there was a difference. It was just that it always felt the same, like a switch in his head flipped from right to wrong, and once you were on the wrong side, it was all flashing lights and sirens and nausea.

"I missed you," Tariq went on. "Believe it or not, I do actually like spending time with you. Which is why I was sad I wasn't going to get to spend time with you."

Phrases were collecting in Paris's mouth. Phrases like *but why* and *how can you* and, right at the bottom, *what's wrong with you*. But thankfully he managed to keep them from spilling out. After all, there were only so many times he could make Tariq tell him he was funny or kind or pretty or…basically okay.

Tariq put a hand on his arm—fingers glinting unguessable colours in the moonlight. "We could have talked, even if we didn't meet up. But you dropped me like a lemon tart."

"Tariq." Paris gave a little gasp. "Too soon. That was the worst thing I've ever seen happen to a lemon tart."

"I'm a bit concerned you're keeping track. And, actually, isn't falling to your death from a great height probably better than being laid out on a silver tray, slowly carved into pieces, and then eaten?"

"Don't say that. How am I ever supposed to eat a lemon tart again?"

"It's fine, just get ethically reared lemon tarts."

And Paris forgot himself for long enough to laugh. Though not for long enough to stop feeling shitty. "I really am sorry."

"Angel cake, it's fine. But I can't have you thinking every minor disagreement is a world-ending crisis. *I* am the drama queen in my relationships and I will accept no substitutes."

"I'm not a drama queen. I'm just…"

Tariq flashed his star-bright smile. "You keep telling yourself that."

Saturday

"I HAVE BEEN looking forward to this moment," said Grace Forsythe, "for the past seven years. This week is bread week, and for the blind bake, we're going to ask you to bake a flat, oven-baked Italian loaf. More specifically, Wilfred…"

Wilfred Honey stepped forward, smiling benignly. "We want you to make a focaccia." He got no further.

"Focaccia," cried Grace Forsythe, "I hardly—"

One hand to his earpiece, Colin Thrimp scuttled over. "Jennifer says: 'You did the *whatever-er, I hardly know her joke* last series, you unoriginal washed-out hack.'"

Grace Forsythe looked genuinely wounded. "I didn't know we were going to do focaccia. It works so much better with focaccia."

"Jennifer says you can go focacc yourself."

"What if instead I were to say *focaccia comin' atcha*?" offered Grace Forsythe.

The time delay between Jennifer replying and Colin relaying the reply was just long enough for Paris to become aware that the room was growing uncomfortably hot again. "She says 1998 called and says you were shit then too. Leave the introduction to Wilfred."

"This recipe," Wilfred Honey continued without missing a beat, "is one I picked up when I were a wee lad touring the world learning about bread. So treat it kind, and it should come out right special for you."

Grace Forsythe shot him a darkly luvvieish look. "Traitor."

The treason of Wilfred Honey aside, the blind bake got off to a good start. Paris had at least made focaccia before, and while that did mean he knew of about six different ways it could go wrong, he also knew at least four ways to stop it going wrong, and that was a better deal than he got on most challenges.

Gradually adding his salt to one side of the bowl and his yeast to the other so as to stop the one from killing the other, he risked a glance in Tariq's direction and was pleased to see Tariq risking a glance back.

Honestly, Paris wasn't totally sure they were one hundred percent back on track, but you could definitely see the track from where they were. Assuming it was a track, not just a well-disguised ditch full of poisonous snakes. He was still feeling low-key like an arsehole, but leaving aside the narrow window when he and Tariq had first been getting together, feeling low-key like an arsehole was very much Paris's default state.

Especially since he'd messed Morag around as well, and while she definitely *would* get over it, because she'd got over it every time, that was sort of the problem. Because there had definitely *been* an every time. Several every times. And, yes, it was probably good to have people in your life who'd forgive you if you fucked up, but probably it was better not to test that quite as much as Paris seemed to.

He needed to make it up to them. To both of them. Not that he was exactly sure how. He certainly couldn't do anything for Morag while he was stuck in a hotel in the middle of nowhere, but he could do something for Tariq. He'd heard there was a nice gastropub in the village—maybe he could take him there? That would be okay, wouldn't it? Saying *sorry I was a jerk, let me buy you dinner*?

Yes, there had been trufflegate, but that had been a very different context because truffles were mega-expensive. And there was also the whole oh-wow-you-live-in-a-palace context. Which later became the oh-wow-you-live-in-a-palace-and-your-parents-are-famous context and then crossed a line to become the oh-wow-you-live-in-a-palace-and-your-parents-are-famous-and-my-housemate-wanked-to-your-mum context.

Shit, he was meant to be baking. But focusing on the baking was what had got him into this mess in the first place. Not that it was a mess, not really. It was just a…just a situation. Because couples had fights. And then you said sorry and then it was okay again.

At least that was the theory.

The yeast, salt, and flour were mixed in the bowl, and Paris was blanking on what to do next. The instructions had just been "make the dough, starting with the dry ingredients," and he knew *basically* what that meant but now his brain was doing its best to sabotage him, telling him that there was a step he was missing or a special technique he was forgetting.

Letting experience take over, he made a little well in the middle and poured oil into it—God, he hoped that was right. He'd made focaccia before; he made focaccia for fun. He knew how this worked. It should be calming.

It was not calming. And he couldn't remember if you put the oil in like that or not.

Forcing himself to move on, he added the water. Honestly, it felt like too *much* water, but in baking, as in life, sometimes not enough felt like too much, and sometimes too much didn't feel like enough. Besides, if he'd learned anything from the past six series of *Bake Expectations*, it was that if you went off-recipe, then the judges would spot it and call you out on it.

Looking up, Paris saw Tariq had already turned his dough out onto the work surface and was starting to knead it. And for a moment Paris's brain switched off and he just watched, remembering how calm and happy it had felt to be in Tariq's kitchen making dinner together, how the confidence that radiated off him made everything seem so much better and less confusing and… No. Focaccia. He had a focaccia to make. He turned his own dough out onto the table with a wet splat.

He had definitely used too much water.

Between proving, stretching, proving again, and then baking there was a whole lot of downtime involved in making focaccia, which gave Paris far longer to sit with his thoughts than he would have liked. But every so often he and Tariq would glance at each other and wave, then go back to sitting quietly on stools waiting for their doughs to double in size, so on the whole the inside of Paris's head was a less awful place to be than it usually was.

He'd decided against the gastropub idea, and then decided in favour of it again, and then decided against it again, and he'd gone through about four different iterations of that. The problem was that it felt a bit half-arsed. Because while there was the occasional place like The Hand & Flowers that had actual Michelin stars, at the end of the day a pub was just a pub and taking somebody to a pub said *mate, I'm sorry your football team got knocked out the football thing*, not *I have made an effort and I am sorry*.

Except that left him with exactly zero ideas.

Rodney wound up winning the round, with Lili coming last. She and Paris had both made the mistake of using too much water ("You didn't have to use all of it," Wilfred Honey had explained. "Sticking to the recipe is good, but you've got to use your judgement and bread is about feelings"), but Lili had also got less of a rise, probably from letting her salt kill her yeast. Still, it had been touch-and-go, and when he realised how close he'd come to utter failure, Paris got that hot-but-sick-but-cold-but-sweating feeling that he'd been having all too often recently.

"I…Yeah," he said in his exit interview, trying to at least avoid crying this time. "That just wasn't—it's week six, so everybody's really good and I suppose I need to step up my game. It's just"—suddenly *avoiding crying* seemed like a more ambitious plan than it had two minutes ago—"I really thought I was but I'm just not and…" He lapsed into silence for what felt like far too long and, judging from the irate look on the camera operator's face, probably actually was. "Still, there's always tomorrow."

Slouching away like he was hoping his own jumper would eat him, Paris went looking for Tariq, who was giving his own interview in the growing shade of a tree. "...pleased, but also, grr." Tariq had a smile on his face that signalled a kind of radiant frustration. "Wilfred said mine was *nearly perfect*, and I thought *yes, Tariq, you have got this* but then he said Rodney's *was* perfect and I just went—" He made a gesture of exaggerated deflation, flinging his arms downwards like he was dropping a basket of laundry. "But tomorrow, watch out, Rodney. I'm coming for you."

"You are *so good at that*," said Paris, only slightly enviously, when Tariq had finished. "My bits are all *I don't know, I guess I didn't do very well but I'll try harder*."

Tariq gave a modest shrug. "I'm sure that comes off fine in the edit. Being unsure of yourself is relatable."

"Oh, don't. You know what I'm like, and it's not relatable. It's just annoying."

"It's not annoying." With an indulgent smile Tariq laid his hands on Paris's shoulders. "Or if it is sometimes a bit annoying, it's not your fault. It's just your brain being...Parisian."

And even though Paris was still swimming in his own bread-themed uncertainties, this felt like a good moment to prove he was a good boyfriend and say a supportive thing. "I thought your focaccia was better than Rodney's."

"Thanks. I mean, it wasn't, but thanks."

"No, it really was. It was more like they make it in Italy."

Tariq laughed. "Let me guess, your parents took you to Genoa and you ate focaccia hot out of the oven while your mum was shooting an advert for Gucci?"

"Well"—there was no way Paris was getting out of this, and the unexpected reminder of those days made thoughts bubble up that he had to fight hard to keep down—"it wasn't Genoa. And it wasn't Gucci. But yeah?"

Without another word, Tariq booped Paris on the nose, and they walked hand-in-hand back towards the house, with Paris still racking his brains trying to work out what the hell he could suggest they do together that was romantic but still achievable when they were stuck in the cheap bit of an otherwise nice hotel in the middle of nowhere.

Actually, that was a thought?

"Would you like to—" A cold tightening in Paris's chest brought him up short, but he pushed through it. "I thought maybe we could get a room in the hotel this evening? I mean," he added hastily, "a twin room. To make up for not seeing each other."

Tariq's attention flicked to the ornate facade of Patchley House, the look on his face hovering between enthusiasm and suspicion. "Is it that obvious I find fancy hotels really exciting?"

There was no way to answer that, because the truth was *no, I was just desperate and suggested a thing at random.* Also it hadn't actually occurred to him that Patchley House was particularly fancy or that staying in hotels was the sort of thing people got excited about. "Yes?" he suggested.

"Oh, come on." Tariq re-booped him. "You get to explore the room, and bounce on the beds a little bit, and the bathrooms are enormous, and there's a mini-bar that I will never use but which I like knowing is there, and they put chocolate on your pillow, and you get a dressing gown and…and…it's just fun, okay?"

This was already going so much better than Paris had expected. "Shall I do it then? Shall I see if I can get us a room?"

"I…" Tariq's eyes narrowed. "I want to say yes. But this feels"—he made an encompassing gesture—"truffley."

"It's not a truffle. It's a treat. And I'm asking you in advance, so you don't feel ambushed. And you don't have to."

"And you're not just overcompensating for ignoring me last week?"

"Well, I am. But does it make a difference if I'm honest about it?"

Tariq considered this. "Maybe?"

"What if we say," offered Paris, slightly too earnestly, "that it's to celebrate you doing well today?"

"I did make a pretty good focaccia…"

"You *did*." Paris's failcaccia loomed in his mind but he did his best to squash it.

"All right," said Tariq, in his sternest voice, which honestly wasn't very stern. "You're getting a provisional yes. But I reserve the right to withdraw it at any time."

Paris gave a nod so enthusiastic he nearly gave himself whiplash. "Okay. Yay."

"I need to go back to my room for prayers, but I'll meet you at reception in about half an hour?"

Paris kept nodding. "Okay. Yay."

And then Tariq bounced off, leaving Paris in that ambiguous state of unfeeling where he couldn't work out how the emotions he thought he should be having lined up with the ones he actually was.

"This," declared Tariq, "is the best."

He was in the claw-footed Victorian bath in their room's cavernous en suite. It was full to the brim with bubbles and steaming-hot water, and Paris was sitting in the doorway resolutely not looking.

Happy splashing noises echoed against marble and gilt. "I haven't had a bath in months. Er—I mean," Tariq went on hastily, "I've washed, obviously. But nobody in their right mind would take a bath in a house with the Daves. Also, I think Gay Dave lost the plug."

"What was he doing with the plug?"

"Oh, he took it off to clean it because it was kind of rusty and a bit gross. But then he forgot where he put it. And then Jewish Dave went to a hardware store to get another one, but it was the wrong size. Sorry, it's not a very exciting story really."

"You could lie and say he…I don't know. Sold it for drugs?"

"What? A bath plug? A rusty bath plug?"

Paris settled himself more comfortably against the wall. "I

suppose…I guess I just don't know very much about drugs? There were loads at school but nobody ever gave me any."

"Would you have taken them?" asked Tariq, slightly incredulously.

"Well. No. I'd have been worried I might die."

"Is there anything you *aren't* worried might kill you?"

"Um. No? But…but…drugs actually might. There's medical evidence and things."

Tariq laughed. "I'm just giving you a hard time. And honestly I don't know, because I'm not exactly Mr. Show Me Your Crack—"

"Show me your what?"

"Yeah, sorry. That came out really wrong. As you can probably tell, I know nothing about drugs either. A friend of mine thought he'd got some weed once, but it turned out to be oregano."

"Didn't he notice?"

"I don't think you and I are representative of our generation's average ability to identify herbs."

There was a silence. "Now I'm scared I'll be baking," said Paris, "and I'll try to put oregano in something, except it'll turn out to be weed."

"Oh, angel cake." Tariq's voice was warm with affection Paris was sure he didn't deserve. "Your brain is a very special buttercup."

Buttercup probably wasn't the flower Paris would have chosen. He'd have probably gone for one of those carnivorous plants with the slippery sides that insects would fall into and then drown in enzymes while they thrashed and flailed trying in vain to escape.

"I'm probably going to have to get out soon." Tariq sounded genuinely disappointed. "My toes are going wrinkly."

"I'm not going to judge your toe wrinkles."

"No, but it feels like a sign from the universe that you have bathed to the fullest extent of bathing. Also I'm losing my bubbles and a bath without bubbles is just an indoor pond."

"I can get you some more bubble bath," Paris offered, still on his best *I will give you the gift of a wonderful evening* behaviour.

"No you can't, honey. I've used it all already."

"I could ask at the front—"

Tariq cut him off with the barest hint of impatience. "Just let me leave the water. I am ready to leave the water."

"I put a towel on the towel rack for you."

"Wow." Tariq's tone conveyed a certain, not entirely undeserved, amount of scepticism. "You must have been so impressed with my focaccia."

"You did really well and I've been really bad and—"

"Okay, let's leave that there. I am appreciating the gesture and this is very nice, and I'm going to wrap myself in a toasty warm towel followed by an equally toasty warm dressing gown and then I'm coming out."

Paris hastily shuffled back into the bedroom and closed the door behind him. Through it he could hear the risey, splooshy sound of Tariq getting out of the bath and entoweling then enrobing himself. When he emerged looking clean and bright and sparkling, Paris had a hard time not staring.

"So…" Paris was pretty sure he'd been intending to start a sentence, but it took him a moment to work out how to continue it. "Room service?"

Holding his robe tight around himself, Tariq curled up on one of the beds. "Really? That runs the risk of getting *very* truffley."

The spectre of the truffles was something Paris was really hoping he'd shed at some point. He was reasonably confident that it was, in fact, okay to spend money on your boyfriend sometimes. "It's just a one-off thing, we're celebrating your victory, remember."

"Technically it was Rodney's victory."

"Well, I don't really want to share a hotel room with Rodney."

"Don't you?" Tariq lifted his brows teasingly. "He's got that whole Daddy thing going on."

"Only because he's literally somebody's daddy. Like, three people's daddy."

"Which shows he's a responsible family man."

Paris perched on the edge of the other bed, well aware that he rated a comfortable zero on the Daddy scale and was barely responsible enough to take care of his cat. "You're not really... into Rodney, are you?"

"No, you insecure muppet. I'm into *you*."

And because they were sharing a hotel room, and Tariq looked adorably fluffy, Paris just about managed to believe it. "Does this mean I can order something?"

Sadly, this made Tariq do sceptical face. "Well...okay. But keep it simple, yeah?"

"And here's me planning on lobsters and quail's eggs."

Tariq laughed. "You know lobsters aren't halal, right? It's that *water creatures that aren't fish* thing."

Should Paris have known that? He should probably have known that. And it *had* just been a joke but he still needed to do better. "Strawberries?"

"Also not fish, but strawberries would be fine."

So Paris ordered strawberries, and something fizzy that was not alcoholic. And, later, they sat on Tariq's bed with a silver dish of locally grown strawberries glistening decadently between them.

"To what I still maintain was the best focaccia," said Paris, raising his glass. And for the tiniest of moments he was by a fountain in Palermo, eating focaccia with his mother and—he crushed the memory.

Tariq lifted his own. "To coming second with style."

There was a pause while they drank and strawberried, and Paris tried not to pay too much attention to the juice shining on Tariq's lips.

"As consolation prizes go"—Tariq smiled—"this is pretty good."

He was right. And it should have been a good consolation

prize for Paris as well. After all, here he was, with his beautiful (very patient) boyfriend in a relatively luxurious room in a quite nice hotel. This was a relationship. An actual relationship. They did things together, they talked, they had fun. Tariq was only annoyed with Paris some of the time.

It was, honestly, everything Paris had always wanted.

And yet he couldn't stop thinking about his soggy focaccia dough and the soft, warm, Italian original that it mocked. Wilfred and Marianne had been fairly nice about his effort, but he'd still basically failed. Everybody watching would know that he'd failed. And they'd say *wow, he was overrated. I guess he just got lucky.*

Which…would be true?

Because it was true of kind of everything. He'd done okay at school because having no friends left plenty of time to study and he'd still only got into UCL because he was doing an unfashionable course. For that matter, he'd only got on the show because of Morag. And only stayed in the competition because the weeks he'd done badly someone else had done even worse. He was only with Tariq because…Why was he with Tariq? Or more to the point, why was Tariq with him?

Why hadn't he worked out yet that Paris Daillencourt was worth nobody's time?

"Um," said Tariq. "Are you okay? Because I am eating all of these strawberries."

Paris started. "Yes, yes, I'm fine."

"And the shell-shock stare is because?"

"I just remembered that I messed up my focaccia. So if I don't nail it tomorrow, I could go home."

There was a long silence. Tariq put down a strawberry in a manner Paris was inclined to find ominous.

"Listen, honey"—it was Tariq's ever-less-gentle gentle voice— "I get the competition is hard, and I have been in your place a bunch of times. But you'll probably be fine and if you're not fine, you've still got three wins under your belt and that's nothing to be ashamed of."

"Except people aren't going to say *that's Paris, he won three times*. They'll say *that's the guy with the soggy focaccia*."

Tariq gave the sort of huffed-out sigh that was never a good sign. "Two things. One, no they won't. Two, you sold this to me as a *let's have fun and celebrate* evening. Not a *trap Tariq in a room and make him reassure me* evening."

"Sorry. Sorry. I just—"

"And I don't want it to be a *Paris says sorry, sorry, I just* evening either. Can we not"—Tariq gazed at him, half pleadingly— "enjoy the strawberries and each other and remember that we've both been given this great opportunity and we're both doing really well with it."

"*You're* doing really well with it. I'm—"

"Oh, come on," Tariq groaned. "You did amazingly. Now you're doing slightly less amazingly but you're still amazing, and why am I still having to tell you that when the evidence is right in front of you?"

What evidence, though? That was the problem with the good stuff: it never felt real. It just slipped away like a dream about butter. Whereas all the bad stuff stuck around, digging into your skin and nagging at the back of your mind, and making you think *but what if they're right*.

Because, well, what if they were?

And, instead of being kind and pretty and worth spending time with, as Tariq believed, he was just…weird and odd looking and boring and messed up and useless and selfish and, and, and—

He took a deep breath. "I can't believe you ate that many strawberries."

"They're really nice and you were checked out for a really long time. So basically it's your own fault."

"Maybe." Paris tried to smile. "And I would feel the loss keenly if I wasn't about to order some more."

For once, Paris had unfucked something he was in the process of fucking. Grinning, Tariq pounced on the last strawberry and popped it playfully into Paris's mouth. Only slightly wary of spraying juice all over the sheets—and, worse, all over Tariq—he bit down, letting the impossible sweetness of summer rush over his tongue.

This was fine.

He could do this.

For one evening, he could pretend.

Sunday

TREMBLING AND CLUTCHING his braided loaves, Paris stumbled towards the judges. "I'm so sorry," he said. "I don't think these have come out well at all. This is all burned across here and the jam's sort of—"

Marianne Wolvercote checked him with an imperious gesture. "Why don't you tell us what you've made, Paris?"

He set his loaves reluctantly down in front of them. "This one is supposed to be spinach, mushroom, and Cambozola. And the other one is a cranberry and cheese coffee braid. But they've—"

Marianne Wolvercote gestured again and Paris fell hopelessly silent.

Meanwhile, Wilfred Honey was frowning. "Now perhaps I'm just being old-fashioned…"

"You, Wilfred?" put in Grace Forsythe. "Never."

"…but I," he went on, undeterred, "am a bit concerned about cheese and cranberry as a sweet."

Oh God. He was going out. He'd made a sweet the judges didn't think was a sweet. He was going out.

Marianne Wolvercote was reaching for her judgement fork. "Well I for one am intrigued. But shall we start with the savoury?"

Through half-closed eyes, Paris watched them carve through his loaf and sample it with a meticulous care it definitely couldn't withstand.

"I'm sorry, lad," said Wilfred Honey, finally. "There's nothing wrong with this, but I'm not getting the spinach. A blue cheese and mushroom filling is always going to hit the spot, but if you aren't careful, it's going to overpower everything else."

Paris hung his head. "I'm sorry."

"I'm afraid I agree with Wilfred," Marianne Wolvercote went on mercilessly. "This is a very serviceable loaf, and the braiding is very neat, but I do think the Cambozola has overwhelmed you rather."

And wasn't that the story of Paris's life: overwhelmed by a slightly potent cheese. He blinked back tears.

Wilfred Honey rubbed his hands encouragingly. "Let's have a go at the sweet."

Marianne Wolvercote knifed it. Then there was chewing.

"I think," she said, "I actually rather like this. It's almost like a cheesecake, which isn't quite what I was expecting. And I do find the tanginess of the cranberry nicely counterpoints the sweetness of the cream cheese."

Wilfred Honey sighed regretfully. "Sorry, but I don't agree. To me, it's neither one thing nor t'other. If it were a bit sweeter, it'd be a good sweet, and if it were a bit cheesier, it'd be a good cheese bread. As it is, I don't quite know what to make of it."

Don't quite know what to make of it was Wilfred Honey speak for *I hate this and I hate you.*

"Mmhm," said Paris. "Thanks."

He retreated to his stool and sat there with what he hoped was an appropriate camera face while the rest of the judging went by in a blur of misery. Both Rodney and Catherine Parr had done well, and Lili had done…okay? Wilfred Honey had really liked the simple homeyness of her cheese braid savoury and her Nutella (other chocolate-hazelnut spreads are available) braid sweet, but Marianne Wolvercote had thought simple had crossed the line into basic.

"I was expecting something quite a bit more artful from you," she'd said.

And Lili had nodded. "Mmhm. Thanks."

Which just left Tariq.

"So," he said, looking shiny and well rested and not at all fucked in the head, "I've made a tomato-stuffed challah and a cinnamon babka."

Marianne Wolvercote assessed the loaves before her. "You

see, I think this is simplicity done right. These are both very classic recipes but, and I'm going only by the initial presentation here, they seem to have been executed to perfection."

"The colour on that," added Wilfred Honey, drawing his fork over the undulating golden surface of Tariq's challah, "is a thing of beauty. It makes you really want to dive in and get a mouthful."

The judges dived and got.

"Flawless," said Marianne Wolvercote.

Wilfred Honey nodded, his cheeks still faintly hamstered. "Aye, that's right good that is."

The cinnamon babka was equally well received, earning a *by 'eck it's gorgeous* from Wilfred Honey, and a look of stately approval from Marianne Wolvercote.

Tariq practically bounced back to his seat.

And then they were released into the gardens for interviews and fretful around-sitting while the judges deliberated.

The judges deliberated for a very long time. Far beyond the point that the remaining contestants could make small talk with each other. Even beyond the point where Rodney ran out of anecdotes about his daughters.

And Paris, sweating in his jumper, knew he was doomed.

Eventually they were called back in and reassembled on their stools.

"Well, this was a tough one," began Grace Forsythe. "But Wilfred and Marianne have finally come to a decision."

The decision was Paris. The decision was that Paris sucked.

"The happy news is that our winner this week is somebody who has sparkled for the last six weeks and is finally beginning to shine—"

There was a ringing in Paris's ears. A roaring in his head.

"—as brightly as the sheen on his challah or the varnish on his nails. That's right: at last…it's Tariq."

Hugs were happening around Paris. He said congratulations. He was sure he said congratulations.

"But now"—Grace Forsythe adopted a pose of theatrical

sadness—"we come to the worst part of my job, which is the part where I have to tell you wonderful people and our beautiful viewers which baker won't be joining us in the semifinal."

Paris. Paris. It was Paris. Why didn't she just say it was Paris?

"Marianne and Wilfred do want me to say that this was a very, very hard decision for them but, after a long, painful discussion, they've decided that this week…"

Paris was the worst. Paris was a failure. Paris didn't deserve to be here. Paris didn't deserve anything.

"I'm sorry, Lili, but we're saying goodbye."

Paris burst into tears.

"Do you, um," asked Colin Thrimp. "Do you need a moment to calm down?"

Paris was still crying. He'd been crying for an embarrassingly long time.

"No." He gave a valiant sniff. "I can do this."

Colin Thrimp squared his shoulders. "Okay. Yes. One more try. Like you're not answering a question: How are you feeling about today?"

"I just…" Oh God. Maybe he couldn't do this. "I'm really disappointed in myself. I thought I…But I…I'm just really disappointed in myself."

It wasn't much but Colin Thrimp seemed to accept that it was all they were going to get. "Thank you," he said, and led his camera operator off to interview someone else.

Lacking the strength to walk much farther, Paris crumpled onto a nearby wall and put his head in his hands. And then time kind of lost all meaning until Tariq Tigger-pounced him.

"I won! I mean, I feel really bad for Lili. But I won!"

A cold hand was squeezing Paris's rib cage. "Yeah."

"And it's the semifinal next week. We both made the semifinal."

"Yeah."

Paris's world was still the tiny cracks of light between his fingers, but he felt Tariq move away from him. "Call me over-sensitive, but you're really not feeling this, are you?"

"I…It's just…" The spectre of rejection laid its icy fingers on Paris's shoulder. He wasn't good enough for any of this. For the competition. For his parents. For Tariq. "I did really badly."

"You did fine."

"I didn't do fine," Paris muttered. "I nearly went out."

"And I've nearly gone out multiple times."

The spectre's fingers gripped tighter. "That's different."

There was a sharp little pause. "And how is that different, honey?"

"I don't mean…I mean…you're not. I just. I was doing really well."

"Yeah, and all that time you were saying it was a fluke and you secretly sucked. You can't have it both ways."

"I'm not having it both ways. I was doing well and I thought it was a fluke and I sucked. And now I'm doing badly because it was a fluke and I suck."

"Angel cake. Please." Tariq put a soothing hand on his back. "Don't do this. It wasn't a fluke. You don't suck. You've had a couple of bad weeks is all."

For a moment Paris just let himself sit there breathing, feeling the gentle pressure of Tariq's hand through his jumper. Trying to focus on that instead of the cold. "It feels really…really hopeless, you know?"

"You're two weeks away from the final, how is that hopeless?"

"It's not that, it's…" He wasn't really sure *what* it was. Only that it was something. It was this scary, lurky, shadowy void of nothingness that sat waiting for him just the other side of failure. "I've just ruined everything. I've fucked up and I've ruined everything."

There was silence again, and perhaps it was just his brain playing tricks like it always did, but Paris thought he could feel a new tension building between them. So he screwed his eyes up tighter and looked away.

"Paris," Tariq said at last, "you know this…you know this is kind of unfair, right?"

"I'm sorry," replied Paris, entirely on reflex.

"I don't think that helps. Like…this was my week. I did really well in there."

That much was true. Because Tariq was great and Paris was shit and he didn't deserve to be with somebody like that and—"Yeah."

"And you haven't even said congratulations."

Hadn't he? He could have sworn he had. Of course there'd been a lot going on and he'd been having a lot of feelings, but he *must have*. Surely. "Congratulations."

In the darkness behind his eyelids Paris felt a rush of movement as Tariq stood up. "Really? Now? Literally the second I said it?"

Fuck. Fuck fuck fuck. He was doing this wrong. He was doing everyone wrong. He always did everything wrong. "No. I mean really. Congratulations, I meant to…I just—I thought I was going home and then I wasn't and then there were interviews and I really thought I did and, fuck, I'm sorry, you're great, you're so great and I suck so fucking much, I'm sorry I fucking suck and"—Paris had opened his eyes now and was looking up into Tariq's face. It was not the face of somebody who liked what he was hearing.

"Oh my life will you *listen* to yourself?"

"W-what do you mean?"

"I mean I know you've got"—Tariq made the *something going on with your brain* gesture that had become a kind of code between them—"and I'm really trying to make allowances for that. But I've been there for you every single time you've done well or done not so well or doubted yourself. And now that *I'm* finally"—he looked at Paris almost imploringly—"finally in with a chance you've spent the whole weekend making it all about you. And when I've said, *can we not make this all about you*, you've made the process of making it not all about you *all about you*."

"I wasn't. I didn't. I just—"

"You were. And you did. And you do."

Paris took a deep breath and tried, desperately, to be less shit. "I'm having a hard time. But I am really happy for you."

"Are you, though?" demanded Tariq. "Is there any part of you that's actually thinking *oh, I'm so proud of my boyfriend right now*? And not *oh, I suck, I'm terrible, I hate myself, and everyone else hates me too*."

There wasn't. There never was.

The enormity of Paris's shititude devoured everything, no matter how special, or important, or beautiful.

Tariq was staring at him with a kind of flat horror. "You know, you could have just said yes."

He could have, couldn't he? "I'm sorry."

"You're always sorry." Even with Paris's usual tin ear for intention, Tariq's voice sounded pained. It would have been better if he'd been angry, if he'd been shouting. Instead he just sounded like he'd been let down. Like Paris had let him down. Like Paris let everybody down.

"In case you haven't noticed, I've usually got something to be sorry for."

"How about"—Tariq twisted his hands in his hair in very visible frustration—"you solve that problem by not doing the things you have to be sorry for in the first place."

"I try but I—"

"Do you? Do you really? Because I used to think it was sweet. I used to think *there's a guy who might make the occasional mistake but always wants to do better*. And then we talked about how there's, like, a medical name for this kind of thing, and so for a while I was thinking *okay, he can be difficult sometimes but he's doing the best he can*. And now I'm starting to think you do whatever you like and make endless excuses and when it hurts someone you get so loudly, extravagantly self-loathing that people have to forgive you and that's—it's messed up, Paris. It's not okay."

"That's not what I was doing," cried Paris uselessly. Because it was, wasn't it. It was what he had always done. "I do want to be better. I just don't know how. Every time, I…It…I *fail*."

"It shouldn't be this hard, Paris. Even if you've got a genuine mental health thing, it shouldn't be this hard."

Paris should have been well out of tears by now but he apparently wasn't. "I know it shouldn't. I just don't—I don't know how to not be terrified all the time."

"Well, I don't know either. I've been trying, Paris. I've really been trying to help you."

"I know you have. It just—it hasn't helped."

"And that's the thing…Nothing helps. I know it's not your *fault*, but that doesn't change how it feels to me. Because, from where I'm standing, it's like unless everything is totally about you and going your way all the time, you fall apart. And then it's my job to put you back together, and that's…that's too much."

"Is that really what you think?" asked Paris, appalled but unsurprised. "I…I came to Birmingham. I did laser tag. I thought you liked me."

"I did. I mean, I do. I'm sorry, Paris. I can't handle this. I really wish I could."

A tiny flicker of defiance was catching inside Paris. Because there was something about this that felt like betrayal. "You said I should tell the truth. That it was important to talk about things. And now you're saying that because I did that, you don't want me anymore."

"That's not it."

Paris couldn't help feeling it was at least *partially* it.

"I…" Tariq trailed off for a moment. Then tried, "I didn't know what I was getting into. I mean, I knew you had *issues*. I just didn't expect it to be this hard this often. And maybe I was arrogant or dazzled because there were moments when it really seemed like you were changing. Like I was getting through to you, like I was helping you see that it's okay. That you're okay. But that was never going to happen, was it?"

This should have been hurting. But it was like cutting yourself on a knife so sharp that you can't feel it and so you just sit there and watch the blood and wonder what you should do about it. The worst of it wasn't even that Tariq was right; it was that Tariq was just catching up with what Paris had always known: that people could only like him for so long before they saw who he really was. "No," he said. "This is who I am."

"I know." Tariq seemed almost on the brink of tears too. "And I'm sorry. But I can't...I just can't."

Paris nodded. "Okay."

After all, nobody else could either.

Saturday

FOUR LORD WOOLTON Pies were lined up at the front of the ballroom. Paris could barely remember making his.

He was just really tired. Even though he'd been sleeping a lot.

Like, *a lot* a lot. Like, so much even Neferneferuaten had got bored and fucked off.

"The best pie," Wilfred Honey was saying, "and they're all very good, is this one."

Rodney beamed.

"The thing about a Lord Woolton Pie," Wilfred Honey continued, "is that it's made with very simple ingredients on account of the war, and so you've really got to bring the best out of them to get something flavoursome. It all comes down to love and respect for your vegetables."

Marianne Wolvercote waved a fork over the three remaining offerings. "The worst, and Wilfred's right it was very close, is this one. The pastry's just a little too thick and it's slightly underseasoned."

It was Paris's.

Obviously it was Paris's.

It was the worst because Paris was the worst.

And for some reason, it didn't even feel worth crying about.

"Are you okay?" Tariq asked, catching Paris up as he trudged back to his room.

"Yeah. Fine."

"You seem really..."

"Really what?"

"I don't know? Like..."

"Like I'm failing a baking show?"

"Like"—Tariq glittered like someone else's Christmas decorations—"you haven't slept for a week?"

"So I'm failing a baking show and I look like shit?"

He sighed. "Honey, I just wanted to make sure you were all right."

"I thought I was too much for you to deal with."

"It doesn't mean I don't care about you. I just couldn't have you in my head all the time."

"Well. The good news is you don't have to. I'm going out this week."

"You say that every week. You even said that on the weeks you won."

Paris shrugged.

There was a long silence.

"Why do you even care?" Tariq asked. "You're only in the competition because of your housemate. You seem to hate being here. I've never actually seen any signs you like baking. Or want to win. So it feels like you staying in the competition isn't fair on you because it's genuinely bad for your mental health, and it's not fair on the rest of us because we fought to be here."

Paris had, at some point in the intangible past, liked baking. He had even, he thought, wanted to be there. Some private part of him, after Morag said *so I signed you up for that fucking baking thing you're always on about because I knew you were too much of a prick to do it yourself*, had thought *oh, that will be nice*. Except it had gone now, like the part of him that remembered how to feel things. That knew how to make Tariq smile. How to make his parents come back. "Sorry," he said.

"Don't say sorry." Tariq threw his hands in the air. "Say... literally anything except sorry. Just—*please*." The look in his eyes was unbearable, a kind of begging look laced with the beginnings of anger. "Stop shutting down on me. Do you...like...Is it because you already have everything that you can't want anything? Did you even want me?"

Paris was going to say yes, but it felt like a trap.

Because wanting things meant losing them.

"Well," said Tariq. "Thanks. Guess that answers that one."

Sunday

"THESE," PARIS SAID, trembling, "are a Kentish pasty main and a plum charlotte. They're both wartime recipes and—yeah."

Marianne Wolvercote looked over Paris's bakes. "Well they're very simple, but that's to be expected from the wartime theme. And I think your plum charlotte has caught *just a little*."

Had it? Fuck. It had. Paris was normally so careful about this kind of thing, and normally had such an eye for imperfections that having one pointed out that he'd missed felt like a fist in the gut.

"I'm being picky," she continued, "but it *is* the semifinal."

Wilfred Honey twinkled soothingly. "I really like that you've done a stale bread recipe. Back in t'days of rationing it was all about waste not, want not, and if your bread went stale, you found something to do with it."

"Shall we start with the pasties?" Without waiting for a reply, Marianne Wolvercote started with the pasties. "So this is just rice, cheese, and carrot, is that right?"

Paris nodded miserably.

She chewed carefully. "I think it's actually very good. It's austere but the flavours are coming through well."

"And," added Wilfred Honey, "it'd definitely fill you up on a cold day."

They moved on to the charlotte.

"Again," said Marianne Wolvercote, "I think this is well done. Obviously there's no spicing because, correct me if I'm wrong, Wilfred, you wouldn't really have been able to get spices."

Wilfred Honey nodded. "That you wouldn't."

"But you've balanced the fruit and your small allotment of sugar exactly right so the sweetness takes the edge off the tartness and it comes together as something quite pleasing."

"Takes me right back this does." Wilfred Honey was smiling. "It looks comforting, it tastes comforting, it's very comforting food."

Not quite sure how to feel, Paris gave a noncommittal head bob.

The judges had been deliberating for a really long time again. Or maybe it just felt like a really long time. Because, with the too much sleep or the no sleep, Paris had no sense of anything. The world was ebbing and flowing around him like he was looking out to sea or standing at the top of a very tall building and trying not to think about falling.

He had a sense he'd done badly. But Tariq was right: he always had a sense he'd done badly.

And in some ways, he was almost hoping he had. Because then maybe he'd be able to stop worrying about doing badly.

Except it never worked like that.

It just meant that instead of dwelling on something that might happen, he'd have to live with something that had.

He'd always known Tariq would see through him, get sick of him, leave him. But when he finally did, that hadn't made it hurt any less.

"...a man"—Grace Forsythe's voice finally battered through the dense fug around Paris's brain—"who gave us an amazing Lord Woolton Pie, surprisingly unvinegary vinegar cake, and of course another splendid cardigan. Congratulations, Rodney. You are this week's winner."

There was a round of hugs and back pats and well dones, and Paris tried very, very hard to participate, even though his hands felt like they were attached to someone else's arms.

Grace Forsythe detached herself from the celebratory group hug. "And now we have the hardest moment in perhaps the whole show. The moment when I have to name the one person who isn't coming with us to the final. And I'm sorry to say that after a long, wonderful journey in which he's produced some amazing bakes, and brought real joy to the ballroom, Wilfred and Marianne have decided that it's time to say goodbye…"

She paused. And the pause echoed endlessly in that vast gilt-and-marble chamber.

"…to Paris."

Sunday

THE LAST EPISODE of a series of *Bake Expectations* always brought the contestants—all the contestants—and their friends and families back together for a big party in celebration of the finalists and, eventually, of the winner.

Paris's family hadn't come, of course. He'd told his parents about it, but they'd been off somewhere exotic and wonderful while he was here, limping back to Patchley House one last time to look from the outside at everything he'd lost and everything he was missing out on.

The day was too hot, the sunlight too bright. And when it was over, all Paris could remember was that his jumper had been too scratchy and that he'd said some things to some people, some of them with cameras.

Then Morag came to pick him up.

In the car, on the way home, he was too tired even to cry.

Autumn

EPISODE 1

Biscuits

💬 ♡ ↻ BAKING IS NOT A CONTACT SPORT. #bakeexpectations

💬 ♡ ↻ Oh why are the pretty ones always so dumb? #bakeexpectations

💬 ♡ ↻ If the one Bangladeshi in the competition goes out because a white guy hit him in the face with a fridge I will ... completely unsurprised. #bakeexpectations

💬 ♡ ↻ If Tanya doesn't win this whole thing I'm not paying my licence fee next year #bakeexpectations

💬 ♡ ↻ im just gona say it paris can hit me with a fridge any time #bakeexpectations #gotohornyjail

💬 ♡ ↻ A Muslim drag queen talking about the environment is peak BBC. #bakeexpectations

💬 ♡ ↻ I really want to fuck Paris. At first, it was because I thought he was hot. Now I just kinda want to make his arse hurt. #bakeexpectations

○ ♡ ↺ Loving Catherine Parr. Great name, great no fucks
attitude #bakeexpectations

○ ♡ ↺ why is everybody being so nice to paris when the shy
thing is so clearly an act #bakeexpectations

○ ♡ ↺ if we have to watch eight weeks of a pretty boy crying
over biscuits I'll resent it but also kind of get off on it
#bakeexpectations

○ ♡ ↺ Can everybody stop defending Paris. If a woman
acted like that you'd all hate her. #bakeexpectations

○ ♡ ↺ Paris is that guy you spent weeks psyching yourself
up to ask out and then immediately discovered was a
self-centred prick #bakeexpectations

○ ♡ ↺ Calling it now: Paris is going to whine his way through
to the final and I'm going to hate every second of it
#bakeexpectations

○ ♡ ↺ paris is a twat #bakeexpectations

BERNARD HAD INVITED EVERYBODY to the viewing party
because of course he had. And he'd done it far enough in advance
that even though he lived in Kenilworth—a place the internet
had called "a boring town full of old people"—Paris hadn't been
able to think of a good reason to say no. It had even seemed sort
of a nice idea about three months ago when the competition had
felt very real and immediate, instead of something strange and
distant he'd done for reasons that still escaped him and he was
now trying to forget.

Not that he'd be able to forget with his face being all over
the TV for eight weeks and all over the internet after that. And
then on Netflix and then not on Netflix until public outrage put
it back on Netflix.

Paris was trudging along a narrow, privet-lined street surrounded by interchangeably neat redbrick houses and cars that

people had been forced to park half on the pavement to avoid blocking the road. It felt suburban even though there was no particular urb for it to sub, and it was slightly disorientating to remember England was full of places like this instead of places like London. Probably he shouldn't have come. It had been a long journey, and he hadn't really stayed in contact with anyone or done anything interesting since the show. So what was he going to say? *Hi, it's me, I'm still me, sorry about everything.* Maybe he should just turn round. He'd told Bernard he'd be there, but nobody would actually miss him.

Then a familiar blue car drove past and Paris wanted to vomit. Or die. Or both. Or at the very least run away back to London. Or the moon. They were sending people to the moon now, weren't they?

The car stopped a little farther on and started doing that awkward shuffle between the kerb and road that you got when the driver had done parallel parking to pass their test but hadn't done it anywhere near often enough to be competent at it. Paris put his head down and tried to walk past quickly, hoping that sheer social discomfort might magically render him invisible.

"Are you actually going to totally blank me?" Tariq had wound the window down and was now comprehensively disproving the invisibility theory.

Paris paused. "What? No. I just thought maybe you wouldn't want me to..."

"Can you at least spot me while I park?"

Paris was still terrified of spotting people while they parked in case he did it wrong and made them hate him. But Tariq hated him anyway so... what did he have to lose? "All right. Um, back a bit?"

The car went back a bit.

Paris made the universal *move your car this way* gesture. That palm-up beckoning motion like you were goading your opponent in a martial arts movie or massaging the testicles of a moose. "Um, back a bit?"

The car went back a bit.

"Forward a bit?"

The car went forward a bit.

"Back a bit. Forward a bit. Back a bit."

"Paris." Tariq stuck his head out the window again. "I'm getting déjà vu and I'm not moving."

What had he expected? It had only been three months. Did he imagine Paris would have miraculously transformed into a functioning human being in the interim? "I know. I'm just really worried about damaging your car."

Although Paris couldn't quite see, he was sure Tariq was rolling his eyes. "This car cost me six hundred quid because my uncle had a friend whose son was going to university and couldn't take it with him."

"What if I damage a different car?"

"Well, given the alternative is that I spend the rest of my life rolling two millimetres forward and then two millimetres back, you might have to risk the jail time."

"Jail time?" squeaked Paris before he could stop himself. It had been a joke, and he'd known it was a joke, but between coming to Kenilworth and seeing Tariq again and knowing that in less than twenty minutes he'd be broadcast live to the nation, he didn't have the energy.

"Oh for..." Tariq let out the long expressive sigh he used in place of swearing. "I can't believe I used to think this was cute."

"If it helps, I can't believe you thought it was cute either."

"Oddly enough, it doesn't help. It just makes me feel like the whole thing was a massive waste of both our time. Now go inside and I'll see you when the show starts."

There were a lot of things Paris wanted to say. Most of them were *sorry*. But some of them were *I know I fucked up* and *I don't think I wasted my time* and *I miss you*. Unfortunately, what came out of his mouth was "But I haven't helped you park yet."

"Yeah. In case you haven't figured it out, I know when something isn't working." The worst of it was, Tariq didn't sound angry or even sad. Just crushingly matter-of-fact. "Seriously, it's fine. Please go."

So Paris went.

The party, such as it was, was already swinging, such as it swung, when Paris showed up, hoping he didn't look as rubbish as he felt. Bernard's living room—which was about as chintzy as a living room could possibly be—was already quite full. For a start it included Bernard's dad, who looked like someone had put Bernard through one of those aging filters you got on Snapchat and was ensconced in an armchair with the air of a man who would fight to the death anyone who tried to take him out of it. But it also included an intimidating number of Paris's former co-bakers.

Joan had taken the only other armchair and was looking like she'd fight to keep it as hard as Bernard Senior would fight to keep his. Tanya was flopped comfortably on one end of the sofa while Lili lounged on a pouffe beside her. It was sort of odd to see them again. What was odder, though, was that Gretchen had shown up.

"Paris," she called up from ground level, having apparently chosen to sit both on the floor and in the lotus position. "Your aura is looking incredibly clogged. Let me give you the number of my crystologist."

"Thanks. I'll…I'll see about unclogging as soon as I can."

She gazed at him earnestly. "No, you really should. It's severely disrupting your chi."

"Sorry." Paris stepped carefully round her and lowered himself onto the sofa, trying to sit far enough from Tanya that he wasn't impinging on her personal space, but not so far away that she'd think he found her repulsive. "Sorry if my chi is…is bad."

Lili had that exasperated look that said *I really wish I could let this go but it will only get worse if I do*. "That's not how chi works."

"Actually," said Gretchen, "I've got a degree in traditional healing practices, so I think I know how chi works."

"Okay, but I'm, you know, Chinese. And it's kind of a thing in my culture."

Before Gretchen could defend the authenticity of her incorrect beliefs about Asian philosophy, Bernard bounced through the door bearing a baking tray upon which lay a pair of braided yeast loaves. "So this is what I would have done if I'd made it to bread week. There's one sweet and one savoury, and I won't lie, I went a bit wild and pushed the boat out because the savoury one's got rosemary in it."

"Rosemary?" exclaimed Bernard's dad from his armchair. "What do you think this is, a French cathouse?"

Bernard cast him a look of loving mortification. "Stop embarrassing me, Dad. I keep telling you, you have to move with the times."

"Well, all right. I'll try it this once, but I don't want you to be getting any ideas. Remember what happened with the spaghetti bolognaise."

"What happened with the spaghetti bolognaise?" asked Joan.

"Ooh." Bernard winced. "We don't talk about it."

"Not ever," added his dad.

There was a pause as bread was sliced and buttered and passed around. The guests were just in the middle of reassuring Bernard that yes it had come out well and no the rosemary didn't make everything taste like an explosion in a soap factory when Tariq came in.

At which point the gargantuan strategic error in Paris's decision to take the second-to-last seat on the only item of furniture with seats remaining became starkly apparent. And for a moment they were staring at each other, locked in the same bleak calculus of social awkwardness. Because while Tariq could have gone and sat somewhere else—on the floor, or a windowsill, or Bernard's dad's lap—it would have looked incredibly pointed.

Apparently deciding he had no choice but to tolerate Paris for the forty-seven minutes or so the show would run, Tariq claimed the middle seat of the sofa. Which put him close. Like two and a half sandwiches close. Like *I am remembering touching you and kissing you and the violet notes of your cologne* close.

"Oh, there you are, Tariq," said Bernard, immediately proffering a slice of rosemary bread. "I was beginning to think you'd got lost."

"Trouble parking."

Tariq's tone was probably neutral. But Paris read rebuke into it anyway. He was about to apologise, but he was cut off by an announcement from the suddenly unmuted TV.

"—xt on BBC Two, a brand-new series of *Bake Expectations*."

"It's starting, everyone," called out Bernard, putting down his tray and flicking off the lights.

And then the room filled up with the familiar theme music as cameras rolled across the British countryside before hovering over Patchley House. It seemed impossible just then for Paris to believe he'd actually been there.

"It's time," said Grace Forsythe's mellifluous voice-over, "for a fresh batch of bakers to brave the ballroom…"

It cut to Bernard and the whole room erupted in cheers. "I think it'll be all right." He squinted towards the camera. "I'm just hoping I don't go out in week one."

Real Bernard was staring at himself without recognition. "Oh my God. Does my voice really sound like that?"

"Yes," Joan told him.

"Crumbs."

"Well I've been baking my whole life…" Catherine Parr had popped up onscreen.

"Really?" exclaimed Lili from her pouffe. "Because she never mentioned it."

Catherine, thankfully present only on television, had folded her arms. "I suppose I just don't have much tolerance for nonsense."

Tariq already had his phone out. "Well, in a characteristic display of poor taste, Twitter loves her."

"Already?" Bernard looked a little shell-shocked. "She's only been onscreen for eight seconds."

"Edgy grandmas are always popular," Tariq told him. "It's that *tells it like it is* thing that's code for—"

"—'racist as fuck,'" finished Lili.

Paris was having trouble concentrating on the show. He was just very…aware of Tariq beside him. The curl of his eyelashes in the light from the TV. The dance of his fingers over his phone screen. The horrible mixture of attraction and uncertainty that, now that he thought about it, characterised most of Paris's relationships.

"Actually," a version of Paris was saying from the television, "my flatmate entered me. And she knows nothing about baking, so I'm probably not supposed to be here."

Oh God. He was too tall. And his hair was too red. And that jumper had felt really comforting at the time, but it made him look like he'd been knitted by somebody's aunt. This was such a bad idea. Except it was a bad idea that had happened months ago. And had now been immortalised by the BBC.

"Aaaand," announced Tariq, "here come the thirst tweets."

Bernard frowned in gentle confusion. "Well, it's not really started yet. If they're thirsty, they've still got time to make a cup of tea."

"Two sugars in mine, if you're making," added Bernard's dad.

A brief silence settled over the room as the company tried to decide who would explain the vernacular usage of *thirst* to Bernard.

In the end, Lili's art school background gave her the requisite lack of fucks. "He means," she said, patiently, "that lots of people want to bang Paris."

"To be fair they're not saying *bang*," Tariq added. "They're mostly saying *lick*. Or doing suggestive baking puns."

"What sort of suggestive baking puns?" asked Joan with the air of somebody who found puns inherently suspicious.

"Oh, you know, *he can stick his roulade in my oven anytime, I wouldn't mind scraping the fondant off his spatula*, that kind of thing."

Joan leaned back in her armchair. "This is why I'm not on social media."

Paris was beginning to think he should probably get off it himself.

"That doesn't even make sense," Bernard was saying. "Because you don't put a roulade in an oven."

"Yes you do." Tanya was weighing in now, and Paris wasn't sure if this was a good thing or a bad thing. "You bake the meringue, then you roll it up."

This didn't seem to convince Bernard. "Oh, you put the *meringue* in the oven obviously. But in my view that's not a roulade, it's just part of a roulade. It's not a roulade until it's assembled."

"Also"—fuck, now Lily was getting involved—"if the roulade is supposed to represent Paris's penis, something wide and flat that's going to get filled with cream and then bent into a spiral—"

"Oh look," Paris said more loudly and squeakily than he'd intended, "the blind bake is starting."

The camera cut away to Marianne Wolvercote explaining that chocolate chip cookies were a deceptively challenging bake because they were very simple so there was nothing to hide behind.

Against his better judgement, Paris slipped out his own phone and started scrolling through the feeds of some of the show's more prolific live tweeters. And people did seem...okay with him? In a slightly licking-focused way but he could live with that. After all, it would be worse if they *didn't* want to lick him, wouldn't it? Maybe? Probably.

Then he opened a fridge door into Tariq's face, and the internet exploded.

Not in a bad way. At least not totally in a bad way. Although Paris winced to remember the experience, it didn't seem to have earned him the immediate ire of a vengeful nation—it wasn't like that time in season five when that woman had knocked that guy's trifle on the floor, then insisted it was his fault for putting it on the end of the bench.

"I'm sorry about the fridge," said Paris.

Tariq spared him a look that would once have been indulgent. "And I told you to drop it. Three months ago."

"To be fair"—unlike the rest of them Joan was actually paying attention to the show—"it actually made pretty good TV."

Illuminated by the glow of her phone screen, Lili was scrolling rapidly. "I think Tanya Saves the Day might be trending."

Tanya grinned. "Oh good, I'll have something to talk to my form group about."

The blind bake finished, cutting to a short round of interviews during which Paris mostly managed to watch himself without wanting to die, and then the baketacular kicked off.

"I'm making bees," said TV Tariq, smiling at the camera in a way he'd once smiled at Paris. "Because I think they're great. I mean, who doesn't love bees? They dance and they make honey, honey. And they're also increasingly endangered because of...I think either climate change or industrial farming? So, y'know. Appreciate your bees while you can."

And Paris drowned in sad. Because the man who liked bees had also briefly liked him. Before he fucked it all up.

"Oof." Real Tariq flinched away from his phone. "That did not go down well in Middle England. Someone with a column in the *Daily Mail* just said *A Muslim drag queen talking about the environment is peak BBC.* I'm not a drag queen, you herrenvolk hack."

"To be fair," Lili said. "It's pretty impressive that they managed to be racist, condescending, and wrong in eleven words."

Tariq rolled his eyes. "If you ask me, they're slipping. They could easily have got in a dig about single mums and Meghan Markle at the same time."

"I'm sorry, Tariq." Bernard offered some consolatory rosemary bread. "I just don't understand all this twittering and what have you. What was it Mum used to say, Dad?"

"*We've arrived and to prove it we're here*?" said Bernard's dad.

"Well, she did say that. But she also said *if you can't say something nice, don't say anything.*" He turned his attention back to the television, where his broadcast alter ego was telling the camera that, while he didn't like to blow his own horn, he thought his biscuits had come out quite well thank you.

"Shortbread on shortbread is also trending." Lili was still monitoring the internet.

Bernard patted his dad gently on the shoulder. "To this day, I will stand by two types of shortbread counting as two types of biscuit."

"I think what's really important"—that was Gretchen, who had been mostly meditating over the episode—"is that you know your own mind."

The room gave a collective wince as, on the screen, her giving hands collapsed into a pile of dust.

"Ow." Tanya made a sound of pained empathy. "It's a lot worse when you watch it back, isn't it?"

Tariq laughed. "Well, normally when you burn your biscuits or knock your cake over, you don't do it in slow motion with ominous music playing over it."

Sometimes Paris felt his whole life was in slow motion with ominous music playing over it.

"I'm at peace," said Gretchen. "All I wanted to do was put love into the universe and I did."

Bernard leaned forward with the doomed sincerity of someone determined to be helpful. "I think the problem was, you put your love in the oven for a bit too long."

"Or," Tariq added perhaps out of belated revenge for the Reiki, "you overworked your love, which was why Wilfred Honey couldn't eat it."

Joan folded one leg over the other. "No, it was a structural issue. The weight was too far forward. So there was far too much torque at the wrists."

"I'm at peace," repeated Gretchen, somewhat less peaceably.

It was strange watching the judging having lived through it—not least because it had taken several hours to film and then been elegantly edited down to about eight and a half minutes of screen time. Paris's biscuits, now that he had a bit of distance from them, actually did look all right. And toxic masculinity aside, he was beginning to wish he'd cried less. He was just about to check his phone, to see what Twitter thought of his biscuits roses de Reims, when Tariq put a hand over his hand.

"Honey. I wouldn't."

Oh God. What had happened. Was it the fridge thing? Had the fridge thing finally caught up with him? "What?" Paris asked wildly. "Why?"

"You know the internet. Everything's either the best thing in the world or the worst thing in the world."

A cold liquid weight had settled in Paris's stomach. "I'm the worst thing in the world?"

"Only until the next milkshake duck comes along."

"But...but I haven't done anything wrong. I mean, apart from hitting you in the face, and you said that was fine."

Tariq seemed to be trying to frame something insulting in a non-insulting way. "It's the law of reality TV. Whoever wins didn't deserve it. Anyone who's a bit confident is arrogant. Anyone who's not confident is whiny and attention seeking."

This wasn't helping. It was just making him imagine all the horrible things people might be saying. And when it came to imagining horrible things, Paris had years of practice.

So he looked. How bad could it be?

"I might," Paris said. "Um. Sorry. But I think I..."

And with that he crept outside to cry in the street.

EPISODE 2

Pastry

💬 ♡ ⇄ Bernard is the hero this country needs.
#bakeexpectations

💬 ♡ ⇄ What is it that makes Paris's face so uniquely
punchable? #bakeexpectations

💬 ♡ ⇄ My husband and I had our honeymoon in Paris. Those
memories are now ruined. #bakeexpectations

💬 ♡ ⇄ Amazing how much better Tariq does when you don't
hit him with a fridge #bakeexpectations

💬 ♡ ⇄ Women like Catherine Parr won us the war.
#bakeexpectations

💬 ♡ ⇄ I still want to fuck Paris but I think it might be
because I hate myself nearly as much as I hate him
#bakeexpectations

💬 ♡ ⇄ why are the judges spending so much time
reassuring a whiny prick #bakeexpectations

🗨 ♡ 🔁　I know he's married but can I marry Rodney anyway?
#bakeexpectations

🗨 ♡ 🔁　I really hope Paris isn't gay because if he is he's setting
us back decades #bakeexpectations

🗨 ♡ 🔁　its unfair. when Massimo dropped a lemon tart it got
a Michelin star #bakeexpectations

🗨 ♡ 🔁　Sing it with me: Ooh-ah, Catherine Parr, I say ooh-ah
Catherine Parr #oohahcatherineparr #bakeexpectations

🗨 ♡ 🔁　On tonight's episode we are shown a Muslim drag
queen making a Jewish donut. #bakeexpectations
#peakbbc

🗨 ♡ 🔁　i am officially upgrading paris from twat to megatwat
#bakeexpectations

PARIS DID NOT GO to Bernard's for the week two viewing party. Nor did he watch the show. He did, however, watch Twitter.

"Are you crying in there?" Morag pounded on the door. "Are you wanking in there? Is it both? Are you cranking? Are you cranking over social media?"

This idea was so repellent that Paris felt compelled to deny it. Though the crack in his voice made it very clear he had, at least, been crying.

"Put your cock away. I'm coming in."

"My cock is already away," Paris insisted as Morag burst into his room and flicked the light on. "I mean, it wasn't out in the first place."

Morag sat on the end of his bed and snatched up his phone. "Stop looking at it."

"But it's like a spider. I'll know it's there."

For a moment, Morag scrolled lazily through the show's hashtag. Then she switched the phone off and skimmed it across the floor underneath the wardrobe. "It's just a bunch of fucking arseholes on the internet."

"And they all think *I'm* an arsehole."

"Well, you are." She waved an imperious hand in his direction. "Look at you."

Pulling a crumpled tissue from his sleeve, Paris blew his nose. "That's not helping."

"Why not? You want someone to tell you how shit you are, I can do it without using up your data allowance."

"I don't want someone to tell me how shit I am."

"You act like you do. Your last Google search was for *Paris is a wanker.*"

"I just need to know."

She wrinkled her brow at him. "What? If you're a wanker?"

"No. If people think I'm a wanker."

"Of course people think you're a wanker. Someone thinks everyone's a wanker. I think Judi Dench is a wanker."

Paris stared at her, aghast. "How can Dame Judi Dench be a wanker? She's a national treasure."

"In my book, anybody within ten miles of that fucking cat movie is a wanker. Judi Dench: wanker. Taylor Swift: wanker. Ian McKellen: double wanker."

"Why," asked Paris, knowing he would regret it, "is Sir Ian McKellen a double wanker?"

"He got a contact wanker from working with Ricky Gervais."

"Is there anybody you don't think is a wanker?"

"No, that's my whole fucking point. People will say you're a wanker whether you deserve it or not. That's their right. Not giving a shit is yours."

Paris picked up his novelty strawberry-shaped cushion that went by the inventive name of Strawberry and squeezed it needily. "I can't just decide what to give a shit about."

"Yes you can, you damp Saxon fuckstain. Now get out of bed, it's your turn to make dinner."

It was a lie. He'd made dinner yesterday. And it was a self-serving lie because he was a substantially better cook than Morag. But it was also, in its way, a kind lie, because she knew cooking distracted him. After a little more cajoling he was up, mostly dry-eyed, and standing in their kitchen area chopping mushrooms.

"I'm sorry," he said eventually.

"Unless you're sorry that you're making me eat a fucking mushroom risotto like I'm a fucking plant, then stop it."

For a weird moment, Paris felt the instinctive urge to reach into his wallet for a ten-pence piece. "Why do you think plants eat risotto?"

"I was just being colourful, don't change the subject. You were about to say that you know you've been shit for the past three months, and we are *definitely* talking about that."

Honestly Paris suspected he'd been shit for a lot longer than three months, but that wasn't a conversation worth having. "What's there to talk about?"

"What we're going to do about it."

Paris transferred his mushrooms into a bowl and started boiling a kettle. "There's nothing I *can* do. I just—I tried to do a thing, and the thing didn't go well and now I'm just trying to focus on uni and—"

"And bingeing the internet until you literally puke. It's not good for you."

The kettle clicked off, and Paris poured boiling water over the mushrooms. "So what do I do?"

Morag, at Paris's direction, found the stock cubes and tossed one over to him. "I don't know. Fucking talk to somebody, fucking talk to *me*. Talk to him off the show you had that thing with."

"He wouldn't want to." Paris had gone very still. "He was at the watch party and—"

Having made her one contribution to the cooking process, Morag dragged an armchair from the sitting space into the kitchen space and flopped into it. "Oh fuck me, is *that* what this is about? I thought you'd been unusually pathetic this week."

"He hates me," Paris said. "And now the whole internet agrees with him."

"He didn't seem like the hating type to me. And if—and honestly this is pretty fucking likely—you've done something to piss him off, I'm sure he'll forgive you if you stop being such a prick about things."

Paris began chopping an onion, which at least gave him an excuse for crying again. "I don't think he will."

"Why? What did you do? Did you fuck his cat or punch his dad?"

"No. He doesn't have a cat."

"But if he had, you would have fucked it?" He couldn't see Morag's face because onions and tears. But he could well imagine her expression. "Paris, that's a much bigger problem."

"I just mean I didn't do anything. I *wouldn't* do anything. It's just—he just—we just…"

From the sound of the leather, Morag was leaning forward in her chair. "You just what?"

"Lots of small things? Maybe. I—I don't really know."

"So," she asked, "you broke up with someone and you don't know why?"

"I know why. It's because I'm rubbish and he saw I was rubbish and he couldn't cope with it anymore."

Morag heaved an exasperated sigh. "You're not rubbish. You're just…who you are?"

"Which"—Paris attacked a clove of garlic with a dangerously sharp knife—"is rubbish. I see it, Tariq saw it, the whole nation sees it. The only reason Neferneferuaten doesn't see it is because she's a cat. And, frankly, a lot of the time she'd rather be on her own too."

There was a long silence. "And what about me?"

"Honestly? I don't know. Maybe it's because I buy all the food and don't charge you much rent."

There was an even longer silence. "Sorry, did you just call me a fucking freeloader?"

"No. But right now, I legitimately can't see what the fuck else you're getting from this relationship."

She stood up. "You know what? Sometimes neither can I."

A few minutes later, he heard the front door slam.

EPISODE 3

"American"

💬 ♡ ⇄   I can't believe Paris won again. #bakeexpectations

💬 ♡ ⇄   Is it just me or does Marianne Wolvercote seriously want to fuck paris? #bakeexpectations

💬 ♡ ⇄   I want Catherine to be my nan. She's bad ass. #oohahcatherineparr #bakeexpectations

💬 ♡ ⇄   American here. Our food isn't like that. It's weird you guys think it is. #bakeexpectations

💬 ♡ ⇄   If marriane doesn't want to fuck paris can i fuck paris #bakeexpectations

💬 ♡ ⇄   Are they trying to ship Tariq and Paris? That had better just be editing #bakeexpectations #tariqcandobetter

💬 ♡ ⇄   So Paris's shy and innocent act was bullshit.:shocked pikachu face: #bakeexpectations

💬 ♡ ⇄   Hey did anyone else see this picture of Paris collapsed in the street? #bakeexpectations

American here. Tell me bread and butter pudding isn't a real thing. #bakeexpectations

Paris clearly knows he's winning the show. He's not even pretending any more #bakeexpectations

I want to tie Paris up, lick butterscotch off his naked body and then punch him in his smug annoying mouth #bakeexpectations

Why is nobody talking about how great Rodney is. Rodney is the best and none of yall fuckers have taste. #bakeexpectations #fuckyeahguysinknitwear

Things I am doing this weekend. Making bread and peanut butter pudding. Nothing else. #bakeexpectations

ive just realised paris looks like jolene if jolene was a man and a complete twat #bakeexpectations

PARIS COULDN'T QUITE REMEMBER what had led him to the YouTube channel loosely attached to the ITV breakfast show *Each Morning*. It could have been a tweet or one of those emails about publicity he sometimes got from the BBC, or maybe Google had told him he might be interested. But there he was, watching regular presenter Morgan Pearson in conversation with *Daily Mail* columnist Christopher Hawkins on a video called *Is the BBC Racist Against White People?*

"Because fundamentally," Hawkins was saying, "the Muslim drag queen went on a baking show and didn't bake anything. Whereas Joan, an ordinary, hardworking white woman who has nobody standing up for her rights or her interests, got eliminated because the BBC doesn't want a fatwah placed on Wilfred Honey or to have the whole show cancelled by the gay mafia."

Morgan Pearson laughed. "I think that's a fair concern, Chris. And you've got to remember the BBC is supposed to be a publicly funded service that provides for the needs of all British people and doesn't pander to special-interest groups."

"You're absolutely right, Morg—"

Paris slammed down the lid of his laptop. He was shaking and he wasn't quite sure why. After all, it wasn't his place to get upset because the sorts of people who always said those sorts of things were saying those sorts of things about Tariq.

In a fit of self-soothing or self-loathing, he opened up iPlayer and found last night's episode of *Bake Expectations*. He flipped to a random point in the middle, and there was Tariq, standing by Paris's bench, smiling and sparkling and doing his terrible impression of Wilfred Honey.

And then Paris was looking at himself looking at Tariq. And then he had to slam the lid of his laptop down again because he was crying.

When he thought back, all he could remember was being terrified, and being terrified of failing, except onscreen he just seemed...happy. Laughing with Tariq like he didn't have a care in the world.

It was probably the wrong thing to do, but he put his laptop aside, pulled out his phone, and called Tariq.

"Um...hello?" said Tariq, with intimidating wariness. "Is everything okay?"

"Yes, I mean no, I mean—"

Tariq sighed. "Never change, honey, never change."

"I'm sorry," Paris yelped.

And then Tariq just laughed.

"I...I saw, you know, I saw the clip."

"Which clip?"

"The one from *Each Morning*."

"Still not narrowing it down."

"The one with him from the *Daily Mail*, where he said—"

"Yeah," Tariq interrupted. "I know what he said."

Paris flailed silently for a second or two. "I...I was wondering if you were okay. Or if you wanted someone to talk to."

There was a deeply ambivalent sound from the other end of the line. "Angel cake, I...It's nice you want to save me from the racists? But that's kind of not what I need from you."

"What do you need from me?" asked Paris, in a sudden frenzy that felt like hope.

"I *needed* you to be my boyfriend. Not just someone who used me for emotional support, couldn't say he wanted to be with me, and then disappeared."

"But I did want to be with you."

"Then where were you when I won in bread week? Where were you after the final? Where've you been ever since?"

"I didn't know how to—"

"I get that. But this isn't how to. If there's one thing my twenty years as a gay Muslim has equipped me to deal with, it's exactly this kind of nonsense."

"And you're really okay?" asked Paris, who couldn't deal with that one guy who kept calling him a twat on Twitter, much less a major news organisation as good as calling him a terrorist.

"Not really, no. It sucks. It's not fair, it's not right, I hate it. But I am who I am, I'm not ashamed and I'm not afraid, and I've got people in my life who'll back me up." There was a horrible silence. "And I'm sorry, Paris, but you had a chance to be one of them, and you blew it."

"Can I...can I unblow it?"

There was another silence. Of at least equivalent horribleness. "I appreciate that you want to try but, right now, I don't see how you could."

"Oh."

And then Tariq was gone.

And Morag was still staying with friends.

And Neferneferuaten was hiding under Morag's bed and wouldn't come out.

I'm kind of having a bit of a hard time, Paris texted his parents. **I really need to hear from you. Please call or text or something.**

"Um," said Paris, squirming in his chair, "so I was, um, thinking of, um, the rhetoric of the extraordinary. In Greek poetry."

Dr. Laughlin looked quizzically at him over her half-rimmed glasses. "Go on."

"Well…" He could do this. He knew this. He'd studied this. Then he'd taken two months off to obsess about baking instead. And now people were calling him a twat on the internet basically every day. "It's about…"

"Were I a more cynical person," Dr. Laughlin continued, "I might think that you'd picked a title that sounded grandiose without actually being able to define it."

His supervisor's office was modern and brightly decorated, but at that moment it seemed to be closing in on Paris rapidly. "No. I mean maybe. I mean I do have—I wanted it to sound right but—it's about divinity."

"Divinity is it now?" Dr. Laughlin was popular in the department, Paris knew—Morag thought she was great, although Morag had unusual taste in people—but he'd always found her terrifying.

"Or immortality?"

"Immortality?" Her eyebrow had stayed raised throughout this exchange, but it now inched just fractionally higher.

Shutting his eyes to block out the sensory overload, Paris tried a few calming breaths. "In"—*breathe*—"in modern western thought"—*keep breathing*—"we see immortality as about just *not dying.*"

"That is quite a big part of the definition, yes."

"But in classical thought immortality is the same as divinity. It's the same as…as extraordinariness." Unbidden his thoughts turned to Tariq smiling at him in the summer light, in a different life. In a world made immortal by the theogonies of set lights and cameras.

Dr. Laughlin tapped some notes into her laptop. "Well it seems like you have some interesting ideas. But right now they feel very scattered."

That was probably the least surprising thing anybody had ever said to Paris, other than *fuck off, I hate you.* Scattered was the default state of his everything. "I think that might be right."

"Some of my colleagues have been saying you're not yourself this term."

"Not myself?" Paris's breath caught.

"You've been distracted, you've been quiet, and you've obviously not been doing the reading. This is probably a bit late, but do you think going on that baking show was the right idea?"

He didn't. It clearly hadn't been. And it hadn't even been *his* idea. It had been Morag's idea. He'd just gone along with it like he went along with everything and..."Probably not."

"You're a good student, Paris, and you could do well this year."

He wasn't a good student. He'd never been a good student. He'd just been terrified of failure. Of course, now he'd failed at baking in front of the nation—a nation that hated him—so it kind of made sense to him that he'd start failing at everything else too.

"Paris?" Dr. Laughlin tapped her fingernails on the desk. "Are you listening?"

He jumped. "Yes?"

"This is exactly what I'm talking about."

"Sorry...I just..."

"I'm not..." She seemed to search for young-person-friendly language. "...*having a go* at you. I'm concerned."

Paris hung his head. Now his supervisor hated him too. "I'll...I'll do better."

Except he wouldn't. He'd go to bed and sleep. Or fail to.

"In my long, long experience," said Dr. Laughlin, "*I'll do better* isn't helpful without a clear idea of what better looks like and how you're going to get there."

That probably would have been good advice. The problem was Paris couldn't think about anything more than about half an hour ahead without his heart seizing and breath strangling. It wasn't that he'd ever been a particular fan of the future in general, but he was sure he could remember a time when the dread hadn't been quite so overwhelming.

He'd once read a...a...something about a Chinese someone

who'd dreamed of being a butterfly and then never known afterwards if he was a man who'd dreamed he was a butterfly or a butterfly who was dreaming he was a man. And Paris's increasingly vague recollections of times when he was less shit were beginning to feel a lot like that.

Maybe he'd always been like this.

And he'd only ever dreamed of being younger and freer and less afraid.

"Paris?" Dr. Laughlin tapped her fingers again. "Do you need to talk to student support and well-being?"

Oh God. Now she thought he was mad as well as useless. "No. I'm fine. And I'll…I'll make my ideas less…And I'll be less…Thank you for your time."

And before she could reply he bolted.

The world was weird and wibbly as Paris staggered towards the bus stop. He kept thinking he was banging into people even though he wasn't, and his pulse kept stuttering faster and faster like one of those YouTube videos where it's A Thing But It Speeds Up Every Time a Thing Happens.

He reached the bus stop.

It was okay. He was okay. Everything was going to be okay. He just needed to get home.

He couldn't breathe.

Like, genuinely not a drill, not just *I ran a bit fast and had a bit of a shock*, properly *something is crushing the life out of me* couldn't breathe.

Oh God, he was dying. He was actually dying.

Here in the street, surrounded by strangers, who were all staring at him thinking *hey, it's that twat off the television*.

"Are you all right, love?" came a voice from very, very far away.

And Paris tried to say yes, he was fine.

But he wasn't fine. And he was so not fine he couldn't even pretend to be fine.

His eyes were full of coloured needles. He could taste blood at the back of his throat. There was a noise in his head like a wineglass.

And he was all alone.

And more frightened than he'd ever been in his entire life.

"Give him space."

"Is he wearing any constricting clothing?"

"I'm calling an ambulance now. No-one else has to call an ambulance."

"Put this under his head. Does anybody remember how to do the recovery position?"

"Hey, is that the bloke off *Bake Expectations*?"

Paris opened his eyes to a blurry ring of worried faces.

"He's opening his eyes."

"I told you, give him space."

"Can you remember who the president is?"

"What are you saying? This is Britain. We don't have a president."

"I tried them roses de Reims. They was really good."

"Um," said Paris.

"Try not to move. You've had a fall."

"Has he got a bracelet? Is he diabetic?"

"The ambulance is on its way."

"How are you feeling?"

"I…" Paris felt terrible. Absolutely terrible. "I don't think I need an ambulance. I think I just…"

Actually he didn't know. He'd just…died a bit? Was that a thing that happened? Did you sometimes just die?

"All right, I'm cancelling the ambulance."

"Don't cancel the ambulance. He might have a concussion."

"Can you remember who the presid—"

"I told you, we don't have a president."

"That's what they always say on the telly."

"Yeah, on American telly."

"How many fingers am I holding up?"

"Everybody stop crowding him. The lad's had a shock."

Paris was becoming increasingly aware that he was lying on

the pavement, looking like a prick. He tried to get up but the pavement had other ideas. Thankfully someone caught him before he cracked his head again.

"Maybe just stay there 'til the ambulance gets here."

"It's all right, we'll wait with you."

"I won't. That's my bus. Good luck on the show, though."

"Um," said Paris, who had now resigned himself to remaining floor-bound for the foreseeable. "Thank you?"

"You're much less of a twat in real life."

They'd said it was probably a panic attack, and he'd need to book an appointment with his GP, but they were going to run some tests to be on the safe side.

And some tests had turned out to be all the tests.

Which meant, until the results got back, there was still the possibility that Paris had a concussion or a brain tumour. Which, if the initial diagnosis was right and it *had* been a panic attack, probably wasn't the kind of thing it was helpful to have swirling around in his head.

He'd been put in one of those little waiting beds, surrounded by plastic curtains, with just enough room for a nurse to stick things in him without getting in the way of more important patients. And every now and then someone would be rushed past who'd clearly been in a car crash or fallen through a plate glass window, and Paris—with his *I fell over because I was sad* injury—would feel terrible for wasting NHS resources.

"What the fuck happened to you, you soft English bastard?" Morag swept the curtain aside.

As Tariq had correctly pointed out, Paris was bad at wanting things. But right then he couldn't think of much he'd wanted more than to see Morag. "What are you doing here?"

"Apparently I'm still your fucking emergency contact."

Paris pulled the thin NHS sheets up to his chin. "God. I'm sorry."

"Oh stop it. Are you all right?"

"I mean, I think so? It was probably a panic attack." He paused. "Or cancer."

"So it was a panic attack?"

"Or cancer?"

"It's not fucking cancer. You're twenty-one, you don't smoke, you barely drink, and you insist on feeding people fucking vegetables."

"Yes but"—Paris blinked anxiously at her—"that's exactly the kind of person who gets cancer."

"Only in a daytime movie on Channel Five."

There was a long silence. Then Morag stashed her handbag and settled into the plastic chair by the side of the bed with the air of someone who was there for the long haul.

"You don't have to wait with me," Paris told her.

"I'm just trying to prove I don't only put up with you for the cheap flat."

Paris winced. "I'm really sorry I said that."

"I wouldn't care but I think on some level you believe it."

"Not because you're…Just because I'm…"

"That's not the non-insult you think it is." Lifting a foot in a cherry-print Mary Jane, Morag braced herself against the edge of the bed. "No matter what your reasoning, you still believe I'm only living with you because you've got a bunch of nice stuff."

"I know. It's just hard to—"

"I'm sure it is. But what you need to understand is that you can hate yourself as much as you want, but there comes a point when all you're doing is making the people who care about you look like pricks."

"Wh-what do you mean?"

"I mean, you've known me a long time now. Do I seem to you the kind of person who'd put up with a worthless piece of shit because she didn't know any better?"

Paris pondered this. And she definitely wouldn't. He had first-hand evidence she definitely wouldn't, because he'd heard her call multiple people worthless pieces of shit to their faces. But following that thought to its logical conclusion seemed impossible. "I do get that," he said slowly, "rationally. It's just...I can't make my brain agree."

"Yeah well." Morag let out a long breath. "That's because, as I'm beginning to realise, you're profoundly fucking mentally ill."

Oh God, he was here again. First Tariq, then Dr. Laughlin, now Morag. "Um...Morag, that's not a very...You can't just..."

"Way I see it, you've got two choices, Paris. Either you're a terrible person who treats people badly and deserves to die alone. Or you've got an actual problem you need help with."

"What was option one again?"

"Oh fuck off. I'm trying to fucking apologise here."

"What? Why? What have you done?"

"In case you've forgotten, I made you go on a TV show that's made you have a total fucking breakdown."

The phrase *total fucking breakdown* snagged at Paris's brain in a way that made him suspect it was accurate, however little he might like it. "That's not your fault."

"Aye, it is. I knew it'd be tough for you, but I thought it'd get you out of your head, help you meet new people, show you that you can be good at something. But you were *definitely* not in the right place for that."

"You were trying to...to *fix* me?"

"'Course. I'm a very practical person. That's why I always carry lube. And fuck talking about your feelings, you've got a problem, you fucking solve it, and I thought this would solve it. But it didn't, and I'm sorry. I should have been more—I don't know..." For a moment, she looked genuinely remorseful. "Thoughtful or something."

"Yeah, I think maybe being thoughtful isn't always your strong point."

"Excuse me, I'm *incredibly* fucking thoughtful most of the time. That's another reason I always carry lube."

"Okay." Paris was still processing and wasn't sure how lube fit into the situation. Although that was an issue that probably solved itself. "I mean, I did go on the show. I could have said no."

"Paris, when have you ever said no to anything?" She paused. "And I am really, really sorry. I've been a bad friend. So have you, by the way. Just so we're being really fucking clear."

"I can't believe you sent me on national television to try and make me...be...not a mess."

"In hindsight, it was a shit idea. But, in my defence, you were being really annoying that week."

"Are you apologising?" Paris asked slightly plaintively. "Or insulting me?"

"Both. Insults are my love language."

"Well...I feel very loved. And I'm sorry I drove you out of the flat and then dragged you all this way."

She made a mildly repulsed gesture. "It's fine. Don't be soppy. And I'll try to be a better friend. For example, next time instead of saying *look, I've entered you for a nationally televised baking competition*, I'll say *go and see a fucking doctor.*"

Paris was still not completely working, insofar as he ever completely worked. He was confused and exhausted and still not totally convinced he didn't have cancer, but he was starting, very slowly, as if he was cautiously peeling open an envelope containing a letter he wasn't sure he wanted to read, to entertain the suspicion that maybe...that just maybe...Tariq and Dr. Laughlin and Morag were right.

And that he might not be stuck forever, feeling like this, being like this, unable to see any other way but this. That being miserable wasn't something he somehow deserved. "Do you think...," he wondered, "...do you think it will help?"

Morag shrugged. "Well, how the fuck should I know?"

And for some reason, just then, that sounded like hope.

EPISODE 4

Cakes

💬 ❤ 🔁 AGAIN?!!! #bakeexpectations #fuckparis

💬 ❤ 🔁 Catherine: serving bums on national TV without batting an eyelid. Legend. #oohahcatherineparr #bakeexpectations

💬 ❤ 🔁 Calling it now. Rodney is winning this. #bakeexpectations

💬 ❤ 🔁 I get where Tariq's coming from. Every couple of years I'll fancy a peardrop and then be like nope. #bakeexpectations

💬 ❤ 🔁 I almost didn't hate Paris this episode. I have contacted my doctor. #bakeexpectations

💬 ❤ 🔁 Thread: all of Rodney's most iconic cardigan moments 1/20 #bakeexpectations

💬 ❤ 🔁 This is your weekly reminder that Paris is a whiny prick whose shy boy routine was clearly an act and

something seriously fucky is going on with the judges
#bakeexpectations

Is it bad I want to fuck Paris less when he cries less?
#bakeexpectations

bernard should cook the queen's birthday cake. it
would be a chocolate sponge with chocolate icing
#bakeexpectations

Bummed Tanya's gone. But at least my Year 8s will
stop asking me if I'm going on the show next year.
#bakeexpectations

Can't believe Rodney didn't win. It takes a real man to
put sugar flowers on a cake pop. #bakeexpectations

okay ep this week. downgrading paris from megatwat
to complete twat. #bakeexpectations

PARIS DID NOT HAVE cancer. Or a concussion. Or a brain
tumour. Or a vitamin deficiency. Or a blood disorder.

What he did have, according to his GP, was generalised anxiety disorder.

Which, honestly, felt like a nothing condition. Just a slightly
more medicalised way of saying "you're a mess and you need to
get it together." Couldn't he at least have had depression? Sylvia
Plath had depression. That was definitely a real thing that mattered. It made people look at you and go *oh, they were so brilliant and yet so tragic*. Whereas anxiety sounded one step down
from the vapours, like he was an elderly aunt in a Victorian novel
clutching at his chest and going *oh my nerves*.

But that was Paris all over, wasn't it? Couldn't even be mentally ill properly.

He'd been given a prescription for some little white pills and
put on a waiting list for phone therapy, which might—at some
point in the future—translate into face-to-face therapy. Some

combination of which might—at some point even further in the future—eventually make him feel less worthless. Although to say that possibility felt dim and distant would be to do a disservice to both dimness and distance.

With his prescription burning his satchel as if its plain NHS packaging was broadcasting a signal to the world saying *Hello, everyone, I am a crazy person*, Paris trudged home. Recent events had added "bus stops" to the ever-growing list of things that Paris tried to avoid, which made travel even more complicated than it already had been.

Opening the door of his flat, Paris was struck by an immediate sense of foreboding that he told himself was paranoia and generalised anxiety disorder. Unusually, he was wrong.

"You've got a visitor," Morag told him, sticking her head out of her bedroom door.

"Paris," called Jennifer Hallet from the front room. "We need to talk."

Shit shit shit shit. Was he in trouble? Had he violated his contract by fainting at a bus stop?

He sidled through from the hall and found Jennifer lounging in one of the armchairs with Neferneferuaten curled up in her lap like Blofeld's cat.

She scratched Neferneferuaten behind the ears. "Nice flat."

"Yes. It's my parents'."

"I know it's your parents'. I know everything about you. It's my job to know everything about you. Which is how I know you're having a total mental breakdown where people can film it on their phones."

"Oh," said Paris. "Sorry?"

"For once you don't have to be sorry. What with the, you know, suicides in the industry, we need to be really fucking on it with what you might call"—her lip curled—"aftercare."

Paris wove from foot to foot. "I'm fine. I've been to the doctor. I've got a little bit of anxiety."

"You'd be amazed how many people do."

"It's not a big deal."

"I decide what's a big deal, sunshine." Jennifer Hallet's usual manner was mildly impeded by Neferneferuaten, who'd wriggled up under her chin. "You're going on *Baker Expectations* in a few weeks so that people can see you outside the ballroom and be all *oh gosh, I thought he was a prick but he's actually a pretty normal person*."

Shit, he was, wasn't he? Part of the deal when Paris signed up was that—barring accidents, emergencies, or a cavalier attitude to getting his arse sued off—he was required to be free to film an episode of *Bake Expectations*' companion show *Baker Expectations* to be broadcast directly after the episode where he was eliminated.

"And," Jennifer Hallet went on, "that only works if you can stand up and speak in sentences. So right now, it's in your interests and ours to get you into therapy quicksmart."

"I'm on a waiting list."

"Look at me, Paris. Am I a person who waits for things?"

Jennifer Hallet did not look like a person who waited for things. "No?" he suggested.

"Do you know what a rhetorical question is?"

"I do, but you keep pausing so I keep answering."

"It's for dramatic emphasis, you rancid streak of—" She cut herself off abruptly. "Sorry. I'm being sensitive today. I came here to tell you that you're in a group. You don't have to go. But if you don't, you're on your own."

"A...a group?"

"It's a CBT thing for people in the public eye."

Having lived with Morag for over a year now, it took Paris a while to realise that *CBT*, in this context, probably stood for "cognitive behavioural therapy." Rather than "cock-and-ball torture." At least, that was what he hoped. "I'm not sure I—"

"Nobody's sure they. Go to the fucking group."

"But I don't like groups," Paris protested. "One of my problems is that I don't like groups."

"Very sensible of you. Colin likes groups and Colin's a wanker."

"Isn't he your assistant?"

She nodded. "Yeah, he's a good assistant. He's still a wanker. But go. It'll help you. And—"

"But what if it doesn't?"

"Then you'll be no worse off than you are now. In fact"—she tickled Neferneferuaten under the chin—"you'll be better off because I'll be a lot less pissed off with you if you start doing what I say."

Paris tried to sit down while remaining standing. And then blurted out, "Everyone on Twitter hates me."

"Gosh, and Twitter is normally so famous for being warm and accepting."

"But it's awful."

"It's not real. Ten million people watch my show. Twelve of them tweet about it. They're just very loud."

"It still feels real."

"And that"—Jennifer Hallet was clearly out of patience—"is what the therapy's for. So go to the fucking therapy."

"Okay," said Paris. Because Jennifer Hallet had an *I'll stay here until I get what I want* vibe and he didn't know how else to get rid of her.

"See that you do." She got up, dislodging a highly reluctant Neferneferuaten. "Nice cat, by the way."

And then she was gone and Paris could breathe again.

It was nearly eleven o'clock, which meant that Paris should be going to bed soon but, in practice, would be up for at least four hours. Neferneferuaten was already asleep, curled up on his favourite cushion in that *possessive* way that was endemic to her species.

He'd taken his pills, which he'd been told wouldn't have any effect for a couple of weeks at least, but he still hoped to feel maybe a bit different. Like someone who'd done something if nothing else. Like someone who was stepping up and taking control. Instead of like someone who was mortally fucking terrified.

And what if they weren't working? What if they made him worse? He'd tried really hard to avoid reading the list of side effects, but that had just turned them into a formless monster waiting to get him. So now they were a very well-formed monster offering him a future full of fluid retention, rectal bleeding, fast heartbeats, slow heartbeats, irregular heartbeats, dry mouth, migraines, hallucinations, heavy periods, movement disorders, persistent painful erections, and the inability to urinate.

Maybe he was better off just fainting at bus stops.

Except no, fainting at bus stops was the worst. And driving his flatmate away in a fit of self-loathing was the worst. And being unable to hold down a relationship because a little voice in your head said they'd leave you anyway was the worst. A little bit of rectal bleeding would be a small price to pay.

Sitting on the sofa with Neferneferuaten on his lap and the intimidatingly huge leaflet of side effects by his side, he wondered if he should text Tariq. Just casually. Just to say *you were right, I needed to do something about my brain and now I am.*

Or maybe that was selfish. Or unfair. Or selfish *and* unfair. Or he'd get it wrong. And Tariq had basically told him that it was too late to make things better between them. That he'd already blown it. But then that had been before. And didn't he maybe *owe* Tariq—well, not an apology, he'd already made far too many apologies, but an update, maybe?

His fingers hovered over his phone. The trouble was, a part of him still felt like he was just making excuses. That sure, he could say *it wasn't my fault I was a shitty boyfriend, I was mentally ill the whole time*, but in the end he'd still been him. He'd still made choices. Choices that made Tariq feel unloved and unwanted.

Then again, maybe that was the point. Maybe taking responsibility for his choices and admitting he needed help weren't opposites at all. Maybe they were the same thing. Either way, he had to try, didn't he? Not trying was how he'd got here in the first place.

Hi. Just thought I'd let you know I've been sort of diagnosed with generalised anxiety disorder. And I'm working on that now.

I know it doesn't change how I behaved or all the ways I hurt you. But I just thought I'd let you know.

It was not a well-constructed text, but the last twelve iterations hadn't been any better. And Paris's brain kept telling him that if he just kept trying, he'd eventually get it perfect, but in a fit of insight that he almost allowed himself to feel proud of, he realised his brain was wrong. Trying something until it was perfect was the same as not doing it at all, because perfection was just a ghost he conjured up to scare himself with.

So he sent it. And as he was about to put his phone down and make the first of what would likely be several attempts to sleep, he got back: **Thanks for telling me. I hope things get better for you.**

EPISODE 5

Patisserie

💬 ♡ 🔁 If there's a hosepipe ban next summer, I'm just going to get Paris to stand in my garden and cry on my begonias. #bakeexpectations

💬 ♡ 🔁 Finally. Win for Lili. Her presentation has been unbelievable for five weeks. #bakeexpectations

💬 ♡ 🔁 WHAT IF FRUIT ISN'T ENOUGH. #askingthebigquestions #bakeexpectations

💬 ♡ 🔁 Did he seriously just break down in tears because he didn't get handed another win he didn't deserve? #bakeexpectations #fuckparis #noseriouslyfuckparis

💬 ♡ 🔁 The thing I hate most about Paris is that he distracts people from how awesome Rodney is. #bakeexpectations

💬 ♡ 🔁 RIP Bernard. This world was never meant for one as beautiful as you. #bakeexpectations

○ ♡ ⟳   guys i was going to grab a banana for lunch today.
But like. What if fruit isn't enough? #bakeexpectations

○ ♡ ⟳   Catherine telling it like it is as always
#oohahcatherineparr #bakeexpectations

○ ♡ ⟳   The only way I can stand to look at Paris is if I imagine
his tears are actually my cum running down his face
#bakeexpectations

○ ♡ ⟳   BENARD NOOOOOOOOOO #bakeexpectations

○ ♡ ⟳   There's just so much going on with the world with
rising income inequality & out of control political
polarisation. And I just keep thinking: what if fruit...
isn't enough? #bakeexpectations

○ ♡ ⟳   ●●●●●●●●●● can i win bake expectations now
#bakeexpectations

○ ♡ ⟳   In other news paris still a twat #bakeexpectations

THERE WAS, PARIS REFLECTED, something odd about having a complete stranger explain the entire way his brain worked with a diagram they could draw in ninety seconds. Thoughts-feelings-behaviours-thoughts, trapped in an endless cycle: something gets in your head, that makes you feel weird, then you act weird, and that puts more thoughts in your head, which makes you feel weirder, which makes you act weirder.

Obviously they didn't say *weird*. But that was the overall gist.

Paris's entire life reduced to a broken-down washing machine that was stuck on spin and ruining all his clothes.

Of course, it was hard to tell how knowing that your entire life was a washing machine helped you stop your entire life being a washing machine.

He looked down at his sheaf of handouts. They were about halfway through the session, and having laid out the original model, the facilitators were now talking about how it was useful to categorise one's worries as either practical (and so to be addressed by clear problem-solving strategies) or hypothetical (and so to be managed purely psychologically). Then they were told to discuss these concepts with the person they were sitting next to. Which meant a room full of people who hated speaking to strangers was suddenly confronted with the need to speak to strangers.

Paris turned to the woman sitting next to him. She was older than he was, but not by much, with dark hair cut in a bob, and those large black-framed glasses that had become trendy again. Something about her seemed familiar in a way Paris couldn't quite pin down.

"Hi," he tried. "Paris."

She offered him a shy smile in return. "Joy. You're—sorry, I probably shouldn't bring it up, but you're the guy off *Bake Expectations*, right?"

Paris nodded. "Sorry, I think I've seen you somewhere too but I can't remember where."

"I'm the one who does the maths on *Got Your Number*."

"I don't watch much TV. Sorry."

"It's an okay quiz show where people do maths problems and I tell them the solution. I'm also sometimes on panel games, and I've done a couple of pop maths things on BBC Three."

"Classicist." Paris indicated himself in a vague sort of way. "So I'm quite scared of maths."

She gave him a playful look. "Is that a practical or hypothetical concern?"

"I think…neither? I think I'm genuinely bad at maths."

"Don't say that. My whole gimmick is making maths accessible to people, so the whole *oh, some people are just bad at maths* culture really offends me."

"Oh God, I've really offended you."

"No, the world we live in has really offended me. Anyway"— she riffled through her notes—"we should probably do the exercise. Go on, Paris. Pick a worry. Any worry."

That legitimately gave Paris choice paralysis. "Um, I'm quite worried I'll do the exercise wrong?"

"Okay." She checked her notes again. "I think the way they want us to phrase it is *what if I do the exercise wrong?* So do you think that's practical or hypothetical?"

"I don't know," Paris squeaked. "I mean, if I do the exercise wrong, I might do this whole thing wrong, which means I might just mess up my brain even more."

"I think," she said gently, "that's hypothetical. Because I don't think any of those things are going to happen."

"Maybe, but isn't the point of this group that none of the things we think are going to happen are going to happen? Which means everything is hypothetical?"

Joy got a very mathematicianey look. "How about we reduce it to its simplest case. What's something that would definitely be practical?"

"Um. What about . . . What if I've left the front door unlocked? Because even if you go from there to *what if I've left the front door unlocked and a murderer comes in during the night and murders me—*"

"You get that as well, huh?"

Paris nodded. "All the time. But I can just get up and check the door. And I think in that case it's a practical worry and I think what they're saying is we need to just check the door once—"

"Instead of twelve times?"

"Yeah. And I think a purely hypothetical worry would be like . . . *what if we all die because of climate change?* Because even though I am quite worried about that, and it might happen, it's not like I can do anything about it."

"That makes sense." She made a pondering sound. "And I suppose that actually there are some things you can put in either box. Like *what if I do the exercise wrong* could be practical because trying it anyway is a kind of a practical solution, or hypothetical because you have no way of knowing if you've done it right or not until you try to do it."

That wasn't quite the level of certainty Paris was hoping for from the magic fix-your-brain technique, but it made something in the vicinity of sense. And maybe *it can be both* was a lesson worth internalising in general. "That sounds right?"

"Cool, then we're nailing this."

They ran through a few other examples, finding some easier to categorise than others. *What if I lose my job* was probably hypothetical unless there was a real way to control it, but *what if I lose my job and can't pay my bills* was more practical because financial planning was a thing. *What if the internet thinks I'm a twat*, they both agreed, was probably neither; it was just a shitty fact of having a mild public profile.

After a couple of minutes, the group fed back, and after what the facilitators at least seemed to think was a fruitful discussion about the value or otherwise of worrying whether you had cancer, they moved on to the next topic. This involved setting goals for their progress over the next weeks, which Paris found frankly mortifying.

He just sat there, staring at a blank form, haunted by the memory of Tariq asking if he'd ever wanted anything, and realising that he might genuinely have forgotten how. But he was also pretty sure that *be better* didn't count as an achievable target.

In the end, he folded the paper up without writing anything. And nobody checked.

The session concluded with a squeaking of chairs, a rustling of papers, and a setting of homework. Which, for the first week, involved keeping a diary of all the things they were worried about.

Naturally, Paris found this prospect extremely worrying. Because not only did he have to worry about what he was worrying about, he had to worry about writing it down.

"So," said Joy, still stuffing notes into a ring binder. "Cured yet?"

"Definitely. You?"

"Oh completely." She paused. "Seriously, though. Do you actually feel slightly worse? Because I think I might feel slightly worse."

Paris wasn't quite at the point where he could be sure what he was feeling. For a start, he'd been encouraged to pay attention to a lot of things he'd never paid attention to before, and so what he was mostly feeling was confused. "It's all…really simple, but also really hard. Which is really annoying."

"Right?" she said, with that *oh thank God, it's not just me* tone that Paris wasn't used to but had heard a lot in the past hour. "Because it's your own brain. Why does my own brain not do what I tell it?"

"Because it hates you."

"Thanks. Comforting. Good to know."

There was another pause, as the rest of the mildly famous people with uncooperative brains filed out of the hall. Both Paris and Joy were sort of lingering, maybe caught in the shared sense that the moment they parted company they'd be once again alone with thoughts they couldn't control and homework they didn't want to do.

"So," began Paris, "what I'm worrying about now is that… I'm thinking it would be really nice if you wanted to go and get a coffee with me or something. But you don't know I'm gay so you might just think I'm trying to hit on you, which I'm not because I'm gay. Or you might just think I'm really annoying. Or think I'm some secret stalker maths fan. And, um, is that practical or hypothetical?"

She frowned in a contemplative rather than *despising you* way. "I'm inclined to say it's practical. But I think you've found a good solution. And if you want to keep it low-pressure, there's a very shit kiosk down the end of the corridor."

"I like low-pressure," Paris told her. "Because it turns out I'm extremely mentally ill."

So they kiosked, and then sat at a small Formica table nursing cups of just-about-okay coffee insulated with corrugated cardboard. Joy had bought a large cookie studded with Smarties, which she'd invited Paris to share.

For a while there was the kind of silence you could only really get between two people who were convinced that anything they said would make them sound like a complete arsehole. Paris broke first.

"I didn't write down any goals," he said.

"I only got one."

Paris got halfway through "What was it?" before realising that it was probably an incredibly personal question. "I mean, you don't have to say if you don't—"

"I want to be able to spend money on myself. Which sounds really first-world problems but, like, I *really* can't spend money on myself. If it's not absolutely necessary, I don't buy it."

"Isn't that just being financially prudent?"

Joy rotated her cup a quarter circle. "There's prudent and there's—I've literally never had a holiday I've had to pay for. My husband and I had the cheapest wedding we could manage, and even though I want kids really *quite badly*, we're holding off because I wake up in the night in a cold panic because I don't know how we'll pay for them. I once wore a pair of shoes with holes in them for six months because I figured they'd last until the snow set in."

"Oh." This had a different-but-familiar edge to it that Paris felt weirdly comforted by. "I'd have thought you were doing okay, if you're on TV."

"That's the thing. I *am*. My job pays well, the show's been running for years, I've got several side hustles, and my husband's got a very stable job at the National Trust. It's just, every time I think *oh we've got plenty of money, we should do something nice with it*, I start thinking *but what if it all goes away?*"

"So," Paris offered tentatively, "I guess that's a hypothetical worry?"

She laughed, pushing her glasses back up her nose. "It's nice they've taught us to do this one thing that helps us put names on our problems but not remotely address them."

"Maybe that's next week?"

"Yes, I'm sure next week they're going to give us the quick, easy secret to not having clinical anxiety anymore."

Delicately, Paris prised away his corner of the Smartie cookie. "Do you think it's actually going to work? I mean, not next week. I mean, the whole thing. Or do you think we're stuck being like this forever?"

"I'm pretty sure we're stuck being like this forever. I think that's just how it works. But you're supposed to be able to get better at dealing with it."

Part of Paris was asking *but what if I don't, what if I'm so rubbish that not even I can put up with me*. But those were hypothetical worries. "I…" Paris's mouth had gone completely dry, which was only partially the cookie's fault. "I…would…I would like that."

"Me too, Paris." She gave him a little smile. "Me too."

That evening, Paris and Neferneferuaten were staring at a blank worry diary and a still-blank goals form.

Neferneferuaten was not being very helpful. Because she was a cat.

Biting his lip very, very hard, Paris took the plunge and wrote the date. Then, after a really long time, he wrote:

What if I get lost on the way to the session
What if everyone at the session hates me
What if this doesn't work
What if it works for everyone else except me
What if Joy secretly hates me
What if I get lost on the way home from the session
What if I faint at a bus stop again
What if that guy has a knife
What if I get home and Morag has decided to walk out again
What if Neferneferuaten has got out

What if Nefernefervaten has just died
What if my parents never text me back
What if Tāriq never talks to me again
What if I have no ideas about immortality in classical thought and
    fail my degree
What if I didn't shut the fridge properly
What if I'm doing this wrong

Exhausted, he turned the page, trying to trap his anxieties like ants. Although, much like ants, he could still feel them crawling. On the paper and in his head.

Neferneferuaten batted irritatedly at Paris's knee.

"I'm trying to do my homework," Paris told her. "So I can… have friends who aren't a cat."

Neferneferuaten widened her eyes.

"No offence," he added quickly.

With her tail curled at a haughty angle, she jumped off the bed and fucked off.

Paris dared to take another peek at his worries. He had a lot of worries. Did he have too many worries?

Sighing, he wrote down:

What if I have too many worries.

EPISODE 6

Bread

💬 ♡ ⟲   **FIRST BERNARD NOW LILI IS THERE NO JUSTICE IN THE WORLD** #justiceforlili #bakeexpectations

💬 ♡ ⟲   **Oh yes. My boy Tariq coming through with the win.** #bakeexpectations

💬 ♡ ⟲   **Paris should have gone out** #bakeexpectations

💬 ♡ ⟲   **Paris should have gone out** #bakeexpectations

💬 ♡ ⟲   **Paris should have gone out** #bakeexpectations

💬 ♡ ⟲   **Paris should have gone out** #bakeexpectations

💬 ♡ ⟲   **Did anyone else notice that Tariq made a literal cinnamon roll?** #bakeexpectations

💬 ♡ ⟲   **I wish Rodney was my dad. He seems like a really good dad.** #bakeexpectations

💬 ♡ ⟲   **Paris should have gone out** #bakeexpectations

○ ♡ ⊡ **Paris should have gone out** #bakeexpectations

○ ♡ ⊡ **Paris should have gone out** #bakeexpectations

○ ♡ ⊡ **Oh my God, stop crying you fucking over-privileged piece of fucking shit** #bakeexpectations

○ ♡ ⊡ **I am now convinced Paris and Marianne are actually shagging. There is no other explanation for the fact he's still in the competition** #bakeexpectations

○ ♡ ⊡ **paris should have gone out. also hes a twat** #bakeexpectations

"FUCK ME," SAID MORAG as Paris trailed forlornly behind her into the twenty-second boutique they'd visited that day. "How have you been intimidated by this for so long? I know your parents are in the rag trade, but men's fashions are so fucking boring I'd've thought not even you could fuck it up. Did you wake up one day and think *oh no, I can't decide whether to wear a T-shirt and a jacket or a shirt and a jacket?*"

"Kind of, actually?"

"Sorry. That was insensitive." Morag lifted a jumper from a pile of identical jumpers which had been lovingly laid on a white cube. "I just mean, as a sex, you could pull your fucking socks up. Literally. Your socks are shit too."

Paris started frantically refolding the jumpers. "Well, I could wear a print dress with tentacles on it, but then one of us would have to change."

"I think you mean *you'd* have to change. Because my sense of style is timeless and also I can *clearly* take you in a fight, you soft English bastard."

There was no point arguing with that. She definitely could. "Maybe this?" He held up a very generic-looking blue-green jumper. "I could wear this."

"That's exactly what you always wear."

"It's not. Look, it's *emerald*. I've never worn *emerald*. This is me fighting against my Intolerance for Uncertainty"—that had been the week's topic in group, the idea being that, to people like Paris, not knowing what would happen was almost worse than knowing a bad thing would happen, like an allergy to the unpredictable—"and I think emerald is pretty striking."

"You'll look like the toilet seat cover in an accountant's second bathroom. Try something else."

"You're supposed to be building my confidence."

"No, *you're* supposed to be building your confidence, I'm supposed to be helping, and I am."

He wasn't going to win this argument. "By telling me I look like a toilet seat."

"Aye, it's like doing resistance training. If you can do this with me calling you a pasty little shite the whole time, think how much easier it'll be when I'm gone."

"I'm not pasty. Am I pasty?"

"No, but look, you actually stood up for yourself."

He hadn't stood very far up for himself. But it counted. "I'm…I'm…going to try on the emerald jumper."

"On your head—or, y'know, chest be it."

Very decisively, Paris swept up a jumper and strode as confidently as he could manage into the changing rooms. Locking himself in a small box that strangers could previously have used for literally anything normally kept Paris restricted to online shopping. But the advantage of going to the kind of stores that his parents used to frequent was that changing rooms were more comfortable than most cinemas and the lighting was expertly designed to make you think that a two-hundred-and-thirty-pound pullover looked good enough to be worth spending two hundred and thirty pounds on.

Paris doffed his existing jumper and donned the emerald jumper. Then stared at himself in the mirror, wondering why he looked much as he always did. Which was to say like a prat. In this case, a green prat.

"How is it?" called out Morag.

"Fine."

"Do you look like an accountant's toilet?"

"I don't think so. But then I haven't seen any accountants' toilets." He re-scrutinised his reflection. Had he really thought dressing in a slightly brighter colour would make him any less fundamentally him? "I guess I'll take it."

It was at that moment that his phone rang. And while he didn't want to be the sort of person who answered his phone in changing rooms, it was Tariq.

"H-hi," he managed.

"Hi. I…" Tariq seemed to briefly run out of steam. "I thought I'd ask how you were getting on?"

"I'm okay. I'm getting treatment. I'm…I'm…" This was really difficult. Because Tariq had told him not to lie to him and then dumped him for being honest. Except he hadn't really, had he? Tariq had dumped him because there was only so much of your own shit you could make someone else deal with. "It's really hard," he finished. "And I don't think my…you know…me-ness is going to magically go away or anything. But I'm doing better. How about you?"

A laugh came rippling down the phone. "You really are doing better. You asked how I am and everything."

"That's mean. I deserved it. But it's still mean."

"I'm…I'm good. But it's weird, because people keep recognising me, and I'm getting a lot of love and a little bit of hate. And if this is what being on TV is like, I think I'm okay with it. But it's a lot."

Mirror Paris was nodding greenly. "It's definitely a lot. But you're great. And you deserve to have people love you because you're great."

"I *am* really great," agreed Tariq, and Paris could hear the smile in his voice. "And everybody is super supportive. It's just… I don't know…It feels like my whole life is changing, and that's a bit odd."

"Changing how?"

"I've got a manager and an agent, and I'm not a hundred percent sure what the difference is. And all these opportunities are coming up and I'm getting all this attention and I guess...I'm scared that if things change, I'll change too?"

Paris sat on the needlessly luxurious bench. "I think...it's hard to tell what's us changing and what's changing us."

"Wow. I can't tell if that's incredibly profound or totally meaningless."

"Yeah. That's how I feel every week in therapy. But anyway"—Paris mustered his words—"I think even if you do change, you'll still be an amazing person. Because that's just who you are."

There was a long silence. And Paris did his very best to be aware of his thoughts and how he was reacting to his thoughts and how his reactions might change his behaviour.

"I hope," he said carefully, "that was an okay thing to say."

"That," Tariq told him, "was a perfect thing to say. I just—"

Morag's voice blasted through the door. "Have you died in there? Have you choked on an ugly green jumper?"

"No." Paris jumped to his feet. "I'm fine...I was just on the phone. It's Tariq."

Morag made a grumbling noise but backed off again.

"Honey"—Tariq's voice had acquired a tone of wary amusement—"not to be crass, but are you on the toilet?"

Paris gasped. "OhmyGodno. I'm in a changing room. Morag's taking me shopping for clothes because apparently I look like a malnourished child who stole his granddad's wardrobe."

"I wouldn't have put it quite like that," said Tariq, "but... yeah?"

"I think I'm going to get an emerald jumper."

A sound of intrigue, best approximated as "ooh" echoed from the other end of the phone. "Send me a selfie?"

Instinctively, Paris wanted to say *no, I'm really bad at selfies*. And that was definitely a true thing, not an anxiety thing. But it wasn't like Tariq was dating him anymore, so even if he looked grotesquely unattractive, there'd be no harm done. "Okay. But I warn you: I'm bad at selfies."

"I'll be honest, angel cake, I didn't have you down for an Instaqueen."

Paris took twenty-eight selfies, found the least worst, and sent it.

"It's taking a while to come through," said Tariq. Followed by "Okay, so, I love the colour. It really makes your eyes pop. But have you thought about wearing something that actually fits?"

"This fits."

"Honey, I'm going to put this simply: no it doesn't."

Paris flapped his sleeves. "I like them like this."

"You know clothes aren't a bag you're delivering yourself in."

"Aren't they, though? In a way?"

"Let me put this simply again: no." There was a thoughtful pause. "Can I give that another try? I get that you don't like attention and that's fine. You don't have to dress like me, although for the record you'd look fabulous in nail varnish."

A warbly sound emerged from Paris's mouth. "Can I start with an emerald jumper?"

"Of course you can. But start with one two sizes smaller. Because, genuinely, wearing clothes that don't fit you has the opposite effect from the one you think it has."

"Nrugh?" asked Paris.

"You see someone dressed nicely in well-fitting clothes. You think *ah, there's a person.* You see someone trying to hide inside their jumper, you think *hmm, what's that guy's deal, why's he made that unusual fashion choice, maybe I should stare at him until I can work it out.*"

"But…but then people will be able to see me?"

"I know, honey," said Tariq gently. "But that's okay."

He stayed on the line while Paris dispatched Morag to get him a smaller jumper. And, once Paris was wearing it, he took another twenty-eight selfies and finally sent one of them.

There was a slightly longer pause.

Then, "Okay, wow. That is *so much* better."

Paris peeked at the man in the mirror. The man who had hands and a shape and…and…was maybe tall in an all-right way? And maybe not so awfully skinny? "What if my nipples show?" he blurted out. "Sorry, I didn't mean to say that aloud."

"What are your nipples made of if they'll fight their way through a shirt and a jumper?"

"Ignore me. I GADed out for a bit."

"GADed?"

"Generalised anxiety disorder."

"That seemed a pretty specific anxiety to me."

"Yeah"—Paris was laughing—"the general is made of the specific. I've now come to terms with the fact that my nipples are not going to show and, even if they did, I would survive the experience."

Tariq was laughing too. And Paris suddenly remembered that he'd been able to do that once—make Tariq laugh—before he'd lost himself and lost Tariq. "Oh, angel cake, do you want to get coffee?" There was a back-pedally-feeling pause. "As friends. Just as friends."

"I'd love to," said Paris, before his brain could find a way to ruin it.

<hr />

They met in London because Tariq was in town anyway to see his manager and/or agent. Paris didn't quite dare to wear the emerald jumper, because—having been told it made his eyes pop—it seemed a bit blatant. But he did wear something new. Something where you could see his wrists.

"Is that," Tariq asked, "a waistcoat? Are you wearing a waistcoat? And a shirt?"

Paris did his best not to look at himself. "Yes. Yes I am."

"I'm not going to lie, it looks really good on you. Kind of preppy, and I'm sure it was disgustingly expensive, but then so was everything else you used to wear and it was really unflattering."

Since he was sort of on business, Tariq was dressed relatively formally in a light brown herringbone jacket over a white shirt and well-fitting black trousers. But his nails were gold and his smile was bright and he was still—for all the exposure and the opportunities— very much Tariq. And that was…lovely. Hurty but lovely.

"You look wonderful too," Paris told him. "But you always do."

They dithered slightly awkwardly while they tried to work how two people who used to be one thing to each other could navigate being a slightly different thing. And then got in the queue together because it didn't feel like a *one of us gets drinks for the other* situation. A few minutes later, Paris balancing an espresso and Tariq clutching a caramelatte, they found a table and squeezed in opposite each other.

Paris's brain was already jaunting off into the wilderness of all the things he wanted to say but didn't know how. So he let it go and tried anyway.

"How's it—" he began.

"Oh my God," came a worryingly teenage voice from the other side of Caffe Nero. "It's that guy and the other guy. From *Bake Expectations*."

Her friend immediately bounced up. "See, I told you they were dating. I have incredible gaydar."

Tariq leaned over the table. "Sorry. Does this happen to you all the time as well?"

"I know I've said I'm doing better," Paris whispered. "But how much time do you think I'm spending outside my flat, honestly?"

The two girls were now approaching excitedly.

"Hiii." The first one waved her hands with the unabashed enthusiasm of someone who'd never seen a day she wouldn't seize. "I'm Ellie. This is Ella. We think you're great."

"I really like," said Ella, directly to Paris, intensely directly to Paris, "how you don't conform to the toxic standards of masculinity that are so pervasive today."

Paris cast a slightly wild look at Tariq. "Um. Thanks?"

"So"—Ellie seemed to be literally bouncing—"when did you start going out?"

Ella elbowed her. "You can't ask them that. It's fetishising."

"No, it isn't. I'm *interested*."

"We're just friends," said Tariq, with crushing sincerity.

Ellie looked even more disappointed than Paris felt. "Oh." Then she brightened up. "Can we get a selfie anyway?"

They didn't exactly wait for, well, consent. But Tariq made affirmative-type noises and did a really good job of corralling the four of them into an Instagrammable position.

"Thank you," Ellie chirped when they were done. "We hope you win. Well, I hope Tariq wins and she hopes Paris wins."

It was disorientating, Paris thought, to have the whole nation invested in the outcome of a competition that, from his perspective, was done and dusted three months ago.

"Good to know." Tariq smiled at them. "I'm keeping my fingers crossed."

And then Ellie and Ella grabbed their takeaway cups and headed out into Trafalgar Square. Paris could have imagined it, but he could have sworn he heard Ella whispering, "Never embarrass me like that again."

"Well"—Tariq leaned back his chair—"check you out, teaching a generation of teenagers to make a stand against toxic masculinity."

Paris laughed. "I was crying because I'm mentally ill, not because I'm making a big political statement. In an ideal world, I'd cry less."

"But," Tariq offered, "other men would cry more."

"Anyway…" With a self-conscious grimace, Paris turned his attention back to his coffee cup. "Why aren't they on Twitter? Being all, I don't know, hashtag Paris Versus the Patriarchy or something."

"Firstly they're too young. They're probably on whatever the thing that's going to replace TikTok is. And secondly"—watching

Tariq counting on his fingers made Paris's heart ache—"there's plenty of people out there supporting you. You just don't pay attention to them. And don't get me wrong, social media is a bad place to find support. Like, that's what friends are for. But you really aren't as hated as you think you are."

"I know. It just felt like it for a long time, and still feels like it sometimes. But I'm getting less bad at dealing with it." Paris risked a shy smile. "Morag and I have this deal where if she catches me looking at people slagging me off on Twitter, she says something worse."

"Does that help?"

"No, but I appreciate she's trying. And actually, I haven't looked in a week. I think it's…" This was hard to articulate. "I think it's a bit like what you said about school?"

Tariq kind of winced. "I'm not sure you should have been totally listening to me. I don't think I got you as well as I thought I did."

"Oh God. Was I that bad?"

"No. I just mean, I…had a lot of ideas about you and me and everything. And don't get me wrong"—Tariq flashed him a winsome look—"some of them were dead-on. But I didn't do a very good job of listening to you."

"I don't really want to play *who was the worst boyfriend*."

"Yeah, I think that's a game neither of us wins."

"Okay, but one of the dead-on things you said," Paris went on, "was that when people have a go at you, it's not about you, it's about them. Because I look back at school and it felt like everybody was spending all day every day hating me personally. But they weren't. They were just occasionally shitty and mostly forgot I existed. And I think Twitter's the same. Like there's this one guy who keeps tweeting about how much he wants to have sex with me or beat me up—"

One of Tariq's beautifully groomed eyebrows twitched upwards. "Er, that's kind of creepy."

"Yes. But also, I'm sure he only thinks about me for the thirty seconds a week it takes him to send that tweet. And when I'm not on TV, he'll find someone else to hate-thirst about. And even the tweets are about his profile and his followers. They're not really about me at all. I'm just...content."

"I think"—Tariq was nodding—"that's probably the best way to think about it."

"Unfortunately I don't think that works for racist journalists."

For the first time since they'd sat down, Tariq looked less-than-sparkling. "The depressing thing is that it sort of does. Half the time, I think they don't even believe what they're saying. They're just trying to attract clicks and shift copy. It's just that they also, y'know, get people who look like me killed."

"I'm sorry," said Paris. "And I know I say sorry too much so I'm trying to say sorry less. But if it helps, this isn't anxiety, it's white guilt."

Tariq grinned. "Thanks. I'll take it. Now can you give the Koh-i-Noor back to India please?"

"I would but the Queen's got it, and she's not taking my calls."

"I thought you guys all knew each other?"

Paris shook his head. "No, I'm British. She's German."

And just like that they were laughing together, like nothing had changed, even though so many things had. Tariq leaned a little forward, smiling. "I've missed you, angel cake."

"I've missed you too," said Paris. Except that suddenly felt like too much, so he developed a sudden and intense interest in the remains of his espresso. "And you know I really am sorry. For how everything went."

"Well, we were younger then."

"It was only three months ago."

"Yeah, but..." The look on Tariq's face was oddly serious. "It feels like forever, doesn't it?"

It did, a bit. They weren't quite back in childhood time dilation, *every summer is a century and Christmas never comes* territory, but the show, and everything before the show, really did feel like another life entirely. Except Paris wasn't sure how to express that without sounding corny, so he just nodded.

"And," Tariq added, "for what it's worth, I'm sorry too. I think we—I don't know, I think we sort of went past each other somehow."

"I think I went past you. I was too ill to realise I was onto a good thing."

That made Tariq laugh again. "Honey, you *knew* you were onto a good thing. You just kept freaking out in case you lost it, and I didn't do a very good job of reassuring you."

"No, no." Paris rushed reflexively to Tariq's defence. "You were fine. You were great."

"I'm not saying I was a monster." Holding Paris's gaze, Tariq took a sip of his caramelatte. "Just that I think you had quite specific needs and I didn't have the first idea how to start meeting them."

"If it helps, neither did I."

Tariq's mug clinked back into its saucer. "It does. A bit. Still, I think—I think it'd go differently now."

Paris's intolerance of uncertainty took a deep bite out of the back of his brain. Now, he told himself, would be a really good moment to say something. He didn't say something.

"Not that I'm saying we should," Tariq went devastatingly on. "Not that we—I think—sometimes things are just too…"

"Yeah." Paris gave a nod that he hoped said *I agree with your reasoning* and not *you have crushed my dreams*. Even if Tariq had done a little tiny bit of dream-crushing around the edges. "There's just so much going on now." And because he didn't want to dwell on how much Tariq didn't want to be with him, he added, "Speaking of which, how did your meeting go?"

Tariq lit up. "Really well. I mean, I think *Strictly* is still a little bit out of my reach."

"No Janette Manrara?"

"Someday." Pressing his hands to his chest, Tariq cast his eyes skywards. "Someday I will live my Janette Manrara dream."

"Honestly...I think you probably will. Although I think they've changed the rules now so you could go with one of the male dancers if you wanted."

"I don't want to go with a male dancer," said Tariq decidedly. "I want to go with Janette Manrara. But anyway, leaving that aside"—he leaned in again—"I can't say much about it. But we're pitching the...you know. The thing we talked about."

Feeling like he was in a spy movie, Paris leaned in too. And, of course, that brought him very close to Tariq's lips and eyes and—oh no. "The show? *Fabulous Halal?*"

Tariq grinned. "You remembered."

"I have anxiety. Not amnesia."

"Yeah, I know. But for a while you...you...were very not there."

"Towards the end. And okay, at the beginning. And maybe a bit in the middle too. But"—Paris gazed earnestly across the table—"I did—do—really like you. And that was your dream. Of course I remembered your dream."

"Baking, showing off, being a little bit famous. It's everything I've always wanted."

"And you are going to be so, *so* good at it."

"What about you, angel cake?"

Paris's eyes flew wide. "Oh no, I'd suck."

"No, I mean. Have you worked out...Have you...Do you, um, want anything yet?"

Well, wasn't that a complex question? "Sort of. I mean it's—there's still a lot I have to work through and mostly I just want to be *better*, but I think that's unhelpfully vague."

"Just a touch."

For a moment they were quiet together, and it was comfortable in a way Paris wasn't used to quiet being comfortable. "I'd like to be friends," he said at last. "With you, I mean."

"I'd assumed from context. And yeah, that'd be nice."

Nice was good. Paris would take nice. It was a step down from *actually I really want to be your boyfriend again* but a step up from *no, I hate you* and also—also he was finding the *no,*

I hate you option strangely unreal. Three months ago, the idea that Tariq secretly loathed and resented him would have wormed its way into his mind like a maggot in a plum, but now it just sort of bobbed there on the surface like a bubble on a river. Bright and distracting if he looked at it, but nothing at all if he looked away.

EPISODE 7

World War II

💬 ♡ ⇄ **Good fucking riddance.** #bakeexpectations

💬 ♡ ⇄ **FINALLY** #bakeexpectations

💬 ♡ ⇄ **And the nation can breathe again** #bakeexpectations

💬 ♡ ⇄ **Seven weeks was six weeks too long** #bakeexpectations

💬 ♡ ⇄ **JUSTICE FOR LILI** #justiceforlili #bakeexpectations

💬 ♡ ⇄ **I am genuinely sad that Paris is…haha jk lol**
#bakeexpectations

💬 ♡ ⇄ **Catherine was robbed. Again.** #oohahcatherineparr
#bakeexpectations

💬 ♡ ⇄ **I notice Paris stopped the fake crying once he realised
it wouldn't save him** #bakeexpectations

💬 ♡ ⇄ **Oh no. Who am I going to hatewank over now?**
#bakeexpectations

💬 ♡ ⇄ **goodbye paris. you were a twat** #bakeexpectations

PARIS WAS IN MAKEUP to make sure he didn't look shiny on camera when Joy popped her head in.

"I just wanted to say good luck," she told him. "Nice jumper."

"Thanks. It's emerald."

She claimed one of the big canvas seats next to him, looking far more at home than she did in therapy. But then, who looked at home in therapy? Well, apart from therapists. "How are you feeling?"

He thought about it for a moment. "Nervous? But I think closer to *ordinary person nervous* than..." It was generally bad form to imply that you knew someone from a support group when you were in, say, a room full of makeup artists. "Than... any other kind of nervous."

"Glad to hear it. And I think it's normal to be a bit on edge before going on camera, especially in front of a studio audience."

"Do you...do you get on edge?"

"A bit. Like, I know some people get incredibly bad stage fright, but that's never been my thing." She grinned. "I think it helps that I just do sums."

"I would find having to do sums on camera the most terrifying thing in the world."

"To be fair, if I had to go on set and bake or translate Latin, I'd be pretty terrified too."

"I *was* terrified," said Paris. "I mean, about the baking. Latin didn't really come up."

"Well, Grace went to Cambridge so you never know."

Paris made a noise a bit like "nerrugh?"

"I'm teasing. You've met her. She's the most terrific old luvvie. She'd never let someone else look bad on camera, and she'd never let someone translate Latin for her."

"You've met her?"

"Everyone's met Grace. She's presented everything, she's on most panel games, and she's done a three-part BBC special on most topics despite the fact she's not an expert on—as far as I can tell—anything except herself."

Paris laughed, feeling somehow reassured.

And that seemed to encourage Joy because, if there was one thing Paris knew as a person with anxiety, it was that being able to relieve other people's anxieties was a very tempting way to deal with your own. "She did a show about the history of maths a couple of years ago, and I consulted for it because they thought that having their maths show presented by a comedian advised by a mathematician was a better strategy than having it presented by an actual mathematician."

"Not got a secret gift for comedy?" suggested Paris.

"Oh no, I'd be terrible. I'll try to tell you a joke and you'll see how terrible I am."

He could see she was trying to distract him, and not so long ago, he would have melted down anyway. But now—although it took a little bit of conscious effort—he was able to accept it. "Go on then."

"Um…" She looked frozen a moment. "So there's this guy who drives a bus. And one day…um. Someone is trying to get on his bus, and he starts the bus and it crushes them. And so he gets fired."

"This is quite macabre."

"I did warn you I was bad at this. Anyway, he eventually gets another job on a bus, and the same thing happens again and he gets fired again. And then he gets a third job on a bus, and it happens again and he gets fired a third time. And then one day he's on the Underground, and this child falls on the tracks and the kid's about to touch the third rail, so he jumps in front of him and lies right on top of it. And then he snatches the kid up and carries him away, and he brings the kid to his mum and his mum says, *I don't get it, why didn't the electricity kill you?*"

The story was sufficiently rambling that Paris had already lost track of what was happening, but he gave an encouraging nod. "Why didn't it?"

"Well, he said, I'm just a terrible conductor."

"Um." Paris blinked. "Why did he say that?"

"Because he was, like, a bus conductor and he kept killing people."

"You said he was a bus *driver*."

"Shit." Joy put a hand to her forehead. "Did I? Sorry, I meant bus conductor."

"Okay. That makes more sense. Um...ha-ha?"

"Don't patronise me." She nudged him gently in the arm. "But seriously, you're going to be fine. Just try and relax, Grace'll take care of you. And I know this is really trite advice but, honestly, just be yourself."

"I think *myself* is a bit of a work in progress."

"Then be a work in progress. People will understand."

"Will they, though? Or will they just call me a twat on Twitter?"

She shrugged. "Well, would you rather be called a twat on Twitter because of who you are, or because of someone you tried to be?"

"I can't help but notice," Paris pointed out, "that either option involves getting called a twat on Twitter."

"Welcome to show business." Standing, she brushed a kiss against his cheek. "I need to get back to the studio. But good luck. I'll watch you on iPlayer when I get home."

He spun his chair. "Did you buy anything nice this week?"

"I bought a Tesco's finest cheesecake," she said gravely. "Baby steps."

Baker Expectations filmed the day before its matching episode aired, and then played directly afterwards on a slightly less prestigious channel. It was hosted by Grace Forsythe and as well as the eliminated contestant, always included two guests, one of whom knew how to cook, and one of whom was professionally amusing. The comedians were usually fine, but the professional chefs could sometimes be more difficult, which made it a bit hit or miss for the bakers depending on who they wound up with. Bernard, for example, had found himself facing off against Gordon Ramsay, and it had been hard to tell which of them was more confused.

"My guests tonight"—Grace Forsythe was seated at a faux kitchen table addressing the camera with the ebullience of a woman with decades of ebulliating experience—"are Perrier-award-winning comedian Gem Hancock and season six *Bake Expectations* finalist Alain Pope."

The two more interesting people stepped past Paris and took their places at the table. The format of the show was such that he was only really needed for the last ten minutes, which meant he had plenty of time to listen to people recapping events he'd mostly forgotten and scour the audience for Morag, who he eventually spotted sitting at the back in a vintage A-line dress with tartan accents.

"I actually thought," Alain Pope was saying, "that this year's semifinal was far more forgiving than the one we had in my year."

Grace Forsythe gave him a look that said *I am being paid to be interested*. "Yes, because you won your semifinal, didn't you?"

He inclined his head with a hauteur that reminded Paris of the people who'd picked on him at school. "I did, yes."

"What you done there," said Gem Hancock, who was shockingly blond and shockingly Estuary, "was made the classic mistake of winning a week earlier than you was meant to."

Alain Pope blinked at her. "Actually, I won several weeks."

"So did Paris. He didn't win the competition neither."

There was affectionate laughter from the audience. Alain Pope managed a tight smile.

"On which subject"—Grace Forsythe herded them expertly past what could have been an awkward moment—"how did we find this week's episode?"

Gem Hancock leaned forward. "Ah, it was well good, weren't it? But tell you what, why's it always posh people what gets food named after them? Earl of Sandwich. Duke of Wellington. Now this Lord Woolton bloke. Why can't the rest of us get that? Why can't I go down the pub and say, I'll have half a Stella, and a plate of Deb What Works Down the Hairdresser's?"

Alain Pope sat back primly. He was a tall rangy man whose quiet confidence Paris remembered being quite impressed by, if not envious of, when he'd watched last year's series. "Well, Lord Woolton was minister for food during the greatest crisis this nation has ever faced. Whereas Deb Who Works at a Hairdresser's works at a hairdresser's."

"Word of advice, mate." Placing a chummy hand on Alain Pope's arm, Gem Hancock flashed him a dazzling white grin. "Don't step on someone else's material. Makes you look a prick." She glanced at Grace Forsythe. "We moving on?"

"An interesting fact about Lord Woolton," Grace Forsythe continued as if it wasn't a complete non sequitur, "is that he actually had a very delicate digestive system. And that's part of the reason the national diet he advocated contains so little salt or spice or, well, flavour of any kind. Which gave British cuisine a reputation for blandness that persists to this day."

"An undeserved reputation," put in Alain Pope, who'd gone a little red.

Gem Hancock nodded. "True. We've got some great grub in this country. We've got the Balti, the vindaloo, the chicken tikka masala."

"I was thinking"—Alain Pope's tone was wary—"more of traditional dishes."

She grinned her dangerous grin. "I will admit, when I look at you, I do immediately think: *spotted dick*."

"And"—Grace Forsythe cut effortlessly back in—"what did you make of our contestants this week, Alain?"

"I actually think Rodney's been underrated so far," Alain Pope said, visibly suppressing any reaction he might have had to the spotted dick comment. "He got a very deserved win this week, and I think he should have had a couple more if I'm honest."

Grace Forsythe was nodding in that *one big happy family way* that was part of the show's brand. "Well, we all love Rodney. He's a dear."

"My favourite thing about Rodney," continued Gem Hancock, "is he always comes in wearing a cardigan and he takes it off halfway through like he's Superman or something." She did a surprisingly evocative impersonation of a middle-aged man taking off a cardigan in a needlessly dramatic manner.

Once the audience's gentle laughter had ebbed away, Alain Pope jumped on the opportunity to speak again. "I also quite sympathise with him because I think more mature men are often under slightly more scrutiny on the show than other people."

"Oh, poor lamb." Grace Forsythe nodded along. "As a sixty-three-year-old lesbian I have no idea what that's like. But speaking of poor lambs and scrutiny, shall we bring on our eliminated baker? Because, of course, five contestants went into this week's World-War-Two-themed challenge and, in this Normandy Landings of baking, one of them had to be Germany." She paused. "Or, I suppose, equally appropriately, had to be Paris."

His name was his cue, though Paris wasn't sure he liked being compared to one of the bloodiest days in military history. Still, he did his best to smile, not to squint into the studio lights or fall over anything, and to walk out like the whole nation hadn't just watched him break down in tears six times in an episode.

He managed to reach the table without having a panic attack. And the welcome from the studio audience was genuinely warm—presumably because they were superfans who loved anything even tangentially to do with the show and had been soundly briefed that warmness was mandatory.

"One moment," said Grace Forsythe just as Paris sat down. Then she reached underneath her seat and produced a comically oversized box of tissues. "Just in case you need them."

Paris winced. But it was fine. It was fine. He knew how he'd come across; he just needed to own it. "I did get quite emotional, didn't I?"

"Yes, very," said Alain Pope, although he'd barely finished speaking before Gem Hancock cut him off with "Don't worry about it, babe, I like a bloke what cries. 'Course, with me, that's all blokes."

Which led to Grace Forsythe corralling them back. "As someone who has been on that set for, as I am occasionally reminded, slightly too many years now, I am deeply aware that, shall we say, passions can run high. Who has not sobbed into a soufflé, wept into a water biscuit, or blubbed into a batch of baklava?"

"Well, I didn't," observed Alain Pope.

Grace Forsythe turned ever so slightly away from him. "Yes, but I wasn't talking to you, dear. So tell us, Paris, was it allergies, were you, as social media occasionally suggests, striking a blow against gender norms, are you just a deeply sensitive soul?"

Honestly, any of those would have been viable—if not wholly plausible—answers. And he was sure Grace Forsythe had offered them as a way of helping him manoeuvre that particular elephant out of the room. But Joy had been right. It was probably best to just be himself.

"Funny story that," he said. "Because I know a lot of people thought the crying was fake or attention seeking or just plain annoying. And, yeah, I can be annoying sometimes—although, social media is right, it's okay to cry if you need to cry, even if you're a boy." He paused. "But actually, the reason I was such a mess on the show was, and I didn't really know this at the time, I've got generalised anxiety disorder."

This wasn't the sort of thing you were supposed to talk about on *Baker Expectations*, so the audience didn't really know how to react.

Grace Forsythe, however, was a pro. "That's very brave of you to share with us, Paris."

He shrugged. "I don't think it is, really. I think you can make too big a deal out of these things. It's part of who I am, like being gay or having a tendency to cook slightly pretentious food. But— like being gay or having a tendency to cook slightly pretentious food—it's not something to be ashamed of. Unlike my Lord Woolton Pie, which was distinctly average."

And then they talked about Paris's distinctly average Lord Woolton Pie.

And it was fine. It actually was completely fine.

It had been three hours and forty-two minutes since Paris had told the British public that he was mentally ill, and he still hadn't checked Twitter. Part of him really wanted to. But he'd got some better words for that part now. Words like *tendency to catastrophise* and *maladaptive coping mechanism*. And while they weren't magic they did...sort of help?

Neferneferuaten was also, in her way, helping. Because she was sitting on his phone. He didn't think this was a conscious effort to help him manage his mental health—because she was a cat—but it was certainly a serendipitous side effect of her inherent feline selfishness.

Eventually, she decided she would rather be on his laptop, maybe because he was using it and she always seemed to take that as a personal affront, so he stopped trying to make notes on the portrayal of the immortal in Greek poetry and reclaimed his phone.

I was on TV again today, he began texting his parents. **I sort of mentioned that**

He stopped. Deleted the message.

And then his phone rang. And the timing was so uncanny that, for the briefest glimmer of a fraction of a moment, he thought it might be his mum and dad.

Of course it wasn't. It was Tariq.

"Hi," he said, fumbling the phone to his ear.

"Hi. Sorry. Are you...Did I interrupt something?"

"No. Not at all. I was just texting my parents but then I realised I..." Paris paused. "Actually I don't really know what I realised. Just that I've run out of things to say to them and I think they ran out of things to say to me a long time ago."

An anxious breath gusted over the line. "Eesh. I can't tell if that's good or bad. Like, the only way my dad could run out of things to say is if there was a kind of time-travel accident and the entirety of the 'eighties got erased from history."

"Your dad's great."

"My dad's a complete muppet. But yes, yes he is." He paused. "He likes you by the way, even though you're terrible at laser tag."

"Thank you?"

"He was very impressed that you sacrificed yourself to protect me."

"Yes," said Paris, laughing. "But only in laser tag."

"Where my dad is concerned there is no *only* in laser tag." Another pause. "But...are you...are you okay? About your parents, I mean? I know we talked a bit about it but, honestly, I never quite understood what the deal was there."

Paris shrugged even though Tariq couldn't see it. "I don't think I do either. Maybe I'm like this flat? They thought I'd be cool to have for a while but then they moved on."

"I still don't know what to say. I mean, you're not a flat. You're a person."

"I am, in fact," Paris told him, "aware I'm not a flat. And I'm not trying to make excuses for them, but I don't think it helps me to think too much about them. Or what they think of me. Or why they...sort of forgot I existed."

"True. You can't let them live in your head rent free." A mischievous note crept into Tariq's voice. "Which, when you think about it, is ironic."

"Hey, if your parents are going to abandon you, they can at least abandon you in a swanky flat in central London." Paris flopped onto his bed and tucked his spare hand behind his head. "Maybe I'll redecorate to make it feel more mine. Maybe I'll make it way less cool. Maybe I'll put plaster flying ducks on the walls."

"Paris. Don't hurt the flat. The flat is beautiful and it's done nothing to you. Also," Tariq went on quickly, "stop distracting me. I called to say I saw you on *Baker Expectations*. And I thought you came across really well."

"I mean, I think they expected me to open with a joke or a self-deprecating put-down, rather than a frank statement about my brain."

"Well, yeah. But if they hadn't liked it, they would have cut it. Magic of television and all that."

"I guess."

"And I know you're right that this sort of thing should be less taboo and we should talk about it more—well, more in mainstream media, instead of just on social media and the occasional tell-all confessional in the *Guardian* or the *New York Times*—but I still think you were pretty brave."

It felt different when it was Tariq who said it. "Thank you. I'm not really very used to thinking of myself as brave. After all, I am literally scared of everything."

Tariq actually groaned. "Are you actually going to make me say the very cliché thing?"

"What very cliché thing?"

"You must know the very cliché thing."

Paris genuinely didn't. "I genuinely don't."

"Fine." Tariq gave the heaviest of sighs and then intoned, "Being brave doesn't mean not being afraid. It means being afraid and doing it anyway."

"Oh, that cliché."

"Don't make me say a cliché, then tell me it's a cliché."

"Anyhow," Paris pointed out, "in my case it's not really *doing it anyway*, it's going to a series of therapy sessions in which you learn a bunch of strategies that might, at some point, help you to do some of it anyway."

"That's still brave to me, angel cake."

Which left Paris absolutely no excuse not to be brave again. "Tariq, I...," he began just as Tariq was saying, "So are you..."

"Sorry," Tariq said. "You go."

Brave was looking scarier by the minute. "Well, I was going to sort of…maybe…ask if you wanted to see me again. But if you'd rather wait or just not, I get it."

"What kind of seeing?" asked Tariq, and Paris tried very hard not to read suspicion into his tone.

"Um. Any kind of seeing." Paris's mouth was going dry. "I don't want to—I mean…" He took a deep breath. Full sentences. This was a time for full sentences. "Obviously, I really liked being with you, you know, in a boyfriending way, and I think it would be dishonest not to admit I'd still like to. But—" Fuck, he was doing so well. "I know when we last met up, we said we were going to be friends, but I also know that sometimes people just say that because it's more polite than saying *we'll probably never speak again*. And if you *do* want to never speak again, that's your call but—well—I hope you don't want that because…" *Honesty and bravery*, Paris reminded himself, *honesty and bravery*. "Because you're one of my favourite humans and I'd be sad if I never got to hang out with you again."

For a moment there was silence on the line. Then at last Tariq said, "Thanks."

"Thanks?"

"You're—you're a pretty okay human too."

"Just okay?" Paris hoped he didn't sound needy, but he was nowhere near better enough not to think he sounded needy.

Tariq laughed. "Well, you're better ahead of at least three of the Daves."

"Which one am I worse than?" asked Paris, letting Neferneferuaten slink lazily into his lap.

"Whichever one left fewest socks in the living room this week." Another pause. And in the gap Paris elected, instead of freaking out about what Tariq could be doing or thinking in the silence, to quietly congratulate himself for not freaking out. Well, not freaking out too much. "But…yeah," Tariq said finally. "I mean—I'm not saying…But let's meet up, hang out, see how it goes."

"We could," Paris began, trying to remember that this was

fine and he would be fine and that being brave meant being scared and doing it anyway. "That is, do you want to do something next week? Like…maybe…we could meet up on Sunday or something?"

He wasn't asking for a date. Not exactly. Just some time. Some space and some time. An opportunity to be somewhere where maybe they could talk. Where maybe Paris could be brave again.

"You know what, angel cake," Tariq replied, "that sounds great."

EPISODE 8

Finale

💬 ♡ ⇄ I never thought I'd say this but I kind of miss Paris
#bakeexpectations

💬 ♡ ⇄ Tariq is smashing this #bakeexpectations

💬 ♡ ⇄ If Bernard was in the final, his gravity-defying
cake would just be a really tall Victoria sponge
#bakeexpectations

💬 ♡ ⇄ Catherine Parr can't win this because the BBC hates
white women #bakeexpectations #peakBBC

💬 ♡ ⇄ I can't get over how fucking adorbs Rodney's family
are. I want to kidnap them and keep them in my
garden #bakeexpectations

💬 ♡ ⇄ i've tried hate-wanking over the other contestants
and its just not the same #bakeexpectations
#bringbackparis

💬 ♡ ⇄ Fucking called it! #bakeexpectations

◯ ♡ ⊏⊐   Well, that's it for this year. See you in time for Strictly!
            #bakeexpectations

PLANNING A NON-DATE THAT could transition at any moment into a date was, in many ways, harder than planning a date. But given the last two dates Paris had planned had involved overcompensating for his intense self-loathing with either truffles or hotel rooms, he had at least done a good job of preemptively managing expectations. At least, that was what he'd told himself as he spent a week racking his brains trying to think of something, anything, that he could do with Tariq that said *I like you and I want you in my life but not necessarily in a dating way, I mean I'd like it to be in a dating way but I don't want you to feel any pressure. But anyway, this is me and I'm trying to do better now and I sometimes am, and I'm sometimes not.*

It would have been straightforward—well, relatively straightforward—to go for another coffee or dinner or to cook something that involved fewer truffles and less being dropped on charcuterie, but that felt almost like cheating. It was the sort of thing the old Paris, who, in many ways, was very similar to the new Paris, would have done to make sure there were enough shiny bells and whistles around to distract Tariq from—oh look, there was that intense self-loathing again.

Ideally, he wanted something special but not too special, personal but not too personal, something uniquely Parisian but not in a bad way. And since he didn't have a dad to play laser tag with, or a bunch of Daves to make curry for, that left him with one slightly weird option.

"So…where are we?" asked Tariq as they got off the train. The train that Paris had ridden on and hadn't frozen or cried or, admittedly, dared to use the loo on despite slightly needing to. Tariq had offered to drive them, but it had seemed unfair to invite somebody to a date and then make them give you a lift and besides, the journey was part of the gift.

"Neversbury."

Tariq looked around. Even the station in Neversbury was

pretty. Not amazing, not somewhere you'd want to actually spend a day, but picturesque in a you-can-see-trees-from-the-platform-and-the-Costa-concession-has-nice-napkins kind of way. "I got that from the big sign saying *Neversbury*. But where are we"—he made one of his expansive, sparkling gestures that Paris had missed so badly—"conceptually."

"So…" Following old instincts from the many years he'd walked this route after his parents had stopped bothering to send the car, Paris led Tariq away from the platform. "Neversbury is a cathedral town, quite an old one. It's in the Domesday Book. It's got a small tourist industry and some nice tea shops, but what it's most famous for is that it's, well, it's where Hawton Abbey School is. And that's where, y'know, I…went to, y'know, school."

Shooting Paris a sly glance, Tariq followed him down the cobbled streets. "I was joking about the uniform thing."

There were, in fact, Hawton boys strolling around in their blazers and boaters and the pointy collars whose name they didn't mention because it belonged to the other place.

"I know," said Paris. "But I wanted to show you something that was important to me."

"Didn't you hate it here?"

"That doesn't mean it wasn't important. It…um. Kind of made me who I am?"

"Honey"—Tariq was laughing at him, but gently—"is that a good thing?"

Paris risked a tentative arm-bop. "Hey, I have medically proven self-esteem issues."

"Yeah," Tariq agreed, "that this place gave you."

"I think it's more complicated than that." There wasn't a great deal of town between the station and the school. Just the mews leading up to the cathedral and Hawton behind. Hawton, with its rooms that had once housed a hundred or so monks before Henry VIII had decided that God and expediency demanded they be moved elsewhere.

They walked slowly across the green around the cathedral towards Paris's old school. "This is probably going to sound a bit Stockholmey, but I think I probably shouldn't blame Hawton. For a start, a lot of"—he made the *Parisian brain* gesture—"is probably genetic, or hereditary, or something and even if it's not, I can't *know* what I'd have been like if…if things had been different."

Perhaps it was Paris's imagination, but he thought Tariq walked just a little bit closer. "It's still okay to admit that something hurt you, though. You don't have to be all *I refuse to be a victim*. I have serious issues with the idea that people have to *refuse to be victims*."

They passed through the gates and into the cloisters. It hadn't changed—of course it hadn't; lab equipment and Smart Boards aside Hawton hadn't changed in centuries. Even old Bridges was there, watching over the entrance, nodding Paris through with a polite "Daillencourt" as he passed.

"I know," Paris said to Tariq at last. "And I'm not—at least I don't think I am. But I don't want to let this place haunt me. And—well—it was five years of my life I'd like to salvage *something* from."

So he showed Tariq around. His old form room, the great hall—honestly a little excessive now he looked back on it, given that it was just feeding a pack of hungry teenagers—the classrooms where he'd learned that he was terrible at maths but good at history and perhaps genuinely interested in classics.

"Daillencourt?" a familiar voice echoed from inside one of the rooms. "Daillencourt, is that you?"

"Mr. Richards?" Age-old instinct made Paris straighten his spine and move to tuck in his shirt even though it was already tucked in.

"Bless my soul, Daillencourt." The tiny, bespectacled classics teacher pottered out of the classroom where he always seemed to be hiding, even when there were no classes, and came out to shake Paris firmly by the hand. "And who's this?"

Paris shot Tariq a reflexively nervous glance, and for a moment it struck him that, ironically, not that long ago he'd have been afraid to call him *my boyfriend* because he was worried about accidentally being overheard by a bigot, whereas now he'd have very much liked to but for the tiny fact that it wasn't true. "This is Tariq," he said, "he's my friend. From the show."

A look of realization crossed Mr. Richards's face. "Oh of course, the show. We've all been watching, Daillencourt. We'll be watching tonight. Do you know"—Mr. Richards turned to Tariq without breaking the flow of his speech—"that Daillencourt here was one of the best classicists I've ever taught. Natural feel for the Greeks. Fine flair for Latin. His essay on Medea and the Invention of the Barbarian was a thing to behold. I still have a copy."

Not quite sure what to say, Paris looked down. "Thank you. I was just—I thought I might show Tariq the woodlands."

"Taking the bikes out again, eh?" Mr. Richards gave Paris a warm look, one that made it feel like it hadn't been two years since they'd last spoken.

Turning to Tariq, Paris gave a sort of semi-apologetic wriggle. "That was the plan. If you want to?"

"That would be lovely," Tariq confirmed. And for once the tiny paranoid voice at the back of Paris's mind that said he was just being polite, that he was secretly mortally offended, that this was all a huge mistake, stayed relatively quiet.

～

The school bikes were, as Paris had told Tariq a lifetime ago, kept in the school bike sheds. Thankfully there were no boys smoking or wanking behind them today. Presumably because it was Sunday, and they'd gone to smoke or wank somewhere more interesting.

"I'm not completely sure," Tariq admitted now that the bikes were before them in all their bikeular reality, "that I've made a good trouser call here."

Paris offered a shy smile. "At least you're not going to get shot by eight-year-olds this time."

"I think you'll find she was nine. And I'd say I'm trying to forget except Fariha put pictures of me sucking at laser tag all over Insta, so mostly I'm just trying to live it down."

"Seriously, though"—Paris did seriously-though face—"we don't have to if you don't want to. We can take a walk instead or hang out in town or whatever."

In defiance of his trousers, Tariq eased a leg over the crossbar and hopped awkwardly onto the seat. "No, no. We're reclaiming your power from an intimidatingly posh boarding school. And I committed to bikes."

And commit he did, wobbling more gracelessly than Paris had ever seen him across the grounds. Embikening himself, Paris—also wobbly at first because it had been a while and, perversely, riding a bike *wasn't* just like riding a bike—set off after him.

"This is harder than I remember." Tariq already sounded slightly out of breath. "When you're a kid, you just hop on and go. But now everything hurts."

"Are you okay?"

Tariq pedaled doggedly. "I'm pushing through it. How often did you do this?"

"Only when I wanted to get away from people." Paris paused. "So most days, actually."

They slowed their pace a little, then slightly more than a little, as they wound their way through the grounds of Hawton and out into the woods that spilled across the never-very-well-defined boundary between the stretches of countryside that the school owned and the stretches of countryside that it didn't.

In a lot of ways, it reminded Paris of their time at Patchley House—albeit with more bikes and fewer buns. The country was different here, of course, each of the shires having their own subtly different flavour of breeze, their own slightly distinct shade of green, but there were still trees above and damp leaves underfoot, and the ground still sloped down to a little brook and a clearing where they could park their bikes and unpack the picnic—the very not-trying-too-hard, although perhaps slightly Waitrose-heavy, picnic that Paris had been toting around with him since London.

He laid his blanket out on a patch of open ground where they could catch the best of the autumn sunlight and began setting up. Tariq helped, digging delightedly into Paris's cooler bags. And Paris couldn't help but flinch at the nearness of him as their hands not-quite-touched while they were hauling out the packaged sandwiches and little pot of carottes râpées that Paris had whipped up in a fit of nostalgia because Sophie had taught him how to make it when he was fifteen, and she'd said it was perfect for a picnic.

"No truffles?" asked Tariq with a look of mock outrage.

"I've learned my lesson. Although I almost considered getting some as a joke. But I thought it might not have gone down well."

Tariq gave a reassuring nod. "Yeah, I'm not sure *I've evolved from the kind of guy who buys expensive beautiful things because he doesn't know how to express himself into the kind of guy who wastes expensive, beautiful things on a throwaway gag* is quite the personal growth arc you were going for."

Paris agreed, although a private part of him wanted to say that if it had made Tariq smile, it would have been worth it. But now probably wasn't the time. "I did get these, though," he said instead. Fishing in one of his many bags, he hauled out a punnet of strawberries and a box of Mr. Kipling Angel Slices. "I hope that's okay."

"Honey, why wouldn't it be okay?" asked Tariq, with that same patient expression that Paris had, fleetingly, appreciated-slash-dreaded while they were together.

"I thought it might be a bit…datey?"

Normally, this was where Tariq would say *no, don't be silly, you're just getting in your head*, but instead he looked down at the strawberries, over to the angel slices, then back at Paris. "Now you've said it, they do bring back some—I mean they're just food but—yeah."

"Yeah." Paris's heart didn't sink exactly, but it was definitely taking on water. "I promise I'm not trying to sneak-go-out with you. Which, as we've established, doesn't mean I wouldn't. I mean I obviously would because I did and I told you on the phone I still wanted to. Oh God, are we going to have to talk about this now? Have I accidentally invited you on a *let's stay in touch, no pressure* picnic that's turned into a *let's have a serious talk about feelings* picnic?"

Tariq laid out a couple of paper plates in a way that seemed like a genuine laying-out-of-plates rather than a desperate attempt to engage with anything except Paris. "Well, when we were going out, the thought of having a serious talk about feelings seemed to cause you actual physical pain, so I'm going to count this as progress."

"Hey, I talk about my feelings all the time now. I talk about my feelings every week in a group of other people who don't like talking about their feelings."

"And on national television," Tariq added.

"It's true." Paris stole a glance across the picnic blanket. "I'm now totally cured and have no further issues or hang-ups." He'd made Tariq smile, which was good. But Paris had been in therapy just long enough to recognise at least some of his own avoidance strategies. "Actually"—he picked at the edge of the blanket—"I'm kind of having a lot of feelings these days. Like, a could-get-quite-boring-to-hear-about number of feelings."

"Honey, I could *never* get bored of hearing about feelings. I *love* hearing about feelings. Plus I live with four blokes in their early twenties, so the only feelings I normally hear about are *I'm hungry* and *I fancy a wank*."

"Well, I'm not used to it," said Paris, only slightly petulantly. "Before I went on the show I was mostly either worried or tired. Then I went on the show and I was either scared or tired. And now I've got all these strategies for coping with being worried or scared, which means I sleep better, which means I've now got time to be…I don't know. Wistful or peeved or optimistically confused."

Tariq seemed to be processing this, and Paris, whose strategies still weren't faultless, was briefly worried it might have been too much. Then Tariq's eyes got that half laughing at you, half laughing with you twinkle. "Please tell me that when you're feeling wistful, you recline on a chaise longue in a frilly shirt and a silk dressing gown."

"I don't have any frilly shirts, and every time I try to lie down on the chaise longue, Neferneferuaten sits on my head. Besides"— Paris attempted to summon boldness from his newly broadened emotional index but got stuck on bashful—"when I'm wistful, it's mostly about this really great guy I dated for a while, and then totally blew things with."

"I've met that guy." Tariq's tone was, ironically, a little wistful. "He's got issues of his own, believe me."

This was news to Paris, who'd spent most his life assuming he had a monopoly on issues. "Are we talking about the same person? Because he seemed pretty together to me."

That got a laugh from Tariq, but not the good kind of laugh, more a kind of oh-honey-if-only laugh. "Okay, so first of all, it's going to get really weird if we keep pretending we're not talking about me here. And second of all, obviously I'm fabulous, but I'm not…" Tariq actually cringed a little. "…I'm not perfect. And I'm not super super proud of how I handled, you know, everything."

"You were incredibly kind to me," Paris said, slightly surprised to find himself on the reassuring side of the *I've been a bad* conversation. "And way more patient than you had to be."

Tariq was still cringing slightly, and it was odd to see because he was normally so the opposite of that. "But I wasn't actually thinking about what you…what you needed, I guess? I just sort of took it for granted that I knew what I was doing. And when it turned out that being kind and patient didn't magically fix your quite complex mental health issues, I felt weirdly betrayed by that."

"You were only trying to help."

"And I did *want* to help," Tariq admitted, slightly tormentedly. "But I think maybe, just a little bit, my annoying kid sister was right and I wanted to help in a way that was about me more than it was about you."

That took Paris a moment to process, because it involved dealing with how the whole you're-a-project conversation had felt back when it happened and how it felt now, and how he felt now about how it had felt then, like he was some kind of emotional time-traveller. Three months ago his self-esteem had been sufficiently through the floor that being the private fixer-upper of somebody who just liked to fix things up would have seemed like the best he could have hoped for even if Tariq *hadn't* been denying the up-fixing aspect of their relationship. In retrospect he was…shit, was he insulted? Was this what it felt like to be insulted and not immediately assume you deserved it?

"So…" For an insulted person, Paris sounded way more shaken and way less righteous than he'd hoped he might. "So I *was* just a project to you then?"

Tariq stopped cringing but only because he went into a sort of overcompensating anti-cringe. "Honey, no. I mean maybe a little bit but mostly *no*."

"But a little bit?" asked Paris. And this time he didn't think that focusing on the bad part of the sentences was completely unwarranted.

"Like I said, that guy has issues. You weren't a project *at all*. I just—looking back I might have sometimes treated you like one and if I did I'm sorry."

The film lid on one of the packs of Mr. Kipling Angel Slices suddenly became highly fascinating to Paris. "It's okay. I mean, it's probably not *completely* okay but I think we both made some mistakes. But I…It wouldn't be good if…Look, I really don't want to be a project."

There was a fraught little pause, which Paris filled by telling himself the universe wasn't going to break.

"You know," Tariq said finally, "I think that's the first time I've heard you unequivocally say you wanted something. Well, say you *didn't* want something. But it still counts."

"I know, right? Check out how far I've come."

The look in Tariq's eyes softened. "I'm checking, honey. I really am. And if I haven't made it clear already, I'm honestly proud of you."

"Thanks." It felt like a moment to bask in, but it also felt like a moment not to be complacent. And a moment to be reflecting and regretting and hoping because apparently it was possible to do all those things at once when fear wasn't flooding your body with the useless kind of adrenaline. "And just so we're clear"— Paris raised a hand holding something flat and imaginary— "these are my cards." He moved his hand down and mimed spreading something over the blanket. "This is me laying them on the table. I like you. I'd like to go out with you again. I still want to be friends either way but. Yeah. That is a thing. A thing that I want. On my own terms and with my own thoughts."

And now, after everything, after the show and Birmingham and laser tag and viewing parties and Twitter and both of them getting shit talked about them on daytime TV, it was finally Tariq's turn to look sheepish. "Yeah. I…" He laughed nervously. "Okay, the new decisive you is pretty cool and all but I—would it be really hypocritical if I said I was in kind of an uncertain place?"

Paris tried to put Tariq at his ease by nervous-laughing back. "Wouldn't it be pretty hypocritical of me to think it was hypocritical of you?"

That was, perhaps, one step too circular for Tariq, who, compared to Paris, was very much an amateur at relentlessly second-guessing himself. "I think that might be a rabbit hole I don't want to go down. I just mean…actually I'm not sure what I mean."

Trying not to disturb his imaginary cards, Paris slid a hand across the picnic blanket to take Tariq's. "I know I've said this before and it turned out to be not super true, but I really do think it'd be better this time…Which"—he thought back to his weeks of all-consuming perma-dread—"admittedly wouldn't be difficult."

"Oh, Paris." Tariq closed his fingers gently around Paris's. "It's not about being better. It's about what it would mean."

This was either very good or very bad, and Paris tried to stay neutral so he didn't tip it either way. "What do you mean what it would mean?"

"Being with you was…It was nice. It was really nice. But wasn't it kind of a showmance?"

"You mean"—Paris's eyes widened—"something we did for the cameras? Because I definitely didn't do anything for the cameras. Probably, I didn't do enough for the cameras."

"No," said Tariq, gratifyingly quickly. "Not like that. Like, when you're doing a play and working really intensely with someone, but afterwards you can't work out if it was about the play or about the someone."

It was beginning to sound like Paris should take his hand back. The worst of it was, it did kind of make sense. Because dating somebody when you were contractually obliged to spend your weekends in the same hotel for two full months wasn't the same as dating them when you were back to your normal life. "I…I guess."

"It also feels a lot"—Tariq's hand was shaking slightly—"bigger and—and realer?"

"Real is good, though, isn't it?"

"Real is…" Tariq thought about it for a moment. "Real? And there's quite a lot that feels very real right now."

"Like the agent and the manager and the maybe getting your own show?"

Tariq gave a little nod. "Like all that. And I'm excited, of course I'm excited, but last year I was a mildly dissatisfied student who liked cooking and thought it might be cool to be on TV. And now I'm having to make serious decisions like do I jack in my course and move back to London to throw everything I am at something that might go away in six months."

What Paris was used to hearing from other people in situations like this was *well, if it goes away in six months, then it goes away in six months*, and he'd never found it helpful. It just reinforced his brain's conviction that the thing he was worried might happen was definitely going to happen. But then Paris's brain—as he was slowly coming to accept—was medically atypical. "If it goes away in six months," he said soothingly, "then it'll go away in six months. I know that between environmental science and acting and all that it probably feels like you've tried a bunch of things, but that just means you're the kind of person who can always find a new thing. It's part of what's great about you, and it's why you'll always be fine. Even if Janette Manrara stays retired."

A few drops of moisture were caught on Tariq's lashes, and he blinked them away. "That's…that's really sweet of you. It's just—even if you're right, I feel like it's probably not the best idea to be latching onto somebody who makes me feel good just because I'm about to do a big scary thing. I don't think it'd be fair on either of us."

"That's one way to look at it." Paris wasn't at all sure he was saying the right things here, but for once, he accepted that uncertainty was just part of doing business. "Except couldn't you also say that you've got all these amazing, exciting things happening and it's okay to want someone to share them with?"

"Maybe?" Tariq didn't sound super certain either.

"It's up to you," Paris went on, more afraid of breaking the flow than flowing to the wrong place. "But if you don't want to be with me, it should probably be because you don't want to be with me. Not because you're waiting for things to calm down. Because both of us, in our different ways, are very uncalm people."

"You're a lot calmer than you used to be," Tariq pointed out, laughing.

"I'm on drugs. It's one of the many reasons I'd make an excellent boyfriend."

"You have been quite persuasive." Tariq picked up the punnet of strawberries and then, apparently deciding it was not quite a strawberry moment, just held on to them, crinkling the plastic slightly. "And we *will* be in the same city for a while."

Paris nodded. "And I can be the sort-of-famous person's partner who follows them up the red carpet and holds their handbag."

"I think you're vastly overestimating the glamorousness of the lifestyle of a mildly popular ex-reality-TV-contestant."

"Also you're going to be so sick of cooking that having a boyfriend who can make dinner for you will be a massive advantage."

"Well, honey," said Tariq, "I can see why I'd want to be in

that relationship. But are you really going to be okay having an incredibly busy boyfriend who still doesn't believe in sex before marriage?"

"Hey, I have a life too. I have a thesis to write and a cat to look after."

"Paris, the other thing is still a thing."

Except it wasn't a thing. At least not a thing that mattered. "I don't care about that."

"You say that now. But what about in a month? Or six months. Or a year."

And this time Paris laughed. "If we're still together in six months, this will be my most successful relationship ever by a long way. I'm not going to say it might not get . . . I'm not going to say it would *never* be an issue or that I don't want . . . you know . . . with you, at some point. In a scary future involving social institutions I don't think either of us are ready to think about yet. But I don't want that more than I want anything else."

Tariq was looking—well, it was hard to say how he was looking. A little bit scared, a little bit hopeful. It wasn't a way Paris was used to being looked at. He was used to looks of resignation and disappointment, not looks that said *maybe* and *if only* and *do I dare want this*? It felt strange and fragile and, if he dared believe in it, just slightly wonderful.

"Honestly," Paris went on, "I know I'm in a better place now but I've actually had quite a rough time. And I thought about you a lot when I was—when things got really bad. And I missed you. And right now, if I could have anything in the whole world, it would just be for you to hold me like you used t—"

There was a soft *pft* as an already neglected punnet of strawberries landed in the grass. And then Tariq had Tigger-bounced right over the blanket and into Paris's arms. It wasn't a romantic moment, not really. But it didn't need to be. Paris had been so lonely for so long that sometimes just a hug was its own kind of magic.

It wasn't everything he wanted. It came with more questions than answers and with layers upon layers of uncertainty that not long ago he would have been completely unable to cope with, instead of only mostly unable to cope with. But it was a start, and wherever it led, Paris knew he'd be able to accept it.

So he let himself stay in the moment—focused on the warmth of the sun and the cool of the breeze, the quiet, reassuring strength of Tariq's arms and the too-familiar violet-and-cedarwood scent of his cologne—and all the what-ifs and what-nows and what-nexts drifted by like bubbles on a stream.

Monday

PARIS WAS STILL STARING at his phone. He'd got halfway through texting his mum to tell her about how he was working on patching things up with Tariq, that he was in the process of patching himself up in a more general, emotional sense, and that things overall were pretty good. But he'd deleted it six words in.

He was over that now. Past it. Resigned.

Morag already knew, of course, and while she was positive, her response was basically *well it took you long enough, you whiny shitebag*, which hadn't been quite the ringing endorsement of his major psychological progress that Paris had been looking for.

He opened up his contacts and scrolled through. It was a short list. Well, it was a long list because the magic of synchronisation meant that essentially anybody who had ever emailed him about a school, university, or show-related topic was in there automatically. But if he ignored all the randoms and people who hated him, it was a pretty short list.

In the end, he found the name he'd been not-looking-for-but-looking-for.

Hey Sophie, he texted, **it's Paris. I know it's been a while and I've been bad at keeping in touch but I wanted to say—**

What *did* he want to say? *My life is good now?* That seemed presumptuous. *Did you see me on the telly?* That seemed presumptuous and narcissistic.

I wanted to say, he tried again, **that I don't think I ever told you how important you were to me when I was growing up. Or how much I've missed you since.**

Then he followed up with **And I know I'm really just some kid whose house you were paid to look after but you were always**

really kind to me and that meant something, even if you didn't realise it.

He stared at his phone for a moment and then, sighing, tucked it away.

But just as he was going to make a start on the washing up, it buzzed. And he saw a reply.

Thanks Paris thats really sweet of you

Then. **I missed you too**

Then. **How are you**

Tuesday

KENILWORTH HADN'T CHANGED MUCH since the last time Paris had fretfully navigated its suburban streets. He was, to be honest, still fretful: he'd had to get on a train and find his way around a place he'd only been once before, and he doubted there'd ever be a time when either of those things was completely okay for him. But it had felt manageable. He didn't know if that was the pills or the therapy or just knowing he wasn't alone. And it didn't matter.

Manageable was…manageable.

Manageable was good.

As he wriggled down Bernard's street, with its half-on-the-pavement cars, he spotted Tariq once again struggling to edge his way into a narrow parking spot.

As he approached, Tariq rolled the window down. "Hey, honey, would you mind"—he made a jerky, over-the-shoulder gesture that indicated the back of the car—"you know."

For a moment, Paris was about to say yes. Because he was better now—he was getting better, and he needed to learn to do things that he wouldn't normally do.

Except that wasn't quite right.

"Actually," he said, "I still think I'd do it really badly. So how about I go inside and get somebody who knows about cars instead?"

Tariq gave him a radiant smile. "Sounds like a good idea."

So Paris pushed his way through Bernard's still-on-the-latch door and poked his head into the front room. It was much the same crowd that had gathered for week one, minus Gretchen, who had presumably lost interest after her elimination.

"Hey," he said, "would somebody who can actually drive mind watching Tariq while he parks, because I'm pretty sure I'll mess it up."

Bernard looked apologetic. "I would, but my sausage rolls are coming out the oven any minute now."

"Can't take a man away from his sausage roll," added Bernard's dad.

"Well, we can't take you away from them, Dad. Never seen someone eat so many. We've had to ban him from going to Greggs."

Joan stood up. "I'll go. Don't steal my armchair."

Everyone was arranged much as they had been last time, and so Paris followed the path of least resistance onto the sofa. "Um." He swallowed because he was Doing A Sociable. "How has everybody been?"

"It's been a bit funny to be honest." Bernard vanished into the kitchen for a moment or two—the scent of pastry and pig wafting through from the hall. "I keep getting asked to do all these things."

"He's had supermarkets," Bernard's dad explained while his son was enkitchened. "Village fetes. A company in London said they wanted him to do a shortbread masterclass—I'm sure I've never seen the like. And there was a club in Swansea that wanted him to be part of a late-night variety programme between two dancing girls and a magician. I said what do they think you are, a French saxophone player?"

Once Bernard Senior had paused for breath, other people could fill in their own stories. "Back to school for me," said Tanya. "The deputy head asked if I wanted to run baking classes for some of the younger kids, but then I pointed out I was already teaching a full timetable, running the chemistry club, and coordinating all of this year's practical assessments."

"Have you considered a different job?" asked Joan, who'd just come back with Tariq in tow.

Tanya shrugged. "All the time, but I kind of love teaching."

"We're just talking about"—Bernard emerged from the kitchen with some sausage rolls he appeared to have arranged into a bouquet—"what we've been up to since the show."

"Oh right." Joan reclaimed her armchair. "I made some really nice banisters the other week."

"What about the baking?" asked Bernard.

"Yeah. Yeah. Made a couple of pies too."

There was a silence after this. Tariq came and sat next to Paris. And it was still awkward, but it was a different flavour of awkward. It was no longer *I know I really hurt you and am convinced you secretly hate me* flavour. It was *I still really like you but don't know if anything can come out of that* flavour.

"Well, I've been in therapy," Paris offered.

Bernard's dad craned his head in Paris's direction. "I don't hold with therapy."

"Come on, Dad." Bernard put his hands on his hips. "Be nice. Besides, you don't even hold with olive oil."

"I just don't see why we need it. Why can't you get beef dripping anymore, that's what I want to know."

"You can." Rising from the pouffe, Lili went to extricate a sausage roll from the bouquet. "You just have to get it from an artisanal dripping purveyor."

"Is she joking?" demanded Bernard's dad.

Paris took a deep breath and did another sociable. "Probably. But she's also right. A lot of more traditional ingredients these days are hard to get in supermarkets because people don't use them. But some of us are going back to that way of cooking—you just need to know where to look."

"See?" Bernard's dad gave a vindicated nod. "And they call that progress."

"For what it's worth"—Tanya put in—"I *do* hold with therapy. We spent more than a hundred years telling young people with mental health issues to buck their ideas up and pull themselves together, and it just plain didn't work. A lot of kids who get kicked out of school need support, not discipline."

Joan lunged forward, snatched a sausage roll, and reoccupied the armchair before anyone could threaten it. "My husband's seeing someone. He had a bad experience in Afghanistan. It's slow but it seems to be working. I'm not going to knock it."

"It's working for me," said Paris. "I think?"

"Well, that's what matters isn't it?" Bernard started offering his sausage roll bouquet to anyone who hadn't yet partaken. "Oh and Tariq, I've got some cheese and onion ones going in next. And even bought a new baking tray for them special."

"Thank you, Bernard." Tariq had that polite tone in his voice you got when somebody was trying really hard to be accommodating while also having a fairly minimal understanding of your needs.

Lounging back on the pouffe, Lili addressed the post-sausage-roll silence. "I got a call from Marks and Spencer."

"Probably trying to sell you something," muttered Joan.

"Actually they wanted me to consult with them on their in-house desserts. They liked my designs in patisserie week. I told them I'd think about it. But honestly, it's not really what I want to be doing with my life."

"You know"—Bernard perched on the arm of his dad's chair—"for a bunch of bakers we haven't done very much baking, have we?"

Joan cast him a *well yeah* look. "It's almost as if we've got other things in our lives."

"Simmer down, everyone." Bernard's dad waved the television remote. "Show's about to start."

They obligingly simmered, and the screen lit up with the traditional panning shot of the grounds of Patchley House.

"Eight weeks ago," came Grace Forsythe's velveteen voice-over, "ten bakers entered the *Bake Expectations* ballroom. Now only the three finest remain to face the toughest challenges in amateur baking and discover who will be this year's *Bake Expectations* champion."

Paris leaned closer to Tariq. "Are you all right?"

"Yeah. Weird watching it back, though."

"I'm kind of thinking I might actually enjoy the show again now I'm not in it."

Back in the eternal summer of television, Catherine Parr was sternly explaining to camera that she attributed her success so far to common sense and British fair play.

"Every time she annoys me," said Lili, "I remember the week she made a row of bums on sticks."

"I'm just still really pleased to be here," Rodney was saying. It was a blue cardigan episode. "Although I think the girls are missing their daddy a bit."

Finally there was Tariq, bright and shining, and honestly it was kind of a headfuck for Paris because this was the version of Tariq who'd just dumped him. Who he'd treated badly and failed to support. Who he'd lost because he couldn't work out how to have anything.

"I am over the moon." Tariq smiled his beautiful, impossible smile. "In fact, forget the moon. I am over the sun. I've been watching this show since I was fourteen. And now I'm here. In the final, somehow."

He gave an adorable little "ahhhh."

"I wish I hadn't said *ahhhh*," remarked real Tariq. "But it was a very authentic *ahhhh*."

"It was cute," Paris told him. "Everyone will think you're cute."

Lili had her phone out. "Three...two...one: yep, it's been giffed already."

"Ahhhh," said Tariq.

Bernard looked up in some bewilderment. "I read on the BBC the other day that I was a meemee."

"A what?" asked Bernard's dad.

"Meemees, Dad. They're these pictures that people send to each other like a Christmas card except it's not Christmas."

Bernard's dad seemed borderline offended by this concept. "And they send each other pictures of you?"

"Yeah, they do. There's a shot of me holding my lemon shortbread and my vanilla shortbread table, and underneath it just says: *It's lemon shortbread on a vanilla shortbread table.*"

"Well what does that mean?"

"I think"—Lili definitely had a *talking to old people* voice—"that particular, um, meemee is something people use to communicate the idea that something is either obvious or that it's doubling down very strongly on one idea. Like this one…" She turned her phone towards the room, which was the same shot except the words *tax cuts for billionaires* and *rollbacks of welfare programmes* had been inartfully superimposed over the various biscuits. "…is lemon capitalism on a vanilla capitalism table."

Bernard's dad shook his head. "And this is what people do with their time these days?"

"I think it's a sort of generational ennui," explained Lili. "It's what people my age have instead of well-paying jobs in a stable economy."

Onscreen, the blind bake was already well under way. It was some kind of layered pandan cake which Paris was sure Catherine Parr would have vehemently resented being asked to make, but which careful editing had reframed her as being charmingly aware that she had limited experience of Thai cuisine. She came a well-deserved last, with Tariq winning by a comfortable margin.

"Something else you learned from your interfaith group?" asked Paris, mischievously.

"Actually, Welsh Dave just really likes Thai food, so I made it for his birthday once."

"How are the Daves anyway?"

"The Daves are…not known for their capacity for change. They asked about you for weeks afterwards, though. They'd say *what happened to that tall quiet guy you really liked*."

Paris gave a self-deprecating smile. "Did you say he was a self-absorbed prick, so I dumped him?"

"No, I said he left me for someone whose housemates didn't talk about wanking over his mum."

The baketacular that year, as they all actually already knew because they'd been to the finale and eaten the bakes, had the open-ended brief of "a gravity-defying cake."

"I'm so glad I went when I did," said Bernard. "Because I could *not* have done this."

Joan glanced briefly away from the TV. "It's just about re-inforcing your joints and getting your loads right. I would have smashed it."

"What would you have made?" asked Lili.

"Staircase."

They watched as the finalists got increasingly hot and increasingly stressed and increasingly convinced everything was going to fall apart any second.

Tariq had a deer-in-the-headlights look. "It's so weird watching it like this. I was losing my mind the whole time."

"For what it's worth"—Lili briefly de-phoned herself—"I loved yours. It was the right mix of quirky and technical."

It was weird for Paris, too, because he could remember absolutely nothing of the finale. He'd been there, because he was contractually obligated to be there, and he'd given one short to-camera interview where he thought he'd said he hoped Tariq won and then immediately panicked about whether that was inappropriate now they'd broken up.

He did, however, like Tariq's bake best—and he didn't think that had just been loyalty and a desire to date the guy. It was an *Alice in Wonderland* tea party with marzipan figures dancing around the cake and a floating teapot pouring into the cup in the middle.

The judges had admired it too. And they'd definitely praised it more than Catherine Parr's three-tiered wedding cake with gravity-defying flowers—which they and Paris thought fulfilled the brief only in the most technical sense. The general feeling, however, seemed to be that Rodney had pulled out slightly more stops. He'd done a multitiered chocolate-and-vanilla cake with each tier seemingly suspended above the last by a cascade of chocolate sauce falling from a silver jug at the top.

"They took ages to decide," Tariq said. "But at least my family was there so I didn't have to hang out with Catherine Parr for three hours."

On the screen, the garden party was in full swing.

"I, um"—a dishevelled figure that Paris honestly took a

moment to realise was him three months earlier had popped up—"I really hope Tariq wins. Because he's…I mean…obviously everyone's good. But I…He's…Yeah."

"Wow," said Tanya. "You really were not in a happy place, were you?"

Paris winced. "And that's the take they kept."

The other contestants all got their own little moment. Bernard had, of course, been rooting for everyone. Lili was Team Tariq.

"I think Rodney deserves it." That was TV Joan, holding hands with her slightly cake-sticky five-year-old son. "He's a great bloke and a great baker, and doing the show with kids is tough."

Screen Tanya was making a weighing-up gesture. "It's difficult because Tariq reminds me of my students and Rodney reminds me of my older brother. I think they both deserve it, to be honest."

And then, at last, with great ceremony the judges emerged, and Grace Forsythe began one of her interminable, artificially tension-building speeches. "And so, my marvellous magicians of mille-feuille, it is time at last to announce the victory of this year's struggle of the strudels."

Tanya rolled her eyes. "She's really running out of baking things to mention, isn't she? We didn't even make strudels this season."

"…after careful deliberation," Grace Forsythe continued, "and painstaking analysis of the fabulous bakes our finalists have made throughout the last eight weeks, Wilfred and Marianne have finally come to the conclusion that the winner…"

She paused.

"…of this year's…"

She paused.

"…*Bake Expectations*…"

She paused.

"Is…"

She paused.

"Rodney."

"See," said Joan. "Called it."

The camera cut to Rodney, who was standing with his family, holding the slightly decorative cake slice and a bouquet of flowers. "I can't believe it," he was sobbing. "I'm just...I can't believe it."

His wife, a short woman in a business-casual blazer, put an arm around him. "This means so much to Rodney. He's given up such a lot for us, and it was past time he did something for him."

<hr />

Paris and Tariq left Bernard's together, mostly because when Tariq had said, "I should probably be heading off," Paris had cunningly replied, "Actually, I should probably be heading off too." So now they were outside and about ten paces from Tariq's car—which meant Paris had approximately fourteen seconds to steer the conversation naturally from *well, that was a nice evening* to *so have you had any more thoughts about giving it another go?*

"Are you okay?" he said instead.

"Well"—Tariq gave him a wry smile—"I'd already been spoiled by being there. So I knew I wasn't going to win."

"Yeah, but seeing it on TV is different, isn't it?"

"A bit. But I'm...I've actually come out of this pretty well. I'd have liked to have been first, but I don't think I needed it."

And that was Paris's fourteen seconds up. Because Tariq's car was right there, a squat blue harbinger of romantic doom. "So, um, good night," Paris said.

"Do you want a lift?"

Yes. For so many reasons. At least one of them being not wanting to get back on the train, but most of the rest being more important and more personal. "Aren't you going back to Birmingham?"

Tariq shook his head. "Staying with my parents while I sort out some things."

"You're definitely—that's definitely happening then? You're going all-in on the showbiz thing?"

"Yeah. It seemed like—like I'd regret it if I didn't, y'know?"

Paris did know. He knew acutely. Although it wasn't being on TV he was worried he'd regret missing out on. "I don't suppose you've…There isn't anything else you're thinking you might want to go all-in on, is there?"

Tariq flipped his hair back with a glittery gesture. "You realise I'm about to be terribly famous and important."

"Yeah, but I'm a mentally ill classicist with a confusingly named cat. I'm a catch."

"You do have some interesting anecdotes about classical sculpture."

"And I can cook at a nationally competitive level."

"Are you sure?" Tariq asked. "I think you probably just got lucky."

"I can't tell"—Paris was half laughing, half squirming—"if you're giving me a hard time or if you're just letting me down gently."

Tariq cast him a melting look. "What do you think, angel cake?"

"I think," Paris said slowly, "I'm going to kiss you and see what happens."

"That's a bold move." The smile on Tariq's lips was sort of familiar and new at the same time, like they were both seeing more of each other than they'd ever been able to. "You've been making a lot of bold moves recently."

"I feel good about all of them, though."

"Spoiler alert: so do I."

If it had been a movie, it would probably have been raining, and they wouldn't have been in Kenilworth, and Paris would not have been pressing Tariq gently against a car door. But none of that mattered. Not the unromantically temperate weather. Nor the banality of the setting. Nor the metallic creak of a put-upon Vauxhall Corsa. There was just the soft sigh Tariq gave as he settled into Paris's arms. And how beautiful he looked with his head tilted up for a kiss, his mouth soft with laughing, and his eyes full of hope. Paris's brain was blissfully quiet as he leaned down and pressed his lips to Tariq's.

His future was still thorns and brambles. Overgrown with what-ifs and what-abouts and but-thens. Except Paris knew himself better now. And he knew how to get help. That help was possible. He had time.

For now, he had dared to want. Dared to ask.

And hadn't broken.

Tariq brushed a tear from Paris's eye with the tip of a rainbow-painted finger.

"It's a good cry," Paris told him. Because it was. Because, for once, he was just sort of happy. Because even though he'd probably never be in a place where his brain wasn't plotting against him, even though he might never speak to his parents again, he could see those things from the outside for the first time.

At the blurred edges of his vision, the glow from the streetlamps seemed to shimmer and dance, as careless as fireflies. It was a trick of the light, of course. Like everything was a trick of the light in one way or another.

But it didn't matter, because—just then—Tariq drew him down into another kiss.

Since Leaving the Competition

GRETCHEN started a small Reiki practitioner's in her home-town of Frome. She expects that business will improve as she puts more positive energy into the cosmos.

CHRIS hopes to one day live down dropping his dessert live on air, but suspects that between his fellow officers and his wife that will never, ever happen.

JOAN is still a carpenter.

TANYA likes to think she's inspiring a new generation of students to follow their dreams, or at least try baking. But she's concerned that she's just encouraged them to pester her to bring in cakes.

BERNARD was invited to open a supermarket in Bermondsey. He agreed on the condition they'd put him and his dad up in a hotel overnight. "It'll be nice to get away for a bit," he explained.

LILI is now in her third year at Central St. Martins. Her most recent project involved designing an interactive environment at St. Pancras Hospital. It is not baking-themed, but she has described her time on the show as "pretty cool."

PARIS is working on his final year thesis, his Lord Woolton Pie, and himself.

CATHERINE has gone back to Sidcup, where she teaches traditional British cooking classes at a local community centre.

TARIQ is launching a BBC Three cooking show called *Fabulous Halal*. When asked what it will be like, he said, "Honey, the clue is very much in the name."

RODNEY was offered a regular spot showcasing recipes on *Each Morning* but turned it down because he'd far rather have breakfast with his wife and daughters.

Grace Forsythe, Marianne Wolvercote, Wilfred Honey, Colin Thrimp, and Jennifer Hallet will return on the next season of *Bake Expectations*!

Available 2024

Acknowledgments

Thank you, as ever, to the wonderful team at Forever, including Amy Pierpoint (my endlessly patient editor), Sam Brody, Estelle Hallick, and Dana Cuadrado. Extra and eternal gratitude to my agent, Courtney Miller-Callihan. Plus appreciation to my authenticity reader, Filza, and my wonderful assistant, Mary.

Reading Group Guide

A Letter from the Author

Hello!

Thank you so much for reading *Paris Daillencourt Is About to Crumble*. I know, I know, it's a really long title.

But it has a dessert pun in it?

I always start these letters by pointing out that this letter is aimed at people who are reading as part of a book club and that, therefore, there is a good chance that you didn't even choose to read this book in the first place. If that's the case, I hope you still enjoyed it. If it's not, sorry. And if you're the one who picked the book for your book club, thank you so much. I guess we stood or fell together on this one, didn't we? I hope it went okay.

Anyway, however and whyever you read this book, thank you so much! I always have trouble with these letters because I get the impression I'm supposed to say something in them that will give you insight into why I chose to tell this particular story in this particular way about these particular people. The thing is I'm a huge believer in the Death of the Author, so I really don't like to interpret my books for people and I think it's kind of important that I not be a huge part of the reading process.

What makes this even worse is that I have, once again, been asked for discussion questions. Do please feel free to ignore these. I'm sure you can come up with far more interesting questions about this book than I can.

But thank you again for taking a chance on my book (if you did).

Lots of love,
AJH

Questions for Discussion

1. Let's start with a nice easy one. Have you already read *Rosaline Palmer Takes the Cake*? If not, sorry, skip this question (but please read it; it's cool, I promise). If so, how do Rosaline's and Paris's journeys differ?

2. Okay, let's try a trickier one. I really don't like questions of the form "why was it important to" or "why did the author think it was important to" because speculating about why I did something shouldn't be your job. But when I was planning out this series, I did make a conscious decision that if I was going to write a book inspired by Various Very Popular British Cooking Shows that it was important to make sure that at least one of them included a British Muslim in a central role. Why might that have been?

3. Less tricky one again. Do lemon shortbread and vanilla shortbread count as two different kinds of biscuit? If so, why? If not, why not?

4. At what point did you realise quite how bad Paris's anxiety really was?

5. I feel like there should be a less wanky way to say this, but what's the role of social media in the novel? Why, if nothing else, does every section of part two open with a page of mean tweets?

6. In a very early draft, I was going to have Paris and Tariq's story unfolding in parallel timelines, with the summer and

autumn segments interleaving with each other. What would have been the advantages of this structure? What would have been the disadvantages?

7. Favourite '80s movie? Favourite '80s band?

8. A major feature of this book is the way Paris's mental health intersects with other people: how their actions can unwittingly make his problems worse, and how his symptoms can sometimes be difficult for other people to deal with. Can you think of some examples? How did you feel about these interactions at the time? Do you feel differently now that you've finished the book?

9. How do Paris's relationship with Morag and his relationship with Tariq reflect on each other?

10. This book is about two people who are old enough to be popular contestants on a reality television show, but assuming it is set roughly around its date of publication, they were both born in the twenty-first century. How old does this make you feel?

RECISES

Paris's Biscuits Roses de Reims

Makes 24 approximately

I was told this recipe is the original, from Fossier, the company that has made biscuits roses de Reims since the eighteenth century. I don't know if that's true. But I hope it is.

I used to enjoy making biscuits roses de Reims because, when they work perfectly, they capture something beautiful and magical and elegant. These days I enjoy making biscuits roses de Reims because even if they don't work perfectly, it's nice to remember that something wonderful can start life as a complete mess.

4 large eggs
200 grams (1 cup sugar) (I use caster, but the recipe doesn't actually specify)
4 teaspoons vanilla extract
A few drops of red food colouring
180 grams (1½ cups) plain flour
50 grams (⅓ cup) cornflour (I believe they call this cornstarch in America)
1 teaspoon bicarbonate of soda (I believe Americans call this baking soda)
Icing sugar (And I believe this one's powdered sugar in America), for dusting

Preheat the oven to 150°C or 300°F.

Separate the egg yolks from the whites of the eggs. Divide the whites into two separate bowls—you'll want one bowl of four egg yolks and two bowls with two eggs' worth of whites each.

Mix the egg yolks, sugar, and vanilla together with an electric whisk. You're not aiming for a particular consistency yet, so just work up through the speed settings and keep at it for about five or six minutes.

Now beat in two of the egg whites (I did say you'd need to keep them apart), then, after about two minutes, beat in the other two (sorry, that's a lot of twos) egg whites and the food colouring (how much you need will vary, so you might have to experiment). This is the point where you are aiming for a consistency. This is basically just meringues, so go for soft peaks, like always.

When that's done, sift the flour, cornflour, and bicarbonate of soda into the mixture, and fold in with a spatula. You want a smooth mixture with an even colour, but I suppose thinking about it, it would be strange to be aiming for a lumpy mixture with an uneven colour, wouldn't it?

Transfer the mixture to a piping bag with a smooth, quarter-inch nozzle, and pipe your biscuits onto a lined baking tray. You want roughly finger-width and finger-length.

Once they're all piped out nicely, sprinkle them with icing sugar and transfer the tray to the oven. Leave it to bake until not-quite brown (you want to keep the pink colour). This can take anywhere from fifteen to twenty minutes.

Remove from the oven, sprinkle with more icing sugar, and return to the oven for another ten minutes or so.

Once they're out of the oven, cut them quickly into rectangles. Or don't. They'll probably have spread in the oven, but sometimes I like to let them keep their rough edges. I feel it gives them character.

They're traditionally served with champagne. But they also go well with coffee. And probably with other things. Sometimes a biscuit will surprise you.

Tariq's Croatian Fig Tart

I should probably say I'm not actually Croatian, so I don't know how authentic this is. But it does feel summery to me, no matter what the judges said.

For the pastry:

- 70 grams (⅔ cup) plain flour, plus more to make a floured surface
- A pinch of salt
- 100 grams (7 tablespoons) unsalted butter, cut into small cubes
- 50 grams (¼ cup) caster sugar
- 1 egg yolk
- 50 milliliters (3 tablespoons plus one teaspoon) double cream

For the filling:

- 500 grams (2 cups) mascarpone
- 6 tablespoons clear honey, honey
- 6–8 figs, trimmed and halved (you'll need enough to cover the tart)

In a lot of ways this is a mega-simple recipe, and I love it. Start off by making the pastry. You can do it by hand, or if, like me, you're just really keen to get on and do something fabulous, you can use a food processor.

Begin by sifting the flour, then adding the salt and butter and mixing it until it gets all breadcrumbly and great, then stir in the sugar.

Once that's done, mix the egg yolk into the cream (you can chuck the white).

Mix the egg-yolk-cream liquid into the flour until it does its magic and turns into dough.

Roll the dough out on a floured surface and use it to line a 26-centimeter flan tin (loose bottomed is best but use what you've got). Then trim the dough, cover it with clingfilm, and stick it in the freezer for 30 minutes to cool.

Touch up your nail varnish while you're waiting. Or get a start on the washing up. At some point you'll also want to pre-heat the oven to 180°C or 360°F (or gas mark 4, if you're old school).

Take the case out the freezer and blind bake for 10 minutes. Use whatever blind baking technique you like best—line it with paper and then fill it with beans or rice or whatever you've got handy that works.

Once that's done, take out your paper and beans-or-rice-or-whatever and normal-bake it for another three minutes.

While all that's going on, mix the honey and mascarpone and then soften it (not too much, just so it pours) in a saucepan over a low heat.

Take the case out of the oven, pour in the filling, and arrange the figs on the top. You can make this look amazing or you can just chuck it in however you'd like. You do you.

Bake for thirty minutes until it's just going golden. Then leave to cool, serve, and enjoy your fabulous, definitely summery fig-and-honey tart.

Bernard's Chocolate Shortbread

Makes two dozen

People keep asking me for my shortbread recipe, and I keep telling them it's just shortbread. "It's just shortbread," I tell them. "Surely you already know how to make shortbread." But my dad says that these days people don't think something is real unless they see it on the telly, then look it up on that internet.

So here's a recipe for one of my shortbreads. It's the recipe I use for chocolate shortbread, which is different from the one I used for the vanilla shortbread and the lemon shortbread on the show. And that's why I still say that two different types of shortbread count as different biscuits, whatever the judges thought.

175 grams (¾ cup) butter, softened
85 grams (a bit more than ⅓ cup) golden caster sugar
200 grams (1¼ cups) plain flour
2 tablespoons cocoa powder
100 grams (3 ½ ounces) chocolate chips

So the first thing you do is mix up the butter and the caster sugar in a bowl. You can do this with one of them fancy food processors, or you can do it with a spoon or your hands like we used to. I use a spoon, because if it was good enough for my mam, it's good enough for me.

When you've mixed up the butter and sugar, add the flour, and then the cocoa powder. The recipe says two tablespoons cocoa powder, but I sometimes use less because my dad doesn't like anything that's too rich. Once that's all worked in nice, you can put in the chocolate chips.

Then you roll the whole thing out into a big long sausage, cut the sausage in two to save space, wrap it in clingfilm, and put it in the fridge to cool down. Then you leave it for an hour or, if you've got the time, a day or two. Just don't do what I do and forget it's in there and then make another load or you'll never see the end of it.

When your dough is all lovely and chilled, take it out, unroll from the clingfilm, and cut your sausages up into little circles about as thick as your finger. Pop them on a lined baking tray in an oven you've preheated to 180°C (160°C for a fan oven, and the nice lady from the TV company says that those are 360°F and 320°F), and leave it for ten to twelve minutes.

Then take it out, let it cool, and enjoy.

Newport Community
Learning & Libraries

Don't miss the first
Winner Bakes All
story . . .

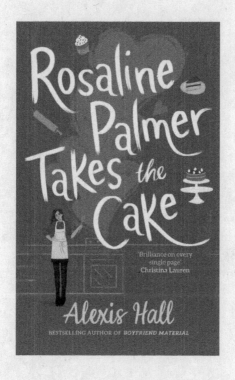

Available now from

PIATKUS

Do you love contemporary romance?

Want the chance to hear news about your favourite authors (and the chance to win free books)?

Kristen Ashley
Ashley Herring Blake
Meg Cabot
Olivia Dade
Rosie Danan
J. Daniels
Farah Heron
Talia Hibbert
Sarah Hogle
Helena Hunting
Abby Jimenez
Elle Kennedy
Christina Lauren
Alisha Rai
Sally Thorne
Lacie Waldon
Denise Williams
Meryl Wilsner
Samantha Young

Then visit the Piatkus website
www.yourswithlove.co.uk

And follow us on Facebook and Instagram
www.facebook.com/yourswithlovex | @yourswithlovex

PIATKUS